THE CRITIC ✓ W9-AYE-603
FROST IS HOT!

"Passion, danger, lots of behind-the-scenes looks at the concert stage and the recording studio—that flapping sound is the reader turning pages at an obsessively fast pace."

—Seattle Times

"An amazing tour de force. . . . Turns the espionage thriller into a magnetic lure which won't let you go even after you have read the last word."

—New England Review of Books

"Ms. Weber is an American concert pianist who writes as well as she plays . . . one of The Notable Books of the Year 1992."

—New York Times Book Review

"Janice Weber knows how to write a spy novel. In *Frost the Fiddler* she observes the conventions of the genre by turning them upside down and inside out . . . beneath her sparkling prose is Ludlum lifted into the unexpected medium of literacy."

—Boston Globe

"High-spirited and engaging . . . the hard-boiled heroine has enough panache to keep readers turning the pages."
—Publishers Weekly

"Makes James Bond look like a Quaker. . . . The web of intrigue is neatly spun, and Frost finds herself caught up in situations she cannot resist even though she knows they aren't safe. . . . Weber's first novel will leave readers dying for more."

—Booklist

"A virtuoso manipulation of hallmark preposterous super-spy novel elements—and it's very, very funny indeed."

—Kirkus Reviews

"A fast-paced thriller . . . will make a good companion on a rainy day. Recommended."

—Library Journal

ALSO BY JANICE WEBER

The Secret Life of Eva Hathaway
Customs Violation

JANICE WÆBER

FROST THE FIDDLER

WARNER BOOKS

A Time Warner Company

WARNER BOOKS EDITION

Copyright © 1992 by Janice Weber
All rights reserved.

Cover design by Tony Greco
Cover photograph by Herman Estevez

This Warner Books Edition is published by arrangement with St. Martin's Press, 175 Fifth Avenue, New York, NY 10010.

Warner Books, Inc.
1271 Avenue of the Americas
New York, NY 10020

 A Time Warner Company

Printed in the United States of America

First Warner Books Printing: December, 1994

10 9 8 7 6 5 4 3 2 1

To J. A. N.

With special thanks to Vincent Bono,
Daniel Killoran, Henry Miranda,
John Newton, and Gilbert Stubbs

I'm Smith. There are only two of us left now. Used to be seven but Vassar got her wrists slashed under the Eiffel Tower, Wellesley slipped into the Bosphorus on Valentine's Day, Holyoke did a swan dive off a balcony in Tokyo . . . bad luck. At least each of them had the foresight to make her death look like a bimbo suicide. Last year Bryn Mawr then Radcliffe vanished in Africa, leaving Barnard and me alone with Maxine the Queen. At least I think we're alone. For all I know, the Queen's slapping another seven debutantes through boot camp. She certainly isn't treating her two survivors like priceless gems. On the contrary, my last few adventures leave a whiff of suspicion that she's trying to cancel me. Of the seven, I've been the Queen's class brat and Maxine seems to resent my outlasting the sweetheart Vassar, who heeled like a champion spaniel, or Holyoke, who would hack off her right foot for America. I'm a patriot, not a kamikaze, and have occasional difficulty taking orders from a lady with an IQ sixty points below my own. Worse, the Queen has the *joie de vivre* of a tortoise. Maxine doesn't like to diddle with reality as if it were fiction. She rarely exploits coincidence, never plays God . . . then has the gall to laugh when I tell her that gambling with my own little life keeps me humble. By now Maxine's half convinced I stay alive just to irritate her; no one joins this outfit without a sensational death wish and I've had many opportunities to indulge myself lately. The ante just hasn't been high enough. Smith's eyeballs will not become buzzard's lunch; Smith's brains will not dribble like slugs over a black leather couch unless the history of the world is at stake. I detest anticlimaxes.

1

*F*ather was a diplomat. I grew up in West Berlin hearing about our great, free country across the sea and actually lived in America for four years before returning to Europe. Now I reside in a grand house near the Grunewald with Curtis my manager, butler, bodyguard: he protects me from the monster Fame. Most nights I'm onstage pressing horsehair over gut, earning megabucks and defending the title Concert Violinist. Just to keep the cover believable I have to practice five hours a day; toss in travel, interviews, rehearsals, receptions; let's not forget the hairdresser and the dressmaker. So Queen Maxine's not left with much Smith. She gets the most mileage out of me after a concert when she knows I'll be wired, near dead, too alive . . . always alone.

Since Hugo there have been a few flirtations but men have a problem playing second fiddle to a fiddle. They fidget watching strangers kiss me in a dressing room and they start unraveling when they call my hotel at three in the morning and no one picks up the phone. They don't like me rolling out of bed at sunup to sniff rosin and they tremble to think how much money I earn. Nonetheless, romance usually stumbles on until they ask me to get rid of Curtis. Then I drop them.

Hugo predated Curtis, so he never had to deal with Beloved sleeping in big house with Black Man. If I hadn't married Hugo Lange, of course, I never would have inherited the big house and I would never have met Curtis. Maxine wishes I had never gotten emotionally involved in the first place: seeing a man die in my bed was, professionally speaking, much more debilitating than killing a man in self-defense. She's afraid that if ever I have to do a little close-range pest control, memories of that unpleasant night will paralyze me. Since I'd probably die were she right, I go to considerable lengths never to put Maxine's theory to the test. The simple precaution of treating men fairly badly has, so far, saved me a lot of useless remorse. And fewer and fewer of them possess that dash of cunning, that mischievous evil, which I find so attractive in the opposite sex. Thus I've remained a merry widow.

I met the Queen during my junior year at MIT, where my father had sent me to study: not every diplomat's daughter graduates *summa* from Berlin's roughest technical school. It wasn't difficult: numbers and I have a certain affinity. They're rigorous and they make sense, something I can't say for the humans I know. Instead of a mother, I received a violin; Father hoped music might feminize me. Early in the game I remember opening a curved case, touching rich, burnished wood, and realizing that here lay not the fount of melody but an exalted branch of mathematics. On my sixteenth birthday I got a Stradivarius; Father wanted me to fly from MIT to Juilliard on weekends for a violin lesson. We fought. I had no intention of living in a country full of imbeciles who kept losing their passports.

"Those aren't the real Americans," my father said, adding that I needed to interact more with teenagers instead of the ambassadors and generals floating through our house all the time.

College was a catastrophe. My roommate spent hundreds of dollars on junk food and hundreds of hours in the bathroom puking it up; her boyfriend thought the Berlin Wall was a rock band. When they weren't screwing on a dead mattress, they were panicking about their grades. Everyone took drugs to go to sleep or stay awake and downtown Cambridge was an anarchic sty. The litter disgusted me. After two months of dormitory hell I moved into my own apartment and bought a gigantic Harley-Davidson for commuting to New York. Father yelped a bit but finally had to concede that it was an excellent way to see the country in which I was born. He was pleased that instead of returning to Europe, I spent my first summer coasting through the U.S. mainland. That, I remember, was an educational trip; the sheer size of America overwhelmed me. In Berlin I could ride maybe an hour before hitting the Wall; here I could chase the sun for days and when the land ran out, I was staring at three thousand miles of ocean. Wherever I stopped, people still spoke English and they were unbelievably kind. The more I rode the more I understood why Americans were so pathetic at foreign affairs.

In my junior year I met Alfred Chung, a Taiwanese student who lived below me. He was nuts about computers and the symphony, he was a foreigner, so we engaged in a heavy platonic relationship. I still look him up whenever I play in Boston. Aside from Alfred, I avoided the other students: those with brains had no elegance and those easy on the eye were murder on the intellect. I wasn't into female bonding and once the Harley arrived, I was never in town on weekends anyway. My classmates knew my name was Leslie Frost; beyond that, I was a cipher.

One aphrodisiacal April dawn, as I was tanking up at a Shell station on Memorial Drive, another motorcycle pulled behind me. Atop a 1000-cc BMW sat a figure in tights and leather jacket. Black helmet, opaque visor nodded at me, floated into the office. Great legs, whatever it was. It returned to the pump. "Where you headed?"

Gender questionable. "New York."

"Mind a little company?"

"I ride fast," I said.

The black helmet didn't move. "So do I."

It followed me to the Mass Pike, where we tried to generate a few sonic booms. Conditions perfect: no traffic, no wind, and my radar detector slept like a stone. Around New Haven

I pulled off the highway, less for refreshment than to see who my clone might be. Parking at a doughnut shop, I unstrapped my helmet. "Coffee?"

Two gloved hands slid the visor up, revealing a dark, patrician face. Her black skin looked twenty, eyes fifty. She blinked at me disdainfully as a Nairobi princess. "Orange juice." Part jasmine, part Sterno, the voice left no doubt that I was expected to fetch.

I did. We drank in silence. "That's some bike," I finally said. She wouldn't be initiating any conversation.

"Thanks." She glanced at my violin. "Are you ever afraid that case might blow off?"

"That's what insurance is for." Nevertheless I checked the bungee cords. My father didn't need a million bucks of kindling.

"I have to be downtown at nine." She held out her empty cup for me to throw away.

Ignoring it, I dropped my own cup into the trash and took off. We hit Manhattan around eight-thirty and she followed me to the underground garage at Lincoln Center. "Thanks for the ride," the helmet said. "Maybe we can do it again sometime."

I'd love to see a cop pull this babe over for speeding. "I come down every Saturday," I told her. "Meet me at the Shell station if you're interested."

The next weekend she was waiting for me. Bit by bit I learned that her name was Maxine and she sang Saturday nights in a club. What she did with the rest of her time remained nebulous. On the other hand, all she learned about me was that I studied at MIT and took violin lessons on Saturday mornings at Juilliard; I had spent enough years around smiling, carnivorous diplomats to learn that one never gave the adversary something for nothing. She was always testing me, though, with her silence, with her cool glances, with strange bursts of speed on a crowded patch of highway . . . I had to wonder what she wanted. My body? She had observed me in enough doughnut parking lots to know that men and I found each other attractive. A singer had no apparent use for a mathematician and if Maxine was interested in my friendship, she would have asked for my phone number by now. I waited her out until the last Saturday in May, then told her that our little trips faced summer recess. Next week I'd be heading west.

Presto: beneath Lincoln Center she invited me to her nightclub. "Don't ride your bike," Maxine said, giving me an address. A dog would think twice about using the area for a shortcut.

I took a cab and arrived just before midnight. Inside, a trio serenaded a crowd that smoked an array of illegal substances. The ladies looked expensive, the men looked as if they could afford them. Above the bar danced a naked woman with breasts as large as her head. I took a seat at ringside and watched them flop back and forth a while, thinking of my physics professor. When the live demonstration of fluid dynamics got redundant I looked around: *hmmmmm*. The only other white face in the joint belonged to the light bulb behind the cash register.

"Hello delicious," said a voice at my elbow. His perfume was a cross between brass polish and bananas. "Sure you're in the right place?"

"This is the World Trade Center, isn't it?"

"Har har! Lemme buy you a drink."

"I've got one." As his hand began strumming my back I wondered if Maxine had sabotaged me in revenge for all those cups I never threw in the trash for her. "Lay off, buddy, I'm not a ukelele."

He didn't laugh quite as merrily this time and he didn't lay off. "Wha'd you come here for then all by yourself?"

Judging by the faces at the bar, we were slowly upstaging the naked lady. It was not a sympathetic audience. "Maxine invited me."

His hand immediately fell away and for the first time I was frightened, not of him, but of Maxine. "That's very nice," he said, retreating into the smoke. I sat undisturbed as a leper

while the dancer tried to slap her big toes with her nipples
and the people around me built up equity in lung cancer. I
had no choice but to wait for the dreaded soloist.

The trio suddenly changed tune as a spotlight hit the curtains behind them. Out walked my travel companion wearing
a gold sheath about four sizes smaller than its contents. To
lusty cheers she slithered across the floor, singing about love
in a low, thick voice, turning to reveal a slit in the back of
her gown running from ankle to anus. I didn't notice any
frilly underwear. The woman had enormous charisma and
played the crowd the same way she played me, with arctic
hauteur: same results, too. When they finally let her leave the
stage she gravitated toward the bar, pausing often to chat with
her devotees. "Nice dress, Maxine," I said.

The tapster gently slid a beer in front of the Queen as the
naked dancer remounted her platform. "Thanks for coming
by. Hope we didn't shock you."

Get serious, honey. In Berlin this show would run in a
family restaurant. "How long have you been singing here?"

"Two years."

She took a little too long to answer and I was suddenly fed
up with the Sphinx routine. "Thanks for the invitation," I
said, standing. "I've got a violin lesson tomorrow."

"Wait," Maxine said, holding my arm. "I know a diner
on Twenty-third Street."

She changed and we walked toward the nearest subway
station. After dark, residents of the neighborhood would find
a dinosaur more easily than they would a cab. Sailing past
five uneasy passengers-in-waiting clustered around the token
booth, Maxine tripped downstairs to the platform. Ahead of
us a derelict stood peeing on the tiles as a blowsy grandma
watched. "Don't you think we should stay upstairs?" I asked.
"It's kind of late."

"What are you afraid of?"

We boarded the Transit Authority's version of a sleeping
wagon. At the next stop two Robin Hoods hopped into the car,
inspected the snoring wretches near the front, and beelined for

us. Maxine's purple bomber jacket didn't exactly blend into the scenery.

The short one pulled a gun. I nearly swallowed my tongue. "Cash," he said. "No muss, no fuss."

I was fishing in my purse as Maxine stood up. "It's in my back pocket," she explained, then ripped the kid's arm sideways. The gun went off, blasting a hole in the glass inches from my neck. I heard his elbow snap but he didn't shriek until Maxine shoved him into the door so hard that his nostrils displaced his earlobes. She didn't show much mercy either for the first mate, who thought he could strangle her from the rear because he was taller. A gun barrel dented his forehead and while he was still conscious Maxine played a little soccer with his scrotum. "This train stinks," she said, yanking me off the seat. We exited at the next station.

My knees shook. "Jesus Christ! He had a loaded gun, Maxine!"

"So what? Did you get hurt?" Her cheeks were flushed, eyes bright, as if she had just made love.

"You broke his arm."

"I dislocated his elbow. Does that bother you?"

Actually, the sound bothered me more than the result. I frowned. "Where'd you learn to do that?"

For the first time I saw the Queen smile: she had bagged me. In the diner she implied she was more than a jazz singer and the next day we rode out to Bernardsville, New Jersey. That's aristocrat country: two miles between mailboxes and dainty-legged horses outpoint the heiresses. At the close of a long, forestal lane Maxine pulled up to a heavy gate, entered a combination onto a keypad. The door fanned slowly inward and I saw a driveway walled by high, impassable hedges. Soon a new wall of hedges blocked our path, forcing Maxine either hard right or left; after several quick turns I realized that we were in a gigantic labyrinth. My nervous system was not amused. I began counting rights and lefts, trying not to panic: if Maxine wanted to kill me, she would have done so already. Unless she was really kinky.

Fourteen turns later she dismounted in front of a stone mansion. I had a feeling its windows were bulletproof. "Who's the architect?" I asked as she unlocked the door. "Ethelred the Unready?"

"I assume you're not armed," she answered. "We're going through a metal detector." We walked into a standard millionaire's living room. Probably not nouveau riche: no Warhols. I didn't bother asking whose home it was. Instead I followed Maxine through mahogany dens, damask bedrooms, waiting. No answers came as we passed an indoor swimming pool, a gym, chemistry lab, a theatrical dressing room.

"Well, what do you think," she said when we returned to the foyer.

In the corner stood a grandfather clock, which hadn't been wound. "It makes me homesick." I was suddenly depressed. "What are we doing here?"

She led me to the kitchen, put a kettle on the stove. "You sent a résumé to the CIA last year."

The poor schmucks were trying to recruit on campus while a couple hundred of my peers called them assassins. That aggravated me; without clandestine information, my father was a eunuch. "How did you know that?"

"Because I read it." She poured boiling water into a pair of Italian mugs. "The CIA never saw it. I wrote your rejection letter."

"Why?"

"Because I want you to work for me."

Work for Maxine? She was out of her mind. "What are you?"

"An international peacekeeping consultant."

Saying *spy* would have saved her ten syllables. I laughed; should have known. Not CIA, FBI, DIA, NSA, either: Maxine was UFO. She began inconspicuously in the army. In the seventies, when the intelligence services got their nuts clipped and a bunch of CIA rejects were publishing their memoirs, she was approached by a general who wished to create a black hole of an agency that didn't have to ask half the U.S.

Congress for permission to wee-wee. He reported only to the president, and only if necessary. Our budget was buried somewhere in spare parts, our accountability was zero, and our mission was catalytic intelligence: to locate trouble and either neutralize it or, better, use it against the opposition. More mature governments had been nurturing, and denying the existence of, such agencies ever since Abel misjudged Cain. Maxine accepted the general's challenge on condition that her agents all be women: better liars. She resigned from the army, became a jazz singer, and began hunting for the Seven Sisters. Naming us after ladies' colleges wasn't exactly original but it beat calling herself Snow White and us the Seven Dwarfs. Before me, Maxine nabbed Vassar, an archae-ologist, and Radcliffe, who wrote sappy novels. Wellesley danced, Holyoke sold bonds. Maxine picked me for the com-puter nerd of the lot.

That summer the seven of us camped with her in Ber-nardsville. Maxine rapidly became known as the Queen, in recognition not of her majesty but of her flair for beheading those who displeased her. The Queen was a monster on body-building and had us swim a mile in ice water before breakfast: said it put the brain in gear for her morning classes in muni-tions, surveillance, survival, chemistry, physics, computer programming . . . I found the technical courses beneath my dignity but the phys ed side of Camp Maxine about killed me: had to abandon smoking, drinking, all thoughts of recre-ational sex. In the afternoon we studied cosmetology, linguis-tics, geography, politics, history, and after supper we slaved over homework in whichever fields Maxine decreed us defi-cient. In the off-hours we took psychological tests: Maxine had to ensure that her initial impressions of us had been accurate. She didn't want any closet Quakers.

The Queen had to check because, unlike the gentler intelli-gence agencies, ours did not compartmentalize: the seven of us had too much talent to be safe little drones who knew only what they needed to know and did only what they were told. Maxine preferred to hit us with a bulging file and an objective.

If we needed additional technical/logistical support, the Queen pitched in; otherwise, she stayed out of our way. Her trust has paid off. No one's discovered us yet and the unlucky ones have all died cleanly. Sure, we're brilliant, resourceful, clawed, but in the end, we succeed because we're American women. The rest of the world considers us about as Machiavellian as the ladies it sees on "I Love Lucy."

By September we had become a pretty sharp troop of Girl Scouts. Shortly before dismissing us to our former existences, Maxine called a meeting in the chem lab. "I see you've all profited from the summer," she began. "The seven of you have lost a total of eighty-four pounds." That got a nice round of applause. "We're ready for a graduation exercise."

With a pair of tweezers Maxine lifted a tiny spot, about the size of a pinhead, from a surgical pad lying in front of her. "I'm going to implant one of these just beneath the skin of your left hand, between thumb and first finger. It will look like a dark freckle."

"What is it?" asked Holyoke. "A transmitter?"

"Poison. You will die four seconds after biting it."

No applause this time. What the hell, I'd go for class dummy. "Is this really necessary," I asked. "What if someone bites it by mistake? Like a pet dog?"

Maxine drilled me with her best evil eye before laying the dot on the table. She rolled it beneath her fingertip. Nothing happened. "The sac can take a lot of pressure." Then she pinched it hard between her fingernails: we watched a clear liquid ooze onto the gauze. "The poison only reacts with saliva. Don't taste it unless you mean it. In four seconds you'll have total cardiac arrest. The toxin, if it leaves a trace at all, will look like household salmonella." The Queen bit the skin between her thumb and first finger. "Easy access. Unless you're stupid enough to get your hands tied behind your back, of course." Maxine didn't have to add that in such a case, we deserved to be tortured to death. "I hope that none of you will ever need this. But there's such a thing as bad luck. Who's first?"

Hotdog Holyoke splayed her fingers across the table and the surgeon slipped her a freckle. With growing dismay I watched the six of them receive postoperative Band-Aids as if they were diamond engagement rings. Finally the Queen looked at me. "Smith?"

"No implants," I told her. "Sorry."

"What's the problem."

"Violin, remember? My left hand is priceless."

Maxine smiled coldly. "How about the right hand."

"I have to hold the bow with that hand. A hair lying across it throws it off balance." My classmates exchanged amused glances: none of them had spent twelve years alchemizing a wooden box into a nightingale.

"Any other suggestions?" Maxine asked. "None that would interfere with your little hobby?"

"Big toe," suggested Wellesley.

"Left tit," said Vassar. "Your lovers will die happy."

Both women are dead now so I won't dwell on their stupidity. I pointed to a mole above my lip. "Put it there."

Maxine held my face under the light. "That's not quite as easy."

"You're the doctor," I snapped.

She should have taken my little hobby more seriously. Maxine received a giga-shock the following spring when my fiddle and I got through the first round, then the second, of a prestigious competition in New York. I'll never forget her face when she came backstage after I'd won. She wasn't her usual walnut brown. She was yellow as a squash, her lips blueberry: the Queen had not planned on Smith becoming a famous violinist. "Well, I guess you did it," was all she said. The Queen doesn't know how to pronounce the word congratulations.

Between outdoor festivals, interviews, and all the other hype burying me that summer, I couldn't get back to camp. As Maxine was probably doing a lot of remedial work and advanced brainwashing with the other ladies, I wasn't missing much. In fact, that year she told me to stay away: didn't want a mob of photographers in Bernardsville searching for the *artiste*. For six months the Queen avoided me, waiting for the publicity to subside. Then I met Hugo at the Vienna Musikverein.

Hugo Lange was a man in his prime, fifty years old, dark and elegant as a Rembrandt. I had always had a major weakness for men of that age. It's the time of life when the successful ones finally become interesting. They're at that gorgeous confluence of passion, power, and, at last, humility. The predilection probably stemmed from my childhood, when so many older men would come to my father's house in Berlin bearing gifts, bouncing me on their knees . . . they were all so strong and clever, so protective of me. Hugo Lange was all of that and a musician besides. He conducted the slow movement of the Sibelius Concerto the way I would have, had I held a baton instead of a violin. After our first performance, we exited off stage directly into bed. His then-wife Nina, a gargantuan soprano, promptly called the newspapers, shrieking that I was young enough to be the Maestro's granddaughter and only lesbians rode motorcycles. Her brassy divorce made Nina more famous than had thirty years of trying to sing *Aïda*. She never thanked me, of course; Nina had about as much class as she had talent. Anyway, Hugo got the house in Berlin, Nina got the London flat. We married in December and Hugo died in his bed in February.

Maxine phoned a week later. "Hello, Smith. How about tea?" Thus the Queen extended her condolences. She couldn't bring Hugo back and she couldn't make the violin go away, but she had come up with a diversion that kept me from biting the little dot above my lip.

Despite her original antipathy, the Queen quickly realized that Frost the fiddler had certain advantages over Frost the computer nerd. I was totally mobile and, on the road, totally alone unless my manager Curtis tagged along to titillate the prurient. If Maxine needed me somewhere, Curtis arranged a concert nearby. People generally left me alone, figuring I was in my room practicing, resting, conjuring the Muse, and of course, mourning my dead husband. Over the years I became known as the Garbo Heifetz, with a soupçon of James Dean, a cover that the Queen and I exploited well.

We avoided guns; too crude. I preferred a ceramic knife that looked like a comb and never got a rise out of metal detectors at the airports. Since I spent so much time onstage, I naturally hauled around a lot of makeup; so far no customs agent, no border guard, had ever looked twice at what was actually a cache of plastics, powders, and devastating perfumes. As for electronics, again I was quite safe. Nowadays no one questioned a Sony Walkman, a portable DAT player, or a laptop computer, particularly in the hands of a famous violinist who spent so much time away from home.

Yes, Maxine had planned everything very well. I probably owe her my life and she subtly reminds me of the debt; over the last eight years, as our band has dwindled, my assignments have become more Byzantine. But so have I. Once my emotions went into hibernation, my brain began to flower like a glorious cancer, feeding insatiably upon itself until I finally became my perfect mate, above banal need, one step beyond love. It's the price of virtuosity. When the solitude and the secrets occasionally strangle me, I go for long, fast rides, always at night, when civilians are asleep and animals are stalking each other. Then it's just Smith goading Divine Providence: if I return alive, then I was meant to live another day.

2

$\mathcal{W}$ *ednesday, 11 October 1989.* I had just had one hell of a stinking rehearsal: Maestro Waldemar Kunz and I thought differently of a Mozart concerto that we were to perform the next evening with the Leipzig Gewandhaus Orchestra. His interpretation was lunatic. The man was a professor from Magdeburg and he'd spent the last forty years annotating Telemann trumpet voluntaries. However, he was about to become very famous. My record company wanted an unknown East German conductor on their roster, figuring this would pump sales in the ever-curious West. "This is one of my favorite pieces," Kunz told me before I had played a note.

"You don't say! Mine too!" I had answered. Thus war was declared. So far I was the loser: one violin didn't stand much chance against a symphony orchestra. Normally I would have canceled the engagement but the Queen wanted a progress report on the Great Reform. East Germans were now trying to replace Communist politicians with the democratically elected variety, assuming that this would be an improvement. The Leipzigers had sparked the ruckus with their weekly demonstrations and town meetings; since I performed there frequently and knew the town well, the Queen designated me Fly on the Wall and expected a little update each time I returned to Berlin.

Rehearsal had ended several hours earlier. I couldn't sleep: the Mozart concerto had aroused memories of other halls, other conductors. I tried the Hotel Merkur pool (closed), sauna (broken), room service *(zzzz)*, a biography of Bismarck: when the couple beyond my headboard began pounding each other to hyperorgasm, it was time for a walk.

I love Leipzig. Within a few years it will probably be destroyed by marauding progress, but that night it teemed with very powerful ghosts. The pollution and decay, the grisly postwar architecture had receded into shadow and now the old buildings came alive, almost whispering as I walked by: Bach composed here, Goethe wrote here, Lenin published here, Napoleon lost here, Mendelssohn conducted here, Luther preached here . . . their spirits all throbbed in the gloom, lost and sad. I wondered where they'd go when the BMW's disrupted their nocturnes.

It had been drizzling and the air smelled of the brown dust that eats lungs and contact lenses. An acrid fog licked my back as I went to the Hauptbahnhof for a beer. As usual, traffic was minimal: spare cash and its corollary, loose morals, were still futuristic concepts there. I brought my glass to a dingy table cluttered with plastic sugar and salt shakers and peered into the terminal. Twenty-eight platforms wide, murals the length of a football field, it was still the most magnificent train station in Europe. Its grandeur had mocked East Germans for forty-five years: who could walk through it without feeling proud of its architects? For a while I sat watching bodies scurry antlike along the gigantic promenade. Now that the secret police had been neutered, the Leipzigers seemed to be walking a bit more buoyantly. Then again, an entire nation had just bagged history's most elusive bachelor—Freedom— and was giddy with triumph. I envied them. They were fresh, vital, on the brink of a great adventure, where America had been two hundred years ago.

Debarking from the Dresden express, a dozen Russian soldiers tromped into the café. I decided I'd better leave while they were sober. Conversation ceased as I walked out: black leather, stretched over the proper sinews, can appear to be molten skin, licorice maybe, on loan from a leering Satan. Men wanted to touch, to taste . . . sorry chaps, this was my uniform, not my vamp gear. Kept the body warm while melding it with the quiet throat of night. Twice, in black leather, I've remained alive by blending into a tree trunk in the Schwarzwald. In city alleys it has bought me five, ten precious seconds. Without black leather I'm naked as raw steak.

On Goethestrasse I followed a pair of lovers into the fog. Visibility poor: a super night for adultery. The Mozart concerto rippled unpleasantly through my brain, snagging at the hundred or so points at which Maestro's interpretation differed from mine, while I strolled toward the St. Thomas Church. Johann Sebastian Bach had been its organist for many years. Now his statue stood outside: contemplation of another frustrated musician might soothe my soul. I crossed the old town square, nodding to one policeman. Not much action for a city of half a million. Everyone was probably inside recovering from Monday night's Up With Democracy demonstration. At Burgstrasse I peered toward bronzed Bach but saw only a dark hulk. No moon, spotlights kaput and they probably wouldn't get fixed for a year or two. Across the Thomasplatz was a solitary bench. If I sat on it communing with an unlit statue, sooner or later a tadpole capitalist would try to sell me something so I searched the square for trees to climb, bushes to crouch behind: nothing. Secrets had had no place in a worker's paradise.

At the edge of the square stood a two-tiered fountain, dry of course. Its gargoyles hadn't spat in decades. The top basin was just my size so I climbed inside and studied the sky, searching for consolation. The chalky clouds offered none and eventually I turned my attention to the old building beside the fountain.

The Thomaskirche was long, narrow, high, a bedlam of acute angles and pointy spires. Allied bombs and now air pollution had eroded the masonry dreadfully. Since that wouldn't do in a major tourist attraction, the authorities had encased the church in scaffolding. They were probably busting to finish repairs by the next trade fair, when thousands of merchants would swarm into Leipzig. Conventioneers would be visiting Bach's gravesite by the busload and would certainly leave impressed with East Germany's concern for its cultural heritage. I lay in the basin waiting for sympathetic spirits to seep out of the old steeple. As ever, all I got was a damp rear end.

Footsteps. Peeped over the edge of the fountain and saw a civilian in Burberry raincoat, low black hat, walking very slowly toward the church. Awestruck, perhaps. I had felt that way too the first time I had stumbled upon Bach's tomb. Some heavy force had flung my soul against a mysterious, final threshold, disconnecting me from my body: for a moment I had floated next to the eternal composer. Then I had blinked and Bach evaporated.

Below, the man slowly circled the statue, gazing at its dull bronze eyes: without lights he could barely tell whether they belonged to Bach or George Washington. Suddenly he glanced in my direction. Felt me. I froze: he froze: in the gloom he could never make out my face in a basin. Or could he? In either case he indicated nothing before wandering behind the church.

Movement above. I looked sharply at the scaffolding that surrounded the steeple and saw a small high door swing open. Out stepped a man who crept warily along the planks, afraid, clumsy, yet full of purpose. My antennae clicked on and I flattened against the marble basin: he wasn't up there to get a better look at Ursa Major. The fellow leaned over the edge of the scaffolding, waved, and a platform holding a big box began inching up the spire. Twice the pulleys squeaked, twice the platform paused . . . a few seconds later I located the ground crew: surprise, Mr. Burberry Raincoat. Now he was standing next to the portable toilet beside the steeple, intently studying the deserted Thomasplatz. Professional. My pulse dipped.

The platform finally reached the chap up above and he began lugging the box along the scaffolding. What was it, a new bell? Too squat. A locker? Dehumidifier. Refrigerator. Tight squeeze shoving it through the little door but he had measured it all out months before. Unless he was CIA, of course. Whoops, here came the Polizei. I slid way into the basin and prayed that the copper's mind would be elsewhere when he walked past the fountain. I had jumped into it on a whim; he might peer into it on a whim also. The rhythm of his footsteps suddenly broke and he changed direction, heading for the steeple.

"Good evening, Officer," I heard Burberry say, voice heavy, twenty decibels overloud, sincere as cheap perfume.

The policeman muttered in reply, the steps continued. Then the little door up in the steeple creaked wretchedly. "Who's up there?" the cop called.

Ffffft, went the silencer. The policeman's nose hit the cobblestones and snapped like an ear of corn. I shut my eyes, sick: Jesus Christ, Burberry! This was Leipzig, not Los Angeles! He had probably seen me. Any second now he'd pop over the rim of this fountain and blow my brains into Jena. Another little *ffft* and my lips would kiss only worms. Suddenly I wasn't ready to die. Burberry hurried toward the fountain—I reached for my white knife—but he continued down Klostergasse.

Time to vanish. No one would believe a lost tourist spiel from me now. The door in the steeple had shut again, secreting man and box. Burberry was off welding an alibi. The cop sprawled inelegantly in the square. I rolled him over. Fifteen minutes ago he had smiled at me; now sightless eyes bulged from defunct organic matter. His face brought back frightful memories so I ran back to the hotel and took a hot bath, wishing I could call Curtis and whimper like a pup.

On my way to rehearsal the next morning I walked by the St. Thomas Church. The body was gone but the Thomasplatz gleamed in the little patch where they had hosed away the blood. Workmen hammered at the steeple as the rickety elevator lurched up and down, this time laden with cement. The little door up top was sealed. By now the coroner had plucked a slug from the cop's ventricle and Leipzig's finest had launched a frenzied interrogation of the local rebels. They'd discover zero, of course. I checked the kiosks for cop killer headlines but today the population would be reading about pesticides in the turnips, big bad America, and that new chimera, Reform.

I signed in at the Gewandhaus, Leipzig's concert hall. Maestro greeted me backstage. "I've been thinking about your cadenza," he said, ogling my purple tights.

"Have you?" I unwrapped my violin. "I've been thinking about your *tutti*."

The rehearsal went remarkably well: nothing sweetens a melody like sudden death. Afterward I lunched with Maestro, who wished to discuss further musical details over a bratwurst. By his third beer, as conversation drifted toward Maestro's frigid and sour wife, I excused myself. If I had a dime for every frigid and sour wife I hear about, I'd have three Stradivarius violins, not one.

Rain piddled through the smog, teasing the mud, as I returned to the St. Thomas Church. Outside the entrance was a chipped plaque.

Thomaskirche, Leipzig
Reinhild Last, Preacher
Oskar Wildau, Organist
Ulrich Moll, Choirmaster
Bach Motets sung by the Boy Choir Fridays at 6

Inside smelled of dust and Martin Luther's Reformation. Between the plain plaster columns hung iron chandeliers, which cast equal patches of shadow and light over the worn wooden pews. No mosaics dazzled the eye, pierced the spirit:

high, narrow windows kept the sanctuary dim as the belly of God. A dozen visitors sat about the pews as the organist in the loft rehearsed a toccata. I walked to the altar, where the composer's dust lay under a slab. A couple stood at Bach's gravestone, minds on that faraway threshold; others wandered among the corkboards that detailed church events since A.D. 1310. Mozart played here; Liszt conducted here; Wagner was baptized here; now Burberry slaughtered cops here. The church was keeping pace with the twentieth century.

The elderly sexton was busy straightening candles above the pulpit as I drifted into the tiny vestry left of the altar. Empty; I had about half a minute. I ducked under the heavy ropes beyond which nice tourists did not stray and began yanking at the dark, heavy doors lining the walls. One of them led up into the steeple. All locked, including the one with bulletproof new cylinder and hinges.

I returned to the altar. Eventually the sexton finished with the candles and resumed his post behind the donation box. Seeing my innocent girlish face, he smiled; I visit this church each time I visit Leipzig and the sexton is a cellist. "I have a few more questions for you," I whispered. Certainly, that's why he was there. I began with more inane inquiries about Bach, watching the sexton's eyes very carefully. You never know about these old geezers. One of them in Prague almost got a flagpole down my throat.

The toccata stopped and a fugue filled the air. "Did Bach play that same organ?"

No, they had had a small problem keeping the original instrument undestroyed during the first World War. The present one was built in 1917.

"How about that organist? How long has he been here?"

"Fourteen years."

"That long?"

"It is not so long. The organist before him stayed sixty years. Bach himself stayed twenty-seven years. It is a life calling."

"How long have you been here, then?"

"Forty-eight years."

"How long has the choirmaster been here?"

The sexton's benevolence cracked a tad. "Two months. His predecessor became ill." Out of habit, he shut his mouth: innocuous words could still become evil little boomerangs. One released them with caution.

I let a moment pass. "The Thomaskirche is a national shrine. You must have auditioned hundreds of candidates."

"We didn't audition anybody," the sexton said. "The state appoints the choirmaster." A couple of Japanese tourists hovered at my side, wanting to ask the sexton the same asinine questions he had been hearing for forty-eight years, so I folded a few deutsche marks into the donation box and wandered far back to a pew beneath the choir loft.

The main doors behind me parted: policeman. His eyes raked us all before he strode down the center aisle for a chat with the sexton. One got the impression that his boots had persuaded many obstacles to move. That made me a little nervous so I dropped to my knees and half pretended to pray. Done with the sexton, the policeman proceeded to the organ loft. The fugue swelling the sanctuary abruptly ended. "Oskar Wildau?" I heard him say. He had no idea how pristine the acoustics were in these old churches. "You are organist at the Thomaskirche?"

"Yes."

"You were here last night?"

"Yes, I was rehearsing with the choir until six. Then I went home."

"You live in the parsonage next to the church?"

"Yes."

"Did you notice anything or anyone unusual here last night?"

"No."

"What were you doing between ten and one?"

"Reading a book."

"What was the title of this book?"

"*The Theory and Practice of Ornamentation in Liturgical Motets of the Fifteenth Century.*"

A short pause. "Do you have any witnesses?"

"No, of course not!"

"What time did you go to bed?"

"Midnight."

"You heard nothing outside?"

"No."

"You saw nothing outside?"

"The lights have been broken."

"What time did you arrive at your job this morning?"

"Eight o'clock."

"Was everything in order?"

"Yes."

"That is all for now. You may be questioned further."

The policeman left. Oskar Wildau tried to resume practicing but his fingers had become macaroni. Soon he came down from the choir loft. I said a quick Amen and caught up with him at the door. Soft innocent eyes: he had fallen in love often, probably with the boys in the choir. "Mr. Wildau?"

He spotted my violin and the mole above my lip. Maxine likes to think it's one of my trademarks. "I know who you are. This is a pleasure."

Poor thing. I took Oskar across the street for a few cream puffs and soon had his life story. Some women inspire wars; I inspire confidences from strangers. The end result is probably the same. Apparently Oskar had been a close friend of the old choirmaster and things hadn't been the same around the Thomaskirche since Ulrich Moll's arrival two months ago. The new choirmaster wasn't very sociable. Didn't live in the parsonage with everyone else but stayed in a room up in the steeple. Said it was quieter there. "But worse," said Oskar in an undertone, raining sugar into his coffee, "Moll's a terrible conductor. The boys don't like him."

Sympathy and consolation poured from my mouth and soon

I knew that Moll's first act as choirmaster had been to put fancy locks in the steeple. Stayed in his room all day and night and not once had he invited Oskar up for a cup of tea. "What's he doing in there?" I asked.

"Composing, I guess. He has to write a cantata for Easter."

"Doesn't he ever go out?"

"He rehearses the boys from two to five in the afternoon. He takes voice lessons on Thursday evening."

Tonight. I couldn't waste such good fortune. "With whom?"

"Madame Bovronsky. She says he's hopeless." The poor fellow had waited weeks to divulge this information to someone. "Forgive me, I'm boring you."

No no no. I consulted a map and a phone book. Bovronsky lived on the corner of Haydnstrasse and Zetkin Park, an arborway named for the eminent socialist pedagogue who now smiled placidly from ten-mark notes. An unflattering statue of Clara Zetkin frowned over her domain; its sculptor had probably been handed several tons of bronze, a pocket knife, and been told the unveiling was in a week. The only logical path from Moll's singing lesson to the steeple cut right past the Zetkin statue. I walked the route over, then returned to the Hotel Merkur to practice the rest of the afternoon. People pay lots of money to hear me hit the right notes.

That night I found my bench and waited. Clouds feathered the moon, leaves rustled overhead: inspired kissing weather. No one seemed to be taking advantage of it. I got a tiny atomizer from my pocket, bit off the cap. Moll was about to inhale some designer perfume. The House of Maxine calls it OS-120: one whiff and it's outer space for two minutes. Most useful for accessing pockets without leaving a prunish welt across the host's neck. Unless I stole his pants, the subject would have no idea that he'd been taken. Come on Bovronsky, send the choirmaster home! The longer I had to wait, the more eyes I imagined behind every bush: New Germany or not, at night the paranoia monoxide in Leipzig still reached hallucinogenic levels. Every spy in the world was there now that the borders had ruptured. A couple million newly unemployed State Police, the beloved Stasi, couldn't all be home reading the want ads.

No lawmen seemed to be patrolling this part of town; they were still saturating the Thomasplatz in case Burberry decided to stroll through the area and play some more with his silencer. That didn't mean a cop might not wander over, of course, and I hadn't anticipated the moon shining brightly as an antitheft device overhead. Increased visibility increased the risk of exposure so I'd have to hit Moll exactly between two lime trees at the curve of the path. I planted a branch there and retreated, becoming aware of leaves fluttering under a far bench, tires whirring upon distant pavement: sound meant life, sound meant death. One had to know the difference.

A shadow bolted past the statue of Clara Zetkin. It was the man I had seen on the scaffolding last night. Hadn't expected him to be moving quite so fast on those stubby legs and now I was a hair off collision pace. He didn't see me until I stumbled over the branch at the curve and went flying into him. Tonight the *ffft* was mine and he dropped like a sodden mattress onto the bench. I ran my hands over his pockets. Nothing in those pants but a titanic erection: Bovronsky must be trying to make a tenor out of him. Tried the shirt and found two keys dangling from his neck, one brass, one plastic (schmuck), so I twisted open a lipstick case and made an impression of the brass key in its ruby stalk. Then I took my American Express card and clamped the key that looked like a popsicle stick against the magnetic strip above my signature.

I buttoned Moll up just as his eyelids began to flutter and yanked him to his feet. "Watch where you're going," I snarled, and ran off. Had I apologized he would have known I was from the West.

Annoyed Polizei still infested the center of town; I was questioned twice en route to the Merkur. A plainclothesman lounged over the hotel desk, studying the guest list with the manager. As I swished by he checked out the black leather legs before returning to his printout and a pile of passports; the manager had already explained what I was doing in Leipzig and everyone knew violinists did nothing but practice and eat barbiturates. "How was the opera?" the manager asked, handing over my room key.

"Superb." Took the elevator up nineteen floors and bolted myself into the bathroom with a little cosmetics case. I pulled Maxine's lipstick from my pocket and dribbled what looked like expensive makeup into one of the depressions from Moll's brass key; in a few moments that tawny liquid would harden into rock. I need only repeat the process with the other side of the key, apply nail file, a little glue, and that heavy door in the chapel would swing open for me.

Duplicating the plastic key would take a bit longer. Embedded in all keys of this type was a line of wee round magnets, some with north poles facing upward, others with south poles facing upward, like a parade of tiny dimes, some heads up, some tails up. Slide this key into a lock and the magnets would either attract or repel a line of tiny pins and tumblers. Eight magnets, two to the eighth possible combinations; twelve magnets, two to the twelfth, and that was only for single-file magnets: once they were inlaid two or three deep, the permutations got a bit thick for the average lockpicker.

To the naked eye, the strip along the back of a credit card is as dynamic as an old shoelace. But pass a magnetic tape reader over it and out springs an arrangement of tiny parallel lines: iron particles magnetized into bar code describing the cardholder's name, account number, credit limit. While reasonably stable if kept in a wallet, iron particles will abandon the bar code if a more attractive magnet comes along. I dug in my cosmetics bag for the green eye shadow and held it under the tap, rinsing the greasepaint away. I lifted out a disk no larger, no thicker, than a quarter. Magnetic tape reader: two thin circles of plastic encasing a solution of alcohol and iron particles. Slide this baby over a magnetized strip and the particles suspended in alcohol would mimic the pattern of the bar code beneath.

I slowly ran the reader across the strip on my Amex card and saw, instead of bar code, an arrangement of clots and voids. The magnetic dots in Moll's key had seduced my Amex card. His north poles had sucked the iron particles into tiny dark circles and the south poles had chased the particles away. I counted eight poles, single file: a simple key, as I had suspected. Moll and Burberry were a low-profile operation.

My wallet contained many credit cards, only two of which actually worked at checkout counters. The rest were magnetic key blanks: came in handy when Smith met door. The bogus Eurocard was the eight-magnet blank. With a travel iron I wilted its edges and peeled back the top layer of plastic, exposing eight tiny magnets in a row. With a tweezer, I turned the north and south poles according to the pattern on my Amex card, ironed it shut again, shaved away the sides: there lay my clone of Moll's key. It was probably the Open Sesame to my execution.

For hundreds of years the boy choir at the St. Thomas Church had been singing motets at six on Friday night. Although this evening's concert would not begin for another hour, older people were already waiting in the sanctuary, staring patiently at nothing. Women, mostly. I watched one claim a seat: she had been sitting there Friday nights through the rise and fall of two empires and this space would remain hers no matter what the present Caesar decreed concerning private property. Standing at the fringe of a small group huddled at Bach's grave, I had a good view of the sexton and the chapel, whence Moll would have to emerge within the next ten minutes to warm up his boys. While he was gone, I planned to inspect his dormitory. It was dicey but ignorance galled me and I couldn't return to Berlin with nothing but preposterous fairy tales for the Queen. Finally Moll popped out of the vestry and hurried back to the choir loft, preoccupied and wan: the sight of forty boys staring derisively at his baton each Friday night no doubt filled him with terror. I liked that. He may have gotten a little sloppy about details in the steeple prior to departure.

Off answering more obtuse questions, the sexton had not noticed me today. I was dressed like a Karl Marx U. sophomore, dark and baggy, with a black beret pulled down over my face. I waited until a few old ladies ran some interference on the sexton then drifted sideways into the vestry, where I stared at a flaking Nativity until the room cleared. Then I pounced behind a cabinet and waited for Oskar's organ prelude to begin. As a deep chord rolled through the silence my hands began to throb: the heart was injecting high-test red into the system now. Smith faced a one-shot performance and the fingers had better work perfectly.

I suddenly heard the voices of tiny angels. No instrument on earth, not even my violin, could make tones that high, that pure. Little mouths opened and out poured a current direct from The Source. Sound split into polyphony, swirled around the dim rafters: ten thousand years from now Bach's counterpoint would still cause souls to tremble. But I had to move. Moll would only be detained for the next twenty minutes. I crept to the locked door, slid my new key into the new lock: the bolt moved elegantly back. With two fingers I floated the heavy oak open and let the steeple swallow me.

Instead of a far-off motet I heard only wind whooshing hollowly through the cavern. There was no alarm. Just enough light seeped past the occasional slats to outline a narrow, uneven staircase. I started slowly up the spiral, feeling my way along the damp outer wall: the Lutherans hadn't installed a banister and Moll was not assiduous with a broom. My fingers ran over rough stones, cobwebs, mold . . . freezing metal.

Lightning rod, I thought first. Usually a copper braid runs from the needle on top down through the steeple, grounding halfway to hell far below the church foundation; naked, forgotten, the braid is harmless except for the once or twice per century that a billion volts might be zapping through it. But the hump on the wall was thick as my fist. Forget the lightning rod, this was hundred-kilowatt conduit. Moll could broadcast the Top Twenty, fry an egg in Zwickau . . . inventive minds had a blast with this much juice. Look at Dr. Frankenstein.

The wind whistled and softly fell away as I went round and round the staircase, following the conduit. The steps were becoming crooked as a crone's teeth. Then the conduit suddenly disappeared through the wooden ceiling and the staircase deadended at an old door. Locked, son of a bitch: Moll's stage fright had not prevented him from securing his apartment. I eased my magnetic key into the slot above the knob, inched the door open. No roommates, please. I had no time for introductions.

He lived alone in a bachelor's sty. The air reeked of ossified socks. Books, papers, bread crusts strewed the floor. Moll hadn't made his bed and from the look of the blankets shoved to the foot of the mattress, he did not enjoy many sweet dreams. No pictures, lamps, no cuddly afghans from Mom, and forget the crucifixes: Moll worshiped hi-fi equipment. Ten choirmaster's salaries wouldn't cover the toys on that far wall. Speakers, tuner, amplifier, CD player, tape deck, video, turntable could have walked right out of the priciest shop on the Ku'damm. Looked like Moll had spent the other half of the gross national product on LP's, cassettes, CD's: Bach up the wazoo, a giant collection of Beethoven . . . the dear boy even had a copy of my Brahms concerto. I was tempted to autograph it.

Walked to his desk and stood a moment behind the computer terminal, a new, compact model with a hundred megabytes more than he needed to cross-reference his record collection. Without knowing his password I didn't dare disturb the oily keys. His desk was locked, no time to crack it, so I picked up the trail of the conduit gliding along the perimeter of Moll's room. In the far corner it disappeared through the ceiling, next to a trapdoor. I pulled a cord and a new staircase unfolded down at me. Cold air brushed my face.

I crawled up into the bell tower. Four iron hulks dangled gracefully in the gloom, swaying with the motion of the earth. For hundreds of years they had tolled weddings, wars, quarterhours: now they hung silent as discredited oracles. Whatever Moll had dragged off the scaffolding the other night stood in the opposite corner so I circled the bells slowly, with utter respect. They were still alive.

An air conditioner. I had one just like it on the roof of my house in Berlin. Mine was in better shape, though. Deep scratches scored the sides of this one; Moll had barely eked it in from the scaffolding. He hadn't hooked it up yet. I stared at the heavy electrical wire snaking over the floor, wondering why Burberry would murder a cop in order to keep Moll's home entertainment system cool and dry. Was possession of an air conditioner punishable by death here? An airplane that had been humming overhead gradually faded toward Budapest and the steeple became still as a crypt. No rush-hour horns, no squealing brakes filtered up from the street; beneath me a major industrial center lay quiet as a Silesian village.

At first it was indistinguishable from the soft wind; then the brain locked in and I finally understood the low, even purring above me. My eyes followed the cooling duct through the last ceiling. There was no time, absolutely none, yet I had to look. I climbed the rusty rungs on the wall and clawed longer than I should have at the seams in the wood until the catch went ping and a tiny trapdoor opened to the topmost level of the steeple. Familiar white heat, half terror, half exultation, glowed in my stomach: I was about to enter sacred ground, reserved for saints and suicides.

There was the most magnificent mainframe I had ever seen. I stared at the rows of tiny red lights, transfixed by their million self-correcting clicks. No wonder Moll needed such a huge air conditioner: the IC's in this baby would generate thousands of BTU's and he didn't want any fried brains this far from a repairman. I followed the conduit to the end of its trail deep in the rumbling beast.

CLOVE QV6   Cambridge, MA

Serial number nineteen. I skidded back down to the chapel. The steeple door sighed shut and I hid beneath a moldering altar cloth, trying to swallow, as Bach's motet faded back into slumbering eternity.

3

After our third bow Maestro Kunz kissed my mouth and invited me to Auerbachs Keller for a postconcert celebration. I turned him down: our performance of the Mozart concerto had not put me in a backslapping mood. Out in the auditorium, applause continued, so the stage crew swung open the padded door and we walked back under the lights. Again I shook the young concertmaster's hand. Since the first rehearsal he had been scrutinizing my rear end with an almost scientific curiosity, as if he had heard it singing lieder to him. "Coming to the party?" he asked, barely moving his lips.

I bowed to the burgundy seats at my right. "No."

Butting in once again, as he had been doing all evening, Maestro kissed my hand and led me offstage. Suddenly I was hungry. Hadn't eaten much between visits to the steeple and concert hall, and the highway back to Berlin was not exactly studded with Burger Kings. If I left Leipzig by eleven I'd be able to catch Maxine's last set at the club: tonight she sang a late show. "Do they still serve that venison with cabbage?" I asked Maestro. Of course, it was a house specialty. "Then I might join you."

We walked to an ancient arcade in the center of town. Inside, next to the statue of a cackling Mephistopheles, a staircase led to the famous underground café. For centuries,

Auerbachs Keller had been a favorite hangout of tawdry artistic types. According to legend, Goethe began writing *Faust* here. Schiller had scribbled poetry on the heavy napkins and Schumann had dined alone every night, facing the wall. Two centuries later the dark beer and low ceilings still ignited the imagination. As the headwaiter led eight of us to a table, glances throughout the room lifted, hovered a moment, dropped.

I sat between Maestro and the concertmaster, who struggled to maintain a modicum of small talk while scanning for nipples in my décolletage. Across the table a few Gewandhaus groupies managed to laugh in all the right places as they blew smoke into the breadbaskets. When the waiter served supper Maestro began telling jokes, pressing his leg against mine at all the punchlines. He was a much better raconteur than musician and only very gradually, between titters and hee-haws, did I feel the extra set of eyes boring into me. I began at the dim corner to my left and worked head by head across the dining room: I've been stared at all my life and the antennae are pretty sharp at distinguishing looks of admiration from looks of targetry.

He sat at a small table stage center with two other men. Graying blond hair, mid-fifties, a man's most dangerous and perfect age, dressed well, irradiating a dense energy . . . his was the classic Aryan face that time distilled rather than dissipated. As our glances met the blue eyes glittered but his mouth remained absolutely still. He knew me. That glacial mask hovering beyond the soft candlelight gripped the muscles in my back: assassin. Maestro suddenly burst out laughing and I recovered my voice but not my appetite. Each time I felt the stranger staring, my throat tightened. Twice he caught me looking at him. My brain had registered that profile before but where, how, came up blank.

As we were drinking coffee he folded his white napkin. Deftly sidestepping waiters and thick chairs, he came to our table. His body looked tough as an old oak; the black suit probably concealed a couple of spectacular scars. Maestro bolted up and vigorously shook his hand. "I'm delighted to see you, Herr Direktor."

"The pleasure is mine." He looked at me. "Good evening. I enjoyed the concert."

Sound meant life, sound meant death: had he just kept his mouth shut I would have driven back to Berlin nagged by the intense blue eyes I had seen at Auerbachs Keller. In a week, as no clues came to me and the post-concert chasm healed, I'd forget about him. But that voice flung me back to a dark fountain, a dank sky. I had heard that same cool "good evening" just before a short *fffft*: Burberry.

"Thank you," I said. "Have we met?"

"I don't believe so. My name is Emil Flick."

"A violinist of exceptional skill," Maestro informed me.

Figured: the instrument fascinated marksmen and sadists. "How interesting."

"Unfortunately I do not have the time to practice anymore," Flick said. "Thus I appreciate all the more those who do." His eyes dropped to the skin below my neck. Perhaps he could see my heart thumping. "I have been following your career for some time. In fact I remained in Leipzig an extra day to attend your concert."

Maestro arched his back. "Thank you very much, Herr Direktor."

Flick ignored him. "Will you be staying tonight?"

"No, I'm returning to Berlin."

Flick extended his hand toward Maestro. "A pleasure."

The hand lingered but I did not take it: he must not feel my fingers this cold. I nodded good night. Flick bobbed between a clump of heads back to his seat.

"I think he likes you," said the concertmaster.

"I hope not."

Maestro was aghast. "Emil Flick is deputy chief of the international trade fair. It is a very important position."

I swallowed cake. "Can he really play the violin?"

No one knew the answer to that so we switched to less metaphysical topics. More coffee at my table, more at Flick's:

each of us was waiting for the other to leave. Every few moments, just as my pulse returned to normal, I felt his eyes lock on me; finally realizing that I had lost this round, I stood up, bid everyone adieu, good show, looking forward to the recordings we'd be making in a few weeks. As I was kissing cheeks, I could see Flick quietly fold his napkin.

He intercepted Maestro and me at the door of Auerbachs Keller, where we discovered that Flick happened to be walking right past the Hotel Merkur, thus would relieve Maestro of chaperone detail. With a fulsome smile the man in tails handed me to the man in the Burberry raincoat. Flick took my violin and we went up the dingy staircase, keeping our mouths shut as our toes chatted with the worn stones.

"I suppose men pursue you all the time," he said as we passed the statue of laughing Mephistopheles.

"That is correct."

We left the arcade and walked quickly past the Thomaskirche. "Then you must think me very rude."

"I think nothing," I said. A clock chimed eleven-thirty. I'd have a hell of a time getting back to Berlin by one. We came to an intersection at the end of the square. No cars, no trams, no bag people: only the traffic light showed signs of life. I stepped into the street.

Flick suddenly yanked me back to the curb. "The light is red," he said. "We don't jaywalk in Leipzig."

I wrenched my arm away. "You don't do a lot of things in Leipzig."

A policeman congealed from the mist and stood a few inches behind us, perhaps waiting for the light to change. I shut up and Flick stared stiffly at the opposite curb, clearing his throat. The moment we saw green, Flick took my arm and stepped tautly forward. I huddled against him like a quivering chick.

"In my opinion, the G Major is the loveliest Mozart concerto," he said, making sure the policeman could hear.

"It wasn't very lovely tonight."

Flick looked carefully down at me. When he spoke again his voice was low, suddenly intimate, one violinist to another. "Don't be silly."

It threw me way off balance. I forced my eyes on a smoke-stack behind the Hauptbahnhof. Even at this hour it was puffing thick white miasma into the night. "Maestro Kunz and I will be recording all the Mozart concertos," I said.

"In Leipzig?"

"Of course." The policeman faded right, toward the opera house. We didn't have to continue this inane conversation, and didn't. Flick accompanied me to the Hotel Merkur, a palatial, sterile sinkhole for Western currency. Overhead hung a modernistic chandelier whose glare hurt the eyes but somehow didn't illuminate the lobby. A solitary Japanese, smoking on a couch, watched us walk to the desk.

"Would you bring my suitcase, please?" I asked the recep-tionist.

The man disappeared into the baggage room. "I'd like to see you again," Flick said.

I looked coolly at his mouth. Our lips were about the same size. "Why?"

Maybe he smiled. "Because you are an artist."

The world contained many artists; none of them happened to be lounging in the Thomasplatz fountain last night. He had seen me. The bellboy finally appeared with my suitcase and helmet; I went to change into riding gear as Flick waited for me beneath the chandelier. "I'll walk you to your motorcy-cle," he said when I returned.

Two teenagers were hovering over the Harley, which hauled more chrome than all the stubby, poisonous Wartburgs in the entire parking lot. I rode the bike in the Eastern sector as much as possible: one fully dressed number like mine wasted about fifty Communist Youth League meetings. Flick watched as I strapped my suitcase, then my violin to the rack. I pulled the helmet on. "How'd you know about the motorcycle?"

I saw his teeth for the first time. White, very white. Men who took care of their mouths were attentive in bed. "I read the newspapers," Flick said. "Good night."

One snap of my wrist and the engine rumbled against my thighs. I shot into the street and kept the speed low, lights down, until the E6. Then I cranked up to the legal limit, which lay solidly in the middle of second gear. East German highways torture me. They are flat, straight, deserted, and heavily patrolled by the police. Fines for speeding cost more than a wad of truffles and of course radar detectors were illegal. They got confiscated and their operators went to jail, there to draft letters of ransom to foreign banks. At least I was making the trip at night, when I couldn't see the blue exhaust billowing from the butt of every vehicle on the road or the milky death cloud lying over the land. Instead of computers, why couldn't Flick have stolen a few catalytic converters, for Christ's sake?

I putzed obediently along at 100 kph. Every so often the Harley would coast by a sputtering Trabant or a little truck laden with pig manure; for a few seconds my headlight would catch a curious face to my right before I reentered a black abyss. No streetlamps, no painted lines, no shoulder, no median, no picnic areas, no billboards adorned the E6 and I wouldn't be seeing many stars for another hour, when the smog dissipated around Wittenberg. Faint lights twinkled sporadically in the distance, barns perfumed the night, and somewhere between Bitterfeld and Dessau, as always, I began to lose grip of the twentieth century. The tires whirring beneath me narcotized thought and I was conscious only of gliding through a sleeping, medieval plain, a Grimm brothers fairy tale.

The concrete suddenly widened from four lanes to sixty: Checkpoint Bravo. I braked at a yellow cement booth, handing my passport to a chubby blond. In the old days, he'd ask me to dismount and would circle the Harley twice, checking for defectors strapped to its underbelly. Then he'd disappear into his shack. Some nights he'd come right out; other nights, he'd play solitaire for half an hour. Meanwhile I'd just wait, trying to look anxious. But times had changed; now the border guards swept East Germans past as if they were dead leaves. They saved the old routines for the old antagonists. In the next lane, a Pole chain-smoked calmly as two guards disemboweled his van. He'd finish a carton of cigarettes before they finished with him.

Eventually I got my passport back and proceeded to the second barrier. "Hello," I said cheerfully, sliding passport and customs declaration under the guard's window. No reply. He put his nose to the glass, impassively observed my mode of transport, told me to remove my helmet. The fellow's eyes flickered from my face to passport to face. Then he flipped verrrry carefully through a little book containing nothing but numbers. He disappeared into a back room.

They were sliding mirrors under the Audi in the next lane. I glanced at my watch: come on, pal, waits made me nervous. I knew it was just one chance in a million but that was an infinity more than zero chances in a million and with each minute another needle of fear pierced my stomach as I peered pleasantly into the empty booth, humming Schubert. The guard finally emerged, returned my passport and I drove to yet a third set of guards, this time English. I was entering Berlin's British sector.

He stared at the Harley. "What were you doing in East Germany?"

"Playing the fiddle."

He waved me home. I blew West: surely this road lay on a different planet. Guardrails and streetlamps sprang miraculously from the earth. The eyes had to adjust to a startling stream of white stripes on the pavement. Trees crowded the shoulder, whispering like exotic, precious life-forms. But it was the grass in the median which always made me cry; I never realize how mud oppresses me until I leave the East. Maybe the Germans would remedy that little problem once they became one big happy family again. A few seconds later I had the Harley up to one-fifty. It's a typical reaction along this stretch and the police leave us alone for the first couple of miles.

I rode down the Kurfürstendamm because it was bright and shockingly clean, crammed with shiny cars and neon and stupid little dogs in argyle overcoats. Punk lovers strolled past whores in pink ski pants as rotund men studied brassieres in the windows. Noise rushed at me from everywhere, a million white lights sparkled from the trees: the color and commotion jolted my nervous system like a bucket of espresso. I buzzed through a maze of side streets to the night-club my brother owns on Urbanstrasse. Chained the Harley to a young tree and slid into a murky foyer. Pressed a buzzer and saw Horst, bouncer, behind the doorknob. His granite face relaxed. "Leslie," he said, opening up. "Where have you been?"

My face burned in this pool of warm air. I thought briefly of striding back into the night. "On the road."

He took my helmet and violin. "Wonderful riding weather, eh."

I looked at his hands in the subdued light. They would fit perfectly over my chilly breasts. "Is Maxine on yet?"

"No, sweetheart."

I pushed the last set of doors. "Thanks."

Jazz and smoke thickened the air. Onstage a pianist played blues. I stood inside the door a moment, sizing the shadows: a dozen habitues, a sprinkling of lovers, and at the bar four new faces. As I ordered a drink they all glanced at me, hoping for what? Deliverance? Not in this town, gang. Blue fumes licked my legs as I walked to a table in the corner. The crowd seemed enrapt in the music, their companions, their cigarettes. I relaxed. No one had come here sniffing for Smith.

Champagne in hand, my brother began making his way across the room as women of all varieties followed his progress: like all of us Frosts, Roland was tall, dark, and haggardly handsome, a pirate with angst. I saw at once that his new novel was not going well; he looked like our father the night the Berlin Wall sprang up out of the ether. "Hello Les," he said, swooping into the empty chair beside me. Roland lit a cigarette. "Rough day?"

My hand fanned the air. "I thought you quit smoking."

"I quit smoking Gitanes." Roland exhaled into the recessed lighting above his head. "What brings you here?"

"I just got back from Leipzig."

"Aha. Let me get you a drink."

The curtains behind the piano parted and out stepped Maxine in a shimmering red gown. Heavy rhinestone earrings grazed her shoulders as she sauntered into the crowd. I couldn't peel my eyes off her, and I am a woman. "She's looking good," I said to my brother.

Maxine gracefully slouched over the piano as a spotlight warmed her mocha shoulders. Half the red gown wanted to melt away and the other half crushed its contents in a pythonian death grip. I wondered where she had gotten it; a rig like that would come in handy next time I had to play an atonal concerto. For twenty minutes Maxine's dusky voice described lust and regret as a mesmerized crowd watched her lips: no one sings blues like an American black. I sipped my mineral water, waiting restlessly for her set to end.

After two encores the Queen came to our table, smiling slowly at the regulars. I checked the room for drifts in posture, unlikely glances: we were alone. Everyone here knew that the violinist was Roland's sister, the singer was his lady, and Roland was slowly putrefying his liver. We had been a happy threesome for some years. At the beginning, it had seemed a perfect arrangement. Roland had fallen for Maxine the moment I took him to her dumpy cabaret on Nordstrasse. He had sent flowers, poetry, jewelry, finally persuading her to sing at his own nightclub: it all fit so well with our cover. By lover's osmosis, Roland had to know that Maxine was more than a singer. She kept her body too well honed, she locked too many drawers . . . no doubt it had increased his desire. I think the Queen had genuinely loved him during the first couple of years. Then she lost five of her seven agents, I got famous, and Roland stopped writing.

"Great show," I said as Maxine took a seat.

The Queen loosed another sultry smile, half onstage yet. She'd need another moment to shift gears. "Thanks." She reached for my brother's champagne.

"No drinking on the job," Roland said, watching her empty the glass. He looked toward the bar. "I'll get you something else."

"Would you, darling?"

He walked off; we had about four minutes. My brother had spent enough years around diplomats to know that Maxine and I were something more than a two-bit mutual admiration society; whether he should be jealous that we excluded him, or outraged that we peripherally included him, was an issue that Roland would probably never resolve. He preferred to see us as cornerstones of his writer's block.

Maxine's eyes flitted lazily over my face. "Tell me you didn't do it."

The dead cop, of course. "No, I didn't do it," I retorted. "Why isn't it in the papers?"

"Maybe they don't want the idea to catch on." She patiently watched me drain my glass. "How was your concert?"

"Terrible." That chap at the bar, the one I had not seen here before, had not budged. He could have a microphone in his eyeglasses, the sole of his shoe . . . that woman catty-corner from us, who seemed to be crying on her lover's shoulder, had just taken a handkerchief from her purse. I didn't like the way it was lying open on the table now, pointing at me. Had Flick sent her?

"They're okay," said the Queen. "What's the problem."

I slouched in my chair, staring at the empty stage. "You know the new Clove QV6 computer? Great brains in a great body?"

"Vaguely."

"There's one in the steeple of the St. Thomas Church."

Maxine coolly studied her long red fingernails. She knew better than to ask how I had stumbled upon this information. "You're sure."

"Serial number nineteen." That shut her up. "We didn't put it there, did we?"

"No."

"Look up Ulrich Moll, the choirmaster. Lives in the steeple with the brains. You know Emil Flick?"

"Deputy chief of the trade fair."

"He shot the cop." Her eyes narrowed. "I saw that, too."

Maxine smiled mirthlessly. "You've had quite a trip." That was the Queen's way of saying *great job*.

Roland was weaving back toward the table. There was time for only one more sentence. "Flick is following me."

Roland appeared with a near-exhausted bottle of champagne for himself, orange juice for Maxine, nothing for his rich and famous sister. "So where are you going next?" he asked me, dropping heavily into his chair. "Tibet? Duets with the Dalai Lama?" His tongue had turned to moss; at the bar he had probably swallowed the upper three-quarters of the bottle. My father should never have yanked Roland out of New York to live in Berlin. The sudden demise of English and the Little League had left permanent welts on his seven-year-old psyche. Had Roland been three, like me, the move would have meant nothing more than a change of bedroom.

"Duncan and I are playing at the Philharmonie tomorrow," I said. "Then we're recording for a few days. Beethoven sonatas."

"Uh huh." My brother neglected to ask for complimentary tickets.

Onstage Maxine's pianist began another moody set and a couple got up to dance, or rather, to neck in a standing position. They didn't care who was watching. Roland eventually shifted his gaze from the ballet to the bubbles in his glass. "So how's Curtis?" he inquired.

I felt Maxine's eye slide in my direction. She never asked, never forbade, but she was vitally interested in the men who perhaps laid hands on me: the Queen didn't want a repeat of Hugo. "Curtis is fine," I said. No further chitchat as onstage a tune slowly boiled over. At that speed it verged on the pornographic and no one really wanted to clap afterward. The two dancers didn't bother to come up for air; even the pianist was staring at them.

I stood up. "Nice seeing you, Roland."

"Leaving so soon?" More champagne slid into his stomach, there to split into piss and hiccups. "Have a nice concert."

"Take care, Maxine."

The Queen finished applying lipstick in a shade between blood and eggplant; she was due back under the spotlights. "Be good."

I quickly walked through the smoke and heat to the door.

She would notice if anyone followed me. The moment I hit the street a gust pressed my throat. I let it whirl by and ran to the Harley before the wind returned to suffocate me. The air had turned sour, the moon had fled, leaving many thick clouds in anarchy. I saw Flick behind every tree so I took a strange, overlong route home.

My housekeeper Curtis met me at the wide front steps. We hurried inside with some skittish leaves. "Have some tea," he said, beating me to the stove. He knew my nerves were confetti: it was the same each time I squeezed past a checkpoint. I threw my jacket across a chair and started playing with the boots.

In one smooth motion he had my tea on the table, my boot in his hand. "Come." Half command, half invitation: I had to obey. He pulled, hesitating an instant as he noticed the little loop of my ceramic knife which sleeps along the inseam. The second boot came free and Curtis put both in the hallway. They'd be polished, the knife sharpened, before morning. "I made some rice pudding," he said. "It's still warm."

Biceps bulged his shirtsleeves as he shifted a heavy pot to the front burner. To please him I swallowed a couple of mouthfuls, whining about the concert, and went upstairs. Curtis dropped off my luggage. I watched him leave the bedroom. Sight of those hindquarters has pulled me out of many a funk: that man's ass is more expressive than most people's faces.

At the door he paused. "Duncan is coming at one," he reminded me. "Dress rehearsal at four. Concert's at eight."

"That blows tomorrow, I guess."

From my window I watched him walk to the garage, checking that I had locked the Harley inside. He hates the thing; it cruises at 200 kph and I'm usually in a rush. Curtis and I had met six years before in an Austrian clinic, shortly after my back intercepted a .32 caliber meteorite. I remember opening my eyes and seeing a black man in the corner reading *Steppenwolf*. Looked nasty enough to be the Queen's brother. "Who are you?" I had said.

"Your new nurse," he had replied in perfect German. "Curtis." No indication if this was first name, last name, or working title.

Switched to English. "I don't need a nurse." Then I looked down the sheets and saw bandages where my left hand should have been.

"First-degree burns," Curtis had said. Now he had a Southern drawl, the kind that wilted a lady's honor. "You could lose a thumbnail."

"Is that so? I have concerts in Edinburgh next week."

"I've canceled all your concerts for the next three months."

"You what? Son of a bitch!" I tried to sit up.

A large hand guided me back to the pillows, maintaining pressure against my chest until I realized that Curtis probably detested his job as much as I did. "That's better," he said, removing a finger from my neck. I felt somehow worse. "We're driving back to Berlin tonight. You can't stay here."

It was not a pleasant journey; my blood kept blowing kisses at the bandages. Curtis has been with me ever since and I still wasn't sure of his real job. Why ask? I wouldn't get a straight answer and he's a terrific housekeeper.

It was almost three o'clock. I went to the fireplace and

pressed an ornamental button in the mantel. To my right a mahogany panel whished open, exposing a tiny closet. A hundred years ago it probably concealed Frau's diamond brooches and Herr's deutsche marks. Once upon a time, Hugo had kept his Brahms autographs there. Now a solitary gun-metal box gleamed at me. I touched the lock with my left thumb. A sensor read my print, the hasp clicked, and out slid my beautiful little computer. I called it Spot: it was the closest I'd ever come to owning a pet. Spot knew all kinds of trivia about the seams of the earth and the scraps in orbit above it. Spot contained an esoteric Who's Who, airline schedules, Ibo history, and it had total recall. Each month Maxine sent me an upgrade in the mail and I melted down the old hunk of plastic, which held more knowledge than I would amass in fifty lifetimes. Brains like that dazzled me. Were Spot a man, I would want his children.

I pressed a small switch above the keyboard. Two red lights peeped on and Spot whirred a few seconds, thawing from sleep. First I hit the East German file, specifically Emil Flick. My pulse withered as his 3-D picture bloomed on the screen. I identified him and Spot began scrolling.

Emil Flick b. 16 August 1936 Brandenburg/
   mother Annaliese musician d. 1945
father Herbert Professor of Physics, Dresden
   University d. 1945
unmarried/heterosexual/siblings 0
Dresden University 1957 Bachelor degree
   Mathematics
1961 Doctorate Physics: Thesis, The Future of
   Optics
Military service: Army discharged January 1962
March 1962: Research assistant, Osteroptikal, Jena
May 1967: Appointed to Leipzig Trade Fair
   Committee to assist with technical exhibitions.
   1975 Secretary, 1981 Advisory Assistant, 1984
   Deputy Chief

Vices: unknown
Interests: amateur violinist
Defector potential: twice approached, results
     negative
Health: excellent

Ho hum, another perfect communist. I tried Ulrich Moll. Spot chewed a few seconds, scanning a hundred thousand names: *kein* dice. No data on Strauss or Wildau either; choirmasters, sextons, and organists didn't generally make these society pages. I put Spot to bed.

Outside, the wind had overturned two potted geraniums and they sporadically rolled an inch here, an inch there, bleeding dirt onto the patio. Who would put a QV6 in a steeple in Leipzig, the middle of nowhere? Why not East Berlin? The Clove was capable of processing fifty million instructions per second. What was Flick doing with horsepower like that? How'd he get it there? Computers of that ilk didn't disappear without months of preparation and a specific purpose in mind. Who was Moll? The most agitating question mark, of course, was Flick himself. Had he seen me in the fountain? If not, why would he pursue me now? Such coincidence resurrected all the old phantoms: that I had screwed up somewhere, that someone was on to me, that I had stepped into quicksand and wouldn't know until it was too late . . . that I was a rook on someone else's chess board now. When the porch lights went out I lay across my bed and stared at the curlicues in the plaster ceiling, seeing Flick's even, white teeth as his voice resounded in my ear, low, purple, just a caress above silence. For those brief moments with him, I had been utterly happy. That was the most shocking coincidence of all.

4

*D*uncan Zadinsky had first appeared to me in a ladies'
room at the Juilliard School of Music. I had just
arrived in New York for my weekend violin lesson
and was in a cubicle changing from road gear into more
classical attire when the door flew open and someone began
crying bitterly into the sink. Braying of that volume, I
thought, could emanate only from a singer; even in grief they
played to the last row of the balcony. I opened the door and
saw a chubby fellow with wild hair.

"You're in the ladies' room," I said.

"I don't give a damn," he snapped.

I washed my hands as the sobbing continued. "Hey look,
it can't be that bad."

"Oh shut up!"

Duncan was ruined. His mother had lashed him to a piano
seat before he was even toilet trained. Then she had taken
him to a famous teacher who told him that he must practice
ten hours a day for twenty years before the world lay at his
feet. I got him just as the twenty years elapsed and Duncan
wiped out in a famous competition: stage fright. Having just
learned—too late—that he was incapable of walking into the
footlights alone, Duncan became my accompanist. The next
spring we won the same competition he had lost. After my
marriage ended, Duncan moved to Berlin. Between concerts

with me, he now gives expensive piano lessons and is writing the definitive biography of his idol, Chopin. Twice a month he flies to London to teach at an exclusive prep school. He resents me as much as he adores me: I am his vicarious everything.

At the moment he was pacing frantically backstage at the Philharmonie. "It's two before eight! Where have you been?"

"Sleeping." Tossed my violin case onto a chair. "What's the problem?"

"Will you get dressed? Look at the time!"

Duncan fell onto the sofa. As I changed into concert clothes I could hear him babbling snatches from Ecclesiastes. When that didn't do the trick, he tried humming the theme from Rocky. By the time I was done, he had lapsed into catatonia; were it not for the intermittent twitching of his Adam's apple, he could have passed for an embalmed bridegroom. I patted his cold nose. "Let's go."

"I can't breathe," Duncan whispered. "My heart hurts. I need a doctor."

I trilled Beethoven in response to his ranting: thus we comforted each other in face of that siren which impels foolish mortals onstage. Someone knocked on the door. "Miss Frost? Mr. Zadinsky?"

Pale as a potato, Duncan rolled off the couch. "I am going to die."

"So am I, baby," I said. "But not tonight." We followed the stage manager to the soundproof door, our last frontier. I could feel my heart lurching against my velvet bodice and for a moment wanted to run back through time and many universes to my father, who would rescue me from all these hideous demons. Then I remembered who I was, or who I was supposed to be. "Duncan?" He looked constrictedly at me and took one shuddering last breath. We walked onstage. Lights warmed my shoulders, burnished his hair. We heard the applause: phantoms vanished, replaced by a much less imposing sea of heads. My accompanist bowed and began the *Kreutzer* Sonata as if he were doing the composer a favor. By ten o'clock it was all over.

His Eminence Harry Paradise, the legendary record producer, arrived backstage first. He had just blown in from London with Emory, his sidekick engineer. Since our first project about six years earlier, the three of us had slogged through dozens of recordings and a sea of booze together, thus considered ourselves a half-assed family. "So that's what we're playing tomorrow," Harry cried, smile upstaged by a fifth gold medallion dangling from his neck. Each time a new divorce goes through, Harry buys himself a trophy. "Sounds awful."

People began trickling in so Harry stepped aside, backwashing me with treacly cologne. As I was shaking hands he began talking Opera with a journalist from some German music magazine. They were still name-dropping thick and fast when the last well-wisher had left.

"You must come with us," Harry insisted to the critic, smelling a feature article. "Our conversation will continue at the Kempinski Hotel."

"See you boys tomorrow," I said, tossing on a green cape.

"Hold it, you can't go home," Harry cried. "We're celebrating our new contract with Kakadu."

"Kakadu Classics?" Media asked.

Harry smiled unctuously. "It's not public yet, of course. We just signed last week. Four recordings a year for five years. Super orchestras, big conductors, the major masterworks . . . maybe a few sonatas with Zadinsky here."

Duncan frowned. He had recently been making a few new stabs at a solo career. Didn't want his obituary to begin with the line *Leslie Frost's Accompanist*.

"Kakadu wants to give unknown American artists more exposure," Harry continued, patting Duncan's arm.

"That's diplomatic of them," the journalist said. "Considering they swallowed three American record companies." Kakadu's headquarters were in Tokyo.

"I'm getting thirsty," Emory announced.

We adjourned to the Kempinski, where Harry and Media resumed a fatuous operatic debate as Emory drank, Duncan sulked, and I scanned the faces in the dining room: no Flick, no appetite. Between rounds Emory told us of his latest bout with Beethoven's Fifth Symphony. He and Harry had now recorded the piece thirty times.

"Why do you do it, Em?" Duncan finally asked. "The music? The money?"

Emory thought a moment. "The beer. Harry and I will only record the piece in countries with great beer." He drained another pint. "We hate Beethoven."

Meanwhile, across the table, Harry and his friend traded intimate musical anecdotes. When that little game staled, Paradise smiled benevolently at me: I was about to become alternative subject fodder. "That's a lovely cape, Les. Green beaver? Where do you come up with these things?"

"Her housekeeper buys them," Duncan answered for me. "The man's taste is extremely questionable."

"I rather like it," Emory sloshed, running a hand along my shoulder. "Reminds me of Harry's second wife. Greta, wasn't it? The one with the bright orange lipstick?"

Harry smiled icily: one topic people never, ever discussed with him was alimony recipients. "Ah, if only your ears were as sharp as your memory," he replied. "We'd have twenty Grammy awards by now."

Before their bons mots could go nuclear, I stood up. "Tomorrow's a big day, boys. Let's get some sleep."

"You can't go! I ordered a special cake!"

Harry had probably ordered a special photographer also. The man lived to see his teeth in newsprint. "Try to have it on the table when I get back," I said. "Along with a pot of coffee for your partner." En route to the ladies' room I scanned every head in the restaurant: someone had been looking at me. I saw nothing but dowagers and waxen waiters. As I shellacked my mouth with lipstick, my mole throbbed. Steady, Smith: this was only postconcert fatigue. I scowled into the mirror and left.

Across the dining room I saw a small woman in a brown coat and hat walk slightly too fast, too straight, toward Harry, Media, Duncan, and Emory, who was now wearing my green cape, hood up. As she breezed by, the woman's cane tapped Emory once on the shoulder. Then she bobbed out the door. Almost immediately my cape began tilting to the right. I reached him just as he toppled to the floor. "Emory!" Slapped his face, took his pulse: out, far out. Meanwhile the Three Stooges stared at me with that childlike wonder of the stone drunk. I tore into the street. The woman had jumped into one of several cars pulling away from the curb. Couldn't stop her now but I wanted her to know that she had hit the wrong target. "Taxi!"

Inside, Duncan and a waiter were attempting to revive Emory as inconspicuously as possible. "Get him out," I said. "Fast."

Harry shook his head. "How terribly embarrassing. A grown man passing out in the Kempinski Hotel. Check please, waiter."

Waiter was hauling Emory away. "Harry, stay here," I ordered. "Duncan and I will take him back to the hotel."

"But I feel terrible."

"You'll cheer up. Look, here comes your cake." I left.

Duncan sat in the back of the cab sliding ice cubes around Emory's forehead. "He's not waking up."

"Take us to St. Hildegard," I told the driver. Emory's pulse was weaker than a worm's. I opened his shirt and saw a tiny swelling on his shoulder: the old cane trick but we all had it down to a science now. Targets felt a small sting and maybe went on for a minute, a day, then bang: heart attacks were best. Infectious diseases were worst. You lay in bed slowly dissolving as your assassin played blackjack in Monte Carlo. "What the hell was he doing with my cape, Duncan?"

"Doing an imitation of Karajan." Duncan stared glumly out the window. "How's he going to do our recording session tomorrow?"

"He's not."

Emory's eyelids began to flutter as we unloaded him at the hospital. I told the nurse he had been taking drugs. After they wheeled him upstairs I called home. "Curtis? I'm at St. Hildegard. Maybe you could do me a favor."

"What's the matter."

I couldn't tell him much over public phone lines. "Emory passed out while we were having dinner. I hate to leave him alone here but Duncan and I have to get some sleep before the sessions tomorrow."

"I'll be right over."

As Duncan paced the lobby, I signed a few autographs. Finally the revolving doors swirled and in came Curtis. I ran over, clinging to his arm as if it were a life raft. "Check the left shoulder," I said. "He's drunk. It might alter things."

Curtis knew which doctor to call. "Why Emory?"

"They were going for me and missed." Curtis frowned; he detested amateurs. "I guess we can go home now, Duncan," I called.

"You don't mind, do you, Curt?" Duncan asked. "It's all my fault. I should have cut him off after five beers."

Curtis gave me the car keys. "Scram."

Next day a biting fog blanketed Berlin. On our way to the Philharmonie, Duncan paused at a newsstand to indulge his masochistic bent for reading reviews. He kept an enormous scrapbook and sent his mother extolatory clippings in languages she couldn't read.

"What did Harry say when you called him last night?" he asked, flipping to the arts section.

"Not much. I may have interrupted something."

"Where's he going to find another engineer at the last minute like this?"

"That's his problem." The security guard at the Philharmonie told us that Harry Paradise had signed in three hours ago, alone. Duncan and I took an elevator to the control room five floors above the stage and followed a stream of cables to a beige door. Behind it blared Beethoven. "Harry?" I called, pushing the door open.

He was seated at a long table which supported a mixing console, a remote control, CD player, various lamps, meters, and electronic toys in addition to a smorgasbord of health food in case the World's Greatest Record Producer felt hollow before lunchtime. Eyes closed, he swayed with the music flowing from the loudspeakers several yards ahead of him. Millions of digital signals, looking like ribbons of static, spilled across the TV monitor to his right. "Good morning," I shouted. "Feeling well?"

Harry turned down the volume. "Any more stupid questions?"

"How's Emory?"

"The doctor says he has to cool it the rest of the week."

"Son of a bitch!" Duncan cried suddenly from the corner.

Harry snatched the newspaper away. "Jackass! Why must you read reviews before a recording session? Go warm up the piano." After Duncan had left, Harry returned to his listening, again blasting Beethoven through the speakers. He was reviewing the tape of the first eight sonatas that Duncan and I had recorded here last spring. Now we were supposed to be wrapping up the last few sonatas so that Kakadu Classics could sell the complete set for many more bucks.

"I'm not thrilled with this," Harry called above the noise. "The sound is grainy. You're playing flat. Maybe we should do everything over again."

I killed the volume. "Pipe down, Napoleon."

"That was an awful cake," he said. "I was humiliated."

"Your partner of thirty years just about dies and all you can think of is cake?" I unlatched my violin case. "Who's replacing him?"

"Chap from London. On Kakadu's recommended list."

"You're using someone you never worked with on my sessions?"

"I've been in this business forty years," Harry announced. "I know what I'm doing."

"Is that so? Do you know your channels are crossed?" I flipped a filter switch. "Doesn't sound too grainy now, does it. Who set up this place, you? It's a mess."

Then pure, silken whistling floated into the control room. I had never heard tones like that before: half bird, half Pan . . . my violin might get that high, but never that ravishing. The lips must purse very tight to hit that altitude, the tongue had to flutter incredibly fast. As Schubert's melody sailed effortlessly on, I held my breath, shocked: here was virtuosity like my own. Wasn't sure I liked that.

A caucasian male mid-thirties, six two, one seventy, entered the control room. He looked the way he whistled: polished and carefree. The gray eyes had seen it all and the smile managed to be both indulgent and cynical. Vertical, his body riveted my attention; horizontal, it could melt my bones. Confronted by our grim faces, he stopped whistling. "You're all set downstairs, Paradise," he said: American.

I turned to Harry. "Good reports, eh? From where, *Gentlemen's Quarterly*?"

"This is Toby Chance," Harry said.

I looked at his mouth again. "I've never heard of you."

"Pity," Chance replied. "I'm quite good."

"All right, let's get moving." Harry pressed the talk-back speaker. "Duncan, why don't I hear any music down there? You're supposed to be warming up."

We heard a newspaper rustle. "Mr. Zadinsky is a stimulating collaborator," Duncan translated. "One day we would like to hear him in his own recital."

"That's very commendable," Harry interrupted. "Now put the newspaper away and get to work." Duncan began to play the *Kreutzer* Sonata. "Chance, go downstairs and check the cables for me. Channels sound crossed."

Toby Chance followed me into the elevator. "I understand everyone had a busy night."

"When did Harry call you?"

"Early this morning. I took the six-thirty flight from Heathrow."

I doubted he had been sleeping alone; the eyes didn't look weary enough. "So you live in London?"

"No, Boston. I was doing a job at Abbey Road." In silence we dropped another few floors. "I've been asking Harry for work for two years."

"I suppose this is your big break, then." The steel doors opened and as I walked past him to the auditorium my own absurdity made me smile. In minutes I would be recording a thorny violin sonata. Last night someone had tried to kill me, the night before that I had found a computer stashed in a steeple in Leipzig, the night before that I had witnessed a murder and perhaps been seen doing so, and what seized my imagination but the dimple on Mr. Chance's chin. No wonder the Queen had a discipline problem.

5

*I*nstead of two thousand faces I saw two thousand square yellow seats spanning the Philharmonie. My footsteps echoed hollowly over the empty auditorium as I walked across the stage toward Duncan, who was bitching at the piano tuner about some twangs near middle C. I stood thoughtfully grinding rosin into my bow while Chance fussed with the two condenser microphones above my head.

Interesting phenomenon, recording. Soon I'd be running horsehair across four violin strings, pulsing air molecules into alternate regions of rarefaction and compression: sound waves. Across the tips of Chance's microphones stretched a sheet of nickel about one-quarter the thickness of a human hair; as I played, the sound waves would vibrate that delicate diaphragm, changing the electrical charge in the capacitor behind it. Two cables would pick up those electrical signals and feed them into a mixer up in the control room, where Harry would rearrange the signals into a nice ratio and dump them into the Sony DAT recorder. That pinnacle of Japanese enterprise would then measure the signal 44,000 times a second and instantaneously assign it a binary number, depending on its strength, between 64,000 and zero; the tape head would convert the electrical signals into magnetic signals and store them on a tiny tape creeping by at a half inch per second. Playback? Sony-san would reverse the process: magnetic signals would revert to electrical signals, this time feeding into a loudspeaker that converted electrical energy back into sound energy, which would travel across a room and vibrate the hairs in a human's inner ear. An electrochemical signal traveling near the speed of light would hit the brain, which would interpret the sounds I had made months, perhaps years before, and initiate another electrochemical mystery known as an emotional reaction in the audience I would never meet. Almost science fiction; however, complex as the recording process might seem, it was Neanderthal compared to the chain of events that enabled my fingers to dance across a violin in the first place.

"Those mikes are too high," I told Chance. "And too far apart." Rather than heed my advice, he began to whistle. "I thought we were trying to match this recording with Emory's."

"You worry about your end, sweetie pie, I'll worry about mine." Chance backed up a few feet. "Would you mind playing something?"

I'd straighten this cocky boy out in the control room. Meanwhile, Duncan needed supervision. He was going over and over a tricky passage, getting more and more irritated as it slipped away from him. "What did you have for breakfast," I asked him. "Caffeine pellets?"

Duncan did not reply. We had played that section dozens of times perfectly; now his fingers were beginning to feel the burden of digital history. I put a hand on his shoulder. "Relax."

I may as well have told him to lay eggs. "I listened to Richter's recording of this last night," Duncan said. "Taken from a live performance. No mistakes! None! Oh God! Why do I even bother?"

"Because it's fun." I opened his score to a page covered with red penciling. "Let's do the last movement. Chance is trying to hang mikes."

We made noise as Mr. Substitute moved his gear a few millimeters here and there. Eventually Harry's voice oozed over the talk-back speaker. "That's super, gang, scrumptious. C'mon up, Toby, roll some tape." Chance left the stage. "All right," our producer finally breathed, about to pronounce his favorite bromide. "Let's make music."

Duncan and I obediently trashed the first movement; he was hyper about notes and I was wondering why I hadn't cut my fingernails. "Not bad," Harry lied when the last squawk faded. "Come up for a listen."

Harry had lowered the lights in the control room to as seductive a level as possible without necessitating the use of his bifocals. As Duncan and I walked in, he and Chance were playing with the faders on the mixing console. "Coffee, anyone?" Harry offered. "Bananas? Demerol? Straight to it, then." Duncan guzzled a liter of grape juice. I watched the digits streaming by on a television monitor as Harry regurgitated Take One. "Well, what do you think?"

"Sounds like shit," Duncan muttered.

"Of course it does." Harry smiled. "You always pull this stunt on me, Zadinsky."

"Give me a break! I have a million more notes than she does!"

"The violin's too present," I cut in.

"You don't like that?" Chance asked.

"I'm not a singer, dear," I said. "Where's our last CD? Play some of it and you'll hear what I mean."

"We've already tested this," Harry said.

"Test it again."

Chance stopped doodling on the take sheets and pressed a button on the second DAT player. "What would you like to hear, madame?"

"Last movement of the last sonata, where we left off in April." He found the proper track and, pressing alternate buttons on the mixer, directed last spring's Beethoven, then today's Beethoven, through the speakers. The four of us began arguing about microphones, recording theory, and the acuity of Harry's eardrums as a rondo rippled over the control room. The producer was not his usual urbane self, lamenting that he hadn't slept, he felt an oncoming flu, he worried about Emory . . . bah. Harry was terrified that Chance would discover what a fake he was and tattle to Kakadu. "All right," he finally snapped, winging a pretzel against the wall, "do what the lady wants! Move the microphones into the zoo for all I care!"

We tromped back onstage, where Chance shifted microphones like a good boy. Once Duncan realized that the producer's brain floated somewhere in the ozone, he attacked the piano with much more abandon and, thus, more accuracy. After a few takes he forgot about tape recorders; I stopped worrying about him and we began making a little headway. Aside from an occasional toadyism, Harry Paradise kept his mouth shut. By two o'clock we had half the *Kreutzer* Sonata in the can. Edited, it would be good. "Lunch," Harry called.

The four of us were eating sushi, compliments of Kakadu Classics, when someone knocked on the control room door. "C'min!" Harry called. "That might be Herbert."

Duncan frowned. "Not that pill you met last night."

A security guard walked in, handed me an envelope. I looked at the return address. "Thanks."

"Fan mail?" asked Chance.

Let him guess. I put the envelope in my pocket and bit into seaweed. We worked until five, when the stage crew had to ready for that evening's concert. Spewing superlatives, Harry flew off to visit Emory at the hospital. Duncan and I left Chance winding tapes in the control room. I opened the letter the moment my cab pulled out of the Philharmonie lot.

Dear Miss Frost,

I understand that you will be performing in Amsterdam this weekend. As I will be there myself, I would be honored if we might celebrate this happy coincidence by dining together afterwards. I have an important question to ask. Please forgive my last-minute correspondence, to which you need not reply.

Emil Flick

Elegant, almost feminine handwriting and no mistakes, probably his tenth draft. Over smoked herring I might inquire how Flick happened to know I'd be in Amsterdam and what we might be celebrating. As the cab pulled up to a wall of rhododendron, I thought about his blue eyes. Twenty-twenty? Unlikely in a man his age. Perhaps I was safe. I unlocked the gate and walked to my front door, noticing that my lawn was dead, my trees were naked and black, even the squirrels quivered in the mist: autumn had capitulated to winter.

Curtis unlatched the door. "How'd it go?"

"Oh, Harry was sharp as a zombie and Duncan couldn't play ten notes in a row." I dropped the violin and aimed for the liquor cabinet. "All systems normal."

"Who replaced Emory?"

"Some wiseass with a nice whistle." I poured a hefty shot of Scotch. "What's for dinner?"

"Go take a nap."

Paused at the foot of the stairs. "How's Emory?"

"Hung over. Would you like to visit him?"

"If I get my work done."

I pulled my computer from its cubbyhole. "Amsterdam," I typed. "Concertgebouw." The great concert hall popped onscreen. "Interior."

Spot offered me a shot of the green and beige hall. Closer: I got fewer, but larger, seats. Finally only one seat occupied the screen. Innumerable backsides had buffed the tough hide until it gleamed. I zoomed in for a rear view, following an arc of upholstery tacks that tautened the leather in place. Again closer: for a moment I stared at the convex head of a brass tack. So Flick wanted to visit me? I'd visit him first. Spot poked under a seat, showing me what I had hoped to see: wire hat rack. For centuries the Dutch had been tucking their headgear below their fannies, sparing themselves time and coin at the hat check. I'd use that wire coil as an antenna.

I put my computer away and went downstairs. Curtis was sitting at his desk jawing about the Bruch Concerto with someone in Salzburg. Across his blotter lay my calendar for next year, jamming up fast. I didn't know whether to laugh or cry so I sat on the edge of Curtis's desk watching his lips cuddle syllables. Finally he hung up. "I thought you were taking a nap," he said, penciling in a date.

"Would you happen to have a dozen upholstery tacks in the garage? Those brass ones that look like little umbrellas?"

The plush lips stilled. "Possibly." He left, returning with a small box.

"Thanks, I'll be in the shop." I went downstairs and began poking around the hundreds of tiny plastic bags I had accumulated during my worldwide forays into hardware stores and electronic supply houses. Someday, when I collected a nice pension from Maxine Inc., I'd become an inventor. Until then, Smith would fiddle with bugs. I located my stash of electret microphones, the kind newscasters liked to wear discreetly on their lapels, only mine were much smaller, custom-made on occasional Sunday afternoons. I began drilling tiny holes into the domes of a dozen upholstery tacks so that sound could pass through; then I broke off their stems and glued a tiny electret mike in their place.

"Leslie," Curtis called from the top of the stairs, "it's nine o'clock. You have a recording session tomorrow."

"Yes, mother." At dinner I asked Curtis to notify Flick's office that two complimentary tickets awaited him in Amsterdam. "Fifteen or twenty rows back," I said. "Let me know exactly where." By the time we finished eating, visiting hours at the hospital were over.

We wrapped up the sessions by noon Thursday, just as Harry was finally pulling himself together. For three days his moods had rocketed between euphoria and bitchiness. He was sneaking gin to the control room in his thermos. Despite my repeated assertions that Harry's behavior was all due to the Emory problem, Duncan took every insult personally and actually walked off the stage twice, the last time forcing Harry to catch up with him in the parking lot, sniveling for mercy.

Chance found it all most amusing. "How can you work with these lunatics?" he asked during the second intermission.

I twiddled my fingers over the violin strings, practicing a slippery little leap. "They inspire me." He didn't get it, of course. Later Chance invited me out to dinner. I smiled, shook my head; the guy was a tad too cute for his own good. But he wasn't a half-bad engineer. Chance had correctly diagnosed the Sony the two times it balked and somehow he made Harry feel like a genius, a skill Emory had failed to exhibit in the six years I had known him. Naturally, Harry and Chance had become thick as twins.

When Duncan and I went up to the control room for the ritual postsession backslapping, we found Harry tossing on a cashmere coat. "Sorry gang, I can't stay," he said. "You'll have to celebrate without me. I've got critical business in Copenhagen."

"Wait a minute, when will the editing be ready?" Duncan cried.

"Ask Chance, he's doing it," Harry called from the hallway. "Bye bye!"

Duncan looked darkly at me; over the years he and Emory had spent thousands of hours together in the editing suite. They had a relationship not unlike that of a very light blond and her hairdresser. "Is Emory too sick to edit or what?" Duncan muttered.

Chance emerged from the machine room. "Emory's fine. I just told Harry that if he wanted a recording engineer at the last minute, he had to give me the editing work as well."

"Sharp little businessman, aren't you," I said.

"Thank you, darling. Don't worry, Duncan, I'm a great editor. You'll come out sounding perfect." He glanced at me. "With Frosty it might be a little tougher."

"Give the job to Emory if you can't cut it," I said, pulling Duncan's arm.

Chance accompanied us to the elevator, probably wondering how to apologize. If I made enough of a stink, Kakadu would hand the editing back to Emory. "Are we still on for dinner?" he asked me.

"I don't believe we were ever on for dinner."

The elevator arrived. "We're flying to Amsterdam tonight," Duncan had to explain as the enamel doors shut behind us. "Thanks, Toby, it's been great."

In reply we heard only high, carefree whistling. "Duncan," I began, then shut my mouth. I needed him docile tonight. "You were terrific."

My accompanist and I tried to sleep on the plane but he was still wired from the sessions and I was ulcerating over midnight at the Concertgebouw. Somehow I had to get rid of Duncan as I operated on a certain seat twenty rows back from the stage. Originally we had been scheduled to rehearse in the hall the next afternoon for that evening's concert; however, since that didn't fit with my new plans, I had Curtis speak with the hall manager, who found a way to bend house rules after Curtis found a way to wire him a thousand guilders. Now Duncan and I had the place from midnight till two in the morning for our dress rehearsal.

I told Duncan that Curtis had screwed up our rehearsal time, a tale that Duncan accepted without question. He hated managers. The antipathy dated back to his days in New York, when he had knocked on a thousand impresarios' doors only to be told that the world wouldn't be needing another pianist until A.D. 2075.

"Midnight?" he squawked. "We only begin at midnight? After a full day of recording? Who does he think I am, Superman?"

"He's very sorry. Says he won't do it again." I yawned. "We can get into the hall as soon as the concert's over."

"Who's playing tonight?"

"Vlado Lobotsky."

Duncan's face greened. The mega-emigré Lobotsky had just won another big piano competition and was making a triumphal world tour as a Chopin specialist, much to the aggravation of the world's other Chopin specialist, Duncan Zadinsky. My accompanist stared out the window for many minutes before asking the steward for a brandy. He didn't say much the rest of the way to Amsterdam; during dinner he fortified himself with genever, mumbling that his joints ached. I had to march him around the canals for several hours before his sense of destiny returned.

We got to the concert hall near midnight. "We must have total silence," I told the security guard. "No vacuuming, no floor polishing." Behind him hung two closed-circuit TV screens depicting the main foyer and the lone piano onstage. Great luck: no coverage of the empty auditorium. "Has the custodial staff finished for the night? Excellent."

The doors to our left suddenly banged open and out strutted Lobotsky with two nymphets. Recognizing me, he ran the Hail Fellow Muse program as his bovines gaped on. "Did you hear my B-flat minor sonata?" he asked.

"We just arrived in Amsterdam."

"How unfortunate." Lobotsky described his standing ovation and his many, many curtain calls. When that puffery choked on its own flatulence, Lobotsky finally noticed Duncan. He floated a hand, as if expecting it to be kissed. "You must be the accompanist."

"No, I'm the violin tuner," Duncan replied.

Nodding goodbye to Vlado, I steered Duncan toward the musty backstage corridor. "He's just another piano basher," I said.

"Is that so? Then why are so many people paying to hear him?"

"Because they're curious. They'll only do it once."

Duncan guffawed bitterly. " 'Did you hear my B-flat minor sonata?' " he mimicked. "Christ!" Duncan had been working on the piece since he was ten. He considered it his private property.

"You play it much better than Vlado," I said.

"I play it better than anyone!" Duncan snapped, dropping his music heavily on the piano.

Eureka, I was saved: running into Lobotsky backstage had been a godsend. We hacked at Bartók a while. "I've had it," I said abruptly, putting the violin down.

My accompanist had been playing with a martyr's intensity. "You want to stop? Now?"

"My neck hurts." I lifted my canvas bag, walked down to seat 20L, just beyond the periphery of stage lights. "Could you play some Chopin? It relaxes me."

"What about our program?"

I flopped into a seat. "We know our program. Play me the B-flat minor sonata."

Duncan didn't need further encouragement. When he was ten notes into his recital, I pulled a carbide tool set from my bag. The seats in the Concertgebouw were of hard, old leather, exactly as Spot had shown. With a knife I pried all the upholstery tacks from the back of seat 20L, six to the right of where Flick would be sitting, just out of range of his professional eye. Dropped the tacks into my bag, loosened the leather of 20L and slid first a battery, then a tiny transmitter, then a single-output computer no larger than a credit card inside. Drew a wire from the transmitter to the hat rack beneath the seat, forming my antenna, then got the box of wee electret microphones I had made out of upholstery tacks. Ten of these mites, arranged along the back of 20L, would pick up as much sound as one normal-sized mike. The tricky part was aiming them at Flick's chair. Otherwise I'd be overhearing the wrong conversation.

Duncan was nearly through with Chopin's funeral march by the time I had wired the ten mikes to the computer inside the chair. Pushed the tacks into the holes in the tough leather, aimed them, and moved into 26L, Flick's seat: gorgeous work, Smith. The chair looked identical to its inanimate neighbors, only now it was radiant, listening. I caressed its smooth leather shoulder; the battery inside my brainchild would die in twenty-four hours.

Onstage, Duncan played as loud and fast as possible, then

ran out of notes. "Great!" I applauded. Poor Zadinsky: superior pianist in inferior packaging. Such a combo was not destined for success in the video age. We soon bid the dozing security guard good night. Much later I awoke, ecstatic and alone, still feeling a man's lips upon my throat. He was part Flick, part someone else. I had been demonstrating the effects of my hands upon ancient violins, mute chairs, and certain protuberances on the male anatomy.

I slept late and woke with a headache. I had been dreaming vaguely, disquietly, of the steeple. Rehearsed with Duncan, tested my receiver, swam, napped: waiting was hell. Sensing an upcoming trauma, my nervous system stifled appetite and began seeping adrenaline into the blood, shorting the connection between brain and tongue. It was no life for the gregarious. That evening I found Duncan backstage at the Concertgebouw raging between toilet and couch, swearing never to touch a piano again. He managed to call me the Antichrist before I shut myself into the bathroom. I slipped on a pair of headphones, heard faint bits of conversation but no Flick. Either he hadn't arrived yet or he was studying the program notes. Speak, baby, speak: I needed to adjust levels. Duncan pounded on the door. "My turn," he snapped. "Fast."

We exchanged places. I switched on the microcassette in my violin case and dabbled the fingers over a few strings as Duncan emerged from the bathroom. "Get that last button for me, will you," I asked, turning.

His fingers were nimble as icicles. "This dress is so goddamn tight," Duncan cried. "Why doesn't Curtis ever buy something with pleats? Does he think I enjoy walking onstage with a half-naked woman all the time?"

"One minute," the stage manager called from the hallway. At once Duncan abandoned the button and began walking in circles, wringing his hands. I walked to the stage door and took several deep breaths, forcing the intellect to quell the terror. We marched into the warm lights, toward Flick. I bowed: Smith incinerated: Frost rose from the ashes.

Intermission. I had played particularly well. While Duncan was attending to his plumbing I slid the headphones on and heard Flick's voice, crystalline. The blood swirled. "Overcast and quite cool," he was saying. Great aim with those mikes, Smith, you're a genius.

"Fortunate," she said. Girlfriend? If the lady wished to seduce her date, she'd better slather a little caramel over that monotone. "What do you think of our friend the violinist?"

Many inches of tape streamed over the tiny head. "A virtuoso," Flick answered carefully.

"She's a whore." Sharp little cookie: twenty rows off, she knew I threatened her. "Last week I read that she ran the Chancellor off the autobahn with her motorcycle. And look at that dress. Outrageous."

The toilet flushed so I stashed the recorder back in my violin case. Out bolted Duncan. "I've decided to play a comeback recital in New York," he announced. "All Chopin."

"What brought this on?"

"Lobotsky. And you, making me play that sonata last night. If I can play it like that after a bottle of gin, I can play it anywhere."

I nodded, Duncan babbled: this time, walking back onstage, I searched the field of heads. Next to Flick I found half a pale face, a puff of red hair . . . her one visible eye scorched me. I bowed, smiling directly at the little viper. Leaned into my violin and she disappeared.

Flick dumped her before coming backstage. I was shaking hands with a Dutch esthete when a Burberry raincoat hesitated in the doorway. As it moved in my direction the heart began slowly patting my ribs: wake up, Smith. He stood silently at the tail of the line, studying my face as I greeted a parade of strangers. By the time Flick had shuffled to the front, a few drops of sweat were inching past my knees. He kissed my hand. "Thank you for the tickets. My friend and I enjoyed the concert very much."

"Where's your friend?"

"He couldn't stay, unfortunately."

Flick lied flawlessly. It was a rare, often fatal talent. Eventually I changed into less constricting dress. Daubed a few drops of perfume on my neck, painted my lips, checked my face in the mirror, and decided that on esthetic grounds alone, Flick should not kill me tonight. "Duncan, are you going back to the hotel?"

"Where do you think I'm going, bowling with Queen Beatrix?"

"Take my violin back for me, would you? Thanks." I handed it over. "This is Emil Flick, the deputy chief of the Leipzig trade fair."

"Hi." Duncan assessed my chaperone. "We have a seven A.M. flight to New York tomorrow."

Flick did not appreciate the compliment. He looked coldly down at me. "Shall we go?" My fingers slid under his arm. Beneath the Burberry sleeve I felt his biceps tense. I drew closer: no firearms on the right side. The three of us left the Concertgebouw.

"A curious fellow," Flick said once Duncan had faded into the fog. "His behavior toward you is extremely contradictory. I'm surprised he plays as well as he does."

"So is he." It was a dank, moonless night, the kind that impelled people to spat and connect flesh. After we crossed a few canals Flick suddenly pulled me into a narrow alley. "Hey!"

He pressed me against a brick wall and stood, two fingers over my mouth, head cocked toward the street, listening. Flick wasn't carrying any weapon on the left side either. I could smell his soap; my lips registered a faint pulse through his gloves. Finally he turned his head. "Forgive me. I had to make sure we were not being followed."

I swallowed inelegantly. "Who would follow you?"

"No one." His breath filled my nostrils: fennel. Sweet. "I'm sorry. I don't want my picture in every scandal sheet in Europe."

I pushed him away. "Then perhaps you should have gone straight home."

In silence, amid backward glances, Flick guided me around the murky canals until he found a tiny, pricey bistro. The *maître d'* took one look at us, assumed the obvious, and led us to a private nook. Flick ordered wine. Normally I wouldn't have touched it but my hands were cold and I didn't want to be too careful tonight: inhibited the antennae. "What brings you to Amsterdam?" I said, looking at his pale, feminine hands. Deceptively strong, like mine.

"I just bought a security system for the fairgrounds."

He could have bought that in Berlin. "Why don't you use a few spare Stasi? There must be a million of them looking for work now."

"I need something a bit more sophisticated than the state police." Flick leaned over the table. I searched his eyes for contact lenses: too dark to tell. "Have you ever been to the Leipzig fairgrounds?" he asked.

"I don't sell tractors."

"There are almost fifty pavilions. Thousands of people come to the conventions in March and September. It creates a certain chaos." He raised his glass. I was curious to know how alcohol would alter him. "You're familiar with the convention center in West Berlin, of course. Someday I'm going to build one like that in Leipzig. In the meantime, I do what I can with the old fairgrounds."

"So you bought a new security system?"

"A computer actually."

Another one? I gnashed a herring. "What does it do?"

"Loops all the smoke detectors, shuts off lights and heat when the buildings are empty, activates alarm systems and infrared motion detectors, counts bodies, issues tickets . . ." Flick suddenly stopped. "I'm boring you."

Not yet, baby. "Maybe you could give me a tour next time I'm in Leipzig."

"Your Mozart recording," Flick said. "When is that?"

"Two weeks."

"We'll do it then."

Wine melted into my bloodstream. "How'd you know I'd be in Amsterdam?"

"My secretary called the Concertgebouw. I try to attend as many concerts as possible when I travel."

"A real music lover, aren't you."

Flick looked intently at me for a long moment. "Yes, I am."

Retreat, Smith. "I suppose the cultural life in Leipzig is somewhat limited," I said. "You have one concert hall and one opera house. And a couple of churches."

Flick laughed curtly. "For political meetings. Not concerts."

"Maybe unification will change all that."

"Maybe." He disapproved, of course: Flick was a loyal Marxhound. "Let's talk about pleasanter topics. You, for instance."

"How boring."

Again his eyes chided me. "Not at all. Playing the violin with fabulous orchestras and conductors, traveling all over the world, recording . . . it's a charmed life."

"That's what everyone thinks." I drank. "I thought you knew better."

"I suppose it couldn't be all that exciting," Flick said after a moment. "Otherwise what would someone like you be doing with a fellow like me?"

I found myself staring at his hands again. The long, slender fingers were beginning to provoke me. "You wrote me a nice note. I liked your handwriting."

Flick detoured into Fiddletown, asking many questions about where I grew up and with whom I studied, listening politely to my answers, all of which he probably knew already. Similarly, I ran a double check on him; his replies corroborated Spot's banal data. We were finally staring, exhausted, at two tiny cups of coffee. His sacerdotal formality, so contradicted by the occasional look in his eye, confused me terribly. I didn't know whether to process the information as Leslie Frost or Smith. Through my soft dismay I knew I was staring at him a little too often.

When he signaled for the check, I glanced at my watch: late. We returned to the damp canals, without talking and particularly without touching, until I impulsively tugged him by the Burberry lapels against a tree. "That was a lovely dinner," I said. His stomach grazed mine. "Do I recall an important question you had to ask or was that note you sent to Berlin just a little joke?"

He stared at me for some time, preparing his next lie. At this range it would be difficult to pull off and I didn't ease my grip until his lips moved. "I would like to take violin lessons with you," Flick said.

I sprang him free, walked away. "That's impossible. I don't teach."

He caught up. "I'll come to Berlin."

"You have no time to practice."

"I'll make time."

"You can't afford what I'll charge you."

"I'll pay anything." Flick took my hand. "Please. This is of utmost importance to me."

I laughed. "What could you possibly hope to learn at your age?"

Flick spoke slowly, coldly, mimicking me. "I had hoped to learn a few of your secrets." He dropped my hand. "It's late. I'm sorry to have wasted your time."

Salvage it, Smith. "I would have to hear you before making a decision," I said, taking his arm. The blue eyes didn't thaw. "Could you play something tonight?"

"My violin is in Leipzig."

"Mine isn't."

We got the Strad from the hotel vault and went upstairs.

"Tune it," I said, going to the bathroom. The lights above the sink stung my eyes and my face looked like a meltdown. I heard nothing, nothing, then remembered that my cassette containing Flick's conversation with the redhead was still in the violin case. Drunken idiot! I bolted out: there he stood staring down at the fiddle as if it were the Christ child.

If he noticed the two cable loops protruding from the compartment in the neck of the case, he didn't let on. "I've never touched a Stradivarius before," Flick said. "It's rather daunting."

"Wood and varnish," I said, lifting it out. As he cradled it under his chin, Flick's face became soft and forgetful. For a moment I believed that he had not been lying to me and that violin lessons were his only pursuit. I let him warm up a while, then settled into a chair, assuming the same judgmental pose my teachers had used to such great effect on me. "What would you like to play?"

Bach of course, the d minor Chaconne. The moment he drew the bow across the first chord I realized that wine or no wine he would never have all the notes but he would have the soul of that dark, majestic masterpiece. I watched his mouth twist here, there: if Flick's finger slipped one iota along the strings, if he put one molecule more pressure on the bow, the Stradivarius would amplify his action for better or worse. The instrument was both a ruthless master and a sublime slave. In the right hands it could make sounds so high and pure that they brought tears to the eyes of tyrants. Only a handful of people alive had that power. I was one of them; Flick was not. Yet he played with a scientist's rapture of acoustics and structure, face altering each time the music modulated into a new key. I sat motionless, strangely at peace. Listening to this man fondle my violin enthralled me.

Flick laid the instrument back in its velvet coffin and sat at the foot of the bed close to my chair, waiting: I had seen him naked. "Why do you want to study with me?" I whispered. It was late, civilians were trying to sleep.

"Nine years ago, I was at a conference in Vienna. I heard

you play the Sibelius Concerto." He didn't have to remind me that my future husband was conducting. "I couldn't sleep afterwards."

Neither could anyone else. "I remember the concert," I said.

"You wore a green dress. Your hair was down to your waist. I watched you tuck that violin under your chin as if you were arranging flowers. Perhaps you don't appreciate the effect this has on people." Flick watched my expressionless face. "I began practicing again after that. Hadn't played in years."

"Why not."

"There was no desire." He went to the window, beseeching the fog. "I have all your recordings. You've always been my idea of the supreme violinist. The perfect combination of intelligence and passion. And recklessness, of course."

I slid off the chair, hooked my fingers in his belt loops. "Spit it out, Emil," I said. "I'm leaving in four hours."

As he blinked, I watched the contact lenses center gracefully over his pupils: twenty/twenty vision. So he had seen me in the fountain. It didn't matter now. My fingers crept along his sides, met at his spine. His nose hovered within licking distance, breath smelled of dark cherries. He stood paralyzed, slowly turning to stone. "This is not what I was after," he said. "You must believe that."

A perfect liar, as I had already observed: he knew we'd be here the moment he stalked my table in Auerbachs Keller. "I'll give you violin lessons," I whispered. "If that's what you're after." My lips daubed his. I felt him flee, smash some black wall: then the tide turned and he crushed me. I had never made love with a murderer before. He was in turn voluptuous, brutal, helpless: each time I awoke during the night, I found him already looking at me.

Duncan watched intently as the stewardess performed her preflight charade concerning water landings and oxygen masks. Before lashing himself to his seat, he studied the exits and the passengers he'd have to trample in order to reach them. We were flying to New York, Duncan to visit his mother for Thanksgiving, I for Kakadu's American launch party. "Who was that guy last night?" he asked, huffing into an inflatable pillow. "You sure took off like two bats out of hell."

"He's a violinist."

"I thought you said he was the director of the Leipzig trade fair."

"What's the problem, didn't you like him?"

"Gave me the creeps."

"Come on, he's been in East Germany all his life. He'll need a while to lighten up." I took a book from my carry-on. "He's actually very sweet."

Duncan pulled a sleeping mask over his eyes. "So's Ex-Lax."

Flick had left that morning just before Duncan's wake-up call. He had not said goodbye. As the door clicked behind him, I lay very still, waiting. The desolation hit like a fireball a few seconds later, bringing tears to my eyes: alas, I'd have to see him again. He had caused a subterranean spring to trickle beneath the dark, gnarled forest of my existence. Eternally naive Leslie Frost rejoiced, imagining the return of lush flowers. But Smith recoiled. Love was the enemy's most gorgeous deception. I crawled tiredly out of bed. In this conflict, Smith and Frost would agree upon only one point: without that trickling spring, I was rot.

On the airplane, I slept. Somewhere over the Atlantic, as a car chase tore silently across the movie screen, I blinked awake. Slipped headphones on, rewound tape a few millimeters, listened.

"And look at that dress," the woman with red hair said to Flick. Strange accent, a lowbred Bavarian flecked with what? English? I hated her all over again. "Outrageous."

"I rather like it," Flick answered. The sound of his voice made my stomach soft.

Murmurs, peripheral coughs: such a long silence ensued

that I thought they had left their seats. "I understand she's coming to Leipzig next month." The woman's voice had dropped a few decibels. "You might use your influence to meet her."

"Is that necessary?" Flick's tone had turned green and slick as Astroturf, just as it had with the cop. "With everything else I have to worry about?"

She issued her orders directly into my ten tiny microphones. "Seduce her. After that, events will take care of themselves." Then a thousand hands began clapping and I heard, very faintly, a violinist unravel the first notes of Bartók's sonata.

I slept the day away many floors above Fifth Avenue. Late in the afternoon Mr. Godo, president of Kakadu Classics, knocked on my door. I was his date for the company's Raid America bash. Having rented a ballroom at the Park Plaza, Kakadu had invited a slew of journalists to gorge now, write later. Several hundred respondents now stood jawboning with managers, publicists, and other professional parasites at the sushi bar. Silver balloons in the shape of gigantic compact discs floated above the ballroom as unemployed actresses mingled with the guests, distributing Kakadu sweatshirts. Placards of conductors, pianists, and Leslie Frost spun gently in the hot air as themes from bland classics floated over the babble, reminding all of loftier ends. Harry Paradise was holding court next to a doomed mountain of oysters.

I wouldn't last long here and Godo knew it, so he wasted no time having a few pictures taken of me with the board of directors. He introduced me to a Swedish conductor famous for his billowy blond hair; the two of us were scheduled to record a schmaltzy crossover album in the spring. Goldilocks and I managed to get caught tête-à-tête by a photographer while Godo blew into the microphone behind the bar. Eventually, when all illumination save his spotlight dimmed, Godo got the last drunk's attention.

"Welcome, everyone," he said. "I know Americans dislike speeches so this will be short.'' That earned an appreciative burst of applause: Godo had evicted the bartenders for the duration. ''We are so proud and excited to be here,'' he read from the top card of an ominously thick pack. ''Today's celebration is the result of many years' effort by many individuals.'' Godo named none of them in his history of Kakadu Classics, which used to be three American concerns before submerging into the Pacific Rim. As he spoke, slides of the company's new downtown offices flashed across an enormous screen. The audience got shots of the board, a panoply of recording equipment, and a CD plant that Kakadu had just bought, the better to crank out product of artists it had snatched from less munificent labels. Here the spotlight crisscrossed the audience, fastening briefly on the Swedish conductor and a sumo-size diva, who smiled prettily into the glare. Before pinning the spotlight on me, Godo blurbed about glasnost, the world dynamic, and Kakadu's new contract with the orchestra in Leipzig. His speech ended in a swash of fraternal platitudes.

Harry Paradise waited until all the lights came back on before calling loudly across the ballroom. ''Leslie!'' He hurtled in my direction, pausing only for a belt of sake. His embrace loosened after the last flashbulb had popped. ''Isn't this spectacular?'' Harry beamed at my chaperone. ''You put on quite a show, Godo-san. I'm delighted to be associated with a company that recognizes the importance of public relations.''

Godo smiled back. ''When are my Beethoven sonatas ready.''

Harry needed a second to slap on a business face. ''Oh that! Any day now.''

''In Kakadu we have tight schedule,'' Godo said. ''I like maybe eight weeks from recording session to CD in stores.''

''As I've already explained, that's a rather inhuman pace,'' Harry retorted. ''The industry standard is ten months.''

''Kakadu has its own CD plant now. No more waiting in line at other factories.''

My producer sighed dutifully. "We lead busy lives, Mr. Godo. I have to plan the editing. Someone has to stitch the pieces together. Leslie has to approve it. This can take many weeks if one of us is on a road trip."

"Eight weeks is many weeks," Godo answered. "I am anxious to have this done in January. I am sure you would not disappoint me with your first Kakadu project."

"Indeed not." Harry turned to me. "You heard us now. No sitting on the tapes I send you any more." Someone beyond my shoulder caught his eye. "Ah, there's another culprit. Chance! Come here!"

Toby Chance brushed my left elbow. "Hello, everyone." He glanced over my dress. "Purple suits you, Frosty."

"I hope you've reserved some studio time next week," Harry interrupted. "I'm sending you the editing of the Beethoven sonatas we just finished in Berlin."

Chance grinned; he knew Harry was bullshit incarnate. "Ready when you are."

"Kakadu wants this out in eight weeks," Harry continued. "We have no time to lose. Are the liner notes printed yet, Mr. Godo? Is the cover photography all set?"

"Miss Frost has her picture taken tomorrow," Godo said. "We print in one week."

Harry accepted the inevitable with a fulsome smile. "Brilliant."

Godo excused himself to pay his respects to the opera singer. "Who the hell does he think he is, the emperor?" Harry muttered. "I have an absolutely killing schedule ahead of me. This is going to be a monumental pain in the ass."

"I have an idea," said Chance. "Why doesn't Frosty come to Boston and sit through the editing with me? We can do it all in one shot instead of sending tapes and scores all over the place."

"You're out of your mind," I said. "And quit calling me Frosty. I'm not a snowman."

Harry's brain whirled, dizzying him. "That's a great idea. I send Chance the first outline and you two finish without me.

I promise I won't feel threatened or jealous. We're all adults here.''

"I don't have a free week until nineteen ninety-five," I said. "Glue your own butt to Boston for a week, Harry. I won't get jealous either."

"Just a suggestion." Chance winked at me. "How's Emory? Back in the saddle?"

"No, he's still fighting a virus. You might end up in Leipzig with us after all." Harry ignored my dismay. "Godo likes your work."

"He likes my prices," Chance said. "I give him the deal of the century. So when should I expect the editing, Harry? Tomorrow?"

"Eh—maybe." Obeying the gravitational pull of an important magazine editor, Harry floated off.

Chance grinned at me. "Have fun in Amsterdam?"

A flashbulb detonated in my face. "Certainly. Excuse me." I said goodbye to Godo.

Chance sidled to the coat check. "I know a terrific bistro in the Village. How about dinner with one of your fans?"

My last dinner with a fan had resulted in severe heartburn. "You're a smart boy. Why don't you stick to microphones."

A white globe above the elevator chimed and the doors glided open, releasing a dozen famished scribes. "I'm serious about editing in Boston," Chance said as I stepped inside. "Think about it."

Not on your life, honey. I didn't need any sideshows. I wandered over to Madison, the street that reminded me most of the Ku'damm, and bought a black hat. Wrapped my ears and face like a mummy's: tonight I preferred to be more shadow than substance. I walked downtown, unwilling to think, aware only of the moon's slow ascendance over neon. Strange to be in a country where people strutted around as if they owned the sidewalks, blew the fat horns on their fat cars as if they owned the airwaves, and God did they litter. I hoped the people in Leipzig wouldn't be taking too many cues from this hellhole of a democracy. A dozen fake beggars accosted me before I even got to Fortieth Street. Oy! New York used to be a great jungle.

In Washington Square I dropped a pile of quarters into a phone and dialed Alfred Chung, my old MIT chum. I call him whenever I go to Boston. He comes to my concerts and afterward we usually wind up in a gritty bar talking computerese. After I left MIT, Alfred remained in Cambridge to bag a few doctorates. Now he ran a software company on Route 128. Alfred was a virtuoso gossip: the area contained many engineers desperate for a little pillow talk minus the romantic involvement. He answered after one ring. "Leslie! What are you doing in town? I didn't read about any concerts."

"I'm in New York. How's Stella?"

"The wife? Still shopping as if life were one giant stock split." Eventually, I rounded the conversation to our favorite topic. "I just read about the Clove QV6. Sounds pretty slick."

"Excellent product," Alfred agreed.

"What's their market?"

"Industrial environments requiring massive data base management and instant response to huge transaction flows."

Banks, airlines, insurance companies. "What do they cost?"

"Seven mil a pop and they're selling like flapjacks."

"Scientific applications?"

"The usual, only bigger and faster. Huge simulations, weather modeling, seismic analysis. The best war games in town. They've already made a fortune off the Defense Department. Just in time, before peace bankrupts us all, ha ha! Why do you ask?"

"I've been thinking of buying some stock."

"Do it. They're bulletproof." Alfred mentioned two microchip companies about to go public in case I felt like utilizing some insider information. "When are you coming to Boston?"

"Not until spring, I think. Shostakovich with the symphony." Ran out of quarters as Alfred was describing his two adorable progeny.

I flew back to Berlin. Maxine called the next day, wanting to go shopping, so I met her upstairs at the crowded KaDeWe for lunch. The Queen's hairdo and my fur coat did a pretty good job of mesmerizing traffic, particularly the East German sort, which was already gaga over such mundane complexity as one hundred varieties of bread. We dropped floor by floor to street level, checking for fleas, before shipping Curtis off with a car full of packages. Then we strolled down the Ku'damm, window-shopping with the hordes. It was almost Christmas again. Maxine pulled me over to a display containing three mannequins, three cashmere sweaters, six erect nipples. "What do you think of that one?" she pointed.

"I think you've got competition," I said. "Flick's taking orders from some Nazi bitch."

Maxine peered at an array of gloves. "How do you know?"

"I wired his seat at the Concertgebouw."

A little smile twinged the Queen's lips: I had amused her. "What did she tell him to do?"

Laughed bitterly. "Screw me."

"Did he obey?"

"He pretended to have a violin lesson first."

Maxine's patient brown eyes read mine. "He's our only lead."

"Only lead? You haven't found anything on Moll?"

"No one's got anything on Moll. He's one hundred percent vapor."

"What about the sexton?"

"He's a civilian. Believe me."

"What about the computer?"

"It was bought by the French meteorological service. Remember that cargo plane crash in September? Clove serial number nineteen was supposedly aboard."

"They totaled an entire cargo plane? How'd they do that?"

The Queen smiled ruefully; there was only so much a boss

could accomplish with seventy percent of her work force dead. "When do you go back to Leipzig?"

"Next week. I'm not going to see Flick."

"Maybe I should put Barnard on the case, then. She's pretty good at separating business from pleasure."

I stared at the sweaters, waiting for illucid urges to pass. "What do you suggest?"

"We've got a massive computer hidden in a country that's falling apart, with no idea how it got there, what it's doing, or who's running it. Zero. Whoever they are, they're good." She shrugged. "Do what you always do. Improvise."

"That's all you can say?"

"I think Flick needs another violin lesson." She tugged my arm. "I'm buying you a sweater. It gets cold up in those steeples."

6

Four delightful days in Leipzig coming up: didn't know if my lungs could stand it. I dreamt, pungently and hollowly, of Emil Flick. Improvise? With a professional like that? Maxine overestimated my suicidal bent. "You are not taking the Harley," Curtis said after I had been crunching Mozart concertos for half a week. "It's going to snow tomorrow."

"Fine, I'll drive the M6."

"Kakadu's sending a limousine. It picks Harry up at the airport, he picks you up here, you go to Leipzig together."

"Three hours in a backseat with Harry? I'd rather be in a TB ward."

"You can practice." Over the past few days Curtis had heard enough slipshod cadenzas to realize that music was not dominating the brainwaves. He dumped a wad of mashed potatoes on my plate. "Eat."

"Is it too late to cancel these sessions?"

"Absolutely."

I poked a few peas with my fork. "Maybe you could come over with me."

That got a soft little chuckle. "In which capacity, manager or bodyguard?" Curtis leaned forward, dropped his voice. "Just do your job."

The limo pulled up outside at ten the next morning. "How

about this snow, Les?'' Harry called, swinging open the rear door. ''Any mountains near Leipzig? We can go skiing.''

''Leipzig lies on the North German plain,'' Curtis informed him as the driver took my suitcase. ''It's totally flat. If your rehearsal's at four, you'd better leave.'' He slammed the door, walked to the chauffeur's window. ''May I see your driver's license, please?''

''What's he doing?'' Harry whispered.

''He's my bodyguard,'' I said. ''Wants to make sure I'm in safe hands.''

''Doesn't he trust me?'' Harry pulled out a pack of cigarettes. ''I'll protect you.''

Curtis rapped on the tinted glass. ''No smoking, Harry. It bothers Leslie's throat.''

Harry testily put them away. ''I hope to God there's a bar in this vehicle.'' He pushed a few buttons on a black panel. All kinds of windows went up and down. ''Damn! Driver!''

Curtis backed away, waving as the limo rolled heavily down the driveway. Harry did not wave back. We rode in silence through Dahlem. ''New coat?'' I asked, smiling at Harry's chinchilla.

''My birthday gift to myself.'' He nestled into the collar. ''I deserve it.''

''Of course you do,'' I reassured him after a few seconds. We passed an old church, its steeple dissolved in blizzard. ''Maybe we should have left sooner.''

''They're not going to start without us, sweetheart. Besides, Chance is probably still setting up his equipment. He only got into Leipzig last night.''

There was another fellow I didn't feel like seeing. ''Did he finish the editing yet?'' Harry played deaf. ''Yoo hoo! Did you send him the editing yet?''

''Of course not. I've been in Madrid recording flamenco music.''

''Godo's going to love that.''

''Godo can go squirt!'' Harry chomped on a zinc lozenge. ''I brought the tapes to work on here. In two nights I'll be done. Chance can take everything back to Boston and begin editing next week.''

When Harry wrote editing instructions in a rush, the result was *Finnegans Wake* in Sanskrit. So far only Emory knew how to decipher it. ''Has Chance done any editing for you before?''

''Calm down. Everyone says he's great.''

Yeah, yeah, he was an angel. ''Where'd you meet him,'' I asked.

''At an audio convention a couple years ago. That's one ambitious boy. I bet he'll start his own record company soon. He's got to outdo his father.''

''Who's his father?''

''You never heard of Chance guitars? The rock star's Stradivarius?''

''No. I don't like instruments you can't play in the bathtub.'' I yawned; Harry's Stygian perfume was slowly knocking me out. ''So why isn't Junior in the guitar business?''

''Ask him sometime. I don't know why you're so rough on the chap. You'd make a good couple.''

I watched the snow buffet a row of firs. ''When's Emory coming back?''

My matchmaker sighed, almost sincerely. Emory still had a fever. Harry was convinced he had picked up some kind of plague in St. Hildegard and was egging him to sue the hospital for a few million marks. We ran into heavy traffic at Checkpoint Bravo. Now that the borders had fizzled, the two Germanys were invading each other, sort of like the old days. Took us an hour to crawl to the man who read passports for a living. ''Please step outside,'' he said.

Harry's sweet-as-manure smile fell. ''What seems to be the problem, Officer?'' he tried to ask in German. ''We're late for an extremely important engagement in Leipzig.''

The guard climbed inside and began feeling around the seats. I watched very quietly as he brought my violin out. ''Yours?''

''Yes.'' Maybe it wasn't the best place to pack plastic

explosives. "We're making a recording at the Gewandhaus this afternoon."

"Where are you staying?"

I showed him our reservations. "What the hell happened to Reform?" Harry muttered as the guard fingered the seams of the trunk. "Out of all these people why does he stop us?"

"Did you have to get such a big limousine? Wear that coat? Sink the smile, would you? It makes you look like a drug dealer."

Harry stared at his Rolex. "My nerves can't take this. I have a session in three hours."

I looked up into the whirling snowflakes, searching for archangels. The mole above my lip throbbed as I thought about the esoterica stashed in my luggage a half meter from the guard's nose. "Relax. We'll be out of here in a few minutes."

We were eventually released with best wishes for a successful recording. The moment we rolled onto the E6, Harry typhooned profanities and pulled out a brandy flask which succored him until Dessau. I balled myself into a corner, bending many demons back into a hole marked Nightmares: I had forgotten how vile two-hundred-proof adrenaline tasted. This trip was not off to a good start.

Outside, snow softened the barren fields. The limo cruised down the highway, spitting slush at lesser vehicles, as Harry and I stared out our separate windows. Soon he opened a few Mozart scores. I hoped the frown indicated he was planning how to squeeze five concertos out of three recording sessions; it would be the musical equivalent of shooting *Lawrence of Arabia* in a month. Why Harry and Curtis had agreed to Godo's insane schedule was beyond me. It probably had to do with money.

We left the highway and slithered through the flat fields outside Leipzig. As smokestacks began to appear along the roadside, the biting aroma of sulfur dioxide infiltrated, then replaced, that of manure. I would be coughing tonight. A couple dozen tinny little Wartburgs wheezed by as we approached the city: rush hour. No Christmas lights, no neon, pet dogs rare as fresh pineapple . . . Flick had lived for thirty years in this necropolis. It was unimaginable. As we passed the Thomaskirche, my pulse stumbled: I was a blind beggar in his kingdom now.

The streetlights clicked on as the limo pulled up to the Gewandhaus. "All set, Harry?" I asked.

He looked as morbid as Duncan before a performance. I felt sorry for him; incompetence must be terrifying. When the chauffeur opened my door, Harry snapped out of his coma. "Let's do it," he said, bounding into the sour air. Suddenly he paused, hands shaking. "You go ahead, sweetheart, I'll just be a minute."

I signed in and walked through a corridor, shiny by East German standards, to a padded door. For a moment, I stood listening to the cacophony filtering in from the auditorium, where the orchestra was warming up. Panic billowed in my gut. I let it bloom, fade, then stepped into the control room.

Unaware of me, Chance stood intently behind the mixer. I had forgotten how becoming his rear end looked crammed into denim. His fingers were slowly riding the faders up and down the console, brightening woodwinds, damping timpani . . . for a guitar vendor, he had a great ear. "Frosty," he said, finally noticing me. "When did you sneak in?"

Unlatched the violin. "How's Wonder Boy."

"Terrific." He began futzing with the talk-back system, nervous but sharp: a natural performer. "Where's Harry?"

"Outside smoking."

Chance nodded toward a spray of red roses lying on a chair. "They just arrived. No card, I checked."

"Maybe they're for you."

"My, we're in a fine mood today! It must be nerves."

Harry came in with Maestro Kunz and the concertmaster. After an emotional reunion, Coach Paradise outlined his game plan to the three of us, taking care to explain that since we had so little recording time, no one could make any mistakes. "Teamwork is the key. Let's begin with the G Major. You

all just played it a few weeks ago so it should be perfect."
Maestro and I nodded in disgust at Harry's garish German
pronunciation. "No time for playbacks so you're just going
to have to trust the balances to Dr. Chance and me. Right,
let's get started! This is going to be tremendous!"

I exited with Kunz and the concertmaster. The three of us
paused backstage, clarifying who would have right of way,
where. Not an ideal artistic situation but time was short. If
this attempt failed, we could always re-record the set in a few
years for another pile of money.

Thanks to Chance's prep work, Harry had little to do but
open his score and say "Roll tape." The orchestra was in a
jolly mood; they were to be paid in West German marks.
Their exhilaration infected me. As soon as my foot hit the
stage, I became lyrical as a black swan. After all, tomorrow
I'd be back in Flick's steeple trying to get myself killed.
"This is too good to be true! We're ahead of schedule!"
Harry cried after sending the musicians home. "We should
have done this direct-to-disc. Baby, you were sensational."
He pumped his engineer's hand. "We make quite a team."

A wry smile nicked Chance's lips. "Anyone hungry?" he
said to me.

I took my roses. Chance switched off his equipment and
locked the control room. The three of us went into the snow
fluffing Karl-Marx-Platz, a cobblestoned steppe between
Gewandhaus and the opera where the locals now held their
weekly anti-Marxist demonstrations. In five minutes, we were
back at the hotel.

Now that capitalists were smelling money in the mud, the
Merkur lobby bustled. A bellboy with one earring lugged
suitcases across the marble as the pianist on the upper deck
played beebop Tchaikovsky. The place still needed carpets,
ventilation, potted palms. "Meet you in ten," Harry said,
stepping out of the elevator.

Chance left at the ninth floor. My room was on the twelfth.
Upon entering I checked for uninvited video: clean and no
one had tried to open my luggage. The country really was

going down the tubes. The phone dirled and my stomach fluttered.

"Hello." Then, not hearing a response, "This is Emil Flick."

"I know who it is."

Considering the fondness of our last farewell in Amsterdam, he was probably expecting a bit more enthusiasm. "How is everything?"

"Fine."

"Your recording sessions start tomorrow?"

"That's right." Like a fool I had invited him to them. "My producer doesn't want an audience. I'm sorry."

"Mmmmm." Flick tried pulling another tooth. "Are you free for dinner?"

"I'm not in Leipzig to socialize."

"May I see you for just a moment, then? In the lobby?"

"In my room." It would be a good exercise in self-control. "Number twelve-fourteen, nine o'clock."

"I've been—"

I hung up on him and went to the lobby. Chance was waiting under the retro-industrial chandelier, whistling Rachmaninoff with the piano player. He had changed into a black cashmere shirt which, ounce for ounce, outpriced caviar. I drizzled three fingers down its front just in case Flick was watching us. "Very nice," I said. "Don't stop whistling."

Chance's humid breath resumed brushing my cheek. We waited another ten minutes before calling Harry, whose line was busy. He eventually trotted into the lobby, spattering apologies about important messages and time zones. The Italian restaurant of his choice was closed so we adjourned to a Japanese alternative on the mezzanine. "Are you sure about this, Harry?" I asked, reading the menu posted near the door. "Where do you get fresh seaweed in Leipzig?"

"I am not going into that blizzard again," Harry sniffed as five Asian businessmen entered ahead of us. "Look, *they*'re eating here." He reminded us that the Merkur was part of a Nipponese hotel chain.

Dinner, like appendicitis, was memorable. After sliding three beers in filthy bottles and a basket of blow-dried inedibilia on the table, the waitress vanished. Harry tried to take up the slack with tales of his flamenco guitarist in Madrid; however, after an hour's wait, he stormed out. "Is he always like that?" Chance asked.

"I think Godo's editing schedule has spooked him." Dinner and three more beers suddenly arrived. I sniffed the brackish fumes rising from my stewpot. "Then again, it might be a new fiancée."

"How many times has he been married? Four?"

"Five. Harry believes in commitment."

Chance prodded a square of vulcanized abalone with his chopstick. When he tried to pick up a shrimp, it disintegrated. Now that Harry was gone, my companion's posture had subtly changed; although there was more room at the table, he was actually leaning closer to me. Chance reached for a beer, nudging a black cashmere shoulder against mine. I didn't pull back: somewhere along the line, though I wasn't sure how, this fellow would come in mighty handy. But I'd have to be brutally careful. He had an ego, a temper, and a great body.

We didn't eat much, but this could hardly be called food. "Thanks for dinner, Toby," I said shortly before nine. "I'd better go practice a little Mozart."

He tossed his napkin onto the table. "Class dismissed? Hallelujah."

In the elevator he pressed Twelve: my floor. Suddenly, violently, I didn't want him bumping into Flick outside my room. My finger poked pale white Nine. When the door opened, Chance only smiled. "Well?" I said. "Isn't this where you get out?"

"You don't think I'm going to my room, I hope." Close door. We swished skyward.

"Where do you think you're going?"

He waited until the doors had opened on the twelfth floor. "Out to eat dinner, Frosty." Chance patted my head. "Sleep well."

As I was slipping the key into my lock, I heard two distant panels whoosh open: Burberry raincoat drifted into the long, dim hallway. A hat shadowed his face and as he walked intently as a cat toward me, I prayed to evaporate from my corner and condense on Jupiter. Then Flick's eyes slowly came into focus beneath his hat brim. The optic nerve rammed the will into gear and I felt a million cool circuits connect deep in my brain; when he halted at my elbow, I had become Smith again.

"Come in," I said, twisting the doorknob. "Thanks for the roses. You shouldn't have."

Flick removed his hat but not his coat. My violin student studied me for a long moment. "How are you."

"Fine," I said cheerfully. By now the redhead must be rubbing her sly hands in glee: her agent had seduced me. According to her game plan, events were now supposed to take care of themselves. By God, I was going to ruin them both. "When's my tour of the trade fair?"

Flick tripped but recovered. "Any time you like. Tomorrow?"

"I have sessions until six. Can I call you late in the afternoon?"

"I'll stay in the office until I hear from you." Flick wrote a number on grayish Merkur stationery. "This is my private line."

In the alcove he hesitated and I saw the welt blossoming under his chin, where jaw grips violin: he had been practicing. It confused me terribly. "I have missed you," Flick whispered.

"Please," I said, raising my hand, "don't apologize. These things happen all the time."

"You're lying to me, I think." He traced one finger over my lips and the mole above them. "We'll get to the bottom of this." Then he left.

I plucked the petals, one by one, from the roses he had sent and dropped them into the swirling bath. When the warm, perfumed water crept between my legs, I murmured his name.

* * *

Two pasty faces at breakfast Friday indicated that the previous evening had not been restful. Having foolishly eaten some sewage from room service, Harry had been erupting since midnight. Chance picked moodily at his canned peaches before shoving off to the Gewandhaus to plug in his equipment. "What's his problem?" Harry asked. "You didn't castrate him last night, did you?"

"I was sweet as a honeysuckle."

"Oh Christ, now the poor sap thinks you like him."

Harry's limo ferried us a few thousand feet to the Gewandhaus. I left him snapping at Chance and strolled onstage to warm up. My fingers were stiff, without steering fluid. I didn't feel Mozartean today and from the looks of the orchestra, they'd rather be out playing in the mud. However, we were professionals, duty-bound to make some nice noise before the sun set. A year from now, accidentally hearing today's performance on the radio, we'd feel better.

Just as we began recording, the lights in the hall dimmed then reeled starkly on. "Hold everything," announced Harry over the talk-back speaker, "we've got a few problems back here." The lights ricocheted twice more; as Chance nursed his delicate gear back to its senses, Maestro Kunz and I rehearsed. Harry finally called us both to the control room.

"What happened?" he cried, rubbing his sore stomach. "Things went like magic yesterday."

"Beginner's luck," I said, watching Chance slide a spare IC card into the Sony 1630: sneeze and that useless machine went on the fritz.

"I must conduct Mahler tonight," Maestro pronounced.

"So? You can't do two composers in one day?" Harry whirled on his engineer, as if electrical snafus were all his fault. "Look at the time!" he shrieked, switching to English. "When's that Japshit going to be fixed?"

Chance pressed a few buttons. "Easy, Harry, we're almost there."

A man entered the control room. "I am Mr. Bamburger, house manager. Did you call?"

Harry smiled fetchingly. "There seems to have been a terrific power surge. The equipment doesn't react well to that. Our recording session has been delayed."

"I am so sorry. Construction crews are replacing electrical lines all over Leipzig. It's because of the trade fair."

"Let me tell you something, Mr. Bamburger. If these sessions go into overtime, you're buying them."

Bamburger misunderstood Harry's German. "That is most generous. Thank you."

"I am losing patience," Maestro interrupted. "Delays are very bad for my concentration."

Harry obliged by reattacking the recording engineer. I had to admire Chance's grace. Ignoring us completely, intent and adroit, he recalibrated a stack of befuddled equipment. Harry was extremely lucky to have him there; had it been Emory, we would have lost the entire session. "All set," Chance said finally, reeling Paradise back from panic. "Onstage, Frosty."

Peeved, Maestro began the concerto at a feisty clip. Every so often the lights in the auditorium would dip, equipment would burp; Harry was not officiating well. Maestro was constantly pushing, I pulling, while the orchestra screeched somewhere in the middle. By late afternoon we had almost struggled back on schedule. I wouldn't call it a transcendent musical occasion.

"We're all going to the Biertunnel," Harry told me afterward. "They make special potato pancakes there on Friday. Coming?"

"No thanks." The boy choir at the Thomaskirche sang motets on Friday. I had a little homework to do in the steeple. "I'm taking a nap."

As afternoon faded into quagmirey evening, I returned to the Merkur and packed a few necessities. Then I walked through the feeble snowflakes to the Thomaskirche. The dim sanctuary still smelled of dust and old women. A sizable audience already cluttered the pews. I took a seat near the back, on the aisle, praying that Flick and his redhead were not here. Eventually my colleague Moll appeared, robe afluster, hurrying toward the boys in the loft. When his footsteps had faded, I pulled my beret low and slid into the aisle.

Bach's bones were still there beneath the bronze slab; the old, homesick force engulfed me as I stared at the simple name etched at my feet. Again I trailed a knot of tourists into the vestry and hid behind a chest in the corner. Gradually foot traffic diminished and a thick hush settled over the church. I became dead with fear. Then, as Oskar Wildau began a choral prelude, my heart slowly began to tap rib, insisting that I must stay alive at any cost, not join Bach yet: that would leave too many riddles unsolved and the Queen would despise me forever. I wiped the mud from my boots and reached the steeple door just as the tiny, high voices of the choirboys enticed God into the Thomaskirche. Again I stood transfixed by that unearthly polyphony—the last music I would ever hear? Then fear fused with a gambler's defiance and I opened the lock a second time.

It was very dark, very cold inside the cavern: snow squalls had muffled the last vestiges of day eking through the grilles. No telling what kind of upgrading Flick and Moll had done since my last visitation so I rechecked for an alarm system: none. There was no one to notify. I climbed the dank staircase, following the icy conduit to Moll's door. In went my magnetic key. As I pushed the raw wood, my teeth edged toward the mole above my lip. I held my breath. Were Flick inside, I'd bite.

But Moll's room was empty. Smelled like a poker pit. Books and clothing still lay in disarray over the floor, this time joined by cigarette boxes, crumpled music paper, and maps. Intricately detailed maps, military quality, of East Germany: as I was admiring them, trying to decipher Moll's markings, the terminal atop his desk suddenly ground its gears. I jumped, nerves sawdust. *Start decrypt¢port(1)¢job 11r prior 00* I read at the top of the screen. So the Clove upstairs was cranking. Since my arrival half a minute ago it had made a few billion calculations. They probably weren't baseball statistics.

Time for a little eavesdropping. I drew a folding pocket computer, the kind marketed as Important Person's Diary, from my jacket. Couldn't plug it directly into the butt of Moll's terminal, he might have a tattletale in the system, so I hitched an inductive clamp to the cable connecting Moll's runt to the mother upstairs. There would be no dip in electrical charge, no strange blip: he'd never know I was coupling signals from his system to my own. The pocket calculator couldn't begin to store that barrage of data so I connected a micro DAT recorder to it, typed *Copy to DAT*, and let the pygmies get down to business while I checked out his apartment.

On top of Moll's amplifier lay a CD. *Music for Krumhorn*? Maybe Moll was an early music nut. Near his tousled cot stood an armoire containing naught of interest to anyone but a reweaver so I picked the lock on his top desk drawer: pencils, matches, drafting tools—gad I detested men without superstition. In the next drawer I finally found, buried in a blather of paper clips, the only personal clue. At first I thought the charm was a tiny tennis racket, or an oar, the type of trinket athletes' girlfriends commonly wore around their necks. Then I noticed the triangular webbing at one end: lacrosse stick. I had seen plenty of them during my MIT days. Students too puny for football but too violent for soccer generally ended up on the lacrosse team. It was an American game, not played in Europe. When I turned the trinket over, I saw *RH '77* engraved in the long handle.

Downstairs the choirboys were midway through their service so I backed out of the desk and pulled the ripcord on Moll's ceiling trapdoor. There were even more cables running upstairs now. Cold air again tweaked my nose as the ladder slid smoothly down to my feet. I darted up to the bells. The air conditioner purred like a giant Manx in the corner, pumping Antarctica to the Clove. Behind it was a splitter with two cables running up to the belfry. I clawed up the final rungs and once again listened in awe to the Clove humming its own frightful motet.

New cables up there too: any more copper and Moll would have to drag in a nuclear generator to power the place. No doubt he was taking advantage of the new electrical lines being planted all over Leipzig. I followed the shiny cables to a shoebox-sized transceiver in the corner. Moll was communicating with someone, not via the phone lines. Too vulnerable. Where was his antenna, then? I crawled back down to the bells and finally saw the extra shadow against the sooty slats. Modest, about the size of a pasta bowl, the antenna pointed at a target smack between the cupola of the Neues Rathaus and the Karl Marx U tower. Southeast. What was southeast? Dresden, Chemnitz . . . Prague? Moll would have to get over a mountain range first and he'd need a giant dish on the other end to catch the slop from such a diffused signal. Then I noticed that the dish tilted slightly downward. The recipient was close, then, possibly very close. Meissen, Grimma, Wachau . . . closer still? I looked outside. Of course: the fairgrounds.

I disconnected my little leeches from Moll's terminal and swirled down the drafty stairwell. As I shut the door, the choirboys were pealing Bach's amens. They held the final chord for a prodigiously long time; as it sailed beyond the rafters, piercing the soul, I smiled. Flick would have many opportunities, on many levels, to annihilate me. I edged back to the sanctuary, exiting to the Thomasplatz with the subdued congregation. None of that kissy-cheeky-pass-the-peace crap here: for the moment, East Germans worshiped undiluted God Almighty. That would change once they got fat and rich. The fountain at the edge of the square was puffed with snow. I nervously circled it and from the Information Center called Flick's private office number. "Sorry to keep you waiting."

"I have plenty of work to keep me busy here," he said. Indeed. "The sessions will probably go into overtime.

We've had a few electrical problems. Could I meet you at four o'clock tomorrow?''

"Fine. At the Gewandhaus?''

And run into Chance? "No, I'll wait at the hotel.''

Flick hesitated a moment. "Do you have plans for Saturday night?''

"Not yet.''

I was in my room at the Merkur, swallowing Scotch, about to take a shower, when Charm Boy knocked on the door. Chance seemed a little surprised when I opened it. "You're back,'' he said, eyeing my bathrobe. "Guess you didn't need a nap after all.''

"I was at the Thomaskirche. The boy choir sings motets there every Friday.'' My hand itched to crawl from his neck to knee. Nothing personal: postmission pyromania. "Takes the mind off the mundane.''

His lips pursed, as if he were about to whistle. "Sorry to be mundane, but have you had dinner yet?''

"I really must practice tonight.''

"Really must? You've played those concertos hundreds of times.''

"Where's Harry?''

"Working on your Beethoven sonatas. Come on, be a sport.''

I stepped back as Chance walked in, smelling of lime and warm beaches. He noticed the bottle on my desk. "Drinking alone? *Tsk tsk.*''

"Rough day.'' I swept aside the map of Leipzig with the little line I had drawn southeast from steeple to fairgrounds. "I suppose your day wasn't much easier. Help yourself. I'll be ready in a few minutes.'' I brought my things into the bathroom, showered the spicy fear off my skin, and quickly dressed.

I found him leafing through a heavy biography of Frederick Barbarossa on the nightstand. "Bedtime reading?'' he asked. "No wonder you sleep well.''

Had he touched my luggage? Whoa, Smith, hold the paranoia. As we left my room, the accumulated detritus of Scotch-
steeple-Mozart bashed my nervous system. "Would you mind
if we took a walk," I said. "I have a small headache."

We stepped into the fetid air outside the lobby. Chance
sniffed the mizzling snow and cleared his throat. "This might
be counterproductive. Maybe a massage might be better."

Nice try, Romeo. We strolled through the Hauptbahnhof,
past the opera, Karl Marx U, along the old ring road and its
many monuments honoring poets and statesmen. None of
them were laced with graffiti yet. "You did well today," I
said. "Not everyone could have saved Harry like that."

"You just have to know your equipment. And ignore the
producer. This one in particular." He steered me around a
wide puddle. "How did you get hooked up with Harry anyhow? He doesn't seem your type at all."

"I had just split with my German producer. Harry let me
do things more my own way. Didn't butt in every ten seconds
telling me how to play. It was a nice change and I got used
to it."

"But he doesn't know his ass from his elbow."

"So what? He leaves me alone."

"That's what you want? To be left alone?"

"That's right."

"Anything you say, Frosty." His glove patted my arm. A
simple gesture, he probably meant nothing by it, yet it made
my throat swell: I was more vulnerable than I thought.

"Harry tells me your family's into guitars," I said after a
while.

"So was I," Chance said, "until I realized that I hated
rock music and the people who played it, drugs, chippies,
press agents, you name it."

"You think classical music is an improvement? Please."

"Look at you. The worst you do is wear tight dresses and
drive fast."

At least he had the courtesy not to say *marry old conductors*. "Vice involves time and effort, dear. I have to practice

and go to rehearsals all day long. It takes a little more skill to play the Tchaikovsky Concerto than it does to shriek at a bunch of twelve-year-olds.''

"I wasn't criticizing.''

We circled a mound of brown coal occluding the sidewalk. "So how did you become a recording engineer?''

He chuckled. "My girlfriend was a violinist. She needed audition tapes.''

"Sucked you right into it, eh? That should teach you to consort with musicians.'' I threw my head back, licked a few snowflakes. "Did she get the job, at least?''

"Hell no. She played terribly. Other things she did better.''

I veered Chance onto Neumarktstrasse. A man had been behind us since the Merkur. He allowed a discreet lead, then followed us into the narrow lane, pausing each time we bent over a window display. I must have made a severe mistake in the steeple this afternoon; now someone was coming after me with a quiet little gun. As Chance babbled about the girlfriend who didn't work out but the studio in Boston that did, I hustled him diagonally across the Sachsenplatz. The tail tried to keep up by scooting along the sides of the arcade. He couldn't risk too long a leash in this murky weather.

Chance curtailed his romantic tragedy. "You're suddenly energetic.''

"Jogger's high. Ever had one?''

"Not from jogging. Where are you taking me?''

Into the woods and over the Elster; I knew a tiny bridge, no traffic, no gas lamps. "No idea. So what happened after you bought the button factory?''

"I built a recording studio in it.'' Chance resumed his auto-odyssey. What the hell was I going to do with him after I flattened the third wheel? Ask him to keep a little secret for me? Maybe I should sit him on a bench, tell him to wait there like a good boy until I returned; no, he'd get popped. Improvise, the Queen had said, so I toted him into a heavily wooded park, the type that inspired pederasty and defloration. The snow hadn't penetrated the firs enough to pad the mud;

our boots smacked lubriciously as we headed toward the river. I kept Chance's mouth motoring as I listened for footsteps. No need to look; the nerves along the spine sensed the shoes gently pressing the muck behind us. Soon we were at the Elster's edge. "What does that sign say?" Chance asked.

"No Pedestrians. Official Use Only." I tugged him along. In the middle of the bridge perched a tiny hut from which one could open a few sluices, collect tolls, salute the carp . . . probably hadn't been mended since Napoleon tried to Frenchify Leipzig in 1813. Its windows were broken, weeds spiked the rotted roof. The current frothed inches beneath our feet. I ducked around the hut and hopped up, planting my butt on the stone balustrade.

"You really should come to Boston and see my place," Chance said.

I reeled him in, twining my legs around his spine, and kissed him ferociously: hadn't had an exercise like that since my school days and I detested impromptu refresher courses. My pulse became heavier as I heard the thumps on the other side of the hut. My hand slid down Chance's back, pulled the little loop on my boot. Out slid my ceramic knife; in another second I might have to shove Chance backward, perhaps into a gun, and follow up with some ground-zero fencing.

Oskar Wildau hurtled past the hut, never suspecting that the blots in the periphery of his vision were actually alive. Dunce! I almost laughed in relief. But why would the organist follow me? Hadn't I given him a dozen autographs already?

Chance disconnected his lips from mine long enough to glance at the coattails receding into the snow; then that extraordinary mouth resumed where it had left off. I would have a small problem with the knife if his hands kept drifting along my arms like that; for a moment I considered dropping the weapon into the Elster but Smith had a tour of the fairgrounds tomorrow, to say nothing of a stroll back to the Merkur tonight. To distract Chance I slid my free glove down to the knot between his legs as my other hand found the sheath in my boot. Steady, Smith: miss now and I'd slice my calf in two.

Done. Chance's mouth was an active volcano so I pushed him a few bits backward, stuttered "This is crazy," but that was really no way to thank a bulletproof vest so I grabbed the scarf at his throat and kissed his face a dozen times. When his hands began slowly unzipping my leather jacket, I detracted the gratitude. "We'd better go."

"What's the matter?"

"I'm getting cold."

"Really? I'm getting hot."

I pulled his hair, hard. "Take a swim, then."

He looked thickly at me, calculating whether pushing me over the edge was worth his career. It took longer than necessary to decide. "Don't play games with me," he said. "I'm not a good sport."

Games? He didn't even know whose court he was on! I unzipped my leather jacket. "Be my guest."

Far away the bells in the Nikolaikirche tolled nine. Chance stood stonily for the full count; then he put his hand between my legs. Found the dangling corners of my jacket, slowly zipped it closed. His fingers lingered at my throat. "Don't ever do that again, Frosty," he whispered.

"I won't." Hopped off the railing. Halfway to the Merkur I pronounced myself too weary to dine; Chance didn't argue and Oskar Wildau never found us again. In the lobby I apologized. Chance patted my shoulder, brotherly everywhere but the eyes. I ate mushy salmon in my room then practiced until eleven. Lying in my cold, starchy bed, I began thinking about tails of one sort or another, none of which made any sense to me so I called Chance to see where he had finally eaten. No answer. I called Harry to see how his Beethoven editing was going. No answer there either, so I read about Teutonic emperors to delay turning out the lights. In the dark I would miss Flick badly.

7

*T*he phone interrupted a cadenza streaming through my head, irradiating my fingers, as I lay not awake and not asleep in my room. Until four o'clock today I couldn't worry about anything but a crisis named Mozart.

"Good morning," Harry said. "Sleep well? Ready to kill 'em?"

I found him alone at the breakfast table with a glass of mineral water. Harry looked as if he had spent the night with an inflatable woman. Beneath the metallic perfume he smelled a little grimy. "Real power breakfast you've got there," I said.

Harry fished in his little lunchbox and lay a colorful assortment of pills on the tablecloth. "Everything here gives me diarrhea. I knew I should have brought my own food supply."

"Finish the Beethoven?"

"*Pfffui!* I went to Magdeburg to hear Kunz butcher the Mahler Third. It was not fun."

Godo wasn't paying Harry those hefty fees to have fun. "Look on the bright side. The sooner you finish planning the Beethoven the sooner you can start the Mozart." I watched him choke down a dozen vitamins. "Where's Chance?"

"At the Gewandhaus. I forbade him to have any equipment failures today."

By the time Harry and I got through with him, the poor fellow would wish he had stuck to guitars. Chance looked right through me when I walked into the control room half an hour later. Couldn't worry about that now; I walked onstage feeling particularly mortal, a little surprised to be alive. Fiddling softly, I watched a trumpeter kiss his mouthpiece, a young woman nestle into her cello. We were a select society, caretakers of an archaic strand connecting mud to the stars. Had I remained a mere musician, my life would have been sufficiently honorable. How strange that this second, ruthless existence ruled my heart.

Still orgasmic over his Mahler concert, Maestro conducted more vitally than he had the day before. The orchestra clicked in and I played as well as I ever would. No blowouts in the control room and for once monosyllabic, Harry rolled tape. There was no predicting the dynamic of recording sessions and he knew this was one of those lucky occasions when the accumulated tedium suddenly ignited. Before breaking camp, the orchestra and I applauded each other.

I remained on the empty stage to patch a few cadenzas. The hall was suddenly very quiet and for the first time that afternoon, I remembered Flick. "That does it," Harry said. "Come on back."

Chance was already packing tapes into neat white boxes. An ill breeze wafted from his end of the control room. "Bravo, Harry," I said. "You too, Sunshine."

Harry stretched his arms, searching for lofty words. "Ah, what a relief! I feel as if I've taken a huge shit! Let's go for a drink."

"I've got to pack," Chance said.

"Leaving so soon?" I asked.

"This equipment has to be in Berlin tonight."

"But we're invited to the opera," Harry said.

"I'm on the first flight to London."

I watched Chance's wide hands bed the amplifier in a road case. "Guess we won't be seeing you for a while."

"Looks that way." Whistling, Chance severed mixer from

recorder. His fury struck me as disproportionate to the offense, but what did I know but the tip of his tongue.

Harry remained neutral; he had to work with both of us. "Maestro's waiting at the Kaffeebaum," he said to me. "It wouldn't hurt to humor at least one gentleman in Leipzig."

Picked up my violin. "Goodbye," I said. Chance kept coiling cables.

As soon as etiquette permitted, I excused myself from Harry and Maestro and walked to the Thomaskirche. All doors locked but I heard the organ playing so I coaxed a bolt or two back. Crept up to the dim balcony and waited until Wildau had finished a cantilevered fugue. "Hello, Oskar."

He jumped. "Who let you in?"

"The door was open." I approached the organ. "You were following me last night. Why?"

Denial flared and crumpled. "To take pictures."

"Pictures of me? Doing what?"

He swallowed tightly. "I needed the money."

"Who was paying you?"

"I don't know. Someone who saw us in the café together. I think he was from a newspaper. It wasn't my idea," Oskar blurted. "It wasn't even my camera!"

Back off, Smith: his voice was rising with each word. I followed Wildau's round eyes to his music bag. Inside was a cheap Japanese camera. "Did you take any pictures of me?" I asked, calmly winding the film forward.

"No, of course not! What are you doing?"

"Just making sure." The film dropped into my pocket.

Oskar leapt from the bench. "You can't have that! Please give it back. Please!" When he began to tremble, I felt sorry for him. Organists were a pitiful lot, all bellows and tremolo.

"I'll make you a deal, Oskar," I said, placing three hundred West German marks on the keyboard. "I'm going to get rid of this film. You're not ever going to take pictures of me again. All right?"

He began to cry; so much for maiden ventures into capitalism. "You won't develop the pictures?"

"No." Maxine would, though. I walked to the stairs. "And I won't tell the police."

Oskar apologized but kept the money.

I returned to the Merkur and crashed: Frost had survived the sessions, Smith had survived the steeple. Who would now survive Flick's tour of the fairgrounds was questionable. Precisely at four, Flick arrived, nicely shaved and pressed but periwinkle around the eyes, wan as a frog's belly. He had spent too many nights croaking to the Clove. "Hello," he said, taking my hand: no escape now. He shut me in his menthol-green Trabant, one of several dozen snuggling the parking lot, and drove to the outskirts of Leipzig. It was like riding in a cartoon but at least he kept his clean. "The sessions are finished?" he asked.

"Yes."

"You're satisfied with the results?"

"Here and there." We passed filthy yellow trolleys, once proud buildings, the rear ends of motorists lost beneath the hoods of their stalled vehicles. There was still so little activity there, no shops, cars, not even that first harbinger of freedom, juvenile delinquents . . . just mud.

Flick pulled into a parking lot, nodded over my shoulder. "Look."

Beyond a long reflecting pond stood a gigantic granite monument maybe twenty stories tall, a cross between an Incan temple and a fire hydrant. "That's the Slaughter Memorial," I said. "To commemorate the Battle of the Nations. On that hill Napoleon ran into the armies of Russia, Austria, Prussia, and Sweden. The little bugger rode back to France in defeat after about fifty thousand men died."

"You know your history," Flick said.

"I read a lot of nonfiction. It's the thinking person's comedy."

As we drove up to the east entrance of the grounds, Flick explained that the Leipzig trade fair had begun over eight hundred years ago. Merchants had come to this East/West hub to buy and sell furs, lace, then books, then heavy industrial machinery . . . the present site was built in the twenties, when the exhibition halls downtown could no longer accommodate the March and September population bulge. Trading partners now displayed their goods in twenty-three halls, twenty-seven pavilions, on a site that struck a nice architectural balance between a sixties shopping mall and a medium-security prison.

"How did you get started here?" I asked Flick, following him to one of the enormous pavilions. Inside, construction workers toiled amid the forklifts.

"Well," he began, "as technology advanced, the fair became more and more an international forum for experts, with greater emphasis on a whole range of technological events. Participants could discuss the latest developments in their field and promote worldwide cooperation in commerce and industry, particularly between advanced and emergent countries. . . ."

I hope he didn't think I was buying this crap. Every time a workman or a cleaning lady walked past, Flick raised his voice and cranked out a few statistics. "We're having a special exposition in March," he explained. "I've been planning it for almost two years."

"The political situation doesn't affect your plans?"

"I don't get involved in politics."

Sure. "What's the subject?"

"Optics. Lasers, actually. My pet field."

Lenses: microscopes, telescopes, mirrors. The East Germans were the best at it. "Who's coming?"

"Everybody."

A couple thousand extras, dozens of exhibitions, no more Stasi posing as visiting Bulgarians . . . Flick could waylay a Trident missile in the chaos. I followed him out of the pavilion, sidestepping a half dozen men working in a muddy trench: more power lines. "What's with the overkill in the public works department?" I asked. "Is this an election year or something?"

Flick responded with a wooden speech about the new generator outside of town which would be zipping an extra three hundred megawatts into Leipzig, keeping pace with the needs of the trade fair and the happy population. I let him gush on as we passed a row of pavilions the size of aircraft hangars. Eyes up, Smith: somewhere, on one of these rooftops, was a transceiver, twin of the dish in the steeple. At least I hoped so. Otherwise my theory was shot.

Flick held my hand as he zigzagged between concrete mixers, dumpsters, and lacustral puddles, finally stopping at the tallest building on the grounds. "There's a nice view from the observation deck," he said. "It's best at sunset."

No elevator, of course. I was winded when we finally reached the narrow catwalk. In the distance Napoleon's Slaughter Memorial glowed majestically in the russet pollution. As I was looking at it, only vaguely comprehending its size, Flick leaned lightly into my back. I stiffened: would he throw me down? No, how stupid, we weren't high enough; he'd have to break my neck up here first. Then his hands crept around my waist, pulling me in. I dropped my head, sagged against him, ashamed; he was only protecting me from the wind and I suddenly recalled that, technically speaking, we were still lovers. We stood that way for a long while, listening to each other's disquiet pulse as Flick's Burberry snapped in the breeze. I turned my head, or rather, rubbed my ear against his scarf. "What's the view on the other side."

"Leipzig." He detached himself, led me to the west balcony. I could make out the Karl Marx U tower and, barely, the steeple of the St. Thomas Church. The sun had sunk below the medieval spires, incarnadining the clouds, blinding foolish mortals. I averted my eyes.

On the roof ahead of us gleamed a dozen satellite dishes from one to ten feet in diameter. They were meant to track man-made bodies flying high above the earth, mostly communications junk in geostationary orbit: the BBC, CNN, Rundfunk this and that, Sky channel. Other dishes, locked on the horizon, were in league with antennas on distant hills. They could be relaying anything from the weather to World War III. "We broadcast heavily from the fairgrounds," Flick said, noticing the direction of my gaze.

I found the little dish he had directed at the steeple. Smack out front, of course: people tended to discount the obvious. "What are those peewees?"

"Army property, police bands . . . those there are for radio experiments at the university. I thought you knew about these things."

Bang went the blood. "What things?"

"You went to a technical school."

"My subject was mathematics, not physics." I locked onto Flick's eyes: sincerity iced the best lies. "Whatever I learned there is obsolete now."

He clucked. "You would have made a good mathematician."

A cloud drifted; sunlight slashed Flick's antenna patch. Suddenly I could see the cable linking the little dish at the front to a ten-foot dish perched on a heavy tripod ten feet away. The gimbal mount would allow it to sweep the heavens, searching for tasty morsels in nongeosynchronous orbits. Spy satellites and space shuttles, for instance. Camouflaged by that herd of innocent antennas, the roving dish could operate in total privacy, talking all the while to the Clove crosstown. What was Flick tracking? Why had he brought me to the belly of his operation? Did he really think I'd see nothing?

"You're chilly. We'll go back down," he said, kissing my ear. We returned to the muddy boulevards. "Well! I think you've seen everything now."

"What about your office? No tour's complete without a look at the boss's office."

His calm blue eyes studied mine. "It's not fancy," he said. "Not like in America."

"So who's in America? I'm curious to see where you spend all your time."

We walked to yet another featureless concrete building. Inside, Flick led me to a door with a cheap nameplate on it.

"My secretaries work here," he said, waving to six desks cluttered with triplicate forms and cigarette butts.

I glanced around. "Where's the computer you bought in Amsterdam?"

Flick looked darkly at me, this time without indulgence. "You have a good memory."

"What do you mean? You talked about it for half an hour in that bistro. Of course you were quite drunk at the time."

"It's in another building." Flick ushered me into an inner room and locked the door behind us. Before turning on the lights, he drew the curtains. "This is my office."

The deputy chief's quarters were large, semiplush, and impersonal. Thick books lined the walls. At least Flick's furniture was made of wood, not plastic, and someone had made an attempt to save a few green plants from extinction. I knew at a glance that he didn't love this place.

Framed diplomas and Certificates of Merit crowded the wall behind his desk. "You earned all these?" I asked, walking to them.

"Of course."

They corroborated exactly the data in my files. I stopped in front of a photograph. "What's this?"

Flick stood behind me, perhaps trying to be helpful, perhaps tempting me to lean against him, as I had on the observation deck. Contact here, however, would quickly escalate into tourism of a different sort, so I tried to ignore him. "That's a trade delegation," Flick said, breathing into my ear. "You might find a few familiar faces there."

I studied the picture. The deputy posed with Erich Honecker and several other load-bearing Communists in front of the Russian pavilion. To his left, I recognized a KGB agent and a British mole. "Very impressive," I said, passing by the portraits of other significant socialists. But whoa: that footbridge. I had crossed it many times, tempted to leap over the edge. "You never told me you were in Cambridge."

"I did, in Amsterdam. You were quite drunk at the time."

Liar. "When was this?"

"Nineteen seventy-seven. An economic symposium at Harvard."

Springtime: the dogwood were blossoming. "We could have walked past each other and not known it."

Flick kissed my neck. "I would have remembered you." He pointed to the next photograph; when his hand fell, it encircled my waist. "We went to Hofstra and Johns Hopkins University that same year."

All three had lacrosse teams. "What were you doing?"

"Promoting the trade fair."

Of course. I inched to the end of Flick's portrait gallery, then noticed a neatly made cot in the corner of his office. "That's very American," I said, finally turning. "Do you sleep with your secretaries, too?"

Flick slowly ran two fingers over my cheek, stopping at my mouth, as if warning me to hush. "Do you sleep with your manager?"

I went to the curtains, parting them an inch. Outside, a heavy bluish cloud was creeping over the fairgrounds, eating pavilions. "Thanks for the tour. I'm sure you must be terribly busy."

"Would you have dinner with me?"

I dropped the curtain. "People know you. We'll get our picture taken and you'll end up in every scandal sheet in Europe."

"We'll go to my place," he said. "I'll make something to eat. Then if you're not too tired, perhaps I could play some Bach for you."

Another violin lesson? Damn him. Damn the redhead. "Perhaps."

We returned to his green Trabant. Flick lurched into first gear and drove to Schönau, one of Leipzig's less filthy districts. We didn't talk much: silence tantalized lust. He finally parked in front of a weary masonry building. Most of its epidermis had slid off. The gutters leaned in diverse directions, none of them horizontal, and the windows probably hadn't been washed since Adolf wed Eva. Near the front steps, little red flags marked off a section of mud heaped with boards, stone slabs, pipe: whether this material had rotted off the building and was destined for the junkheap, or whether it was a stash of repair parts decaying for want of a carpenter, I could not say. It was below what I would have expected of the deputy chief of the trade fair. "What's the matter?" Flick asked.

"I hate mud."

"It's going to get much better here."

A strange comment from a pillar of the ruling class. I followed him upstairs to a corner apartment full of blocky furniture and dark rugs. It was very tidy, the complete opposite of Moll's sty in the steeple. The air here smelled sweet yet decayed, like German history. Flick hung up our coats and told me to wait a moment. I watched him cross the room and, again without turning on the lights, draw the drapes. He returned to my corner, halting just beyond arm's length. "May I get you some wine?" he asked.

"You may take me to bed."

After a pause, as if he thought I was kidding, Flick hiked me to the bedroom. He didn't bother closing the drapes and he left no doubt that, unlike our previous duet in Amsterdam, this time he intended to have me. Never forgot his manners, though. Never gulped. Flick peeled off my clothing piece by piece, thoroughly investigating whatever he had exposed before proceeding to the next patch. Eventually I was lying on his bed naked and whimpering. He stood up and looked at me head to foot. For a horrifying, humiliating moment, I thought he was going to leave. Then he began to unbutton his shirt. No rush at all: just like Hugo. Drove me mad but I kept my mouth shut. He didn't need to hear me beg; we both knew who was in charge here.

He finally returned to his bed, less to make love than to continue probing for a hidden weapon. Didn't say a word and as the ballet thickened I realized that he wasn't homicidal, wasn't rabid with desire: he was testing. I nibble you here? You press two fingers there. I twist here? You roll there. The defensive reactions are automatic and I had to struggle not to give in to them. It was perversely romantic.

"Bastard," I said finally, turning my back.

His fingers rested on my shoulder before creeping over flank and knee, wandering back along the trembling seam between my legs. As the seam dissolved, his fingers continued up my vertebrae, stopping only at a long ridge beneath my ribs. Flick carefully traced the .32 caliber scar until all the liquid on his hand had evaporated. His mouth on my ear, he whispered, "What happened here?"

"I fell off a horse."

"When?"

"When I was twelve."

"In Berlin?"

"Vienna. Would you like a doctor's report?"

The mouth dragged toward my nipples. He stayed there a long time, monitoring pulse. "Tell me," Flick said, "why did you do that in Amsterdam?"

"I did a lot of things in Amsterdam. So did you."

"Why seduce an old man? A lapsed violinist. A bureaucrat. A perfect stranger, actually. It makes no sense."

"You started it and we drank a lot of wine."

"That's all?"

I found his eyes in the dim light. "You remind me of my husband."

Surprise and perhaps hurt swept his face. Flick withdrew to the other side of the bed. Then he went to the window and stood with one hand on the heavy drape, looking at the blueblack sky. Eventually his gaze dropped to the ground and remained there. For the first time I looked at his body without thinking of it as a piece of his arsenal. He had aged frightfully well, much better indeed than Hugo, who considered conducting an advanced form of weight lifting. This man still had shoulders and thighs and fifty years of self-denial in that rear end. The fixtures on the front he was born with. The two masses counterbalanced each other and when he breathed they both moved with him, gravid yet weightless, like the bells in the steeple. Bodies like that didn't go to bed alone for fifty years without some overwhelming objective.

I joined him at the window. He had been staring at a graveyard. "What's the matter?" I whispered. Was comparing him to Hugo an insult? Even when I ran a hand over the welt on Flick's chin, he didn't move.

I went back to his bed and drifted asleep. Somewhere in a heavenly calm dream, he slipped in beside me, found my mouth. That strange, soft peace flooded through me again. "Why were you angry with me at the hotel?" Flick asked.

"Nerves."

He chuckled quietly. "I don't think so."

I awoke much later, as he was strumming my back. "Scar fetish, dear?" I said.

"You have a staggering assortment of slight imperfections. Scars, warts, moles, calluses . . . I've been inspecting them." Flick rolled me over, touched my upper lip. "This is my favorite, though. It's really you."

"Where's my dinner."

He dressed and went to the kitchen. As he was cooking, I took the opportunity to inspect his bathroom: nothing there but soap and cracked tiles, zip in the toilet tank. No red hairs anywhere. We ate old meat and canned vegetables, talked music. Loath to make his violin lesson worse than necessary, my pupil drank only water. He finally stood up. "You get dressed while I do the dishes."

"What for? I can hear fine just like this."

"I can't play fine with you just like this."

I left his bathrobe on the kitchen floor and went to his living room. "I'm waiting," I called from the couch.

He turned a light on. "What are you doing?"

"I'm teaching you to concentrate. Go tune your violin."

"You're joking."

"How do you expect to play well if the least little thing throws you?"

"You naked with your legs spread is a little thing?" He was angry. "What is this, some kind of game? How many teachers did this to you?"

"Let's understand something, Emil. In the bedroom, I'm your slave. In the kitchen, I'm your guest. In here, I'm your teacher and you do as I say."

Still he didn't move. "This is not what I had expected."

"Will you stop saying that? Teaching has come a long way since the last time you took lessons." I swung my ankles off the couch. "All right, I'll get dressed." At the door, I paused. "You should never have slept with me, you know. It complicates things."

When I returned to the living room, Flick was running a few arpeggios. He had turned on an antique lamp behind the piano; as he played, its tassels vibrated gently under the domed shade, dappling the rug with shadow. I sat on the piano bench. "Play me an A-major scale, four octaves," I said, then noticed the shelves just beyond the periphery of light.

Flick's CD collection was even larger than Moll's. He seemed to have the entire Deutsche Grammophon catalog plus a few dozen samples from each of the major European labels. Unlike Moll, who sorted by composer, Flick had arranged his library by manufacturer, so that their logos ran continuously from spine to spine, tiny installments of a great epic.

I tortured him with a few more scales. "Not bad. That's a rather nice violin."

Flick handed it to me. "I've had it since I was a boy. My teacher gave it to me."

"For good behavior?" I played a few notes and gave it back. "How many hours a day have you been practicing?"

"Four."

"When?"

"Two before breakfast, two before supper. I don't intend to waste your time."

I suppose that was a declaration of love. He played a Bach partita for me. Since his audition in Amsterdam, Flick's fingers had made a remarkable comeback. Nevertheless, he was a tricky student, steeped in German tradition but lacking the technique to glorify it. I went through the partita with him note by note. In two hours Flick played maybe three phrases without interruption. He seemed to enjoy getting cut off; I would have stormed out of the room in tears long before. But I was a performer, half stallion, half mouse. He was a scientist, parched for knowledge. Or maybe he was just acting under orders from a redhead. I tried not to think about that. "When was the last time you had a lesson?" I asked.

Flick smiled forlornly. "Well before you were born."

When I stood up, my back hurt. "I think that's enough for tonight." As he put his violin away, I wandered behind the piano. "Where'd you get all this?" I asked, running a finger along the plastic cases. "You must have the biggest CD collection in East Germany."

"Exhibitors do all they can to get special treatment at the trade fair."

I took the jewel box on top of the CD player. Never heard of the label. The magenta artwork was awful. "*Music of Leon Jurkowsky*? Someone really thought this would earn a few points with the deputy chief?"

Flick snapped the lid shut. "I bought that myself. It's quite interesting."

I would never have pegged him a contemporary music fan, but then I hadn't pegged him a satyr either. We didn't speak much after that: battle fatigue. Later Flick drove me back to the Merkur, pulling into a corner of the parking lot for a few furtive adieus. "You don't want to be seen with me, do you," I said. "Am I really that bad for your reputation?"

His mouth traversed my fingertips. "I don't care about my reputation, darling. But I don't want any interference."

"Who'd interfere? Have you got a girlfriend stashed away or something?"

"No. Please don't misunderstand. I don't want anyone else to touch us. To even know about us. You're my most private property."

"Most men would want just the opposite."

His tongue paused. "I'm not most men."

I took my hand away. "What do you want from me, Emil?"

He looked out the window, toward the grandiose fountain at the entrance of the Merkur. "Hope," he said. "Just hope. That's not too much, is it?"

Too much? It wasn't enough. I wanted to infect his thoughts every second he was alive. I wanted him to crumble without me. Then we would be equal. "No, it's not too much."

I tried to crawl into his lap but couldn't wedge past the damn steering wheel. Trabants weren't really cars; they were a form of birth control. By the time Flick kissed me good night and really meant it, he needed a shave. The bells at the Nikolaikirche tolled four as I left the car and watched his chintzy taillights pale into the gloom. I turned wretchedly toward the hotel entrance then stopped short: Harry Paradise was scuttling across the parking lot, walking as fast as possible without breaking into a run, trying to look both invisible and legitimate. The exercise would have been more convincing had he not been wearing that ridiculous chinchilla coat. Listening to Beethoven sonatas, eh? I'd ask who the lucky lady was in the morning.

8

*T*he next morning I received no wake-up call from Harry Paradise, nor was he at breakfast. When the limo pulled up to the Merkur at nine and still he hadn't emerged for his matutinal vitamin glut, I went upstairs to pound on the door. "Harry!" Some tortured animal bayed within. "The car's here. We have to leave now." No reaction so I got a maid to unlock the door. Ripped the covers off his bed, exposing a slumbrous form in black silk pajamas. "Rise and shine, Casanova."

His five gold medallions clinked as Harry rolled over, slowly achieving consciousness. "What are you doing in here? Such colossal gall! Get out!"

"It's ten o'clock. You've overslept."

"Oh God! My plane's at two!" He bolted into the bathroom. "Damn you, why didn't you call?"

"The phone's off the hook." Clothes, scores, cassettes buried the furniture and Harry's night table looked like a branch of Upjohn. "I'll pack your pills, you get dressed."

"No, no, don't you dare touch anything! Leave!"

"Give me your key, then. I'll check out. Step on it."

Desperately hosing off his cold cream, Harry made no answer. Soon, in silk pajamas and his enormous chinchilla coat, he leapt into the limo with an empty suitcase and two hotel laundry bags. "Let's go," he shouted to the driver,

117

spilling the contents of his bags all over the backseat. "I have to make a two o'clock plane to Paris. Millions are at stake."

The limo surged forward. "What now?" I asked.

"A live recording of Gilda Poissonnette."

Never heard of her. "What does she play?"

"She's a tap dancer. Her boyfriend's a sheik. Can't this damn car go any faster?"

"Sure it can. Then we'll be arrested." I watched him fussily arrange a few items in his suitcase. "Did Chance leave all right last night?"

"By six. I don't know what you did to him, but I hope you're happy."

"When are you seeing him again?"

"London in about two weeks."

"Maybe you could apologize for me. I was a little rude to him."

"Apologize for yourself, you spoiled brat!" Harry tried to housebreak his hairdo. "God Almighty! If you didn't play the violin, you'd have no redeeming social value whatever."

"Thank you. So why did you oversleep? Spend all night finishing up the Beethoven?"

Harry salved his cold sore. "I went to the opera with Kunz and his wife. If you recall, he invited us both."

"What'd they sing, *Carmen* twice?"

He looked strangely at me. "What's with you today? *Traviata* once. Then I went to bed. I've been so exhausted lately."

Harry was a terrible liar. It made me wonder how he had become such a successful producer. "You promised Godo that editing weeks ago," I said. "Soon he's going to start screaming."

"He's got to find me first. Don't you dare tell him I'm in Paris."

I shut my eyes, blocking out Harry and his romantic misadventures. The man was my record producer, not my bosom buddy. I had more important items to think about. Take the steeple-trade fair-satellite connection. What was Moll tracking up there? Was he gathering or sending data? Both?

Did it have any relation to the optics exhibition Flick had been planning for two years? I'd know a lot more once my computer analyzed the tape I had made in the steeple. How about that lacrosse stick I had found in Moll's desk? *RH '77*: had he gone to school in America? As what, an East German computer specialist? That was a laugh. I thought about Flick's coincidental trade delegation to the States in 1977. Of course he had met Moll. Then I wondered where the redhead fit into all of this and how she thought I might fit into all of this. That made no sense whatever, nor did the little episode with Oskar Wildau following me with a camera. Last, I thought about Flick leading me straight to the satellite dishes at the fairgrounds. Intentional? I would be a fool to think otherwise.

The imbalance of questions to answers eventually put me to sleep. I awoke when the Mercedes ran out of highway at Checkpoint Bravo. Traffic both ways was horrendous and the guards weren't any zippier about letting malcontents cross the borders than they had been for the last forty years. As we nudged to the head of the line, I felt my stomach gently curdle, as always, on a million ifs. This morning I had packed in a postcoital rapture; now I realized that, Reform notwithstanding, the contents of my cosmetics case alone could hang me. Had I dismantled the inductive clamps properly? How about Wildau's film? My tapes? Where were those steeple keys? I rolled down the window. "Hello," I smiled, handing over our passports.

The guard checked my papers then studied Harry, who was rifling the laundry bags, trying to locate the customs forms he had been given upon entering East Germany. "Do you have anything to declare?" the man asked.

"No sir! Nothing whatsoever!"

I felt the guard hesitate. Then, as if he were shooing flies off a cow's nose, he waved us through. Our limousine joined the next line, and the next, finally rolling into Berlin an hour later. The delays drove Harry alcoholic. Between slugs from his flask, he cursed the Germans, the border guards, Reform, and inevitably, me. If I had played perfectly at the recording sessions, Harry reasoned, he wouldn't now be burdened with this gigantic editing job.

"Guess what," I said. "You wouldn't have that editing finished even if I had played perfectly." Harry was obviously trying to teach Godo some convoluted lesson in respect. As we barreled past the Schloss Charlottenburg I asked what he was doing after Paris.

"Nothing. I desperately need a rest." Harry engorged a handful of vitamin C pills. "It's hell being number one. You have no idea."

At the airport I wished him success with Gilda and the sheik. As his chinchilla swirled into the terminal, Harry reminded me to keep my mouth shut.

The car took me to Dahlem. "Welcome home," Curtis said, as always checking the eyes, the mole above my lip. Both disturbed him. "Success?"

"Barely."

He caught up with me in the kitchen. "Hungry?"

I heaved my jacket on a chair. "Did anyone call?"

"Maxine. She'd like you to stop by the club tonight."

"No one else?"

Curtis paused; possibly he smelled Flick in my hair. "Were you expecting someone else?"

"I guess not." Between mouthfuls of cherry strudel, I reported the week's musical highlights to my manager, who listened solemnly less to words than to intonation: he had standing orders to check for stress fractures. Had the new engineer worked out? Fine technically, problematic on all other counts. Harry? Worse than ever. Godo would probably call looking for him today. "Tell him he's tap-dancing in Paris."

Curtis smiled scornfully. "And how's Mr. Flick." He waited. "The fellow who runs the trade fair."

"He had a violin lesson." Enough of this kaffeeklatsch; I had work to do. At the kitchen door I paused. "That scar on my back," I said. "Are the medical records in Vienna straight?"

"Yes." Curtis didn't have to ask why. "Duncan's coming at three o'clock to rehearse."

"Rehearse what?"

"Your Beethoven series in New York begins Thursday. He wants it to be particularly good." The comparison with my own attitude was obvious. Curtis could never let me forget that music was a brutally competitive profession.

I sighed. "Anything else on the agenda?"

"Not much. Two interviews tomorrow morning. I'm trying to leave you plenty of time to practice. You're pretty busy next month."

Duncan arrived in time to finish off the cherry strudel. I tried to keep my eyes open as he told Curtis all about his plans for a comeback recital and the many appointments he had made with music promoters in New York. Naturally, our rehearsal was useless.

After Duncan left, I went to my room and pressed the button over my fireplace. The mahogany panel to my right slid open and out came brilliant Spot, awaiting my fingerprint. I touched the computer's cold face, tapped in our passwords, and started with an easy question. What was flying over Leipzig? Spot began at low altitude with the genus/species of many migrating birds. I skipped them and got passenger airlines. Then my computer ascended to a celestial river: weather balloons, television/telephone satellites, senile sputniks, space stations, above that military eyeballs, telescopes, spare parts, radar, probes. Everything but the Virgin Mary was floating up there. As usual, the two superpowers were the road hogs. Uncle Sam was cluttering space with ever more pebbles in weapons networks. Spot found a heavyweight launched by the Soviets in 1988 for "meteorological research and long-range biological experiments." Above that, way above, were a half dozen CCCP gnats which looked like ultra-high-flying radar launched while Mother Russia was rhapsodizing about glasnost. Bottoming the list were two UFO's, purpose unknown, belched from China.

One of these fabulous birds was warbling to Moll's Clove.

I didn't have the capacity to chase it down now so I plugged in the DAT cassette I had made in the steeple and told Spot to identify.

My computer whirred a few seconds as digits streamed across the screen. On and on they went, billions of them. "Parallel mathematical calculations," Spot concluded.

"Explain," I typed back.

Chomp, chomp. "Computer-generated code, language unknown, not possible to decipher at this time. Need larger sample."

Sorry, that's all the sample I had. Damn! I was going to have to ask Maxine for help. She and her general had access to the NSA vaults in Fort Meade. They were going to have to compare my tape with the NSA's tapes of all the satellite transmissions it had overheard around Leipzig recently. If she could match my coded gibberish with something on file, she'd at least know which satellite the Clove was trying to penetrate. I sighed; it would probably take a while. One didn't poke into those vaults without airtight clearance.

Next I peered at American colleges, asking for an RH '77. My computer found thousands but only sixteen cross-referenced with lacrosse, at Harvard, Johns Hopkins, Army, Syracuse, Hofstra, U Mass Amherst . . . when my spine suddenly flared, I recessed, weary of the tangled mess born of a few moments' meditation in a damp fountain. Before lying down, I called the murderer.

"Hello darling, did I interrupt your practicing?"

"No, I just finished. I was about to go back to my office."

His voice made me foolish. "I miss you."

"Yes." Flick sighed.

Yes? What the hell kind of answer was that? Why the sigh? "What are we going to do about this?" I asked.

"I don't know. Perhaps we should do nothing."

"Are you serious?"

For a moment Flick let the static speak for him. "I must go. Thank you for calling."

Something had happened. Had I made a mistake at the fairgrounds, the steeple, his apartment? My brain regurgitated every tiny word, each gesture, deducing everything and nothing. I went to the window and stared dolefully into the night, just as Flick had from his bedroom window a few hours ago. The wind blew and leaves rushed desperately across my roof, hounded by twigs. I listened to the sudden, startling silence as they hurtled off the edge.

Curtis knocked around midnight but I was already changing into road leather. Seeing my attire, he frowned and shut off the lights. "Come here." I went to the window. Outside, the moon glared at spindly trees. "It's been there since you arrived," he said, pointing to a Trabant parked up the street. "The car's registered in Leipzig."

"To whom?"

"A former Stasi."

I let the curtain drop and pulled on my boots. Curtis followed me to the garage, frowning when the Harley roared. Such noises reminded him that he worked for an endangered species. "I won't be long," I said.

Just in case Bozo was asleep, I gunned the Harley inches from his Trabant. It lurched into gear and wheezed after me into the Grunewald. Would Flick have me followed? What gall. I sped into the forest. Poof, gone: the Trabant might as well have been a tricycle. It was a fabulous night, one a witch would kill for. Even the rocks seemed alive, fragments of a sentient moon. I flew at the wind, leaning lower and lower into the curves of the road as the trees reached for my boots, murmuring thickly to each other. We were all much too alive, in ferment, denying winter even as its breath paralyzed us. I looped through the dark paths again and again, looking for the Trabant, finding only a couple leaning against a tree, kissing passionately. Last time I had zipped by they were hardly holding hands. Didn't want to see them horizontal next time around so I blew out of the Grunewald into a manmade thicket of steel and glass, maintaining speed the fifteen kilometers to Roland's nightclub. No Trabant there and my nose was numb; I had been out a little too long.

"Just saying hello," I told Horst, rubbing my hands.

The Queen was in her dressing room playing with feathers and jewelry. As we entered she glanced at me in the mirror. "Could you bring some tea, Horst? That's a doll."

He left. "Put your lobby camera on," I said.

She smiled wanly. "Can't you lose people any more, Smith?"

I tossed the DAT onto her sequined lap. "Translate this if you can."

"What is it?"

I told her that we could probably kiss off war games, advanced logarithmic functions, weather forecasting, and other pedestrian uses of wide-load computers: the Clove was infatuated with a satellite, linking up through a dish at the fairgrounds. "Clever," she said. "Whose satellite?"

"That's your job. You're going home for Christmas, aren't you? Drop into the NSA bank and start comparing notes. It's in code, by the way. Try to break that while you're at it."

She slid a white feather behind her ear. "How is Mr. Flick?"

On the overhead monitor I watched a couple hand their furs to Horst and go into the club. Thinking he was alone, he rifled their pockets. "Difficult."

"Smitten, poor thing." He or I? She didn't say. As Maxine reddened her lips, a bartender set down two cups of tea and left. "How was his violin lesson?"

"All right. He's been practicing." Flick was none of her business any more. "Did you find anything on the organist?"

"Oskar Wildau was born in Leipzig. He went to school there, he lost his virginity there, he'll probably die there. He's nothing."

I tossed her his film. "He was following me."

"Is anyone else following you? The Mayor perhaps? The Erlkönig?" The Queen sighed, rouging her tawny cheeks.

"You made yourself a famous violinist. Don't cry now if people are curious."

My brother strolled into the dressing room. It was hard to tell whether Roland had been sleeping or awake for the last forty-eight hours straight. "Having a little tea party, girls?"

"Hello Rolly," I said. "How's everything?"

He kissed me sloppily. "I wrote one word today. *The*." Roland turned to Maxine. "Ready to sing? Or do you need more tea?"

She was powdering her nose. "Two minutes, darling."

The door slammed. "What's the matter with him?" I asked.

"The family malady," Maxine replied, sliding her feet into hot pink slippers. "Confusion of fantasy with reality. What's your next move, or shouldn't I ask?"

"I'm going to New York on Tuesday. Duncan and I are playing at Lincoln Center. Then we hit the Midwest."

The Queen frowned. "More concerts?" She cheered up when I mentioned I had a few lacrosse players to run down. Maxine began to hum lightly to herself: my signal to leave. Suddenly she stopped. "Did you tag Flick's phone? His car?"

"No time."

The melody resumed, this time with an infuriating grin: reminded me of Chance and his whistling. "Professional courtesy?"

"I had no time."

"Learn anything about the redhead?"

"Oh lay off, will you? Christ!"

Realizing she had hit the panic button, Maxine asked no more questions. I found Roland at the bar confabulating with a vixen. Onstage a saxophonist breathed on a note as if it were the tenderest portion of a lover's anatomy. I slid an arm around my brother's shoulder and tugged him to our table in the corner.

He dumped himself onto the banquette. "Now you're a chaperone service?"

I watched his lips curl around a cigarette. If Roland weren't my brother, I'd find him quite attractive; he emanated a sharp, dark despair which challenged a woman's curative powers. "I'm a little worried about you. Maybe you should get away from Berlin for a while. Go to the Bahamas for Christmas. Write your book there."

"What for? I like it here."

Maxine began to sing with the saxophonist. She wasn't in very good voice but in her field huskiness could pass for ardor. "By the way, a fan of yours came in," Roland said.

"Oh?"

"An older man. I think his name was Emil. Know him?"

I swallowed a surge of familiar, lemony bile. "When was this?"

"About two weeks ago. Came in by himself, sat at the bar for an hour. A few ladies tried to pick him up."

"What did they look like? Any redheads?"

"I don't remember. Not to worry, they didn't succeed. He looked pretty grim so I introduced myself."

"What did you talk about?"

"You, of course."

"Wouldn't happen to remember the details, would you," I said.

"General consumption, Sis. He talked about your violin most of the time. And a few questions about Curtis. Wanted to know where you two had met."

"What did you tell him?"

"I said you picked him up during a motorcycle trip. That's right, isn't it? I think he wanted to know if you were sleeping together." Roland's highball joined the half dozen that had preceded it. "Hope you don't mind if I pulled his chain a little. He's obviously made the mistake of falling for you."

"Did Maxine see him?"

"She was off that night."

A few feet away the Queen draped herself lazily over the bass player, as if he existed solely to cushion her elbows. "Duncan and I are going to the States for a while. Maybe you could come with us. Father would love to see you."

"What's going on? You trying to get me out of Berlin or something?"

"Of course not. I think you need a break."

That got a terse laugh. My brother kissed me goodbye as Maxine took a series of slow bows. "That old boy had class," he said. "What does he do?"

"Sells tractors. Tell Maxine if he comes in again, eh?"

Roland understood. I could only hope that he'd watch his mouth next time. Out in the street, the Trabant waited under a flickering lamp.

Over the winter Duncan Zadinsky and I would be playing all of Beethoven's violin/piano sonatas at Lincoln Center. Three concerts, third Thursday of the month. Kakadu Classics was sponsoring the jet lag. In anticipation of his upcoming appearances in America, Duncan had gotten his hair permed, thinking that frizz would deflect attention from his bald patch and give him an artsy flair. Finally, overcome by the inequity of giving piano lessons while I played concertos with heavy orchestras, he had booked Alice Tully Hall, where he would be playing an all-Chopin recital in March. While in New York with me, Duncan planned to speak with publicists about press coverage of this important event. Critics and managements would be invited, overwhelmed, and presto, a superstar would catapult into living legend. Duncan talked about little else, lashing through our rehearsals in Berlin with a ferocity usually reserved for the midlife crisis.

The trip had sordid extra-musical aspects for me as well. Now that Kakadu Classics had spent millions of dollars engorging a slew of American companies, Godo-san decided that it was time to infiltrate the Billboard charts. He hired an advertising agency that, after months of deliberation, designed a phantasmagorical purple logo appealing to all ages, races, and IQs. He signed on artists with the gusto of a major league baseball manager and plowed a fortune into state-of-the-art equipment. Every effort was made to remove the stigma of white European music from Kakadu's line without insulting the ninety percent of the market who bought classical music regardless of its origins. The product was handsomely packaged, slightly suggestive, available everywhere . . . all Godo needed now were a few catchy personalities to convince the American consumer that Beethoven was the cocaine of the nineties.

Hoping I would become as lucrative in America as I was in Europe, Godo chose me to lead his first charge. Before launching the Beethoven sonatas in a sea of green, however, he was anxious that I have a little chat with Kakadu's marketing department. Curtis insisted upon attending our meeting at company headquarters. We had spent too many years building Smith's cover to have it subverted into farce; on the other hand, Kakadu had been laying a lot of golden eggs on Leslie Frost lately and my manager thought we should try to accommodate Godo as much as possible.

We met in Kakadu's holly-festooned East Side offices. After welcoming us to America and chatting the number of minutes recommended in his corporate handbook, Godo led us down a beige hallway to the War Room, where we would be meeting his marketing staff. En route I noticed that my manager was turning a lot of heads; when Curtis chose to pack that musculature into a dark wool suit, libidos of both genders sizzled. We walked through heavy bronze doors into a panoramic suite, where Godo introduced us to a table of execs with granite smiles. A Ms. Sydney Bolt, an unholy union of claws and styling mousse, stood up.

Ms. Bolt delivered a banal speech about how thrilled the folks at Kakadu were to have me, yet at the same time, how difficult it would be to interest busy Americans in esoterica like the *Kreutzer* Sonata. Therefore, the marketing department had to sell not a violinist, but a personality, to the uninitiated. To avoid any misunderstandings that might lead to embarrassment, she passed around a news release upon which Kakadu's sales campaign would be based. *Expatriate Comes Home*. The article went on to describe how, racked with visions and longing, Leslie Frost would return to America after a long exile following the scandalous death of her husband, famous conductor Hugo Lange, cut down in his prime by . . . well, never mind the headlines, his hotheaded wife Nina had dropped the charges.

The paper fluttered unread from Curtis's hands, skidding toward the center of the polished table. "This is offensive and totally unacceptable."

"But think of the press you'll get," Ms. Bolt cried. "These are the great American themes of the nineties! Mysticism and litigation!"

"Go to hell," I told her.

That just bounced off her shoulderpads. She looked me over. "Are you having an affair with anyone significant?"

America had degenerated since I was last in contact with it. I glared at Curtis. "Why don't you try the recluse approach?" he suggested. "No press contact whatever. That's mystical."

Bolt's oversize earrings jangled. "A recluse? It took weeks to schedule all these interviews. I can't call them off. It would jeopardize my credibility with the national media."

The underlings tried to earn their salaries. "Maybe you could talk Harley-Davidson into a rally at Lincoln Center," said a tweedy reed. "Get out there in tight pants and cheerlead."

Brainstorm struck a blond. "Was Beethoven gay?"

Bolt leered at Curtis. "Are you chaperoning this tour?"

"No ma'am."

Godo was getting lost. "What about the violin?" he interrupted. "Miss Frost plays the violin extremely well."

"Boring," Bolt snapped. "I'd have better luck selling mosquito bites. No offense, we're just trying to move product for you. Plain vanilla violinists just don't cut it in this country."

Funk settled on the round table. "I guess we could always play up the women's angle again," said the tweed.

"We could get your violin stolen," offered the blond. "It's worth a couple million bucks, isn't it? Ransom, rewards, all that stuff."

Ms. Bolt's fingernails raked the air. "I've done it already."

"Perhaps you could find a boyfriend," Curtis suggested. "Leslie and he will go out to eat. Someone can take a few pictures." He turned to me. "Acceptable?"

I didn't answer.

"We'd have to find a suitable candidate, of course," Bolt said. "I need to maximize impact."

"With your wide range of influence, I'm sure it won't be a problem." As Curtis stood up, Bolt nearly bit her pencil in half. "I would expect to be informed of your intentions beforehand, of course."

Godo accompanied us into the hall. "Sydney Bolt is excellent, no?"

"Worth every yen," Curtis replied.

With two soft bongs the elevator doors parted. "I understand your Mozart recording in Leipzig went well," Godo said, stepping inside.

"Who told you that? Harry Paradise?"

He grimaced delicately. "No. I have not been able to reach Harry at all. Mr. Chance told me. I am anxious to hear the tapes very soon. Along with the Beethoven sonatas. They are done now, aren't they?"

"You'll have to ask Harry. He's in Paris with a tap dancer."

While Curtis lunched with Godo to hash out a few pecuniary matters, I returned to the hotel to pursue the *RH '77* engraved on Moll's little lacrosse stick. I'd start with the registrar's office at Hofstra University. Spot had come up with a Reginald Heller '77 who played lacrosse there. "Hi," I said, "this is Rowanda Moruna calling from the personnel office at Vimco Limited in New York. I wonder if you could help me, like I'm checking the job application of Reginald Heller, a guy who says he got outta Hofstra in 'seventy-seven. Zat true?"

"I can't give that information over the phone. You'll have to write a letter."

"Letter? I can't write so good. My boss will be super pissed if she finds out. You ain't able to tell me? Like this is secret atomic information or somethin'? I got an emergency situation here."

The woman sighed. "What did he study?"

"I can't read these long words very well. It looks like mathmatism."

I heard keys tapping. "I have a Reginald Heller who graduated nineteen seventy-seven. But he got a degree in hotel management."

"Hotels? We're a computer company. I think the schmuck's making this up."

"That's very possible. People do that often these days. Our records show his current address as Houston."

"Zat in New York? No? Shit! I'd better ask my supervisor about this," I said. "Thanks a lot."

Richard Hennigan, Amherst '77, went from Philosophy to Divinity School; Roger Hershey, Syracuse '77, majored in French; Richard Hirt, Harvard '77, studied economics. He was still in school pursuing his doctorate. None of the registrars seemed surprised at the bogus job applications and the more stupid I sounded, the less they questioned my own credentials. My list was getting too close to dead end when I tried Johns Hopkins. The registrar's office found a Reiner Hofmann '77 who studied electrical engineering.

"Did he get a doctor's degree in 1981?" I asked. "With high honors?"

The fellow chuckled. "Try again, sweetie. He only lasted two years here. Then his student visa expired."

"You mean he's not an American engineer? Jeez, my supervisor's gonna hit the roof! The office already looks like Bombay."

I practiced the afternoon away while Curtis hobnobbed with artistic directors. Duncan returned to the hotel about four o'clock, hysterical. He had been out selecting the publicist who would make him the most famous for the least cash outlay. "I hate this country," he cried, flopping across the bed. "It's perverted."

I put the violin down. "What happened."

"You know how much this recital is going to cost me?"

"Forty thousand bucks."

"That's five face-lifts!" Duncan shouted. "That's down payment on my chalet in the Schwarzwald!"

"I'd go for the real estate if I were you."

Precisely what he didn't want to hear. "You think I'm not worth it?"

"Please, I've heard enough advertising slogans for one day." I forced him through a dress rehearsal and then bought him a steak. Trying to calm him, I explained that nowadays fame on the concert stage boiled down to nothing more than playing the same six concertos with the same egomaniacs year after year. Duncan didn't believe it. That evening a hyperventilating Sydney Bolt interrupted a jigsaw party to say I had a date with Luke the Apostle.

"Who's that," I asked.

"You don't know? Where have you been for the last eon, dear heart?"

I dropped the phone on the bed. "It's for you," I said to Curtis.

He picked it up and listened for a time. "Does he speak English," he said. Another long silence. "What does he get out of this?" Duncan and I finished connecting the edge pieces. "No skinny dipping. None."

"Is that how he gets jobs for you?" Duncan asked. "Sheesh."

Curtis finally hung up. "Tomorrow night you're having dinner with Luke the Apostle." He resumed his seat at puzzleside. "He's a rock star."

"Oh come on! Couldn't she dig up a Shakespearean actor or something?"

"She's going for the beauty and the beast angle, culturally speaking. I think it's rather clever."

"In the old days, all musicians had to do was play their instruments," Duncan whined. "What the hell happened?"

Curtis inspected a puzzle piece. "Television raped the imagination. Stick to Europe, Duncan. That's my advice."

Demoralized, Duncan went to bed. "I don't like blind dates," I said to Curtis. "What do you think you're doing with this boyfriend business?"

"I'm managing your career." Curtis tried to yawn.

"Now where are you going?" It was only ten. "Bolt invited you out, didn't she?"

"It's strictly business. Like you and Mr. Flick."

Professional warning or my butler's idea of a joke? I watched his perfect rear end leave the room, wondering if Bolt would be handling it later. The idea did not appeal.

9

*L*uke the Apostle had burst on the rock scene several years earlier with a song urging all American boys to seduce their mothers. It was a big hit but Luke hadn't been able to follow up with any more platinum, so his record company ditched him. Distressed, Luke spent a year sleeping with actresses, then, after the birth of his third illegitimate child in five months, decided that he must make a serious go at resurrection. Things started revving up, particularly in the preteen market, with a slick commercial for shoelaces. Luke snagged another record company and hired Sydney Bolt to give him a new image.

As we drove to a chichi restaurant in the Village, my date disgorged paeans to his publicist; she was our only point of intersection. First she had Luke pass out on the steps of the Lincoln Memorial and say he had been struck by a vision. Then he got a haircut, on one side anyway, and wore John Lennon ripoff glasses to look thoughtful. When Luke began writing songs about abstinence, parents forgave him. Bolt wanted him to be seen with serious women, so he had been dating the daughter of an astronaut and a famous ice skater, neither of whom had become pregnant. So as not to lose touch completely with his former audience, however, Luke the Apostle still drove a pink hearse. "Sydney's a genius," he said. "She knows the temperature of America."

I watched a few pedestrians try to peer through the smoked windows. "Sort of like a giant rectal thermometer."

Once they saw the mutation parked on Houston Street, the inquisitive pressed their noses to the window of the restaurant where Luke and I were swallowing dainty bits of monkfish and a bottle of pink wine. We dead-ended dozens of conversations in a futile effort to find a topic, other than Bolt, in common. Autograph requests ran about fifty-to-one in Luke's favor. "This is embarrassing," he said finally. "Any dope can play the guitar. Not many people can play the violin. I mean, there are no frets on a violin. How can you play without frets?"

You practiced ten hours a day for twenty years, jackass! I studied my watch for the umpteenth time as Luke scrawled his signature across a napkin. "Speaking of instruments, do you play a Chance guitar?"

"Of course. They're the best." Luke ordered another bottle.

"Why?"

"They're ergonomic. Copacetic. The company gives you personal attention. I've played them all my career."

A woman across the room was staring avariciously at my diamonds as her companion filled their goblets with mineral water. "Do you know Toby Chance?"

"Ha ha!"

"About your height with black hair and gray eyes? Wears a lot of cashmere sweaters? Takes baths?"

"How's the son of a bitch doing? Married again?"

"I don't understand."

Uncapping his fountain pen, Luke autographed the rear end of someone's jeans. "I guess he keeps it quiet now that he's trying to go legit." Chance's first wife was now one of the sassiest actresses in Hollywood. The second was a champagne heiress about ten years his senior. He met them both at guitar parties.

"What happened?" I said.

"He dropped them. Each time he got more bucks and

they all still adore him.'' Whoa, another gluteus maximus to autograph. "Wish I knew his secret.''

"Does he have children?''

"Not from those two. How do you know Chance? You don't look like a party animal, no offense.''

"He's a recording engineer. We've done two projects together.''

"Toby makes records now? That sly motherfucker.'' The Apostle glanced at the door, slid a half foot closer. "There's Arty. Pretend you don't see him.''

Leaning into my ear, Luke mimed the whisper-sweet-nothings charade as a photographer shot half a roll from the doorway. When that little parody bobbled, my date dropped a couple hundred bucks on the table and hustled me through an awed crowd to his hearse. We drove a few blocks, waiting for the photographer to catch up, and shot another jam session at the steering wheel. Arty wanted us to look surprised and annoyed, as if he had interrupted a merger. "Let's go dancing,'' Luke said when the camera stopped clicking.

"No thanks. I have to practice.''

"The violin? Now?''

"This isn't enough material, guys,'' Arty said. "I can't go back to Sydney with just this.''

The two of them looked pathetic. "Get in,'' I told Arty. We tanked uptown, past gaily decorated Christmas trees and many furred bipeds. The night was crystalline and cold, intoxicating as a vodka martini, and suddenly I couldn't stand the thought of shutting myself in a hotel room with that dead violin while Manhattan writhed like a gilded Medusa, so I told the Apostle that dancing sounded all right. We headed back downtown to a deafening SoHo pit where I lasted long enough for Arty to get a few action shots. Then I lost them.

The next evening Duncan and I played at Lincoln Center. It was a dull, vexatious dream from opening note to closing bow. Every other woman in the audience looked like a pint-size redhead and Duncan played many decibels louder than he should have. The Apostle showed up sloshed at Kakadu's reception afterward, wondering where I had disappeared the night before. As he pressed my hand to his mouth, announcing that he had just composed a love ballad, Arty shot a few mementos of the occasion. I was in a foul mood: I had played off center and Curtis wasn't doing much to keep Bolt's red talons in her pockets. Across the room Duncan got drunk on gassy champagne and began bad-mouthing pianists whose managers were at the reception. When their unctuous smiles suddenly became grotesque, I walked out.

At the door Bolt seized my arm. "I've seen the pictures," she whispered, as if we were debutantes comparing dance cards. "They're fabulous. We'll take them a long, long way."

I smiled at her exquisite makeup. "I'm so happy for you." I went alone to a movie, a French farce without a scintilla of social message. For two hours I sat in the dark recalling my last, unreal conversation with Flick. Would he drop me, *thud*, like that? No. Impossible! The redhead must have changed her orders; he would have to obey. That would explain everything. Nevertheless, my pain was just as great.

Later, Curtis knocked on my door. I didn't bother turning on the lights; he knew where the damn chair was. "You played well tonight," he said.

"Not really." I listened to spinning wheels and blowing horns twelve floors below: polyphony, Twentieth Century American school. "Can we get rid of Ms. Bolt, Curtis? She disturbs me. This whole city disturbs me. I want to go home."

"Too late," he said. "Sorry, Les. We'll just have to run with it for a while. Don't take her too seriously. She's just doing her job."

A lady cackled drunkenly in the hallway. "I'm quitting this business," I said.

"Which one?"

Tomorrow Curtis would be going home for Christmas and I would be without him for a while. But I wanted him to leave. It was one of those nights when my insides were tinder and one little puff could burn a verdant forest to the ground forever. "Where's your friend?" I asked.

"Out advertising." Curtis kept his rear end fused to the chair until he thought I was asleep.

Duncan and I played a few concerts in the wintry Midwest. While he practiced Chopin, I walked along the wide streets distancing myself from the Flick problem. Cunning, history-poisoned Europe was very far from here; one was tempted to believe that it didn't exist at all, or if it did, too bad. I itched to get a motorcycle and disappear across the plains. When Duncan went home to Cleveland, I flew to Washington to visit my father. For several days we attended a round of ambassadorial Christmas parties, just like the old days but now the men all reminded me of Flick. Everyone talked incessantly, joyfully, about the collapse of the Wall. Maxine never called although she was probably beavering right down the street at the NSA archives. I spent afternoons at the library reading arcane textbooks about lasers, trying to figure out what Flick was up to at the trade fair.

I knew only that he was planning a laser exhibition and that the power lines all over Leipzig were being replaced. Perhaps that was just coincidence. However, over the last decade, the superpowers had been heavily into the develop-ment of high-energy lasers. Unlike low-energy lasers, which were currently used to guide smart weapons to their targets, high-energy lasers were the actual weapons: the "death rays" so beloved of sci-fi writers were slowly becoming reality. The Soviets and Israelis were particularly fond of them. They were rumored to have blinded other spy satellites by burning out their electronic eyes with an intense laser beam. Without eyes, of course, surveillance satellites were functionally dead, although they might continue to orbit. *Hmmm.* Flick could have a lot of fun with a toy like that. But there were a few problems. Building a laser was the easy part. Finding the target was more difficult, as was getting the beam through the atmosphere. Rain, clouds, smoke, and fog all obstructed light. Even on a clear day, the atmosphere absorbed a small fraction of light passing through it; if an intense laser beam were focused on a target far away, thermal blooming would cause the beam to spread, weakening it significantly by the time it hit target.

The best way to bypass atmospheric distortion would be to aim the laser at the target with mirrors. Sensing equipment would have to record the weather conditions, rapidly process the data, and immediately correct the mirror positions. Flick had the computer and the locating equipment; he probably had the laser; did he have the mirrors? I didn't know. But the East German opticals industry was about the world's best and they would be out in force at the next trade fair.

Maybe December was a bad time of year to attempt scientific research; maybe I was more worried about Flick's behavior than that of his equipment. Whatever the case, the more I read about lasers, the less I understood what he would be doing with one on the fairgrounds.

One afternoon, weary of chasing chimeras, I drove my father's Lincoln to Baltimore. Most of its students and faculty had fled Johns Hopkins University for the holidays. Those few remaining tried to look occupied in the libraries, gyms, and administration buildings. In the morgue designated Alumni Office, I displayed an engraved business card, explaining to the sole occupant that I was a lawyer wishing to locate a client's brother, possibly a student in the sixties. That fable got me into a sanctum smelling of cracked leather where wealthy alumni went to discharge their debts to higher education. The woman directed me to a crop of yearbooks and went to make tea.

As her plaid skirt turned the corner I pulled '77 into my lap and immediately found the choirmaster. Then known as Reiner Hofmann, Moll was smiling from the back row of the lacrosse team. In the class photo section, I saw an archetypal nerd who sang in the chorus but belonged to no fraternity, no debating team, not even a foreign students club: instead of a descriptive paragraph, I saw flat white space beneath his picture. "Any luck?" the woman asked, bringing a tray.

"Not yet, I'm afraid." I lingered another half hour poring through hundreds of pages of youth w/ long hair. All that rebellion looked so sloppy now.

Just before five o'clock, as sleet pelted the rolling campus, I returned to the brick administration building. Behind the glass door of the admissions office all but one diehard had gone home for the day. She was over sixty and sharp as a saw, seething authority, as if once upon a time she had changed Mr. Hopkins's diapers. Careful, Smith: this lady would know that I didn't belong here. I stayed in a utility closet across the hall until her shoes clacked trimly by. Waited, waited. When the door at the end of the corridor slammed, I let myself into the admissions office. Her verbena soap still tinged the air. As a streetlamp outside percolated blackness into many shades of gray, I crept past the poinsettia on her desk to another glass door. Had to unlock that one too while the flying ice outside scratched at the windows, looking for me. Security here was a joke. Then again, who gave a damn about Joe Blow's grade in sophomore calculus? I hardly needed a flashlight with those fat black numbers on all the cabinets. Ah, there was '77, Year of the Choirmaster. Splayed his file on the floor and poised a camera over the paltry six pages. Moll was neither a bad nor an outstanding student, just an invisible one, the type whose face professors could never quite correlate with a name. I replaced the nebbish's file and strolled out, passing a few bodies in the hall. No one questioned me: I wore a suit and a pleasant smile. God, I loved spying in America! It was about as risky as shooting rhinoceros from a helicopter!

Back to Washington for more parties, more distinctive men, all shadows of Flick. Roland called once, drunk, asking where Maxine was. The Capitol was drenched in red; as the days slipped by, each holly wreath, Santa outfit, light, ball, and ribbon began to remind me of that woman with red hair who had drawn me into her vicious little circus, all too confident that I would jump through her flaming hoops. She began seeping into my thoughts and dreams, like Flick only much denser, more ruinous, obliterating Christmas. If my father detected my lack of seasonal gaiety, he said nothing; I had always been a moody child and holidays were hell on widows. When he left for skiing in Vail, I flew back to Berlin.

As the airplane touched down, the passengers cheered. They had come to join the New Year's party. No one seemed to mind waiting an hour for a cab; the delay gave bubbly strangers the opportunity to trade war stories and utopian forecasts. Traffic remained thick all the way to my house in Dahlem, where dozens of East Germans strolled along the sidewalks checking out the real estate. My stomach curled when I saw the Trabant still waiting for me at the end of the tall hedges. I went inside. Without Curtis my house was overlarge and underheated, a fortress built for people who threw a lot of parties for a lot of friends. I unpacked in the depressing silence, then, against my better judgment, called Flick's office. "Working hard?" I said.

"Who's this?"

"Baron Munchausen, you bastard. Listen, I must see you. Are you free?"

"Ah—eh—I am not sure."

At least getting shot in the back was clean. Verbal shrapnel bloodied everything. "Well, I am." I hung up.

Work was the best antidote so I pulled a score off the shelf and began learning a new concerto. When that got ugly, I went to the darkroom and swished the film of Moll's transcripts through a few chemical ponds. The doorbell rang; I ignored it. The caller persisted so I stomped upstairs, switched on the cameras: Flick at the iron gate. His beautiful, grim face startled me. Looked as if he had come to snap my neck.

I unlocked the gate. He didn't smile. "I can't stay long."

I pointed to his green car. "Put that in the garage. It's warm." His Trabant chugged in alongside my blue M6 and died, perhaps of mortification. I brought him into the kitchen.

He looked quickly around: it was as big as his entire apartment. I didn't apologize. "Hungry?" He swallowed only fragments of cake, malady stomach knots caused by border crossings. I knew the symptoms well. "So what brings you to Berlin?" I asked. "Bananas? You look awful."

Leading with his mouth, Flick backed me against the refrigerator. I was able to stay on my feet until his fingers began splitting my zipper. Then I dribbled toward the floor. He kept raising me by putting a hand between my legs and lifting. "Where's your housekeeper," he whispered.

"In Alabama."

Flick took me by the hand and strode into the dining room. No mattress there so he continued to the next door, Hugo's study. I recognized the preoccupied eyes, the drastic need to fuse with flesh: Flick was in danger. Only one antidote for anxiety of that sort so I brought him to the deep old velvet couch and unbuttoned him as fast as I could, famished for that magical flesh I wanted to devour forever. Ah, the weight of him, the smell of him . . . it wasn't elegant but ferocity had its own breathtaking beauty and I had to have him sunk, stuck, anywhere there was an opening. Where there wasn't an opening, I wanted to cover him with my skin, absorb as much of that peace as I could in the few moments I had him before the long night returned.

Flick suddenly rolled to the side. "Oh God," he croaked. "I can't stay away from you."

So what? Was I a curse? I pounced on top of him, sliding him inside again, where he belonged. I had to hear him sigh at the mystery of it all, had to hear his gasps and his seismic groans when he knew he wasn't going to escape my hold without paying with a tiny splash of his soul. There he went: bliss, oh God what bliss, so divine, so brief.

Afterward I lay on the couch like a rag doll, all flax no bones, as he tugged my clothing back to its former position. I watched him dress. "Now you're leaving?" I asked. *Zip*, answered his pants.

I followed him to the kitchen. Flick was trying to eat the cake again. A massive chunk of him didn't want to be here. It didn't correlate to the previous quarter hour and for the first time I realized that maybe Flick didn't want the redhead to know he was seeing me. I wiped a few crumbs from his lips, trying to make sense of it. "Don't ever leave me like that again."

He bit my finger. "I'm sorry. It's been a bad time."

"Can you tell me about it?"

Shook his head. Maybe he just shuddered. "A thousand stupid little events." He raised his ice-blue eyes. "How was New York? I understand you went dancing. And driving."

"Where'd you hear that?"

"I read that. So did a few million other people. It's all over the newsstands."

"You mean Luke the Apostle?"

I explained my recent business meetings but Flick didn't get the connection between dinner for two and sophisticated market forces at work. "Do you like him?" he asked.

"I don't like or dislike him. He's the same relationship as an exhibitor at your trade fair."

"Really? I don't sit on the laps of exhibitors at the trade fair."

I withdrew my hand from his arm. "Don't you have anything better to do than read that crap? Publicity is nothing but fairy tales."

"Is it? I'm never sure with you." Flick put his napkin down. "Why did you call me here? Please don't say violin lesson or I might wring your neck."

In this condition he might, so I led him upstairs to my bedroom. Didn't switch on the lights. I pulled the curtain a bit to the side. "See anything unusual out there?" As he found the Trabant parked up the street, I felt an interior wobble. But he said nothing. "Are you having me followed, Emil?"

He stared for a long time. "No."

"My housekeeper is upset. Curtis wanted to call the police but I said I'd speak to you first."

Flick looked stonily at me. "Why speak to me?"

"Because this only started after I went to the fairgrounds

with you." I slipped my arms around his waist; he visited so seldom. "Is someone afraid you're telling me military secrets?"

His gaze shifted back to the street. "Who's inside?"

"A man. He's been following me everywhere."

Flick chuckled bitterly. "He's seen me pull into the garage, of course."

"Who cares? You're allowed to visit, aren't you?"

Quietly disengaging me, Flick stepped back from the window. "Would you mind coming downtown? Walking a bit?"

In his position I would have done the same, although I would have asked more subtly. I grabbed my green beaver cape, the one with a couple of tiny holes in the shoulder, and hopped into his Trabant. On the passenger seat was a package from a big record shop on the Ku'damm. I looked inside. He had bought the latest release of *Parsifal*, the Liszt 1838 *Transcendental Etudes*, a CD of bassoon concertos.

Flick backed quickly into the street. "I keep asking for your Beethoven sonatas," he said. "Apparently they're not yet released."

"Are you kidding? They're not even edited." I was a little angry at him for stopping at a record shop en route to my house. I thought I had a little more pull than his damn CD collection. "Bassoon concertos?"

He glanced in the mirror. "You're right, we are being followed."

Flick drove downtown, joining the Christmas traffic choking the Ku'damm. He puttered into the gnarled, off-color streets of Kreuzberg, where the minimum-wage sort lived, and popped into an illegal space. For the moment, vehicles with East German plates would be immune to parking tickets. "Where are we going?" I asked.

Flick wrapped his hand over mine. "For a walk."

He meandered until our chaperone had found a parking space, then led me impassively past the singing crowds at the Friedrichstrasse crossing. Berlin wouldn't have another Christmas like this until the millennium. However, I couldn't work up much enthusiasm for the hundreds of lachrymose reunions happening all around us. They didn't seem to be affecting Flick either. In the grand sea of history, he and I were the unseen coelacanths miles below the waves: surface hurricanes didn't impact us much. In ten minutes Flick had drawn me back into Turkish Kreuzberg. Sparse activity there. The locals were either inside smoking or at the Wall watching the competition flood into the labor pool. "You seem to know your way around," I said. "Do you come here often?"

"I did as a child."

My computer had no record of that. "What for?"

"My mother brought me to Professor Zwinger for a violin lesson every Friday." He glanced tensely over his shoulder; this conversation existed solely to pacify me. "I was her little Kreisler." Flick steered me behind a brewery.

"Where are we going?"

"Please do as I say." He slipped an arm around my shoulder. "Laugh as if I just told a joke, eh?"

I obeyed. Eventually he tucked me into a loading zone between two dark buildings. When our disciple turned the corner, Flick jumped him. "Who are you?" he whispered. No answer so my boyfriend squeezed the man's neck, as he had recently promised to do to mine, and asked again. Now nothing but muddy gurgling so Flick flung the man's head into the brick wall. The beating was professional and utterly merciless.

"Stop," I cried as the man sank to the cobblestones. I wasn't sure he'd ever get up again. "You'll kill him!" In response Flick calmly gutted the man's pockets. I ran away.

He overtook me in the middle of Viktoria Park. "I had to do it. He was following you."

Liar! I laughed, maybe shrieked; Flick used his fists as judiciously as he did firearms. "Get away from me."

"No. This is a bad part of town."

"Oh Christ, am I ten years old?"

He hustled me to his car. "Get in."

"Take me to my brother's," I shouted. "You know where

that is, don't you!'' Flick drove the few blocks to Roland's. His skin looked pale, unreal as wax. I hopped out, slamming the door as hard as possible: the hinges would never recover. ''I don't want to see you again,'' I screeched, running into the club.

Horst jumped from his post in the coatroom. He looked at my green cape. ''Not riding tonight?''

I reeled against the wall, gulping loudly. ''Would you tell me if that Trabant's gone, please.''

He peered outside. ''Nothing. Is someone annoying you?''

''Not any more.'' I caught a packed bus back to the Ku'damm and wandered stupidly among the blessed, lucky Germans: for them, it was a good time to be alive. I passed the record shop where Flick had just made his purchase. Seeing the late-night browsers jamming the aisles, I was suddenly, morbidly, curious to hear what had upstaged me. ''Would you have a CD of bassoon concertos,'' I asked the clerk, mentioning the soloist. My voice wobbled dreadfully.

He recognized me. ''That's a coincidence, Miss Frost, someone else just bought a copy of that tonight. I think it was our only one.'' He checked the racks: all gone. ''Care to order it?''

''Sure.'' I autographed a CD for him. ''Who bought it? A man with gray-blond hair? Burberry raincoat?''

''Yes, that's the one.''

''Was he alone?''

''Yes.''

''Does he come here often?''

''I hope not. He's quite difficult.''

''What do you mean?''

''He ordered some Gregorian chant that hasn't come in yet. Said he had driven all the way from Leipzig for it. The way he carried on, you would think we crucified him.''

''The poor bastard lives for his recordings.'' About now, driving past Dessau, he would have realized that tonight's visit must never be repeated. Emil! I burned with remorse and longing. ''When do you expect that Gregorian chant?''

The clerk shrugged. "I couldn't say. A day, two weeks, two months. These small labels are so unreliable."

"Would you send it to me when it comes in? I often go to Leipzig and could deliver it personally." He agreed because I was famous.

I went home. My kitchen still smelled of cake and now I ached: for those few moments at my table, wiping the yellow crumbs from his lips, I had been sublimely happy.

The phone rang. "I have the flu," coughed Harry Paradise from London. "Must have picked it up in that cesspool Leipzig."

"Maybe you got it in Paris. How was the tap dancer?"

"Awful beyond belief. Listen, you've got to help me. Godo just called. He's about to sic the Japanese navy on me."

"He wants that Beethoven you promised him last month, I suppose."

"Baby, do me the favor of your life. I just called Chance. He's free between now and New Year's. You've got to go to Boston and do that editing for me. My head's going to roll if it's not done soon. What's your schedule for next week?"

I checked Curtis's date book. "I have four days free."

"Thank God! I'll book it."

"Wait a minute, I didn't say I'd do it."

"You have something better to do? After all I've done for you?"

"Chance is mad at me. I was a little rude to him in Leipzig. He doesn't want me bothering him."

"He's crazy about you, you fool!"

Until Maxine returned from Washington, my satellite investigation was stymied. My laser theories were rubbish. The redhead was still calling the shots. My house was a tomb. Flick was lost. Berlin was full of ecstatic natives. Maybe I should evacuate the area for a few days. "Let me think about it."

I returned to my darkroom, where I had been working before Flick had disrupted yet another evening, and finished developing Moll's transcripts. The people at Hopkins called him Reiner Hofmann. He was there on a West German scholarship to study computer science and had managed to remain a perfect median dope. Couldn't have been easy for a brain of Moll's caliber to maintain flat C's in Statics & Dynamics, Calculus VI . . . I'd go nuts having to deliberately play out of tune for two years. Moll only slipped once, in Fourier Transforms. Alongside a C + his professor noted that perhaps Hofmann had a reading disability: why else would a student who asked such brilliant questions in class bungle every single exam? Moll had only let himself go in chorus, straight A's. Every semester his teacher wrote increasingly laudatory comments about his very nice voice, fine diction, excellent training, whoops last semester demoted to D: our naughty boy had missed the spring musicale, which was Prof's idea of a final exam, without furnishing a proper medical excuse. Silly, Flick could have forged one for him; in April '77, the deputy's trade delegation was visiting America. Moll's absence had deeply distressed his music teacher, the only fellow at Hopkins who seemed to have taken a personal interest in him. A long paragraph describing the incident made the most riveting reading of Moll's entire file except for the little postscript at the bottom of the last page, after the final 2.34 grade point average. Reiner Hofmann had drowned in a swimming accident in Crete four months after skipping his spring musicale.

That was just swell. I muddled away on my violin. Didn't go very intelligibly, so I pulled a prize champagne from the cellar, sampled heavily, and returned to the green velvet couch in Hugo's study. After his death, I used to sleep there; the clutter deluded me into thinking that he was just out of town conducting. Gradually, as the terror of returning to my own bed eased, I spent less and less time in the study. The scent of Hugo's pipe faded from the drapes; Curtis moved the plants to a sunnier room. I came here now to look things up and, on rarer occasions, to ponder where Hugo had gone. Eight years later, his books and autographed pictures, his baton collection, were still where he had kept them. Hugo's old violin was still in the corner cabinet, undisturbed, along with an old oboe and a battered trumpet. The consummate conductor, he had studied every instrument in the orchestra. It was only one reason so many people admired him.

Flick was usurping a lot of memories. History seemed to be repeating itself although now that I was older and weaker, the surprise bursts of happiness nearly killed me. Was my painful little romance proceeding according to the redhead's plans? Had events really taken care of themselves, as she had so confidently predicted at that concert in Amsterdam? Frost the Puppet: the idea turned my thoughts dark and cold . . . I sat for a long time wondering why Flick had really come to Berlin tonight.

he day after Christmas I landed in Boston. Compared to Berlin, the town was a morgue: no Fusion to celebrate. Frozen, unsmiling bodies hammered the sidewalks as a bitter wind chiseled flesh. Overhead, the sun glared coldly at leftover merchandise still posing in windows. Shoppers almost winced now at the sight of tinsel: once again, an orgy of giving and receiving had not altered the fundamental impression that the holiday was an updated version of burning at the stake.

Predicting blizzard, the cabbie dropped me at the Ritz. I had a bouquet of orchids sent to Chance and retired to the tub: my head ached, bah, the whole psyche dehydrated at the thought of dallying hours in a studio with Charm Boy Toby while so many evil stars floated above us. While the plane was crawling over six time zones, I had amused myself by writing *Moll*, *Flick*, and *Redhead* across the top of three sheets of paper and then listing everything I knew about them. Flick's and Moll's pages had filled up fast; the redhead's was blank. I had no idea where these people had met or who was running them, even less idea what they were trying to do. Had the redhead factored the end of the Berlin Wall into her plans? Or had it caught her by surprise, as it had everyone else? On a less objective note, I tried to determine how much of my Boston trip was Flick backlash and how much was humanitarian sacrifice for Harry Paradise. By the time we were over Newfoundland I had decided that it was strictly comic relief. Smith had no idea how to proceed with her case.

As the sun fell, shattering into many golden splinters, I went out again. Crossing the blustery Boston Common, I saw that everyone had gone home to television and saturated fats, leaving the paths blank; even the hardiest drug dealers were opting for inventory over frostbite. I walked through a lifeless Combat Zone and past Chinatown. Chance's studio occupied a former button factory on Sleeper Street. The whole area was now rehab heaven. Beyond the sputtering streetlights I could see that he had done a classy renovation on the old building. The exterior, all glass block, brick, steel, managed to look homey yet impregnable. Money oozed from the mortar. I pressed an engraved doorbell, probably a housewarming gift from one of his former wives. "Hello," called the intercom.

I hadn't expected a woman's voice. "Leslie Frost," I announced. She buzzed me inside. At the head of a long flight of steps was an industrial-strength door that slid open as I approached.

Toby Chance's grand designs were not limited to matrimony. His office foyer was a nice cross between the Rheims cathedral and Caesar's Palace. Way above my head floated a skylight. I turned to the perfect blond receptionist who was arranging the flowers that had preceded me from the Ritz. No man would mind waiting half a day here if she sat at the front desk. Evidently the boss didn't keep his female customers waiting. "Would Mr. Chance be in?" I asked.

She smiled blandly. "Is he expecting you?"

"He'd better be." As she rang for him my knees trembled, jet lag, so I strolled behind the Christmas tree dominating the reception area. On its branches hung dozens of cards from Chance's clientele, the largest and crassest one bearing Harry Paradise's signature. Just reading the message gave me cavities.

I heard footsteps but no whistling this time: through the

garlands I watched him pause at the front desk and read my card twined to the bouquet of orchids. Zero reaction. He was still furious with me for teasing him on a bridge in Leipzig. I must have been the first woman to give him a hard time since he stopped teething. Chance walked slowly toward the glittering tree. "Hello, Leslie," he said finally, turning the corner. No holiday kiss, not even a handshake, smile extinct and the eyes looked haggardly intense, like Flick's: coasting in the top tax bracket was a full-time occupation. "Never thought I'd see you in Boston."

"Likewise."

He posed the requisite inquiries about my flight and my Christmas, not quite listening to responses as much as scenting the air, trying to gauge my mood. I was politely sterile. "How long will you be in town?"

"As long as it takes." I removed my hat. "Harry did send the scores, didn't he?"

"They arrived this morning." Chance took my coat, careful not to graze my neck with the back of his hand as he usually did. His eyes ran over my body, though: perhaps I was forgiven. We walked back to the blond receptionist. "No calls, Mona," he said.

She took a better look at me as Chance headed down a mahogany staircase. I followed him round and round the spiral until we were well below ground level. He had buried his studios in the earth, away from noise and daylight: in this line of work, silence was golden. Floors were cork and the walls a deep sea green, punctuated by sconces which seemed to phosphoresce rather than actually shed light. If I stared at them, they began to swim ever so delicately, so I kept my eyes on Chance's dark head bobbing several steps ahead of me. I missed his whistling; without it, he seemed a little cruel. We paused in front of a heavy door marked Studio C. "Are you sure you want to work tonight?" he asked. "Jet lag and all?"

That was no invitation to dinner; he was trying to get rid

of me. So much for Harry's powers of reconciliation. "Of course I want to work. That's why I'm here."

He opened the door to a gorgeous studio of blond oak and black ash. I stood on the threshold a moment taking in the damping panels, the diffusers, bass traps, the speakers and editing desk so meticulously arranged about the suite: move any of them one inch and the acoustic would alter. Walls, ceiling had to be two feet thick and the floor probably floated on a cement slab, neutering any vibrations from the outside world. Even the duct system was inaudible; Chance had spent a fortune creating the perfect catacomb.

He motioned me to a chair beside his at the editing desk. The pencil lying on top of it was the only item in sight without a five-digit price tag. "I just finished the first movement of the *Kreutzer* Sonata," he said, sliding behind the latest Sony editor, about half the girth of the previous model; in a few years, at current rates of miniaturization, the Japanese would be selling equipment the size of a hamburger. "Maybe you should hear it. I tried to follow Harry's directions exactly."

I sighed. "That was a mistake."

My job was supposed to end at the recording session in Berlin; Harry's job did not. The producer was responsible for listening to all of the takes, choosing the best of them, and sending a plan to the tape editor so that, when all the snippets were hitched together, I would sound as if I'd been playing perfectly. Ideally, I should not be involved in the editing process: my idea of perfection differed drastically from Harry's. He didn't mind a couple hundred sour notes and squeals if the musical line came through; I preferred accuracy to sincerity. It had taken us a few years to adjust to the other's viewpoint. I usually received a tape of Harry's first attempt and sent him a long list of emendations. He did a second edit, I sent a second barrage of commentary: when we got down to five or so articles of war, we ran the "you get this I get that" routine. Each project was like a friendly divorce.

Chance pressed the Forward button. Signals flew from the

editor through a cable under the floor; somewhere in an isolated machine room, the master reel clicked into position and began to wind past a tape head. Silence: then the two speakers at the corners of Studio C emitted a shrill chord. "Whoa!" I said, punching Stop, flipping open Harry's marked score, a mess of blue pencil lines and rubber eraser boogies. "Take twelve? Is he kidding? Duncan was still adjusting the piano bench until take twenty."

"Maybe he meant twenty-one," Chance said. "It's much better."

"You listened to the other takes? Why didn't you change it, then?"

"Because Harry's the producer. I'm following his instructions."

"Harry's fired," I said. "I'm the producer now."

"Would you like to be the editor also? You seem to know where the important buttons are."

I reclined in the chair, shut my eyes. "Start at the top again, would you? Maybe Harry just blacked out on the opening sequence."

No such luck. Splice points didn't quite match. Too many entrances were a little off; balances were uneven. Harry had even chosen a take with Duncan sneezing. All in all, it wasn't awful, but it wasn't great and, mostly, it wasn't my final word on the *Kreutzer* Sonata. At the sessions, Duncan and I had placed every note right at least once; Harry had somehow overlooked those moments. "Oy," I said when the first movement had ended.

"Maybe he's going deaf," Chance said. "Like Beethoven."

"Where's the phone?" Harry's housekeeper in London informed me that her employer was in Morocco for the holidays. Sorry, incommunicado, he needed a rest. I hung up. "When does Godo expect this?" I asked Chance.

"Yesterday."

"Did you do any of the second movement?"

"I tried." Chance pointed to the score. "He wants to start

with take forty. Only problem is, take forty is still the first movement.''

"Maybe he meant fifty.''

"Look at the track sheets. Fifty begins at the coda.''

I had expected to spend maybe ten hours in Chance's studio, putting the finishing touches on Harry's work. Repairing this blowout would require sifting through every minute of session tape and constructing a completely new editing map. I'd be in Boston a damn week. "Thanks very much,'' I said, standing up. "It's been educational.''

"Where are you going?''

"Back to Berlin. I think it's in Harry's best interest to get burned on this project.''

Dismay leadened Chance's face. "You just got here. You can't leave.''

"Why not?'' I turned the handle on the thick door. "I have better things to do than cover my producer's incompetent ass.''

Chance opened his mouth then bit his pink tongue. "I'll drive you back to the hotel.''

Slight headache, would have preferred to walk, but I was curious to see what he drove. Halfway up the spiral staircase, my circulation failed. The vision reeled and I was suddenly in Moll's dark steeple, mounting toward the Clove. I grabbed the rail and hauled myself forward, struggling to separate one cold dream from another. At the landing I was out of breath, a little feverish. Perfect Mona, still arranging flowers at her desk, sent me a knowing smile as her boss retrieved my coat.

There were two cars in the garage. One was a Jeep. Chance drove the Cobra. British racing green, mint condition, horsepower-to-weight ratio a suicidal six-to-one, cruising speed about one sixty, two out of four gears were entirely unnecessary, and there were only a handful left on the planet. A Stradivarius on wheels. I was shocked that he would take it out in the winter: that was tantamount to my playing the fiddle in a thunderstorm. As Chance backed onto Sleeper Street, I held my breath, listening to the rumbling V8. I'd slice off a toe for a test drive. He handled the Cobra the same way I handled my Strad, somewhat recklessly, considering its insurance premiums. Must have been a gift from his father. "Please don't leave yet," was all he said at the Ritz. "I'll call you in the morning. And thanks for the orchids."

Maybe it was the Cobra; maybe I wasn't ready to go back to a stalled riddle; somehow I still hadn't made return reservations when the phone rang seven hours later. "Did I wake you, Frosty?"

"Better luck next time."

"How about breakfast? I have a present for you."

"Couldn't give it to me last night, I suppose."

"No. Get dressed. I'll pick you up in twenty minutes."

Hunger carved my insides. The Cobra slid in front of the lobby as I was pulling my gloves on. "Get in," Chance called, flinging the door open before the porter could even step out from the heat lamps.

"What's the big rush?"

"Sticky buns. They come out of the oven in eight minutes." Chance looked me over. "Sleep well?"

"Like a rock." Christmas lights were still flickering over the dark Common: blue, the color of frozen death. "What are you doing up so early?"

"This is not early, honey. I'm on European time myself." He ran the light on Boylston Street. "We're getting a blizzard today."

"Then forget the buns. Take me to the airport."

"Don't you listen to the weather reports? Logan's already closed." Chance cut off a milk truck. As the Cobra pulled onto Sleeper Street, the first flakes dashed in front of its headlights. I still couldn't believe he had the gall to drive this car in this weather; such daring bordered on disease. "You're about to be snowed in." He began to whistle.

I scowled as his garage door yawned. Chance led me through an inside door to the other side of the factory building, which he had made into living space. Yeast and cinnamon perfused the air; as my host headed for the kitchen, I looked

over his gigantic loft. Here again, as in the studios, the architect had worked with kinky dignity and no budgetary con-
straints. A single-lane bowling alley skirted one side of the
room; leather furniture puffed like giant mushrooms under a
copper mobile suspended from the beams. He could probably
fly a kite in here if all the ceiling fans were turned on. But
no stereo system, no CD collection: when Chance left his
office, he was through with music for the day. "Where's the
swimming pool?" I said, hiking to the kitchen.

"Downstairs."

"Where do you sleep?"

"Upstairs."

"I don't see any upstairs."

"Most people don't." As milky dawn seeped through the
skylights Chance set breakfast on the table. We didn't eat
long; the food ran out.

"So where's the big surprise," I said.

He took me through a passage which eventually opened
into a downstairs shop lined with dysfunctional chunks of
recording equipment. "The infirmary," Chance said. The
repair shop led to an air-conditioned machine room, where
rack upon rack of digital equipment hummed and blinked in
response to commands from the editing suites. A maze of
copper cable slithered up to an elegant new 48-track machine
in the corner; sales tax on that baby alone amounted to down
payment on a nice condo. Someone had risked a lot of money
here. I was impressed: Chance operated the audio equivalent
of Moll's Clove.

Next to the reverb units was a machine I had never seen
before. Its name, Yaba, and its contents were Japanese.
"What's this?"

"My new toy. One of those end-of-year purchases for tax
reasons."

"What does it do?"

"You'll see. If you stick around, that is. Come on."
Chance sat me in Studio C and pushed the Play button on the
Sony editor. I heard the first movement of *Kreutzer* again,

this time Chance's version: seamless, intense, diamantine. Someday, in real life, I would like to perform the piece as faultlessly as that. When it ended I sat in my chair, a little afraid, staring at him: from many inferior bits he had created a lustrous Frankenstein. "When did you edit this?" I asked.

"While you were sleeping." He hit Pause. "Comments?"

"It's great," I said. "Why did you do it?"

He leaned far back in his chair, half yawning. "I don't want you to leave, Frosty. You just got here."

It was gentler than admitting he wanted fifteen thousand bucks in additional editing fees from Kakadu. "When are you going to finish the rest of it?"

Chance stood up. "I'm going to bed, sweetheart. Your shift just began. There are the session DAT's. There are the take sheets. There's the score. Start planning. I'll come back around lunchtime." The two-hundred-pound door softly slammed.

When I yanked it open he was halfway up the spiral staircase. "I didn't come here to do this," I shouted.

"There's the coffee," Chance called, pointing to the kitchenette. "You're snowed in." He disappeared over the landing.

I stood a long moment wondering why I wasn't more incensed at being a prisoner in Charm Boy's button factory. Only one obvious answer, so as snowflakes obscured the skylight I returned to Studio C and began listening to the session tapes of the second movement, choosing what went where, for how long . . . torture. Some takes leapt out, obviously good or bad; others only gleamed upon more subtle listening. Each iteration of a musical passage had its own special geography; to favor one take over another was a subjective, painstaking process involving science and, ultimately, intuition. Listening too hard made one mad.

I took a break around eleven o'clock. Mona was upstairs drawling into the phone so I strolled into Chance's machine room for another peep at his new toy. The Yaba was a reference disc system, or, in the vernacular, a CD-While-U-Wait machine. I had read about them but had not seen one before. They cost sixty thousand bucks a pop and the Japanese had just unleashed them on the market to spare people like Harry the agony of waiting for a test pressing from the CD plant. Now, in the time necessary to play the master tape, the Yaba could produce a CD clone. The unit was selling well in rock studios, where immortality could often be measured in minutes and seconds.

Chance returned around noon. "Where's my lunch," I said.

He leaned over the score. Had just taken a shower; smelled like a baby with muscles. I didn't want to see how many buttons on his shirt he had left undone. "Nice work, Frosty."

I penciled in a final direction. "Put this together. Call me at the hotel when you're done. I'm taking a nap."

"Why don't you sleep here? It's more efficient." He found his place on the master tape. "You know where the kitchen is. The stairs to my bedroom are in the pantry."

The sooner we finished, the sooner I'd get home. I slept on his living room couch. Some time later, through a wan dream, the brain perceived footsteps. I opened my eyes, fingers already steeled, ready to strike: didn't know where I was until I saw Chance approaching with a tea tray. "I'm all caught up," he said, pouring me a cup. "Your turn."

Now he slept, I worked. Early that evening I finished the editing instructions for the *Kreutzer* Sonata and turned Studio C back over to Chance. He'd pick me up again tomorrow at five. Two more days like that and we might have the Beethoven album done. I walked back to the Ritz as snow still eddied downtown, stultifying traffic. Recent recipients of sleds and skis were defying the deadly slopes of the Common. I was in a perversely light mood, as if I had spent the day diving off cliffs: desperate projects like this one sharpened the brain. I hadn't expected Chance to be such a deft editor. Hadn't expected a setup like that button factory, either. Perhaps this was no typical tinsel American. Flick only drifted back to me once, as I fell asleep. I put him out of my mind: Smith was on holiday.

The Cobra slid through the virgin drifts at five the next morning. "Ready for Round Two?" Chance asked cheerfully, dropping a fax onto my lap.

From Curtis: Luke the Apostle was singing in Worcester the next evening and my presence backstage was highly recommended. Sydney Bolt had plans. I balled up the fax and threw it on the floor. "What's for breakfast."

"Hash." The car skidded daintily around a mailbox. "Need a chaperone?"

"Who gave you permission to read my mail?"

"I called Luke last night," Chance said. "You seem to have made a heavy impression on him. I think he's afraid of you, like everyone else."

"Did he tell you about this Beauty and the Beast bullshit? It's a joke."

"So play it like a joke! Have a good time!"

"That's not my style, dear."

"Oh, forgive me. I forgot. You're a serious musician." Chance veered into his garage. "Let's go to the concert. It should be fun."

"I came here to edit, not to watch some maniac gargle with a microphone."

He patted my knee. "Of course, Your Highness."

Breakfast was not cordial. I shut myself in Studio C, approved Chance's overnight work, and began attacking the next sonatas. Two tickets to Luke's concert, along with a gelatinous fax from Bolt, arrived. Godo called, anxious for a progress report. Harry remained unreachable in Morocco, curing his stress.

Chance and I wilted around six. "Enough," he said, rolling his chair from the editing desk. "Dinner?"

"Sorry, I'm seeing an old college friend tonight."

Chance didn't ask for details. He walked me past already sullied snowdrifts to the hotel. The temperature had dropped twenty degrees since morning; one inhaled judiciously, aware of bronchial frailty. "I owe you an apology," he said suddenly.

"For what?"

"For my rude behavior in Leipzig."

"Forget it."

"I misjudged you." He helped me across Arlington Street. "You're only half the pain in the ass I thought you'd be." I began to vaguely understand why his former wives still adored him. At the Ritz he tweaked my cold nose: a strange, almost painful gesture. "Don't stay out too late," he said. "We've got a big day tomorrow."

I met my old MIT chum Alfred Chung in a fish restaurant in the Back Bay. There I would definitely not be recognized; the yuppie clientele did not concern itself with the affairs of violinists unless their instruments were on the block at Sotheby's. I had told Alfred I was in Boston to approve a new recording; my former classmate now sat at the bar, networking with a derelict executive. "Hi Alfred," I said. "Nice tie."

Bright red, company logo in orange smack center. It was the diamond tack, though, that made me cross-eyed. "Like it? A present from Stella."

We reminisced a while then got down to serious gossip about the computer business. Alfred was perplexed as to where his next millions would be coming from. Companies all along Route 128 were fizzling while the whole industry bickered about trade barriers and Asian knavery. The software people were obsessed with copyright infringements and viruses; nobody was inventing anything these days but lawsuits. I told him to forget about Massachusetts and build a few plants in Eastern Europe, where the real action was going to be.

"Stella only speaks English," he said. "And there are no stores."

"So leave her home." I pumped him again about the Clove

QV6. Alfred couldn't tell me anything more about the computer but he could tell me all about one of its vice presidents, who had just resigned, or been fired, for undisclosed reasons. Maybe it had to do with the news broadcaster he was sleeping with. Maybe not.

After a few drinks, we adjourned to Alfred's Beacon Hill town house. Wife Stella, a video addict, waved as we passed the television room; the kids were upstairs taking a bath with nanny. It was a real American success story. Alfred led me to his playroom, which looked a lot like Chance's and Moll's playrooms except that here the toys were hot-rod computers plus the peripheral printers, modems, and black boxes which Alfred would ultimately aim at the patent office. As the rigors of corporate management steadily eroded his faith in government and humanity, Alfred was spending more and more of his nights alone here. Now he lived to hack; it was the ultimate form of gossip, after all.

Before switching on his newest black terminal and several modems, Alfred planted a bottle of Scotch between us. "Look," he said, tapping many keys.

I watched him fly through reams of gobbledygook. Finally two columns appeared on the screen. The left column contained the names of ritzy restaurants, fur salons, jewelry shops; the right column, figures. "What is it?"

"Stella's Amex account," Alfred said. He took the cursor down the column. "See that?"

WINSTON HABERDASH 450. What is it?

"That's my tie," Alfred said.

"She paid four hundred and fifty bucks for that?"

Shhhh. Alfred typed. WINSTON HABERDASH 450 vanished. "Isn't that magnificent?"

"Not bad. Where can I get the software?"

"Luckily, I'm an honest fellow." Alfred reinstated the account. "Go ahead, try me. I can probably get you into anything. Except the Star Wars computers. That's my next project."

"Let's find Harry Paradise's account."

My producer was enjoying his usual low-profile vacation in Morocco. So far he had spent about five thousand dollars at the best hotel in Tangier; maybe he was eating gold-plated chicken. "Can you add to this list?" I asked.

"I can do anything."

"Send Harry a bill from Kreutzer Music Repair. About three thousand bucks."

Alfred began typing. "Playing a little joke?"

"He deserves it. How long will it take him to sort this out?"

"I'll make it come back four times. Lots of finance charges." Now that Alfred was warmed up, he hacked into the UPI computer and reversed the score of tonight's MIT-Brandeis basketball game, which MIT had lost. Then he cut into the American Airlines schedule and created a bogus flight to the North Pole.

Alfred began hacking into the payroll of his father-in-law's furniture company: about time Stella got a raise. As his fingers flew over the keys, he explained what he was doing with all the modems and passwords. I listened for quite a while, trying to keep up with him: wasn't easy after an evening of nonstop Scotch. Eventually I steered the topic my way.

"Say Alfred," I asked, "is the Clove QV6 any good at breaking codes?"

"Sure." His fingers never stopped flitting over the keys. "What kind of codes?"

"Computer generated."

"They're pretty complicated," he said, staring at the screen. "The bits are probably rotated. Then they're compressed, then they're scrambled. That's just the beginning."

Blah. "I suppose military code is the worst."

"By far. It has to be. I mean, you don't want some smartass kid in Wyoming shooting off an SS-20, do you?" Alfred peered at the screen then picked up the phone. "Forget cracking military codes. I've tried. They're impossible. It's easier to steal the computer that generates the code. Or kidnap the programmer."

I scowled; the redhead may have done both. "I suppose even the Clove would need plenty of samples."

"Correct. The patterns are unbelievably subtle. Whoa! Watch this." Alfred increased his wife's next paycheck by four thousand dollars. "Direct deposit," he said proudly. "She'll spend it before they catch on."

We had a few more drinks, played a few more tricks. Then I noticed it was after midnight. "Have to go, Al."

"But I haven't shown you those black boxes," he said. "They're awesome."

"Next time."

The Cobra swerved in front of the hotel about five hours later. "Have a nice evening with your old flame?" Chance asked. "You look a little tired now."

"He's not an old flame and I'm not tired."

"Touchy, aren't we? Never mind." Chance gunned the Cobra around a tight corner, heaving me against his arm. Breakfast consisted of stale biscuits in Studio C as I listened to more damn editing. He stood behind me, arms crossed as the tape slithered past the heads.

"Pass?" he said when it ended. "Good. Buzz me when you've finished the last sonata." The heavy door snuggled into its frame.

I hadn't slept well; playing with Alfred's computers reminded me of Moll. To break the code, Moll and the Clove needed samples, many of them. But from where? Had the redhead penetrated a ground station? Was she getting tapes of hundreds of transmissions between earth and that satellite? Then how would she get that information to Moll? Definitely not over the phone lines. Mules? Too unreliable. Maybe she delivered the data herself. Maybe she had ten men like Flick working for her.

I forced the brain back to music but the sonata in front of me blurred again and again so I mounted the long spiral staircase from the studios and fell asleep on a couch near Chance's Christmas tree. The hell with this project: I was sick of Beethoven. I needed to go home and start hunting again.

An indeterminate time later, I was awakened by a hand on my shoulder. Judging by the light infusing the upstairs, hours had passed. "For you," Chance said, handing me a phone.

"Who is it?"

He pointed to the number displayed in its base. "Recognize that?"

It was my number.

"Hi Curtis," I said. "When did you get back to Berlin?"

"Yesterday. Where have you been?" my manager demanded. "I've been on hold for five minutes."

"Sleeping." Chance was still nestled at my side, one hand over my hip now, pretending to search for coins in the seams of the sofa. "We'll finish up this afternoon."

Curtis couldn't care less about the editing. "About that concert tonight. You're going." He didn't have to say who had issued the order. "Leslie?"

"I heard you." Downwind, Chance tried to repress a smile. "Do you mind," I said, putting my hand over the phone. "This is a private discussion."

"Is it? Ask your manager who's driving you to Worcester."

"Son of a bitch!" I lobbed the phone over the railing. "I told you I'm not going to that concert!"

Chance watched the phone arc delicately through the air and barely moved as it smashed against the tiles downstairs. "That was a Christmas present," he said quietly.

"Take it back. Tell them it doesn't work." Why would Maxine send me to a rock concert in the middle of Massachusetts? To punish me for taking a few days off? I scampered down the spiral staircase, slamming the door of Studio C behind me.

When I emerged later, the tiles were swept clean of phone pieces. Chance was monkeying with the Yaba in the machine room. "I'm very sorry," I said. "Please let me buy you a new phone."

Chance didn't even look up from his calibrators and fancy screwdrivers: back to Miffed Man mode. "How many splices have you got for me, Frosty?"

"About fifty. Then we're done."

"I'll pick you up at nine." No inflection: all emotion was fixed on the meters in front of him. "Try not to be late."

Fresh air mitigated distemper so I took a walk. I knew what the problem was: Smith tailgating Frost. Soon she'd run her off the road again. Above the trees, brilliant black sky became pierced with stars: angel dust, the real kind. Some of those tiny glints were satellites and by now, perhaps, Moll owned one of them. I ducked into a giant record store on Newbury Street. Went to the floor with the least customers and browsed through the latest classical releases, mostly turgid rehashes of the Top Twenty. The big companies were still on a Mahler binge so I pulled a few dozen titles from tiny labels: marimba sonatas, harmonica concertos, Sousa fanfares, Polish lieder . . . an assortment for Flick. For myself, I asked for a copy of the Leon Jurkowsky CD I had seen in his living room. Flick had found it interesting. Wasn't in stock, of course; that would have been too easy. No, I didn't care to order it. I wouldn't be back in Boston for a long time.

At the hotel, for the first time in a week, I practiced the violin. On New Year's Eve, I would be playing the Brahms Concerto in Potsdam. The fingers remembered their routes, the whole edifice sounded better for the break, but with the opening note, Flick began seeping from brain to blood. Boston had been no diversion at all. I had done nothing here but waste time. I was tempted to skip the Apostle's concert and take a plane home tonight. In ten hours I could be in Leipzig delivering presents.

Fealty to the Queen prevailed and I was waiting on Arlington Street when Chance pulled up in his green antique at nine o'clock. "Dressed for action, I see," he said, appraising the black leather wrapping me head to foot.

My jacket squealed against the seat. "Still mad at me?"

"Mad? Just because you wrecked my favorite Christmas

gift? Acted like a two-year-old? Of c- urse I'm mad. You have a way of ruining every good time we have together.''

I had no reply to that so we rode in silence onto the desolate Mass Pike. Not much traffic: a month of crapulous merrymaking had temporarily stupefied the population. I watched the needle in the dashboard climb past sixty, seventy, finally rest southeast of ninety. As the Cobra glided by a long forest, I suddenly wished I were on my Harley, slithering like a bat through the night, swallowing icy black air, thinking my own thoughts. This man still ruffled me.

We passed the miles talking about fast cars. ''Where'd you get this one?'' I asked.

''California.''

He had probably bought it with alimony from the actress. ''Investment?''

''Hell no! Fun.'' He grinned at me. ''Isn't that what money's for?''

I had no idea. Money was just there, like trees. I didn't pay much attention to it because my supply wouldn't become extinct before I did. ''Don't you ever get tired of fun?''

''No. I get tired of other things. Like easy women.'' The Cobra zipped past a Porsche. ''And difficult women.''

As we pulled into Worcester, a senile mid-state metropolis, Chance finally began to whistle. He snuggled next to a fire hydrant a block away from the Centrum and drew a little flask from his jacket. ''I forgive you, Frosty. Really. Here's to our first date.''

I watched his lips slowly surround the pewter neck. ''This is not a date. It's a business trip.'' I drank anyway.

Chance took my arm as we walked to the Centrum. ''Stay close, honey. I'll protect you from those big, bad teenagers.''

I watched five of them squiggle through the turnstiles into the fulgurant auditorium, where Luke the Apostle had been perforating eardrums for the last hour. I took a little box from my pocket. ''Try two of these.''

Chance shook it. ''What are you offering?''

''Earplugs.'' We entered the blinding din. The Centrum

was a hive of jittering bodies and hyperlymphatic aromas. Onstage, Luke appeared to be receiving fatal jolts of electricity, ricocheting between microphone and keyboard as a posse of spotlights tried to run him down. He sounded like a castrato Godzilla. A crowd of audiotropic humanoids surged the stage although they had paid thirty bucks a head for reserved seats.

For some time I observed the mass hysteria, trying to determine how so little talent could generate so much lucre. If nothing else, Luke the Apostle was a spry gymnast. He could play five solid chords on his guitar and every so often he made a noise that could be construed as a musical tone. Beyond that, he was an artistic thug: wind up any exhibitionist, aim him/her at a blithering riot, and the result would be identical. Finally I had to conclude that the real creative genius behind all this was Sydney Bolt. "Is that one of your guitars?" I shouted once in Chance's ear. He nodded yes, sliding an arm around my shoulders.

The soloist swished behind a screen for a few moments while his ensemble violated a dozen drums. Again, volume was the propellant; the act got so loud that I had to supplement my earplugs with a finger. Were these people all deaf? When Luke reappeared in a black outfit with clouds of fringe, I tuned out and retreated to thoughts of my concert in Potsdam. Perhaps Flick would be interested in driving there with me. First we'd have dinner. All would be forgiven. Then I'd get his fingers in my mouth again . . . I hardly noticed when the Apostle took the mike and began baring his soul to the Centrum. Whatever he was saying, it was probably shallower than his rhinestone rivets.

The lights went down and only after Luke began to sing again, by some miracle softly this time, did I notice an icy, flat gleam among the bodies milling in front of Chance and me: camera lens. The man holding it was twenty years above the local median age. I looked casually away, cruised the crowd, saw another camera, another, another. They were circling the area like a pack of hyenas, looking for someone. My skin slowly contracted as the heart notched into a tertiary rhythm, beyond sport and beyond fear: Smith's frequency. Coaxed the earplugs out, leaned into Chance's neck. It was a good place to hide my face. "What's going on," I whispered.

"Luke wrote a little love song," he said, wafting warm air into my ear. "It's about a lady with a mole above her lip."

As a spotlight glossed over nearby heads, I picked up a soft blur of red hair. From the shadows two serpentine eyes pricked memory and this time I saw her whole evil face. She was petite and reminded me of a lizard. Flick's age. For an instant, as our glances met, the hate in her eyes just about burned a hole through me. Whoa, Smith: don't react: she doesn't know you know. Instinctively, to insult her, I dribbled my lips over Chance's neck. It was the second time I had used him as a handy prop. When I opened my eyes, she was gone. "Meet you at the car," I said.

"What? Where are you going?"

Hunting for reptiles. I melted after her into the thick dark crowd as onstage, Luke the Beast pointed toward my empty chair, calling for his Beauty to acknowledge him. Sorry, Ms. Bolt: tonight the spotlights would only find Chance with his mouth open. The little monster was heading diagonally across the floor, wriggling past bodies easily as a newt over brookstones while I snagged on many wayward appendages. Never looking back, the redhead pulled further and further ahead of me as Luke, slowly realizing that his little serenade had flopped, went into a rain dance. His whirring tassels soon had the crowd back in the act, lathering toward Grand Finale. Forward motion was impossible. I piddled to a halt.

Didn't even feel the hand above my elbow until the ulnar nerve was pinched flat screaming against bone, goddamn, that was my bow arm so I ripped ninety degrees right, got two fingers an inch deep in rib before Maxine caught my wrist. "Whoa," her mouth said. In the blue light from the stage her face looked like a liver with eyes. The Queen dropped my arm and receded into the melee.

I followed her to the ladies' room, an epicenter of juvenile trauma. Girls of all hues and dimensions packed the place, crying, pawing their clothing, performing oral sex on their cigarettes. Maxine was waiting for me next to the rubber dispenser. "Having fun?" she asked. "I didn't think you'd ever peel yourself off that poor man's neck. He is gorgeous, of course."

"She's here," I said. "The redhead." Maxine's eyes flew quietly over the room. "Relax. I lost her."

"What's she doing here?"

"How do I know," I croaked. "Following me, like everyone else." Both our brains searched for the blip that could have put Flick's viper on my tail. We came up with nothing, so I turned to the Queen's stony profile. "How was Washington."

Maxine had gone there before Christmas with the DAT I had brought from the steeple. She had been comparing the coded gibberish on my tape against the thousands of transmissions the NSA had monitored during my latest trip to the steeple. All she could hope for was a match: she'd have no idea what anyone was saying, but at least she would know to whom Moll was talking. "He's contacted a Soviet satellite," Maxine said. "Unmanned. Launched almost two years ago. Tactical surveillance. On board is a nuclear reactor."

Big deal. Many late-model satellites carried nuclear reactors. They were a slick alternative to solar energy panels— except when the craft crashed, of course, spewing tons of radioactive debris over the countryside. After the Canadians received an unannounced crater from the Soviets a decade ago, the superpowers made a lot of noise about traffic safety and mutual abstinence. The upshot, of course, was merely a rise in secret launchings. "Ocean surveillance?"

"Probably. With an infrared laser." Maxine paused as a twelve-year-old got product from the condom dispenser. "Looks absolutely harmless."

Sure. With a nuclear reactor aboard, a satellite could launch a second craft to Mars or power a slew of on-board computers. It could keep boosting itself back to its original orbit, defying the earth's gravitational pull, which inevitably dragged all satellites to their deaths. "The NSA doesn't know what it's doing?" I said.

"They think it's routine surveillance." Maxine wasn't about to call anyone's attention to it by asking a lot of questions. "Contact with earth is minimal. The satellite links with a ground station in Morocco and another in central Russia. After leaving Africa, it flies out of range for two minutes before the Russian station picks it up. Leipzig is in the center of the dead zone."

"It must be flying low then," I said.

"Only one hundred miles over Europe. Eccentric orbit. It's probably assigned to the South Pacific and the North Atlantic."

If Moll was clever enough to get to the satellite when it was out of range of its ground stations, then he was clever enough to erase his tracks. First, of course, he'd have to break its code. After that, he could tell it to do anything.

The Queen knew what I was thinking. "The tape you gave me is over a month old. You'll have to go back to the steeple. We need to know if he's broken the code."

"I have no more concerts in Leipzig."

"You have a boyfriend in Leipzig."

"I just told him off. Can't go crawling back now."

She waited as a pair of ten-year-olds fed their life savings to the rubber machine and disappeared into a toilet together. "Crawling might be very good for you. Too bad you lost the redhead." Maxine zipped up her jacket and cut smoothly into the crowd.

Outside, Luke was telling everyone he loved them and good night, drive safely, look for his new CD in all the record stores. I left the arena and leaned against the Cobra's priceless green hood as a cavalcade of imminent date rapes streamed by.

"What happened to you?" Chance demanded when he finally reached the car. "Running away like that was pretty rude."

"I hate cameras." The engine bucked alive. Chance pulled

onto the street and headed toward the Centrum. "You're going the wrong way," I said.

"Afraid not." He swerved into a private alley. "This is a business trip, remember? Many people expected you to say hello to your boyfriend and get your picture taken."

My boyfriend was in Leipzig and my ears hurt from chasing his boss through pandemonium. "Who's paying you?" I asked Chance.

He kept his eyes on the road. "To do what?"

"To exhibit me. Godo? Bolt?"

"Be reasonable, sweetheart. I promised your manager and the president of your record company to look after you." He braked near a police line. "Come on, Luke's waiting."

"Go to hell! I'm not leaving this car."

"Then I'll bring your boyfriend out here. Powder your nose for me like a good girl." Taking the keys, Chance went into the Centrum.

When the Apostle and a dozen cameras finally appeared, I was back on the hood of the Cobra, acting like Leslie Frost again. There was no real choice here. "Nice show, Luke."

The Apostle was high as a lunar eclipse: postconcert anguish, rock music variety. Over an ostinato of clicking shutters we talked about rhinestones. "That was a nice touch, you disappearing," Luke said. "Sydney will like that. It adds incredible drama. Maybe she can blow it up into a lovers' quarrel or something."

"Why wait for Sydney?" I said, slapping him across the face. I gunned the Cobra out of the driveway, spitting gravel at the press corps.

Chance eventually found me back at the fire hydrant. "Sorry," I said. "I had to hot-wire the ignition. It was getting so cold." I opened the passenger door. "I'm driving, dear. You owe me."

Angry again, he got in. "You're pretty unbelievable, you know that?"

"Simmer down, sweetheart. I'm only trying to sell a few records."

Considering its age, the Cobra was still a sparky little number. Above one-twenty it rattled and rolled, and there wasn't much of a muffler, but it was still able to go zero-one hundred-zero in fifteen seconds. The rear end didn't like patches of ice. "Where'd you learn to drive like this," said Chance finally, clutching his knees in terror.

"The autobahn." I rocketed by a Honda. "Germans respect suicide."

Chance didn't say much all the way back to Boston. Over the last few days, he had seen my personality change violently a half dozen times. Just before midnight, I jammed to a stop in front of the Ritz. "Thanks for letting me drive. That was the most fun I've had all week."

He looked dubious. "Are you all right?"

"I'm fine!" I screeched, grabbing the door handle. "Good night!"

Chance put his hand on my arm. "Wait." He took a small, flat package from the glove compartment. "For what it's worth, Happy New Year."

I opened it. Looked like a CD but had no markings anywhere. "What's this?"

"Your Beethoven sonatas."

"From your new machine?"

"Serial number one."

"Does it really play?"

"Come to my place. I'll demonstrate."

Sorry, my vacation ended an hour ago. I shook my head. "Thanks for everything. Really, it's been great." I got out of the car before he could put his hand on my arm again.

Chance met me in front of the headlights. "What's the matter?" he repeated. "You're not yourself."

"Rock concerts upset me. I wish we hadn't gone." I kissed his pink mouth. "You were great to put up with me."

The gray eyes held mine a moment. "Stay a while, Frosty."

Kissed him again. "Can't." I ran into the hotel.

* * *

Berlin was still delirious, Tegel bedlam. Before heading home, Curtis crawled the car through downtown so that I could get another taste of history electrifying the sidewalks. Everywhere, Germans crushed each other, crying, singing, drunk with joy: the third world war had ended and they had actually managed not to lose this one. Naturally the ubiquitous media stooges were covering this year-end windfall as if it were the return of the Messiah. Their spotlights and bullhorns were generating an unholy Blitzkrieg at the Reichstag. Somehow all the commotion reminded me of Luke the Apostle's rock concert. "Nice," I said to Curtis as he puttered toward Dahlem.

He frowned; both of us knew that while Berlin partied, legions of spies were running wild, snatching the opportunities which bloomed only in chaos. "Get any practicing done?" Curtis asked, passing a choking Wartburg.

"Not much. This trip was no vacation."

"You didn't sound too happy when I called." He passed a couple showering in champagne at the foot of the Siegessäule. "Thanks for hanging up on me, by the way. I appreciated that."

"Thanks for pimping me at Luke the Apostle. I appreciated that, too."

We turned to less incendiary topics. No sooner had we stepped into the kitchen than the phone rang.

"How'd everything go?" Harry Paradise asked anxiously. Whatever he had in his mouth put up a good fight before commuting to his esophagus. "I've been thinking day and night about you."

"The Beethoven's finished. Your editing notes were a disgrace."

"I know, I know, baby! Life's been a disaster lately."

"Godo has the master," I said. "You can relax."

"What? You sent Godo a master? Without my artistic approval?"

I almost hung up on him. Then I remembered all the trouble

he was going to have with his credit cards. "Get Chance to make you a DAT."

"Gad, that will take forever! You don't have a copy?"

Not for Harry. "What's the problem, don't you trust my artistic judgment?"

He folded immediately. "How did Chance do? Can he edit all right?"

"He can edit fine. I assume you're free to work on the Mozart concertos now. Godo wants them right away."

"I'll get to them next week. In an hour I'm leaving for Toulouse. Work," he added quickly. Slobbering gratitude, Harry hung up.

Hearing a loud snort, I went to the office. Curtis was reading a newspaper article that had just been faxed over. Without a word, he handed it to me. It was a picture of me slapping Luke the Apostle in the face. Nice tonsil shot: the photographer had caught Luke's mouth wide open. The caption offered a silly hypothesis of what Luke could have said to have precipitated such a whack. *Terrific work!* Sydney Bolt had scrawled in the margin.

"Don't keep me in suspense," Curtis said. "What did he say?"

"Nothing. He just caught me at a bad time."

"You've given Sydney a lot of ammunition, you realize. I'd better tell her to restrain herself." Curtis picked up the phone. "Well, don't just stand there! Get practicing! You do have a concert tomorrow night, don't you?"

I quickly checked my desk for meaningful mail. No envelopes from Leipzig, so I went to the music room and wrestled with the Brahms Concerto. It was in worse shape than I thought. After a few hours I conked out, ate, then practiced some more. Glamour? Adventure? This was the life of a lone mad dog.

The next day, New Year's Eve, I told Curtis to go dance on the crumbling Wall. I drove to Potsdam alone. The orchestra was onstage, about to begin the *Meistersinger* Overture, when someone knocked on the Green Room door.

I had been expecting him. Still, the sight of Flick's exquisitely lined face caused all systems to shudder. He had timed his appearance perfectly: we had about eight minutes and there could be no nonsense here. "Come in."

He looked at my dress, I looked at his face. Flick hadn't slept much since his little boxing match in Berlin the week before. However, the pallor probably had less to do with me than with great scientific discoveries. "I had to see you," he said. "I've been miserable."

Yes, yes, I'm sure he had cried his eyes out worrying about my broken heart, worrying about the man he had beaten to a pulp. If he was so abjectly miserable, he would have been camping out on my doorstep for the last five days. Ah, men were all alike: paying customers came first. "Nice of you to come," I said noncommittally.

"Where have you been?" Flick asked. "I've been calling."

"In Boston." A pastel image of Chance blurred before me. "I had to get away for a while."

Flick slipped a hand into his Burberry pocket and withdrew a little box. "It was my mother's," he said, handing it to me. I opened the box. Lying on blue velvet was a ruby pendant, antique, extravagant: before I could thank him, Flick began his resignation speech. "I came to say goodbye. I cannot see you any more."

Protest? Never. I calmly put the necklace on. The ruby quivered between throat and breast like a voluptuous drop of blood.

Flick stared at it for a heavy moment. "Forgive me," he continued. I was gratified to hear that his voice had changed for the worse. "I should never have become involved with you. The situation is impossible."

"What situation?"

He paused, simmering, on the verge of confession. Then he recovered. "The trade fair will be requiring my full attention for the next two months. I won't have a minute to practice. Seeing me would be a waste of your time.''

Ah, wrong: seeing him beatified time. I was about to rebut when the stage manager knocked. ''Two minutes, Miss Frost,'' he called from the hallway. Flick put his hand on the doorknob.

''Wait,'' I said, ''here's something from Boston. I had a feeling I'd be seeing you tonight.'' I gave him the package of CD's I had bought. Marimba sonatas, harmonica concertos . . . perhaps one of these nights, alone in his drear living room, Flick would come across the first pressing of my Beethoven sonatas and pine for me. ''I hadn't intended them to be a goodbye present.''

Flick was staring at the mole above my lip: he was still torn between the redhead and me. I waited, silent as a tree. ''I won't forget you,'' he said finally.

Were there sweeter declarations of war? I picked up my violin and began fiddling softly. After a moment the door clicked behind me.

11

The next morning, I found Curtis in the kitchen with a rolling pin. "Happy New Year," I muttered, slumping at the table. "What's all this?"

"*Springerle*. We're invited to your brother's." Oh joy, Roland's annual New Year's orgy. Curtis's biceps billowed under his sleeves as he flattened the pale dough. "I hear you were a ball of fire in Potsdam."

"I was." Too bad Flick hadn't been able to stick around to hear it. I watched Curtis sprinkle aniseed over his handiwork. "Any terrible movies playing?"

He named five from Hollywood. We went to two and a half of them, then drove to Spandau. My brother used to live right down the street from Rudolf Hess. After the poor bugger died, they tore down his jail. Now my brother lived right down the street from a supermarket. Curtis parked near the British barracks and we walked toward the noise.

Like most drunks, Roland threw great parties. His formula was simple: tsunamic quantities of booze plus wall-to-wall degenerates. Through the smoke and bodies I saw a trio strumming in the corner; before this soirée broke up, they'd leave a dozen new cigarette burns on my mother's piano. It didn't bother me any more. "Happy New Year, Roland," I said, finding him at the bar.

The red around his eyes had widened to cheek and nose.

"Hi Les, Curtis. *Springerle*?" He snatched the tin of cookies.
"Super!"

Scowling, Curtis watched him totter away: he hated to be
reminded that Roland and I were flip sides of the same coin.
We hit the bar, then the buffet table, where the Queen stood
carving a ham. Her paisley bodystocking could have been a
tattoo. "Hi there," she said, lifting Solomonic eyes. "So
glad you could make it."

I drank, Curtis kissed her cheek. "We wouldn't miss this,
Maxine. It's tradition." After a few friendly inquiries, he
wandered diplomatically down the buffet table, mounding his
plate with knuckles and cabbage.

Maxine lay an iridescent pink slab of ham across a platter.
I couldn't take my eyes off her carving knife: in slow motion,
she was slitting throats. "Any hot mustard in the house?" I
blurted.

The blade paused. "I'll check."

We went to the kitchen. Around the counters stood intense
pairs oblivious to movement beyond each other's nostrils.
Roland? Probably vomiting into another family heirloom. I
tailed the Spandex into a pantry. "You'll be happy to know,"
the Queen began, "that Oskar Wildau took pictures of nothing
but naked boys. Naughty naked boys. You're not even on the
film so you can forget about him. Have you been able to get
any more information on Moll?"

I had been toying with the idea of breaking into the Ministry
of Education in Bonn and lifting his file. It wouldn't be
quite as simple as pilfering the offices at Johns Hopkins,
unfortunately. The ruthless tactics of the Gestapo were still
openly practiced by millions of German secretaries. "No,"
I said. "I'm working on indirect approaches."

Maxine dribbled her finger along a parade of little jars.
"The redhead's on to you. It worries me."

"Come on! It's coincidence."

"Don't flatter yourself. Why was she at that rock concert—
in Worcester? Do you think she's a fan of Luke the Apostle's?"

I remembered her face, still and pale as a death mask, targeting me across a frenzied auditorium. "I'm working on her," I lied. "Give me another week."

"You've already had ten weeks."

"I've had twenty concerts and a dozen recording sessions."

"Not to mention two eminently successful violin lessons." The Queen inspected the label on a crock of pickles. "They've been planning this operation since the satellite was launched. It's airtight. You're not."

"She thinks I'm just a stupid violinist," I repeated. "So does Flick."

"Why would he waste his time with you then?"

I pronounced the impossible. "Maybe he loves me."

Maxine's laughter tinkled over the potatoes. "Oh please! The man's a professional! So's she! There's a reason for dragging you into this."

"Can you think of one?" I almost shouted. Maxine had a gift for identifying sore points and poking a needle into them.

She handed me a jar of mustard and a tiny cassette for Spot. "Whatever it is, I'm sure they're going to regret it. We're running out of time, Smith. Cut the pajama parties." She left the pantry.

I joined the drunken wallflowers lining Roland's apartment. In the middle of the room, Curtis was dancing with a ravishing blond whose hands were rubbing his rump as if it were Aladdin's lamp. As time wore on he seemed more and more likely to grant her wishes, so I called a cab.

Roland caught me leaving. "Wherrr you going?"

"Home."

"Without yrrr bodyguard?"

"He's got the night off."

"I'll drive you back."

"No thanks. You're drunk."

"Am not. I'm getting into the mindset of the characters in my novel." My brother staggered after me into the street. "This is all research."

"How long has this research been going on, seven years now? Your dedication amazes me."

Roland swayed delicately backward. "My dear sister," he said. "What would you and Maxine do without a handy derelict?"

"The same as we'd do with a literary success, I think. Try us." I immediately regretted my words. "Listen, Roland. I know a good clinic in Austria. Maybe you could spend a month there. Clear your head."

"My head's very clear." Roland stuck a Gitane between his lips and finally got the match within ignition range. "Maxine's seeing someone else."

"What? You're out of your mind."

"Where has she been the last two weeks then? Or should I say, the last two months?"

"Working."

"Come on," Roland snorted. "She's hardly home any more. When she is, she's asleep. I know when she's been up all night with someone else. She smells different."

"That's stress, not sex! Don't tell me you can't tell the difference by now."

Roland threw his cigarette into the snow. "You two saving the world again? Pardon me while I choke."

"Jesus, you're a pain in the ass!" I cried. "Why don't you give us a little support for a change?"

My brother lurched back to his party. "I'm not yrrr puppet," he called from the doorstep.

I stalked into the Grunewald and after many miles emerged in Dahlem. Unlocked my fortress and got a great champagne from the cellar. Then I sat in my dining room staring at the empty chairs around the long mahogany table. In better days, artists and diplomats ate here, laughing, drinking all night long . . . I cackled in the dark: Hugo wouldn't even recognize me now. All the soft edges were gone. A round of firecrackers exploded in the street and, faintly, I heard people singing. What were they so damn delirious about? Ruling the world again? Bah, they could have it!

Phone. "Hello, Frosty," said Chance. "It's not too late to wish you Happy New Year, is it?"

"No." I refilled my glass. "What's new?"

"Nothing. I miss you."

"That's nice."

"It's not nice. I got used to you running underfoot here. How was your concert in Potsdam?"

"Unforgettable." My glass was emptying fast. "And you? Out partying?"

"I stayed in bed reading poetry. Andrew Marvell, to be exact."

"All by yourself?"

"Yes."

"Hard to believe."

"Why? I hate New Year's Eve more than any night of the year."

"I thought you liked parties. Not to mention women."

"Liked. Past tense. What's that noise?"

"Champagne being poured into a glass. This is me drinking it." I gulped.

A short silence. "Are you drinking alone again?"

"It's my hobby."

The line hissed as the telephone link jumped to another satellite. "Harry called," Chance said. "He was at the airport on the way to Nice."

"He told me Toulouse. Hope he gets on the right plane."

"Did you really tell him I was the best editor alive?"

"Of course not."

"I didn't think so. He asked for a DAT of the Beethoven sonatas we just finished. Would it be too much trouble to send him that reference disc I made for you?"

Sorry, that was at the bottom of a box in Leipzig. "I gave it away."

"You did? Can you get it back?"

"It was a gift."

I could feel his lips pucker around a whistle. "No problem. I'll run off a few copies. Say, I'm going to be in Vienna this week. What do you think about getting together? I have some free time between sessions."

"I've got concerts in Switzerland. It's not too practical." I finished the bottle. "This week anyway."

Long silence, cadenced with a sigh. "Is it good champagne, at least?" Chance asked.

"The best."

"I do miss you, Frosty."

A sizzle, a boom: brilliant white light jagged through the dining room. Out in the street, revelers cheered. "Are you free on the twentieth? Duncan and I are playing the second Beethoven concert in New York. Maybe we could have dinner. If Bolt hasn't scheduled another sideshow with Luke the Apostle, of course."

"I'll take care of Luke."

I kept him talking for half an hour. Subject matter immaterial: the sound of his voice consoled me. Outside, my neighbors welcomed a dazzling new year. I crawled the wide, empty staircase to bed, wondering if perhaps it wasn't time to get a young man between the sheets for once in my life. Someone with warm skin but no history . . . someone who didn't need orders to seduce me.

Before leaving for Switzerland, where I would be playing several concerts later in the week, I fed Maxine's cassette to Spot. It contained information about the Soviet satellite Moll was contacting: weight, length, launch date, mission. The craft flew an eccentric orbit, perigee one hundred miles over Leipzig every twenty-five hours. As Maxine had said, it looked exactly like an ocean surveillance satellite. There were plenty of them in the sky, all hunting submarines. On board was an infrared laser which measured the waves and perhaps searched for schools of upset, phosphorescing plankton, then fed the information to a computer. Submarines, no matter how deep, caused tiny differences in the surface waves; by analyzing the wave patterns and the clouds of disturbed plankton, a computer could tell if the variations were caused by whales or submarines. Running the computer as well as the infrared laser required energy, hence the onboard reactor. Looked perfectly normal. Damn.

Since Maxine was getting anxious for results, I decided to mosey through Leipzig en route to Switzerland. Not to visit the steeple, however. No more visits to my friend at the trade fair, either. I intended to tag Flick's car, as the Queen had suggested on numerous occasions. Now that he wouldn't be driving to Berlin to see me, I was curious to know where he was going instead. To another woman, perhaps. A redhead.

I made the transmitter first. It would end up in the ceiling of Flick's Trabant, wired to the cabin light. It would draw about three watts, the maximum I could siphon off without flattening his battery. The transmitter would convert chemical energy from the battery into radio waves that would creep along the roof of the car and radiate omnidirectionally through all space: extraterrestrials with a big enough receiver could pick up the signal on Pluto. My tiny receivers would only be able to track Flick within a couple hundred kilometers. They were more tedious to put together: antennas, batteries, RF/IF amps, oscillator, phase comparator, computer all had to squeeze into a box the size of a car radio. The receivers would convert the radio waves from the transmitter back into electrical energy: by analyzing the phase of the radio wave, the comparator could pinpoint the direction of Flick's car. I programmed the computer to log the signal every sixty seconds and store it on a microfloppy. On my way back from Switzerland, I'd gather the five disks, download into Spot: knowing the latitude/longitude of each receiver, Spot could triangulate the location of Flick's Trabant at sixty-second intervals.

When the receivers were finally finished, I visited Curtis's office. "What's the weather forecast?"

He looked up from the booking calendar. "Clear and cold."

"What's the border like."

"As easy as it will ever be. Why?"

"I'm thinking of taking the Harley."

Boiled spinach would have reacted more enthusiastically. "You have a rehearsal in Basel Wednesday at eleven. I've got you on a flight tomorrow afternoon. It's the middle of winter."

"I have to stop in Leipzig for a few hours."

"How many hours?"

To stash a transmitter in Flick's Trabant and five receivers around the periphery of town? "Four. If I'm lucky."

Curtis's fingers trilled on the desktop as he calculated the number of hours between my arrival in Switzerland and my first rehearsal with a finicky conductor. "Maybe I should drive down with you. I haven't visited the people in Basel in a few years."

The M6 pulled into the street late that evening and eddied with a sea of Germans to Checkpoint Bravo. Curtis woke me a few miles outside of Leipzig. He got some heavy coffee down my throat, dumped me behind Napoleon's Slaughter Memorial, and drove slowly away. I waited a moment, acclimating to the black, sour night. As usual, no traffic and no lights. I could hardly make out the fairgrounds at the foot of the long reflecting pool. I removed my first receiver, dropped the knapsack into the bushes, listened. The frozen mud was my only witness.

I had wanted one receiver high and this monolith rose twenty stories above the earth. At the foot of the monument I found one very imposing, but infantile, lock on a chain. Swiftly defeated that and pushed the gigantic door inward. Silence. East Germans would discover alarm systems about a month after they discovered capitalism. I began climbing the endless spiral to the top of the memorial. The cold, hollow stillness reminded me of Moll's steeple, only this was ten times higher and there were real bats in the belfry here. The stakes were the same and I almost panicked about halfway up, when I was too deep to retreat and the thighs began to incinerate. Finally I pushed the tiny door to the observation deck and stood panting with a brisk wind and a pack of twisted, neglected antennas. I attached my receiver to the northern face of the Slaughter Memorial and ducked back inside before the breeze blew me over the edge.

My knees were smoking by the time my feet again touched mud but I retrieved the knapsack from the bushes and jogged twenty minutes northeast. There, in a tree, I nested the second receiver and continued to Eutritzsch, a dilapidated slum behind the Hauptbahnhof. Found another tree, this one in a cemetery. Third and fourth receivers went near the zoo and the sports stadium; the fifth settled in Clara Zetkin's park, in a tree not far from where Moll had first lent me the keys to his steeple. I now had a ring of receivers around Leipzig. They would follow Flick no matter which direction he drove.

I reached his street in Schönau around three-thirty. Flick's Trabant was parked in front of his apartment. I looked up: all lights off. Perhaps he was asleep. I picked the Trabant's cheap lock and slid onto the driver's seat. Oh God, the smell of him here brought back insane memories. I unscrewed the overhead light, slashed a rectangle from the padding between ceiling and roof of the car, and packed the transmitter into the little grave I had made for it. Hitched it to the light-bulb socket, stuffed the antenna into place, then got the hell out of there. If Flick didn't detect my rancid terror here in the morning, he needed a new nose.

So far I had passed only a handful of people: Leipzigers were not yet nocturnal creatures. That took cash and temptation. Nevertheless, the adrenaline began to fade only as I ran far, far away from his Trabant. The streets were so dark, so ghoulishly still. I caught a tram and rode with the predawn shift toward the Hotel Merkur, where I waited, exhausted, in a corner of the parking lot. Curtis would come by in a few minutes.

As the M6 pulled into view, I saw a tall figure striding into the front lobby. I was standing so far away from the entrance that it could have been a hallucination, but I thought he wore a chinchilla coat. Harry? Again? It was about the same time of night I had last seen him scurrying back to bed there. Wasn't he supposed to be in Toulouse?

Curtis swung open the door, looked at my muddy boots and filthy face. "Enjoy yourself?"

"I did my job," I said, climbed in, and thudded asleep. In half dreams I kept seeing Oskar Wildau taking pictures of naked boys. Strange.

I played cleanly in Switzerland, thus received clean reviews. During the week, Curtis assumed the role of a one-man sanitarium, never drifting beyond shouting range, ensuring that I ate, exercised, and mainly slept according to his idea of a healthy regimen. No phone calls in or out, no interviews: my primary responsibility was to inhale as much fresh air as possible. The Swiss left us alone, of course.

My tour ended with the Brahms Concerto in Zurich. Curtis waited tetchily backstage as I tormented the conductor and signed a few autographs. Then he veered me into the dressing room. "A storm's coming," he said, handing me a mound of black leather. "We'd better leave now."

Snow meant footprints and I was no winged fairy. This time Curtis let me drive, so we got to Leipzig while night still ruled the land. Again my rounds began at Napoleon's Slaughter Memorial: after cracking the gargantuan padlock, I ran up the spiral and found my receiver dangling over the northern face exactly where I had left it a week earlier. I ejected the floppy and darted back to the mud. They'd find the receiver in a year or two and wonder what it was all about . . . like the skeleton of some prehistoric beast, it would spur their imaginations but reveal nothing. As I was running northeast the first puny, premature snowflakes began to flutter through the poisonous air.

I plucked the second, third, fourth receivers from their arboreal nooks. My luck ran out, as always, in Clara Zetkin Park: the fifth receiver was gone. At first I didn't believe it.

Thought I had climbed the wrong tree. Then I saw the figure gliding along the bushes. Maybe, strolling through the park one day, he had seen a glint in the bare branches. Maybe the wind had blown the receiver on his head as he was gathering acorns below. Maybe he was just hunting hedgehogs tonight and maybe he had been tailing me since the Slaughter Memorial. I wasn't about to hang around and find out: this was not the time to get caught with my pockets full.

Long way to the ground but I jumped, rolled, ran. The man wasn't particularly swift but he didn't have to be: I had left a decisive trail of footprints in the snow. I crashed through alleys, vaulted a few fences, came out near the woods where I had once led Chance over a rickety bridge. The far half of the bridge had rotted into the water and now there were two of them behind me. Dive into the Elster and I'd wreck the floppies so I yanked myself up to the roof of the dilapidated little hut and leapt like a mad animal on top of the first one to run beneath me: two neat cracks as his skull, and my ribs, bashed the stone balustrade. Before passing out, he got a fist in my face.

As I spun on my remaining roadblock, a slice of steel gleamed in the dark. Oh, now we were playing with knives? What did he hope to gain by that, my purse or my chastity? "I have your box," he said, tapping his chest. "Interesting."

I didn't reply: that would identify gender. He advanced a few steps, circling, waiting for me to make the first move. I tried not to let him down. Reaching toward my boot, I pulled a leather loop: out slipped the white knife. My opponent's grin drooped but still he didn't run away. Mr. Sandbag moaned from the sideline; in a moment he'd recall whose acrobatics had split his head. I had to wrap this up.

I advanced toward him, conducting beats with my knife. His eyes wavered as weak dawn eerily phosphoresced the blade: I could be signaling an army. Yet he dared not look around and check. The moment he turned his head I'd slice it off. So he backed up unsteadily toward the hut.

Perhaps he didn't hear the approaching wind because the

white blade had hypnotized him. But when someone's creeping at you with a nine-inch razor, all six senses have to zip into overdrive, or you're tartare. When the squall hit, triggering an avalanche of weeds and slate off the roof of the hut, I charged his throat. Startled, he raised his knife—bah, only one in a hundred would have the brains to keep it low and dig in under my ribs. I kneed him. He staggered, grunting, and I helped him into the river. After a thick plop he floated swiftly away, gargling brine with the eels. Swam about as well as he dueled.

I scanned for witnesses; zero. As the sidekick began nibbling mud, I retreated to the dark riverbank, clawing through dead wood and malodorous muck until I got back to a main street. The one old woman I passed shrank away from me, maybe afraid I was the law. In a rush I have that sort of walk. Eight minutes behind schedule: not having found me at the zoo, Curtis would be cruising the ring road now. If I didn't intercept him by the third circuit, he was to drive back to Berlin alone. I waited forever behind the Schauspielhaus until the M6 finally curved into view.

Curtis looked at the head-to-foot mud, then his rearview mirror. As he pressed the button that reclined my seat below the window line, I felt the car softly accelerate. "You're bleeding," was all he said, dropping a handkerchief into my filthy lap.

I winced as the car rumbled through a few potholes. I would never know who those men were, how they had found my receiver, whether my fifth floppy would end up at the bottom of the Elster or in a police laboratory. I would never know if those men had recognized me, or indeed, if they both had survived. Tonight I had spawned a plague of uncertainty which would weaken me for a long time. Only one thing I knew for sure: I had fought viciously to stay alive. It hadn't been for Queen or country, though. I had wanted to see Flick, feel that strange peace, again. As Curtis eased onto the snowy E6 and began speeding away from him, I felt my eyes burn. Acid air, acid life.

The car purred past Bitterfeld. "What would you do," I asked, "if someone ordered you to seduce a woman?"

"That depends upon what she looked like."

"What if she looked good?"

Curtis passed a half dozen trucks before answering. "I'd follow orders," he said. "Every chance possible." He pulled off the highway about forty kilometers out of Leipzig and got some fresh clothes from the trunk. I was in no condition to flirt my way past any border guards.

We got home by midmorning. In the kitchen Curtis held my face under a halogen lamp. First he inspected the mole above my lip: intact. Then he looked at the cut.

"A roof fell on me," I volunteered.

His mouth distended scornfully as he swabbed the area with a murderous disinfectant. "What is this? Raw sewage?"

"Mud."

He didn't cap the bottle. "Any more abrasions?"

"No."

"How are your hands?"

"Fine."

"Let me see." He turned them over. "What's this."

"I must have slid into some cement."

Curtis had to help me to my room. "I should call a doctor."

"Forget it, nothing's broken." I lurched for the bathroom. "Don't you dare tell Maxine about this." The door snapped tersely shut. I hadn't seen Curtis this angry in years; on the other hand, he hadn't seen me this battered since I waylaid a bullet in Austria.

First I took a hot bath. My body stank and my bones felt slightly awry; all joints squealed. Then I fed Spot the floppy from my receiver at the Slaughter Memorial. For a week, every sixty seconds, it had been recording the direction of Flick's Trabant. That added up to a little over ten thousand calculations. Spot digested the data and asked for the exact position of the receiver. "Leipzig," I typed. A grid of the town appeared onscreen. I found the monument, marked an

X. Inserted the remaining floppies, pinpointed their locations, and told my computer to start triangulating.

The printer next to Spot began eating paper. I scanned the thousands of entries giving me minute/compass position of the Trabant: the car seemed to have remained most of the week at a standstill, at three locations.

Illustrations, please. Spot popped a street grid of Schönau, Flick's neighborhood, onscreen. In upper left corner I read date/time; in the upper right corner, compass position. A red dot appeared on Flick's street and began to pulsate at 4:14 last Wednesday morning, when I had put the transmitter in his Trabant. I advanced past six o'clock, seven: the dot remained still. Around eight o'clock in the morning the dot commuted to the fairgrounds and sat there until six that evening.

Then the dot began moving toward Bitterfeld, an industrial pit thirty kilometers north of Leipzig. The dot didn't stop there but continued into the countryside, finally resting in what looked like a field. I asked Spot which town I was looking at.

"Rösa." Nothing lived there but cows and farmers. The Trabant remained stationary until ten o'clock. Then it returned to Schönau.

The whole cycle began again the next day. Flick arrived at the fairgrounds at eight, stayed all day, left for Rösa about seven that evening. He returned home at eleven o'clock. A pattern seemed to be emerging so I asked Spot for a week's summary of Rösa.

The printer whirred and I got a surveyor's map with five red dots in the corner of a farmer's field, next to what looked like a barn. I put Spot away and tried to get some sleep. Tomorrow night I'd join the hoedown.

Duncan called the next evening. He had just returned from teaching in London and had been listening to the DAT of the Beethoven sonatas which Chance had sent. Now he wished to make a few corrections.

"Too late," I said. "The master's at the CD plant. It's going to be on the shelves in two weeks."

"What?! I have twenty fixes! Where's that slimeball Paradise? I'll kill him."

"Don't bother. I did the editing."

"You? Why? When?" I explained my recent week in Boston. Duncan remained aghast. "How could you do this to me?"

"Calm down. The best takes are in the master."

"*Your* best takes, you mean. Cripes! Can't I leave you alone for a minute?"

"Listen to the session tapes if you don't believe me." I was in no mood for Duncan's fits.

He finally agreed to come over so we could listen to his cassette together. "Then we can rehearse."

"Rehearse what?" I asked.

"We're playing at Lincoln Center next week, remember? Or are these recitals so ordinary you forget them?"

An hour later, Curtis delivered Duncan and a platter of cookies to the music room. Over the holidays my accompanist had acquired a fluffy purple turtleneck and a new tier of midriff bulge. "My God! What happened to your face?" Duncan cried. "Did Luke slap you back?"

"I slipped on the ice." I hobbled to the DAT player.

"You're not going to New York like that, are you? The newspapers will go crazy." He sat next to me on the couch. "Does it hurt?"

"Not any more." I rearranged the ice bag. "Let's hear the Beethoven. If you find twenty mistakes I'll give you a thousand bucks."

Duncan listened attentively to three long sonatas, chain-swallowing cookie after cookie. "I don't understand," he said when the DAT had ended. "It sounds so much better on your system."

Of course it did. My speakers weren't a high school graduation present from an uncle in Cleveland. I shifted weight off my swollen hip. "You weren't serious about rehearsing, were you? I can't hold the violin under my chin very well."

Instead, Duncan played the Chopin sonata for me again. I'd probably hear it another fifty times before his comeback recital in March. He revived himself with a few sandwiches, then looked at his watch. "Eight o'clock?! I'm late for a lesson!"

"I'll take you home."

"No no, you don't look too good. Go to bed."

"I've been in bed all day. Curtis!" I called at the foot of the stairs. "I'm going for a drive."

My housekeeper's face loomed over the banister. He knew he wasn't invited and he couldn't stop me. "Don't be too late," was all he said.

In the garage, I handed Duncan a helmet. "What? We're not going in the car?" he said.

"The car's dirty. Do you want a ride or not?"

Duncan gingerly hoisted himself over the rear wheel. "Try not to crash, okay? I have a big future ahead of me."

After I dropped him off at his place, I continued on to Leipzig. Considering the hour, traffic on the E6 was heavy. I reached Bitterfeld around eleven, Rösa shortly thereafter, and drove several times past the field where Flick had so faithfully parked his Trabant: nothing there but a few weeds and one ramshackle barn waiting for a puff of wind to put it out of its misery. Amenities aside, it was a good place to tryst. I left the Harley behind a dead silo and limped across the turnips toward a line of elder trees. There, in the frozen mud, I waited. Occasionally, far off, I would hear a sputtering car or the foul zip of a motor scooter. But nothing moved here, not even rabbits.

Putta-putta-putt . . . finally, Flick's Trabant came rolling cautiously along the dark road. He suddenly killed his headlights and edged down the dirt path. Twenty meters from the barn, the Trabant stopped. It was almost midnight.

For an hour, nothing happened. I stared at his car, wishing

I could see inside. God it was miserable in this sticky, cold muck. Once, Flick rolled down his window, taking a hit of fresh air, and I heard, ever so softly, a lone, mesmerizing violin: Frost playing Bach. It was one of my early, proud recordings. I had been more confident then. After a few moments he closed his window, cutting off the music. Silence returned to the poisoned field. My clothes were damp now and as the numbness rolled up my legs, the strange peace returned. I found myself blissfully content, fused to the mud within shooting distance of this unreachable man. Perhaps pheromones were God, then. The brains, the wills driving Frost and Smith had not been able to compete with a few instantaneous chemical reactions. So I was only a beast after all: no surprise. No comfort, either. The molecular theory of love might absolve me from guilt, but it could never explain the wonder, or reduce the pain.

At two o'clock, the car door opened; again I heard Bach. Flick walked to the barn and peed. Then he drove slowly away.

I rolled back to Berlin. As promised, Curtis was waiting up for me. When I shuffled in from the garage, he put his book down. At his elbow was a bottle of Scotch. Not for him, of course; Curtis detested the stuff. "Back shortly, you said? It's almost four o'clock." It was the closest he had ever come to asking where I had been.

"I had an appointment," I said.

"With what, a muskrat? You're covered with mud again. Would you mind not tracking that over the kitchen floor?"

I sagged against the doorway. "Maybe you could get my bathrobe for me."

When he returned I had shed the jacket but was still fighting with my boots. "Sit down," Curtis said disgustedly.

"I can't."

Almost twisted my legs off but he finally had two boots on the doormat. "What about the pants," he said.

"I'm not a cripple," I snapped.

Curtis pretended to read his book. When I had struggled

into the bathrobe, he pushed the bottle toward me. I was swallowing a hefty belt when he put the book down and loosened my bathrobe. The bruise over my ribs was taking on the hues of Gauguin's Tahitian canvases. Curtis studied it as if he were an art student. "Were you in a fight?" he said finally.

I refilled the glass. "They didn't walk away from it."

"Why can't you tell Maxine about this."

"She already thinks I'm losing it."

He passed a smooth brown hand over my yellowing pelvis, checking for broken bones. "Is this personal?"

"Yes."

Curtis closed the bathrobe. "You can't win, then."

"I know that."

He heaved a long Southern sigh. "What would you like me to do."

"Just stick around." I drank.

For two nights I returned to Rösa and sat in the rotten turnips watching Flick. Most of the time he stayed in the Trabant. Just before leaving, he always walked slowly around the barn, stretching his old legs. Then he peed and drove home. And throughout, very softly, Frost the fiddler serenaded two cold, vigilant lovers.

On the third night, as he got out of his car, Flick's walk was exceptionally tense. For many minutes he waited alongside the barn, immobile as Bach's statue at the Thomaskirche. Was someone finally coming to meet him? I looked around, heard nothing. The odor of the air changed but it made no immediate sense so I ignored it and continued to focus on Flick. Gradually the light altered and I could see his face. But it was too early for sunrise. Then I realized the roof of the barn was on fire. A perfect ring of flame maybe a meter wide was growing rapidly outward, eating thatch. Not possible, the roof was damp, no one here was playing with matches, the circle of fire was too perfect and Flick was running neither away nor toward it, he was just staring agape, as if he saw a miracle. When the flames had nearly engulfed the roof, he hurried to the Trabant and sped away.

I left my little ditch and yanked open the barn doors. Vibrant yellow light mottled the cavern but there were no bodies dead or alive, no signs of activity inside. Heat pressed the top of my head. Crack, went the sky: a beam crashed to the floor, disintegrating in a fusillade of sparks. An odd metallic ring rolled unevenly from the debris. I went over and turned it over with my boot. Nice wiring job, that. I sighed, somewhat disappointed: Flick had not been waiting these long nights for anyone after all. He had been waiting for the fire.

The following night, I was in Leipzig, at the foot of the Slaughter Memorial, wandering in the mud with a portable receiver. Moll's steeple, Flick's dishes, Napoleon's monument were all points on a line and I intended to pick up the radio waves that spilled past the fairgrounds: although Moll only had to broadcast a mile to Flick's dishes, there would already be a little slopover as his signal from the steeple diffused through space. I twirled my antenna this way and that, finally picking up an intermittent burp from the steeple. I adjusted my meters, made sure the DAT was running: right on schedule, for two minutes, my meters went crazy. Then the barrage stopped cold. I packed my gear and got out of there.

I reached Roland's club very late, when the bartender usually nicked the lighting a couple hundred watts and the mood of the patrons downshifted from bonhomie to suicide. Onstage a pianist's hands wandered languidly over the keys, peddling commiseration. My brother sat at his corner table equidistant from Maxine and a bottle of gin. "Hi," I said, sitting so that my good cheek faced the Queen. The bum leg I left sticking into the aisle. "Thought I'd swing by before going to New York tomorrow."

Roland half raised his head. "What's that smell? You been playing with a skunk?"

Maxine's fork continued twirling a mess of pasta. "Leaving again? How long will you be gone this time?"

"Two days." I helped myself to the gin. "That was a great New Year's party. When did it finally break up?"

"Yesterday," Roland said. "We ran out of champagne." He stood up. "You really smell awful, Les." He tottered toward the bar.

"Why are you sitting like that?" Maxine asked.

"I'm constipated, all right? Moll's broken the code."

Her jaws momentarily relinquished the pasta. After me, how would this woman ever entertain herself? "Go on."

"I put a transmitter in Flick's car. He's been going to a field in Rösa every night. Parks next to a deserted barn and waits. No one ever shows up."

"Sounds thrilling," Maxine said.

I swallowed another dose of joint medicine. "Tonight, the barn caught fire. Flick watched then drove home."

"Flick burned down the barn?"

"No, Moll did."

"Moll comes with him to Rösa?"

"No, Moll's still in the steeple." Maxine couldn't bring herself to say *I don't get it*, so I continued. "Moll picks up the satellite every twenty-five hours, correct? Then he's got two minutes all by himself to do whatever he wants with it." I leaned over the table. "He had a detonating device with a signal enhancer on the roof of the barn. It received a weak command from far away telling it to go off. Poof! The barn began to burn. Spontaneous combustion."

"Get serious."

"Have you ever set leaves on fire with a magnifying glass? Moll did the same thing from one hundred miles up with the laser aboard that satellite."

"That's impossible," the Queen said. "He doesn't have the technology. Nor the energy."

"Why the hell do you think the satellite's carrying a nuclear reactor?"

She looked upset. It was worth ten years in the mud and a broken hip. "Are you sure about this?"

I tucked the DAT into the banquette near her lap. "That's

tonight's transmission from the steeple. I think you'll find he's broken the code.'' I saw Roland heading back to our table. ''Make my brother some meat loaf, would you? He says you've been neglecting him lately.''

I flew back to smutty, humorless New York. The morning of our concert, second in our Beethoven series, I met Duncan at Lincoln Center. He had been in Manhattan for several days already, neutralizing the jet lag and chatting up a slew of publicity agents, most of whom had accepted tickets to tonight's show only after Duncan mentioned the party Kakadu Classics was throwing afterward. ''Why didn't they teach economics at Juilliard?'' he cursed as we signed in at the stage door. ''If I had known that musicians outnumbered jobs ten thousand to one, I would have become a dentist.''

''And spent your life drilling teeth? Please.''

Duncan heaved his music across the piano. ''Do me a favor. Don't wear that dress with the silver sequins tonight. I want those bastards to look at me, not you. And give me at least three big bows. Kiss my hand as if you couldn't have done it without me.''

''I do that already.''

''Do something extra, then.''

''I'll kiss your feet.''

''Don't you dare!'' he shrieked. ''This has got to be dignified! We walk out, we play, we bow. The muse is God.''

I hugged the violin to my chin. ''This is America. Amusement is God.'' Duncan played a brilliant dress rehearsal. Then, remembering that even muses had to look telegenic, he kept a string of appointments with hairdressers and facialists. I spent the afternoon reworking Beethoven. Chance called, hoping I was free for a late dinner.

Shortly before show time, I found Duncan backstage, ranting as usual. The dressing room smelled like a funeral parlor. ''What's all this,'' I said, looking at the wall-to-wall bouquets.

"Luke-baby sent them. Every card says 'I'm sorry.'" Duncan inspected my face. "At least the swelling's gone down. Doesn't look as if he slugged you any more." My accompanist scooted into the bathroom while I changed into concert dress, trying to focus on a moribund Beethoven. It was difficult to play scales in New York while Flick was burning down barns in Germany.

The toilet flushed. "My God!" Duncan cried, stopping short at the threshold of the bathroom. "Are you ill?"

"What's the matter now."

"Your dress—there—there's so much of it! You're all covered up!"

My ribs were taped and my swollen hip wasn't up for skintight satin yet. "Now you don't like chiffon? You're always whining about my tight clothes."

"I got used to tight clothes. This throws me off now." Duncan searched the back seam. "Where are the buttons? Where's the zipper I have to pull up?"

"This dress doesn't have any."

"Jesusmaryjoseph!" he cried. "No good luck buttons? No good luck zipper? I can't go onstage without any good luck buttons!"

I took a little box from the violin case: Flick's ruby. "Put this on, then." Duncan's icy fingers brushed my neck. "Feel better now?"

"No!" He plummeted to the couch. "I have bad vibrations about this concert. Those flowers are making me ill. That swine probably sprayed them with some kind of cocaine aphrodisiac."

The stage manager knocked on the door. "One minute, Miss Frost."

"It's one minute Mr. Zadinsky too, you oaf!" Duncan shouted, then clutched his head. "I can't go through with this," he whimpered.

I pulled him to his feet. "Think Beethoven."

"With all those managers and publicists out there?"

I left the dressing room. Duncan caught up as I reached the stage door. "Remember, the muse is God. Don't step on my dress."

We sailed into the footlights. Duncan launched fervidly into the first sonata. One would never know that thirty seconds ago he had almost been puking with fright. Two brains engorged data from twenty fingers/four ears, ran a million billion calculations: out slid Beethoven. I was in the slow movement, wooing the G string, when the first rose fell at my feet. A slash of scarlet, a tiny thud: Frost ignored it and kept playing, but after the third plop, Smith whooshed to life. Roses? Here? Illogical. I put the fingers on autopilot and glanced at the floor. The flowers seemed genuinely dead, crushed, not oozing liquid or vapor so I fiddled, waiting for the next to fall, and traced the trajectory. In the loge nearest the stage sat Luke the Apostle and Sydney Bolt.

Fortunately, Duncan's nose was buried in the music when the roses arced in front of me. We took several bows and walked offstage. "Just a minute," he called, running to the bathroom.

I motioned the stagehand to the peephole. "See that man standing in the loge?"

He put his eye to the door. "The guy with the white cape?"

"Get him out of there."

"Is there a problem?"

"He's throwing things at me."

The stagehand hesitated. "Did he buy a ticket?"

"I don't care if he bought the house. Get him out of there."

"Wait, he's leaving."

Duncan soon returned. "Is that audience noisy tonight or what?" he asked.

"House lights are down," said the stagehand. The loge was empty when Duncan and I returned onstage. No more roses dropped at my feet as we played the first movement of a late, sublime sonata and for a few moments I was profoundly grateful to be a living violinist.

"Hot shit!" someone in the orchestra yelled. "Luke loves you, baby!"

Startled, Duncan missed his next chord. He never recovered, nor did the audience. Luke interrupted three more times before intermission. I played on, waiting for an usher to yank him away. Didn't happen, of course: Bolt had bought off the staff. I wasn't about to oblige her by interrupting the performance so I edged closer to my addled accompanist, playing almost into his ear. Duncan wouldn't think about leaving the piano while I was on top of him like that.

He saved the hysterics for backstage. "How could you do this to me?"

"Sorry, Duncan. I didn't know a thing about it." Dragged him back for three more bows.

He stomped ahead of me to the dressing room. " 'Luke loves you, baby!' Mother of God! Why didn't you walk offstage?"

"Then what? Wait for a dozen ushers to drag him out of the auditorium kicking and screaming?"

Someone half knocked. In piled the Apostle with retinue. "Hi, guys," he said. "Thought I'd say hello now. Can't stay for the second half."

"Son of a bitch!" Duncan cried, lunging at him. "You've ruined my life!"

Sydney Bolt, stunning in a chartreuse pantsuit, edged toward her photographer. "Better get this, Arty," she said under her breath.

A stagehand finally pried Duncan's thumbs from Luke's jugular after they had knocked over a row of bouquets. "You maniac," the Apostle rasped, staggering beside me on the couch. "You've crushed my throat."

Duncan next turned to Bolt. "Are you responsible for this outrage?"

"Outrage?" She smiled. "Certainly you mean event."

"One hundred agents came to this concert specifically to

hear Duncan Zadinsky! This is a recital, not a fucking hootenanny!''

"I'm helping your record sales," she said. "You should be grateful."

"Grateful? I'm going to sue the shit out of you!"

Now he was finally talking on Bolt's wavelength. "You don't understand," Bolt tried to explain. "Luke didn't mean any of it."

"Will you get this bitch out of here," Duncan screamed at the stagehand.

"I need a few pictures," said Arty, kneeling before the couch.

Duncan kicked him with his shiny black shoe. "Leave my dressing room!"

Bolt turned calmly to me. "Could you please control your pianist, dear?"

"Get out," I said.

"Kakadu's not going to like this." Bolt retreated nevertheless. "Come, Luke. Off the floor, Arty. We've got other places to go tonight."

The Apostle lingered in the doorway. "I wasn't just shouting, Leslie. I really meant what I said." He looked at Duncan. "Sorry for the hassle. Sometimes you've just got to roll with it, man." The white cape left.

A little mayhem did wonders for my accompanist's concentration: the second half of the concert came frightfully close to perfection. Audience wanted encores and afterward, a flock of teenage girls crushed backstage, hoping to see Luke but settling for autographs from the piano player, who was about the same gender. I was saying hello to Godo when Chance appeared.

"Beautiful concert, Frosty," he said, kissing my cheek. "Despite everything." Again I smelled that delicious froth of limes and flesh.

"Ah, Mr. Chance! You come to our party?" Godo asked.

"For a bit. I do have other plans for this evening."

We finally got Duncan away from the girls and into a

limousine, which may have been a mistake. "Mr. Godo," he began the moment it rolled into Central Park, "you must get rid of that slut. What's her first name anyhow? Attila?"

Godo feigned ignorance. "You have problems?"

"Did you see what she had that stupid man do? How would you like someone shouting at you when you tried to recite a little haiku?"

Godo suddenly smiled. "You are in the newspapers tomorrow. That is not good?"

Duncan sighed in exasperation. "What did you think of that disgusting spectacle?" he asked Chance.

The soft whistling stopped. "Luke was just doing his job, Duncan. You're in show business, after all." The limousine pulled in front of an Upper East Side skyscraper. "You might bear that in mind for the next hour or two." He swung open the door.

"I thought he was above this," Duncan muttered to me. "Do me a favor, would you? Stick to that old fart in Leipzig."

Chance assisted me from the limousine. "Let's go, Duncan," he called from the sidewalk. "Your admirers are waiting."

I lasted half an hour at the reception, long enough to shake the critical hands and endure yet another Kakadu-loves-America speech. Then I told Godo I had an early plane in the morning. "You cannot stay?" he said. "I think Mr. Apostle comes later."

Across the room, my accompanist was expostulating upon rock music's roots in satanism. "I'm sure Duncan will give him a rousing welcome," I said. Chance added a few apologies to my pile and we left.

"You really don't like parties, do you," he said in the elevator.

"Too many bodies at close range." I leaned against the mirrored wall. "Like rock concerts. Where are we going?"

"To a fine restaurant around the block. You'll like it."

Chance took me to a penthouse high above the East River. Again, as in Boston, I found a plethora of leather and cherrywood. Recessed lighting soothed the eye. Near the window was a table set for two. "Is this your place?"

He took my coat. "I got tired of hotel rooms."

I followed him to the kitchen. It looked like "Star Trek" with a sink. "You must do a lot of business in New York."

"Enough. Do you really have an early plane tomorrow?"

"Nine o'clock."

Chance pulled the cork from a bottle of wine. "Don't you ever take a vacation, baby?"

"From what? Cheers."

As he tossed some rare-breed salad, Chance told me about his latest recording projects: opera in San Francisco, Mahler in Baltimore, Tchaikovsky in Chicago . . . this week he'd be recording brass bands at the Manhattan Center. "Too bad you have to leave," Chance said. "We could have a great time here."

I looked out the window. "New York used to excite me. It doesn't any more."

"Why not? It's the same, only worse."

"It's not the same. Violence I understand. Anarchy I don't."

"You've lived in Germany too long, my dear. Makes you forget what the rest of the world is like." Chance submerged a pair of lobsters in boiling water. "We're forty floors above the battlefield. Don't you find that exciting?"

"Not any more." I studied the glistening lights on the Triboro Bridge. Such a beautiful night, such a doomed land. It was run by rock stars, publicists, and Japanese.

Fine food and drink improved my disposition somewhat. Chance kept conversation frivolous: one could prattle for hours about the provenance of each vase and chair in this apartment. We ended up on an Italian couch while lazy and licentious jazz, Maxine's style, burbled in the background. Across the room, the pendulum of an Art Deco clock swung lazily back and forth. Midnight here? Six o'clock in Leipzig. I wondered if Flick was practicing his violin before breakfast.

"Tired?" Chance asked. "You're moving a little slowly tonight, I notice."

"I fell on the ice last week. Cracked a few ribs."

That called for brandy. When Chance sat back on the couch, his hip was touching mine. He slid an arm around my shoulder and, with his free hand, lifted the ruby pendant around my throat. "Very pretty." He let it drop. "I've never seen you perform before," he said. "It's quite riveting."

"How so."

"You don't move, your face has no expression at all, yet there's an enormous psychic energy streaming into the auditorium. What are you thinking of? Art? Death? Love?"

"Mathematics."

"That's all? How do you play with such passion, then?"

Ah, such strong gray eyes: he would never understand the terror or the desolation of it all. "I'm passionate about mathematics." A sudden, tiny bolt of lightning struck my ribs. I stood up, stretched. The pain ebbed. "Leg's asleep," I told Chance.

He rose; we danced slowly, dreamily, forty floors above the anarchy. "You don't trust me, do you," he whispered. "Think I'm just a flash in the pan." Why reply? I was so comfortable. I put my head on his shoulder. "Do you trust any man?" Chance asked.

A minute rippled by. "My housekeeper."

We swayed around the room, gently brushing the other. When the music ended, Chance disengaged himself. "I'll take you back. It's late." I raised my mouth but he kissed my forehead.

12

Within minutes of my flight's departure from JFK, the champagne began to flow: sentimental tourists were still celebrating the end of the Wall and journalists were toasting the media bonanza of the decade. As the plane broke into the blinding sunlight above the clouds, I thought about Choirmaster Moll. Unlike Flick and the red-head, he had my unreserved admiration. Clove or no Clove, the man was a virtuoso. Cracking the satellite's code was in itself awesome; targeting a tiny barn from one hundred miles up—now that was genius.

Theoretically, Moll could burn holes anywhere in the planet now. What for, though? He could do a lot more damage with dynamite. Two years ago, when the satellite was launched, when they had planned this operation, could Flick and Moll have known that East Germany would be disintegrating? They got the Clove in September '89, as the population began hemorrhaging in earnest. What with demonstrations, rupturing borders, Stasi stampeding for cover, no one would be paying much attention to a few boxes going to the trade fair. A monumental coincidence, to say the least.

Supposing that Redhead & Co. were loyal East Germans, what could they be trying to do? Turn the clock back? Spark a few spectacular fires in Berlin, Dresden, call in the troops, plead for Russian backup . . . there were still plenty of Soviet generals itching to stomp out the democratic contagion before it spread east. If Moll was working with the Russians, however, why had he gone to so much trouble to penetrate their satellite surreptitiously? Unless that was part of the deception, of course. The possibility of renegade Russians was not impossible, given the uncertainty of events there as well.

Information was money, which brought me to a second, less noble theory. Acknowledging imminent defeat, perhaps the three of them intended to sell their treasure to the highest bidder and disappear to South America. In the past, Germans had found this a popular method of dealing with reversals of fortune. However, I couldn't see it. Flick had been hibernating in Leipzig for thirty years. He wasn't interested in money. Selling out one's country for a few bucks was now an American specialty.

No, Flick was doing something more elegant than that. I remembered him leading me through that gigantic pavilion at the fairgrounds, talking about the laser exhibition he had been planning for two years. How about all those power lines being dug all over Leipzig? Flick would have the lenses and, now, the energy to make himself a tremendous laser. What would he do with something like that? Now?

Flick, Flick, forget Flick. Moll was a less rancorous enigma. When I got home, I studied Reiner Hofmann's file again. Born, educated in Berlin: all his credentials were in perfect order, of course. If I called every school on this list, they would certainly know of Reiner Hofmann. A body answering to that name had studied there. But I hesitated to ask too many questions about him here on home turf: Flick and the redhead, I was sure, had planted a few informers along the way. I would be safer poking into America.

Once again, I looked over Hofmann's transcript from Johns Hopkins, and despaired: it was so perfectly, inhumanly anonymous. None of his teachers had paid the slightest attention to him but Professor Wesley Wilkins, the chorus director. I read the professor's comments after one semester of song:

Lovely, well-trained voice, by far the best tenor in the chorus. Carries his entire section. Grade: A

After the spring semester:

Acquitted himself superbly during spring musicale. The best vocalist at Hopkins in years. Does not wish to do solo work, claims stage fright, which argument does not convince me! Promises to reconsider next year. Grade: A

A rhapsodical third semester:

Voice in top form after a summer of rest. Inspires the entire chorus. After much persuasion, has agreed to sing the Evangelist in the St. Matthew Passion next spring. A talented, diligent pupil, a pleasure to work with. Social skills are also improving tremendously. Grade: A

And finally:

Inexcusable absence from spring concert very disappointing and distressing to those who had relied upon him. A most unfortunate situation for the chorus. Many hours of rehearsal wasted. Grade: D

I phoned Dr. Wesley Wilkins in Baltimore and introduced myself as Frau Tubsch from the Interior Office of Higher German Education. I was finishing a report on German students in America in the early eighties. "I see your name on the file of Reiner Hofmann, who studied chorus with you at Johns Hopkins University. Would you perhaps remember him?"

Long pause. "I remember him. A tragedy."

"Yes, most unfortunate. All that scholarship money

wasted! If you would please answer a few questions, Professor Wilkins, I would be most grateful. First, I see that Herr Hofmann receives grades of A, A, A, D. Did something happen?''

''He missed the spring concert, which I consider my final exam.''

''What was the reason for this absence? Was he ill?''

''I don't think so,'' Wilkins replied. ''He just didn't show up.''

''Did he oversleep? Forget?''

''How could he forget? He was singing the main role! We rehearsed for weeks!''

I could feel the long-buried exasperation slowly rising: Wilkins had forgiven nothing. ''This is rather unusual. Could you give me further details?''

Wilkins sighed. ''The chorus was to perform Bach's *St. Matthew Passion* at our spring concert. After much effort I finally persuaded Reiner to sing the role of the Evangelist.''

''He needed persuasion?''

''He was acutely shy. He only blossomed when he sang.''

''Then why did he miss his concert?''

Again, Wilkins paused, exhuming bitter memories. ''A day before the concert Reiner called me in tears to say he could not sing the following night. Stage fright was his explanation but I didn't believe that. Of course, I went to his dormitory to give him a pep talk. He wasn't there. Hadn't been there for two days.''

''Where was he?''

''I don't know. He apparently spent a lot of time away from campus. No one knew exactly where he went although he did mention an aunt in New York.''

Aunt, my foot. ''What did you do to replace him, poor man?''

''I hired a substitute. We had to print an announcement in the program that Reiner was ill. He never apologized to me, you know. Just went back to Berlin.''

"I am so sorry, Herr Professor Wilkins. This reflects so badly on all Germans. If Hofmann were alive I would demand an investigation. You would have a written apology."

"It's a bit late for that, I'm afraid." Wilkins cleared his throat. "He had a very special voice. Like a dark sparrow, perfect for Bach. And so well trained . . ." His voice trailed off.

"Yes, yes, Germans are very fine musicians," I agreed, trying to encourage him. "It's in their blood."

"Reiner came to my home a few times to sing Schubert lieder," Wilkins reminisced. "They were very special evenings. He had such a gorgeous sense of phrasing and color . . . his teacher must have been heartbroken. Students like that are not ordinary, believe me. I often meant to write a note of condolence to him but didn't have his full address."

No problem, it was right here on Moll's transcript: he had studied with a Professor von Ditsch at the Berlin Conservatory. I was about to furnish Wilkins the particulars when he said, "I still remember the name. Professor Berger. Poor man."

Wilkins and Moll had probably been sitting on the professor's divan, a little tipsy, having just read through *Die Schöne Müllerin*. Wilkins had asked an innocent question and for once maybe, overcome with postperformance dementia, Moll had blurted a truthful answer, little guessing that many years later his adoring professor would still recall every syllable from his lips. "Such an awful tragedy," Wilkins repeated. Had he known Hofmann was going to drown in two months, he would never have given him a D in chorus. He was just so upset at what had happened.

"Any professor in Germany would have given him an E," I said. "You must not feel badly, Herr Professor Wilkins." Wilkins's day was ruined nevertheless.

After hanging up, I wandered into Hugo's library, repository of many books about German choral societies, German instrument makers, German so on and so forth. Once upon a time I had seen a Who's Who of German musicians here.

Curtis walked in as I was up on the ladder. "What are you doing? Get down before you fall."

"Give me a break! I'm completely sober."

He came to the bottom of the ladder. "Looking for something?"

"Where's that book Hugo had about German musicians? I want to look someone up." In front of me I only saw opera scores. "Did you move all the books around?"

"No. You're looking in the wrong place. Hold on." Curtis wheeled the ladder three sections over. "I wish you'd get down. You don't need any more cracked ribs."

The book was nowhere in sight so I descended. "Why the hell can't I ever find anything in here?" Looking for Professor Berger via the conservatories in the phone book would take all day.

Curtis handed me a fax. "Let me look. You read this."

Another newspaper clipping, from Chance, this time a photograph of Duncan strangling Luke the Apostle backstage at Lincoln Center. *Pianist Strikes Back*, the text began, nearly labeling Duncan a cuckolded accompanist. "Famous at last," Chance had written on the bottom.

I threw it into the fireplace. "Lovely."

"You'd better start looking for another pianist," Curtis called from the heights. "He's going to be impossible." He searched a few more shelves before quitting. "Sorry, no such book. Maybe Hugo's ex got it in the divorce settlement."

I brought a phone book to my room and flipped to Berger. There were only about two thousand of them in West Berlin so I found the music school listings and began with the Albrecht Music Academy. Was a Doktor Berger teaching voice there? Never heard of him, the woman said. Perhaps I would like to study with Doktor Schlitz instead.

No thanks. I called two dozen music schools and got the same response. Dead end, Smith: Choirmaster Moll had not slipped after all. For a moment there, I thought I was a little cleverer than he. Next I tried the Vilnius Institute of Musical

Arts. "Good afternoon. I would like to study voice with
Doktor Berger. Would he have an opening for me?"

"You want to study with whom?" a rickety voice answered.

"Doktor Berger. I've heard such wonderful things about
him."

"One moment, we have no teacher of that name. You must
study instead with my husband, Doktor Johannes Vilnius.
Singers come to him from all over the world. If you don't
like that, you study with me. I teach Italian opera."

God help those poor throats. I began again at the top. "I'm
sure it was Doktor Berger, the voice teacher."

Crack, went the phone. "Hannes! Hannes!" the woman
called. I heard a lot of shuffling. "She wants to study with
Doktor Berger."

"Johannes Vilnius," said a gruff voice. I asked a third
time for Professor Berger. "You have made a mistake. Berger
has never taught here and he never will. He is a total fraud
who knows nothing about singing."

I swallowed carefully. "I'm so sorry. Perhaps I should
study with you instead."

"That would be wise," Vilnius advised me. "Berger will
ruin your voice in two months, believe me."

"But he was so highly recommended! I don't mean to
offend you, but I was told he was the finest voice teacher in
Berlin."

"Dreck! Never has been, never will be! Who told you this,
one of his Communist sycophants at the Hochstein School?"

Of course: Berger taught in East, not West, Berlin. "I
don't remember," I said. "Thank you for warning me." I
hung up, having ruined Vilnius's sleep for weeks to come.

It was rather late in the day but Maxine had said I was
running out of time and this was my only lead so I packed a
mousy brown wig and a pair of heavy eyeglasses into an old
purse, dressed in a funky sweater, boots: my Karl Marx U
outfit. Before leaving the house I painted the mole above my
lip pink. Anyone looking that closely would see an irritated

pimple, not the famous upper lip of Leslie Frost. Camera, recorder, lipstick: I was ready to go visiting. "Curtis," I called into the office, "I'm going shopping."

One look at my outfit and Curtis knew what I was shopping for. Frowning, he scribbled another date into my engagement calendar.

Louring clouds palled the midafternoon sun, ice stiffened my lawn. At the Botanical Garden, depressed dogwalkers kept their eyes to the ground, where flowers had once bloomed. I boarded the S-bahn, riding to the Friedrichstrasse crossing with hordes of East Germans. Six months ago, these cars carried mostly sad old Berliners and their little baskets of food to kin on the unfortunate side of the Wall. Now the train was crammed and festive with young blood.

Guards waved the crowds through the gritty turnstiles: no more stopping to pay twenty-five marks' extortion at the border. One block into East Berlin, the air already started eating my lungs. The streets were immediately filthy, the masonry pitted, windows broken, oh Christ what had these fools been doing for the last forty-five years? As day faded, I dipped into an alley, emerged wearing my wig/glasses. Like everyone else, I looked like an extra in *The Maltese Falcon* now.

The Hochstein Music School had once been a burgher's mansion. Now it was a dingy ruin. I could never decide whether the East Germans really didn't have the money to fix up these places or whether they purposely let them decay as a posthumous insult to those who had so proudly built them. I turned a loose doorknob and entered a derelict foyer. Upstairs, a student's lips locked in mortal combat with a clarinet reed. Behind various doors floated the sounds of instruments and physiognomies in agony. Long ago, I had made noises like that for hours on end. Maybe that was why Roland still hated me.

"Yes?" said the old woman at the desk. Observant, suspicious: crones like this were the lifeblood of a police state.

"I would like to see Doktor Berger."

"What for?"

"I am interested in taking voice lessons."

"What's your name?"

"Lily Braun." I gave her an identity card.

"He's not taking any new pupils." She handed it back.

I looked very, very disappointed. "Does he have a waiting list?"

"No."

"But I've come all the way from Jena," I whined.

"You'll have to go back." She returned to her industrial-strength typewriter.

"I must see him," I said. "This is extremely important."

"He only comes in on Thursday afternoon for three pupils. Believe me, he does not have time to see you, Fraulein Braun. Ten people like you come here every week hoping to study with him."

I forced a few tears under the heavy eyeglasses. "It will take months to earn enough money for another train ticket to Berlin."

She handed me a sheet of paper. "Write him a note, then. Not here on my desk! Go to the library!" She pointed across the foyer. "And be quick about it. The school closes at six o'clock."

Might as well play this hole through: I tiptoed across the desiccated oak floor, which probably hadn't been varnished since the state became landlord. A heavy door opened to a quondam dining room now stuffed with shelves and desks. Overhead, two bulbs glared in place of the uprooted chandelier. A haphazard array of ancient class photographs hung from nails in the rosewood paneling and above that, the sooty plaster displayed a nonstop maze of stress fractures. If the original owners survived the war, they'd probably drop dead if they saw their place now.

Nodding at a sour librarian, I sagged into a chair near the wrecked fireplace, wondering what to do. My ribs hurt. I wasn't going to leave Berger a note: that meant fingerprints, handwriting sample . . . coming here was a mistake. I had been too eager to connect with someone who might tell me anything about the choirmaster. I should have posed my questions over the phone: no witnesses, no stupid wigs to hide the famous fiddler, no hassle with guards at reception desks. Besides, what could Berger have told me about Moll/Hofmann except that he heard the boy sing for an hour each week?

Zero. Typical. As if to reprimand me for my foolish haste, some dour professor's portrait glared down at me from the mantel. Terrible, merciless eyes. As I got up to leave, I read the tarnished plaque on the frame: Herbert Zwinger, Professor of Violin, 1910–1945. My stomach tightened hideously as I recalled a stroll with Flick in Kreuzberg, just before he nearly beat a man to death. *My mother brought me to Professor Zwinger every Friday*, he had said, pulling me along to that dark alley. *I was her little Kreisler*. My head began to pound: was Flick's picture hanging here on the wall?

"The library is closing in three minutes," the old woman at the desk called. "Bring all books to the front."

Class of 1922 . . . 1926 . . . 1913 . . . 1958—couldn't these people hang history in chronological order, for Christ's sake—1927 . . . 1930 . . . I looked—no, that little boy was not Flick, wrong eyes—1935 . . . 1936 . . . 1937—I found him in the middle row, 1944—such a sad creature. The upper right corner of the photograph was ruined but there he was, poor little wise man. Next to him stood the redhead. Her eyes had never changed. I pulled out my camera, shot the faded photograph and for the hell of it old Zwinger over the fireplace as footsteps tapped in my direction. "The library is closed," she said, rounding the bookshelves. "Didn't you hear me?"

"I was just looking at the pictures." I pointed to the class of 1944. "Only seven pupils?"

"All violinists," the librarian said. "Professor Zwinger insisted on keeping the Hochstein School open throughout the war."

"What became of them?"

She shrugged. "They never returned. Not one."

"And Professor Zwinger?"

"He was killed in the Battle of Berlin."

"He wasn't in the army?"

"They wouldn't take him. He had lost a foot in the previous war."

I studied seven youthful faces. "I wonder who they were."

"No one knows," the librarian said. "The school records were destroyed in an air raid. Fortunately, our director had moved the library to a safer place several days before."

In the confusion Zwinger had probably overlooked that last picture. I thanked the librarian and left. Embroiled in argument with two horn players, the woman at the front desk did not see me leave. No note for Professor Berger? Didn't matter; I would never be back. In the first lake of black between streetlights I yanked off the wig, shook my head in the cold night: seeing Flick again, even as a boy on paper, deranged the nervous system. The sudden confrontation with his eyes started the fever all over again.

For a change, I returned to Dahlem without a layer of mud. "Hi Curtis," I called, going downstairs to the darkroom. "I'll be right up."

I bathed the film in chemicals, reversed the negatives: Professor Zwinger's face coalesced on blank paper. I hung him up to dry. Stern, unforgiving eyes, grim mouth: lessons with him must have been terrifying. I imagined little Emil's knees shaking as he opened his case, tuned his violin . . . somehow that upset me so I held the picture of Flick and his classmates under the light. Water damage obscured the face of the boy on the far right. As for the remaining six, not a smile among them. Somber faces, reflections of a mortally wounded nation. Whereas the redhead's eyes glistened coldly as shards of glass, Flick's were sad, direct: both children had probably already seen enough horror for a lifetime. He still looked at me that way when we made love.

"Dinner's on the table," Curtis called from the top of the stairs. As we ate, he talked about the new engagements he had booked. It was his way of reminding me that no matter how preoccupied I might be elsewhere, Frost the fiddler could not be ignored. "Your flight's at ten tomorrow morning," Curtis said. "Rehearsal's at two. This is your first Tchaikovsky Concerto in London." Translation: don't screw it up. "Harry called while you were out. He's throwing a party after the concert."

"What's the occasion?"

"Maybe he wants to thank you for doing his editing. Says he's invited the most important people in the kingdom." Curtis tried to interest me in another piece of shepherd's pie. "You're going, of course. You've got to be seen more."

"I'll go for a few minutes. That's all." Maintaining visibility was the downside of the music business. "Have you heard from Duncan? I wonder how he's dealing with that picture of him strangling Luke."

"Of course I haven't heard. He's famous now."

"I hope you're happy," I said. "This never would have happened if you and Bolt hadn't foisted that boyfriend crap on me."

Curtis took the dishes to the sink. "Just widening your options, Leslie. One day you might be grateful." What was that supposed to mean? I got up from the table.

Took the photographs to my computer and began experimenting with a new program Maxine called Wrinkle: Feed Spot a face and it constructed that same face ten, twenty, fifty years down the rocky road. The program came in handy when certain eremites let a few decades slip by between mug shots. First, a bit of quality control: I had Spot scan a slight boy with dark hair and steady eyes. Flick's youthful face appeared on the screen. Year? 1945. Age? Nine. Nationality? Diet? Health? Profession? I punched in a stream of variables and asked for Flick in 1960.

Flesh dissolved from his face, leaving only a 3-D blueprint of Flick's skull. I watched it slowly bulge and thicken as Spot added age and possibly wisdom. After he turned seventeen, the growth tapered off and my computer filled the gulleys with eyes, nose, ears: not a bad-looking specimen of manhood. I suddenly ached. Missed him terribly. No word since New Year's Eve, perhaps no words evermore. I wiped Young Master Flick, c. 1960, off the screen and instructed Spot to slap another thirty years and a million daily defeats on that smooth face. Again the flesh vanished and a remarkable likeness of Flick emerged onscreen. In real life he had fewer lines, less puffiness, but Spot had forecast the eyes all too well. "Identify," I typed, leaning far back in my chair. As I stared at the white ceiling, remembering how sweet he had felt inside of me, Spot grated through a few million files. Beeped.

EMIL FLICK, I read across the top of the screen. DEPUTY CHIEF, LEIPZIG TRADE FAIR. CONTINUE?

Escape. I had Spot eat the redhead and asked for a menopausal version of the pigtailed brat. Considering the dearth of information I could offer about her, Spot again came up with a fairly good facsimile of the woman who had told Flick to seduce me. Same thin mouth, same beady eyes: a violinist? I couldn't picture it. She'd play coldly as a reptile. "Identify," I commanded.

Not in the system. I proceeded to the next boyish face in line. Spot identified him as an Austrian diplomat, deceased. The next face was that of a Russian physicist, deceased. I got a British security agent, a Hungarian finance minister. No one in America, no one in West Germany, no professional musicians, and all of them dead. I squinted at the last child in line. Taller than the rest, older and in long pants. His posture was that of a leader but his face was blurred beyond recognition. Water damage. Spot couldn't put him back together again. Bad luck: he looked like the class heavy. I posted his body onscreen and panned slowly from the neck down, searching for distinguishing marks. Nothing irregular except a watch chain with triangular links. He wore the newest, cleanest shoes of the bunch: Dad must have been an Obersomething. If he was alive, he could be the courier who brought the redhead's data to the steeple. If he was dead, then Zwinger's little cadre was down to two diehards, same as the

Queen's. Wouldn't that be precious. I ran Zwinger through the ringer. Spot never saw him before.

I put the computer away and practiced for several hours. Instead of Tchaikovsky, I heard the voice of Professor Wilkins as he described the student who had broken his heart. If Wilkins hadn't been in love, curious and adoring, so insignificant a detail as the name of Moll's music teacher would never have stuck in his brain for so many years. And what about old Vilnius? Would his senile mind have remembered the name Berger had he not hated him for the last half century? I despaired of ever forgetting Flick: both hatred and love scribbled over the heart with permanent ink. Perhaps as the weeks passed and I heard nothing from him, as the desire still flared but the senses received no relief, love would begin to choke on its own breath. It would die slowly and terribly, disbelieving his silence; over the rot would creep a film of contempt then, finally, a smooth black hatred which nothing, not even Flick begging on his knees, would be able to crack. And many years later, if left undisturbed, the shield would lose its density, become porous as old wood. Resignation would grow quietly as moss in the fissures . . . once begun, was the sequence inevitable? Forests decayed, glaciers dissolved in an icy sea: the death of love was no less natural an event. Just slow, horribly slow. Flick, fading, would be with me the rest of my life.

As I was about to leave for London, Duncan finally called from New York. "I found a management," he reported. "And a publicist."

"Great! Who?"

"Bolt and Associates," he said proudly.

"Are you kidding? She's not even in the music business."

"Who cares? She's got big elbows and a big mouth."

"Isn't she expensive?"

"She's giving me special consideration."

"Isn't this rather sudden, Duncan? Two nights ago you were calling her Attila the Hun."

"She got me on 'Good Morning, America' with Luke the Apostle yesterday."

"What did you talk about? Chopin?"

"Luke did most of the talking," Duncan admitted. "He's a real shit. On national television he calls me Ludwig van Romeo, then he wants to take me out for lunch afterwards as if nothing happened."

I sighed. "You realize what she's doing, don't you?"

"She's making me famous. Getting me jobs."

"What happened to all that talk about artistic integrity?"

"What's the matter with you?" he cried. "After a lifetime of struggle I finally get a break! Aren't you happy for me?"

"Duncan, I'm delighted. Really. This happened so fast, that's all."

"I'm still your accompanist," he said. "Won't hold any of this against you. Hey, I've got to get off the phone. Someone from *USA Today* is calling in two minutes. I'm going to edge a little Chopin into this interview."

It would never end up in print: Luke the Apostle delivered more bang per column inch. "Talk to you in a few days. Don't forget to practice."

Just a wild idea, rootless and irritating as pollen, but I wondered if Sydney Bolt was something more than a publicist.

I flew to London for a few passes at the Tchaikovsky Concerto and a round of interviews with pale Englishmen. The rain never abated, nor did the traffic in Burberry raincoats. Bored, I kept to my room. Didn't feel like practicing, too tired to exercise, too edgy to sleep, no way I could drink: a man's tongue between my legs would have been beneficial . . . never mind. The afternoon eventually ended and I played a tight, fast performance at the Barbican. The audience appeared appreciative, the daring young conductor exhilarated. He had managed to keep up with me. I walked directly back to the dressing room, in case Flick happened to be there waiting on a white horse. Instead I got Harry Paradise.

"Sensational, baby!" he cried. "We've got to record that again."

"Twice is enough," I said, accepting his operatic kisses. Despite many maintenance sessions in beauty salons, the tan he had acquired in Morocco was jaundicing. It clashed nicely with his lime green ascot. "How's everything?"

"Busy! Crazy!" Harry stepped grandly to the side as enthusiastic strangers and their ballpoint pens aggregated around us. "Yoo hoo! Andrew! Bryce! Over here!" Harry introduced me to two of Britain's finest journalists, dear friends of his, of course. "Wasn't she something?" Andrew's eyes consumed Flick's ruby pendant upon my breast. Bryce stared stupidly at the mole above my lip. They both shook my hand, enunciating consonants.

"We'll talk later, *chez moi*," Harry confided. "Now I must go home and open the bar. Don't be too late, darling, I'm serving dinner at eleven." The gracious host swept out of the dressing room, affording many lesser mortals a glimpse of his magnificent chinchilla as he herded Bryce and Andrew ginward. I began shaking hands and scrawling my name over proffered programs. After the last trenchcoat had cleared the dressing room, I waited another quarter hour before concluding that if Flick was in London, he had neglected to stop by.

I cabbed to Harry's new flat in Golders Green, whence he had invited dozens of intimates for an Occasion. By the time I arrived, Harry's bar had unhinged tongues and inhibitions; the hubbub reminded me of my brother Roland's parties but here the drunks actually took themselves seriously. Harry stood in a corner of the large room, not so much pouring drinks as passing an upturned bottle over a row of empty glasses. "My God, Leslie!" he cried, swallowing a tiny pickle that was dangling from his lips. "You're alone!" It wasn't leprosy, was it? Harry handed me a dripping glass of Scotch. "Where's the harem? Chance? Luke? Duncan? Curtis? I never get you all to myself like this." He turned to an eavesdropping stranger. "Could be dangerous, haha!"

As Harry's mediocre whiskey blistered my tonsils, I looked

around the room. "Nice place, Harry. Why did you move again?"

"Living space! Expansion!" I nodded. Relocation probably had less to do with square feet than with the round palms of his newest ex-wife, fifth or sixth, I didn't remember and never asked. After the third, even Harry got hazy. "Like it? I spent a bloody fortune fixing it up." He took my elbow. "I'll give you a tour." Naturally everyone within earshot clamored to join us. The host could not refuse.

A long procession shuffled to his boudoir, done entirely in red velvet and zebra skins. The bed would sleep four walruses comfortably. "I wanted something dramatic here," Harry explained, igniting the fake logs in his plastic fireplace. "A cross between Lucrezia Borgia and the snows of Kilimanjaro."

"How erotic, Harry," breathed a tall woman in a wig made entirely of red feathers.

We shuffled through a few guest bedrooms loaded with antiques from Harry's mother, who had a predilection for bears, antlers, and obelisks. "Worth a fortune," Harry told us. "I'll never sell them, of course." Evidently none of his ex-wives had wanted any.

One of Harry's intimates was studying the carvings in a dark armoire. "I say, this is quite gory!"

"That's Hansel and Gretel," Harry replied. "You've obviously never read the Grimm brothers in the original version."

"These were in your room when you were growing up?" the woman in feathers asked. "Didn't they give you nightmares, Harry dear?"

"On the contrary." Harry took her arm. "They stimulated my imagination."

She returned his lubricious leer. I didn't like her at all; she reminded me of Hugo's gaudy ex-wife Nina. "Where did your mother get these fantastic objects, Harry?" she asked. "Certainly not here in England."

"Ask Sotheby's, not me! They come on hand and knee every six months!" Abruptly retreating, Harry led everyone to a heavy door at the end of the hallway. "This is my new listening room."

A colorful galaxy of LP and CD jackets covered the pale walls. "I produced all of these recordings," Harry announced. "At last count, nine hundred sixty-eight. Every artist you might imagine is represented here. Every label. Every act from panpipe to grand opera." He pooh-poohed the ensuing chorus of admiration. "It's nothing! Don't forget, I've been around for almost as long as the Queen Mother, ha ha!"

Photographs, Grammy awards, framed letters from the famous festooned every available inch of space. In the middle of the room was a billowy couch surrounded by four telephones, piles of marked scores, hundreds of DAT's and cassettes containing raw material from recording sessions. Along the far wall I saw an extravagant array of audiophile equipment and scads more CD's, compliments of people wishing to curry the great producer's favor. "Well, what do you think?" Harry asked me.

"Great." The whole mess reminded me of the worst elements of Moll's steeple and Flick's office at the trade fair. I wandered over to Harry's gigantic desk. He had been writing a vitriolic letter to American Express contesting charges from Kreutzer Music Repair. On top of a FedEx package lay a fax from Godo demanding when the Mozart concertos would be finished.

"You haven't finished the Mozart yet?" I asked. "I don't believe it. Godo's going to skin you alive."

"If Godo wants to work in America, Godo's got to work on American production schedules," Harry retorted. "I'm sending this all to Boston. Chance is going to finish it for me. Like he did with the Beethoven."

"Oh? When did he volunteer for that job?"

"He hasn't yet. But he will. Perhaps you would consider pitching in again. I understand your stay in Boston wasn't exactly unpleasant last time." Harry's gold medallions glinted in my face as he turned to the crowd. "I just got a test pressing of *Also Sprach Zarathustra*. Would anyone be interested in hearing it?''

While he dithered with his equipment, I strolled by the CD's lining Harry's listening room. One pass around the four walls and my social obligations would be fulfilled. Then I'd leave. The first, low notes were rumbling from Harry's speakers when I spotted a square of bright magenta at knee level. Stop: I had seen that CD before. In Flick's apartment.

I bent down, coughing slightly as the cracked ribs protested. Sure enough, Leon Jurkowsky's CD hung in front of me. Obviously Harry was not very impressed with the project, or he would have hung it at eye level. As trumpets blared, I lifted the CD off the wall and read the back cover.

THE MUSIC OF LEON JURKOWSKY
© Vuota Corda Inc., Tarrytown, NY
Recorded 19–20 June, 1989, at The American
    Academy of Arts and Letters, New York City
Producer: Harry Paradise
Engineering: Emory Morse
Digital Editing and Mastering: Naja Ltd., London

Typical fly-by-night operation. Poor Leon had probably evaporated his life savings on the project. Aside from his family members, maybe fifty people had bought copies. Didn't matter. He was immortal now. I replaced him in his lowly post and glanced along the nether tier of Harry's achievements. Despite his titanic reputation, Harry did a lot of work with tiny labels and unknown artists: even a beggar's money was green and Harry believed that it paid to know everyone on the off chance that one bum in ten thousand might squirm through to the big time. Also, Harry loved to work with people who thought that his name added cachet to a project. Those who engaged him for the first time generally had no idea how tenuous was the link between fame and competence. I continued warily along the walls, reviewing the efforts of musicians and highly untalented graphic artists. The krumhorn disc hung knee-high just inside the doorway.

I had seen this one too, months ago, in Moll's steeple. Again I took the specimen off the wall and read the backside, searching for outstanding coincidence. Nix: Harry had recorded this for a small German company that specialized in antique instruments. Other than his name and those of the musicians, there were no credits at all.

"Leslie! How are you, luv?"

Emory Morse, Harry's longtime recording engineer, embraced me. I hadn't seen him since his run-in with a cane in the Kempinski Hotel. Minus his pink cheeks and beer belly, he looked awful. "You look great, Emory. Feeling better?"

"I'm almost out of the woods, the doctors tell me. It's been a long winter."

"That was some vicious virus."

"They think I must have caught it when Harry and I were in Kenya. A mutant strain of diphtheria. How that bastard escaped I'll never know."

"Nothing sticks to Harry," I said. "Not even streptococci."

Emory smiled dispiritedly. "Anyway, I'm much better now. Doing a bit of editing in the afternoon. Getting my strength back. Maybe I can come to Leipzig with you and Harry next month. What did he say you were doing? The Sibelius Concerto?"

"That's right." My turn to smile without enthusiasm: I had assumed Chance would be recording it.

Emory took my arm. His fingers were unusually hot. "Say, I hear you've got a new boyfriend. A rock star? That's sensational, Les."

"Where'd you hear that?"

"It's all over the papers." He leaned into my ear. "Is he any good in bed?"

I hung the krumhorn CD back on the wall. "It's all lies. Publicity."

"That's my girl, deny everything." He winked. "Maybe you'll tell me when we get to Leipzig. We'll have more time then."

Behind us, Harry suddenly replaced *Zarathustra* with *The Four Seasons*, arranged for marimba. "My latest hit," we heard him announce loudly.

I pointed to the krumhorn CD. "Did you record this with Harry?"

Emory peered at it. "Can't say I did, luv."

"How about the music of Leon Jurkowsky?"

"Who?" I showed him the disc. "Oh. That was an alimony job. Harry has to do about five of those a month. See all these CD's? Everything from the waist down is an alimony job."

"Vuota Corda," I mused aloud, taking Jurkowsky's CD from the wall. "Strange name for a record label."

"Quite," Emory agreed, saying no more.

I turned the CD over. "Who would start a record company in Tarrytown, New York? You know what happened in Tarrytown? Ichabod Crane ran into the headless horseman." Emory nodded uncertainly. "Never mind. That's just a bit of American history." I ran my finger along the list of credits. "And what's this? Naja Ltd.?"

Emory peered at the name and shrugged. "I guess they're the people who mastered old Leon, eh? Probably a bunch of Indians, judging by the name."

An ice cube hit Emory in the shoulder. "Are you two shits talking about me behind my back again?"

"Sharp ears, Harry," I said, replacing the CD. "Very impressive."

"So how was Oslo?" Emory called.

Harry was too busy with the lady in red feathers to respond. "He was in Oslo?" I asked Emory.

"Over New Year's. I think it was another alimony job."

Harry had told me Toulouse and he had told Chance Nice. I chuckled, recognizing the signs: he was probably courting again.

Harry and his feathered friend sauntered over. "What are you doing out of bed, Emory?" Harry demanded.

"I'm better now. You did invite me here." Emory looked around. "What's the occasion, anyway?"

"Does there have to be an occasion? Can't a fellow round up his friends and have a good time?"

"I don't recognize anyone."

"You've been out of commission for months, chappie. I've met a lot of important people in the meantime."

At each other's throats, just like the good old days. I kissed Harry's professionally tucked cheek as the lady in red feathers eyeballed my jewelry. "Thanks for inviting me."

"Leaving so soon?" Harry accompanied me to the door. "When will I be seeing you again? Leipzig, I guess."

"It's sooner than you think. By the way, how were your sessions in Toulouse?"

Harry's gin-saturated breath flew humidly over my face. "Excellent."

Congratulations from Godo and Bolt awaited me in Berlin: the Beethoven sonatas had edged onto the Billboard charts. "This is just the beginning," Bolt had scrawled ominously across the top of her fax, adding that a side-by-side display of Beethoven and Luke the Apostle would be distributed to all major record shops within the week. Godo's fax was less effusive. He wanted to capitalize on this surge of interest and release the Mozart concertos at once. I smiled: not if Harry Paradise had anything to do with it. He'd need a week just to find the session tapes in that mess of his. If he thought I would be going to Boston to bail him out again, he was in for a nasty surprise.

Maxine called, wanting to go shopping for new work clothes so I met her downtown. Nice new hat but she looked a little cocoa around the eyes, obviously worried sick about me. We began at a tiny boutique on the Ku'damm where dresses struck an exquisite balance between opulence and nudity. Renata, the owner, was delighted to see us: not all of her customers backed up their oohs and aahs with credit cards.

"I'm playing the Sibelius Concerto in Leipzig next month," I told her.

"Sibelius." Renata shut her eyes. "Purple and black. Brooding and fantastic as the sky before a storm." She went to her back room.

The Queen held an orange gown against her body and studied the palette in a long mirror. "When are you going back to Leipzig?" she asked.

"Four weeks."

She eyed the embroidery on an ice-blue dress. "Has Flick called?"

"No."

"Written?"

"No."

"Have you called him?"

"No."

"Written?"

"Of course not."

The Queen sighed. "Brilliant."

Renata beckoned me to the dressing room, where I tried on a purple-and-black number. Beneath the cascading silk, the dress was constructed ruthlessly as a bathysphere. I stepped into the showroom, where Maxine was sitting in a chair usually occupied by lecherous old bankers. She watched my reflection in the triple mirrors. "Not bad," she said finally.

In appreciation of her enthusiastic support I bought her the orange dress. Suppurating compliments, Renata showed us out, managing to smile brightly at us between scowls at the East German window shoppers agog at the price tags on her mannequins. "You will play beautifully, I'm sure," she called, slamming the door before any of them tried to slip inside.

Maxine and I stopped at a dim Hungarian café. The pastries were stale and the coffee weak, but no one bothered us there.

"So you found Zwinger," Maxine said, sloughing off her coat. "Whoever that is."

She had already read my report on the Hochstein Music School but I gave her an oral version anyway, starting with poor, devoted Professor Wilkins in Baltimore and ending with the class pictures in East Berlin.

"Unfortunately, Zwinger's disappeared," Maxine said when I had finished. "No one can identify him."

"Did you find Professor Berger?" I asked.

"Berger sang at the Deutsche Oper for years. Now he's a vocal coach. Spends all his time trying to screw sopranos. I think that Moll's studying with him was purely coincidental." She stirred her coffee. "Flick or the woman probably recruited him."

"Not Zwinger?"

"If Zwinger's alive, he's almost ninety years old. Of the original seven children, only the woman and Flick are left. I would think one of them's in charge now."

"What about the boy in the picture whose face is blurred?"

"Good luck finding him." The Queen whisked a few crumbs away. "You were correct, by the way. Moll's broken the code. He did instruct the satellite to fire on the barn. Then he erased his commands. It's all on the new tape you gave me."

So much for congratulations. I frowned. "Moll couldn't have broken that code without a hell of a lot of samples for the Clove to play with."

"Correct. Any idea where he got them?"

I looked earnestly across the table. "The Sears catalog?"

Maxine's jaws clenched; jokes affected her like bee stings. "Unless the redhead makes her own deliveries, I'd say you've got another player out there," she said.

"That's all I need!" Gad, this coffee was bad. I pushed it away and stared at pedestrian traffic instead. So many people . . . *pfuii*. I had about as much chance of finding the redhead as I did of detecting a new planet with the naked eye. "Moll must be a pretty good shot by now," I said after a while.

"To what end? I've been monitoring Russian ground stations. They don't suspect a thing."

"Maybe we should tell them."

"I'm sure you can come up with something more clever than that."

"Give me a few ideas."

"You could kidnap Moll," the Queen said. "That would put a damper on things."

"Come on! We're not the KGB!"

"You could find the redhead. I'd enjoy meeting her. We seem to have a common thorn in our sides."

"Find her yourself. I'm not your fucking dating service." Whoa, Smith: this was a discussion between two seasoned professionals. "How am I going to find her? All I have is a picture of a kid with pigtails and a voice on a tape. That's nothing."

"You could persuade Flick to tell you what this is all about."

"We've been through this already, haven't we, Maxine? He wouldn't tell me if I were the last woman on earth."

"So drug him."

"Why don't we just blow up the steeple and call it a day?"

"You'll never find her, then. She's got the answers to most of your questions. Not Flick." Maxine finished her cake. "There's a laser exhibition at the trade fair scheduled for March fifteenth. That's three weeks away. It makes me a little nervous."

"You nervous? The world must be coming to an end."

Exasperated, the Queen pushed her chair from the table. "We're close, Smith. Closer than you think. Don't get sidetracked now."

"I want this over with," I said. "One way or the other."

"Then find the redhead." Maxine paid for the coffee.

13

*I*nstead of going after the redhead, I spent a week in Austria with an Italian conductor who couldn't count very well. Evidently the poor man was agitated by recent political events: night after night, as he dined at the snootiest restaurants and swallowed the rarest wines, he bemoaned the collapse of Communism. Finally I told him to move to California if he felt so terrible. He was a shoo-in for tenure at Berkeley.

It snowed beautifully in Vienna, particularly at the airport. I had to take the train back to Berlin. As it crept through Prague, Dresden, then that final Deutsche Demokratik wasteland, I stared numbly out the window, narcotized by the stuffy cabin and the unmitigated gray outside. I hated February. It was a dank, shrouded corpse of a month, a travesty of faith. I had become a widow on an afternoon just like this, as mist drowned the streetlights and Berlin submerged into night. Inside, shivering humans threw logs on their fires, rooms glowed, blood thawed and thickened in rebellion . . . eight years already. I hardly remembered my husband any more. When I looked at his picture, read his name now, it didn't connect: we had been apart so much longer than we had ever been together. Was the blunting of memory really part of the healing process? Or was it a rehearsal with death? Senility was probably my last hope. As I lost my grip on reality, maybe Hugo would come back to me, fresh and intense as he had once been. I would find that mysterious serenity again. It haunted me; I wanted it back. For years I had pursued it through great music, through the Queen's labyrinths. It had not reappeared until the night Flick spoke to me in a medieval café. That was before I had heard a stranger's voice tell him to seduce me, of course. How I wished I had never wired that seat at the Concertgebouw! My dreams would still be warm, sweet, full of Flick, uncorrupted by an edgy voice saying oh so confidently, *Events will take care of themselves*. Drove me mad.

The train reached Berlin around dinnertime. I politely swallowed Curtis's potato dumplings, then went upstairs to my bedroom. For a long time I stared at the picture of Professor Zwinger and his seven charges, trying to distill logic from the murky emotions those young faces aroused. Interesting idea, taking a band of children like that, scattering them around Europe at the close of the war. They had grown up into diplomats, physicists, directors of trade fairs . . . where was that girl in pigtails now? How about that boy on the end, the one identified only by a watch chain? Did they still play their violins? Or, like Flick, isolated and uninspired, had they put them away years ago?

I went to the window. Outside, the moon lit my garden, creating a feeble, inchoate mate for itself in the snow. So we were all violinists. How fitting, how perverse. Think, Smith: find her. I shut my eyes, tumbling into an abyss between pain and peace, realizing that I would have to go back to the violin that a teacher had given his young pupil many years ago. A while later I went downstairs and told Curtis that I needed to take a drive, clear the brain, no thanks, didn't need company. He knew where I was going.

Since my last visit, Leipzig had suffered a plague of potholes. Sooty snow patched the curbs. I got to Flick's apartment shortly after midnight. He was gone, of course, abetting the local arsonist. I waited patiently on his stoop, inhaling the pestilential air, listening to drops of water fall into the mud beneath the rotted eaves. An hour passed; across the street, an upstairs window suddenly went black.

As the Trabant finally rattled toward me, I felt my body warm quietly to life. From my black nook I watched him park and furtively close the driver's door. He looked up and down the street, at cars and windows, in trees, before moving: finding my transmitter in his car must have shaken him up. I was glad that he was afraid. When he saw me sitting on his cold stones the Burberry raincoat abruptly stopped. He put a hand into his pocket before continuing cautiously, lethargically, as if he never wanted to reach me. I wondered if Flick was carrying his gun now that he knew someone had tagged his car. His feet dragged to a halt inches from my boots: paranoia and I waited for him to pull the trigger. As the seconds slid by, I gradually saw that he was stupefied not with suspicion or hatred, certainly not joy, but with a profound fatigue. "Surprise," I whispered. He didn't move. "How are you, darling?"

Why didn't he just shoot and put me out of my misery? Flick bent stiffly over, brought me to my feet. From his pocket he pulled out only his keys. We went inside, upstairs to his cold apartment. He hung up our coats. "How long have you been waiting." His voice was low, gritty with exhaustion. I had thought I'd never hear it again.

"Not long." His eyes watched mine inspect his face. "You've been working too hard," I said, running my fingers over his chalky cheek, along his jaw: the violin callus had completely disappeared. "And not practicing."

As Flick kissed the side of my head, the peace returned. "I've missed you," he said.

I brought him to the couch in his living room and went to the kitchen to make tea. When I returned, he was lying on his back, asleep, still as death. I knelt at his side, lay my head on his arm. If I had had a tail, it would have been wagging. He drifted awake, nodded off again. I looked around the room. Frayed but touchingly neat: nothing had changed. I went to the piano, opened his violin case, and sat

in the rocking chair by the lamp with the tasseled shade. Held
Flick's violin under the light, studying the graceful curves,
the exquisite grain of the wood. I peered into the sound holes
to read the old German script that indicated its maker.

W. A. Simler 1848
Kassel

"What are you doing?" Flick whispered.

How long had his eyes been open? I put the violin under
my chin and tuned, watching him. Very softly, I played the
Bach partita that he had been listening to in a stygian field as
fire came from the sky. When I had finished, he said nothing.
Didn't blink, didn't swallow. Then his eyes flared and I was
certain he knew who I was. I had left him so many clues,
after all. It wasn't that I had surrendered our long game of
cat-and-mouse. I just didn't want to be alone any more.

"Come here," Flick said. I sat on the floor in front of the
couch. He stroked my hair as the radiators hissed. The gesture
was paternal, melancholy. "Why did you come tonight?"

"I haven't seen you in so long." My hand edged up his
chest. "I get lost."

His warm finger brushed my lips, the mole above it.
"Where have you been?"

"New York. Switzerland. Austria. Around."

"How was it?"

"They didn't throw any tomatoes." I rested my head on
his lap. "I'm so tired of it."

Now his fingers slowly twined my hair, traced the gulleys
in my ears. "You mustn't give that up," Flick said.

"Why not? I'm nothing but an entertainer."

"Shhh. You're an artist."

The night we met in Auerbachs Keller, Flick had said he
wanted to see me again because I was an artist. "What does
that mean?"

There was no reply for so long that I thought he had drifted back to sleep. Then he said, "It means you're different. You have an obligation to keep playing so that the rest of us can occasionally . . . rise above the mud."

I kissed his stomach, moving toward the warm, pulsing bundle that alone lifted me out of the mud. Flick trembled before the artist's art; Frost trembled before a cylinder of flesh. Who was the nobler savage here?

"Very romantic ideas," I said after a while. "Very German."

Flick slowly sat up and drew me onto the sofa beside him. His hands drifted over my back, moving gradually around to my stomach. Then he lifted my sweater, just as Curtis had that night in the kitchen. Flick stared at the yellowy bruise on my ribs with the same sort of look that came over people's faces as they stood at Bach's grave. "What happened," he whispered.

"I slipped on the ice."

Flick smiled tiredly. Out in the street, a car door slammed. He let the sweater drop. "You should go."

At the door I nearly fell to his feet, begging him to let me wake up beside him just once in my miserable life. I wanted his children. I wanted him to come home to me at night. I wanted to be the payback for his first fifty years. He held my coat, slipped the sleeves over my arms, and I didn't even sigh. Condemned again to solitude: it was the price of virtuosity, on the stage, in the field. At the landing, I looked up. Flick stood at the head of his stairs. Before I got into my car, I glanced toward his window; he was there, too. My M6 purred to life and I drove quickly back to Berlin. In the morning, after he considered the ramifications, I knew he would be coming after me.

For once, Curtis was not in the kitchen waiting for me, so I went straight to Hugo's study. I was nosing along the bookcases when he suddenly appeared in the doorway. "What are you doing up there again? Do you know what time it is?"

I looked down from the ladder. "There was a book on German instruments here once. I need to look something up right away."

"Which instrument?"

"Violin. Violin makers. W. A. Simler."

"Hold on." He pushed the ladder to the corner. "This is the string section."

I checked it out. "What the hell happened to all of Hugo's books? Damn it, every time I look for something, it's gone."

"What's the title."

"*German Instrument Masters* or *Makers* or something. It's up here, I know it. Hugo read it all the time. It's got a green leather cover."

"Half the library has a green leather cover. Do NOT lean over the ladder like that!"

I stomped down to the floor. "You find it then."

Curtis's perfect rear end, curved and taut as a basketball, ascended the ladder. Within a few moments he located the book. "Get to bed now," he said, going to the door. "Duncan's coming at nine."

I opened the frayed page to *S*. Sanders, Seckersohn, Simler: one lousy paragraph separated me from another dead end.

> SIMLER. Violin makers of Kassel. The earliest were by Wolfgang Amadeus (1780–1848); thereafter by his son Johannes (1821–1858); grandson Franz (1850–1918); great-grandson Karl Amadeus (b. 1882). The Simler violin is known for its solid workmanship and purity of tone. The family has kept precise construction records which have furnished musicologists and historians with valuable information concerning the craft of violin making in earlier times.

So much for Simler. I went to my room and shut out the light. Now that I had seen Flick again, the longing was pungent and physical. The cycle had started all over again: night by long night, unrelieved hope would fade into a wide, flat thirst that made a desert of my soul. He was a mirage. I should never have gone back to his apartment, back to the peace.

The phone rang. I pounced on it, certain that only one voice could be at the other end.

"Les?" said Harry Paradise. "Why isn't your answering machine on?"

I fell back on my pillow. "God damn you, this is my private line! It's four o'clock in the morning."

"Sorry, sorry! You weren't asleep anyway, were you." Harry didn't wait for a reply. "I've been tossing and turning all night. The stress is killing me, baby. I can feel a colitis attack coming on." He forced himself to cough. "Listen, you've got to help. I'm in a jam."

"Again? Didn't I just get you out of a jam?"

"Yes! Yes! That's why I'm calling! I know you're going to New York this week. You're playing with Zadinsky at Lincoln Center."

"I'm not going to Boston again," I said. "If you didn't finish the Mozart by now, that's your problem."

"Oh Jesus, don't say that! I have enough problems to kill ten ordinary men!" Harry coughed more sincerely. "Chance said he had the time."

"Fine! He doesn't need me up there distracting him."

Harry became desperate. "You don't understand! He said he'd only do it if you helped."

"Looks like you'd better make another deal, Harry. Why couldn't you finish the editing? We recorded the Mozart two months ago. You knew Godo was dying to get it done."

"I've had other things on my mind."

"Like what? Ladies with red feather hats?"

"Have you been spying on me, you bitch? You're as bad as my mother!" Remembering the original purpose of his call, Harry quickly changed the topic. "Tell me you'll do the editing, Les. I won't ever let this happen again."

"I don't have the time. Really."

"But Chance is mad about you. And so filthy rich."

"And I'm not? Good night, Harry." I hung up before he could remind me of everything he'd done for me. Then I was back in the dark hunting, maybe fleeing, a phantom named Flick.

Curtis was not pleased to find me curled up in Hugo's library in the morning. I had wandered there around sunup because Flick was everywhere and nowhere in my bedroom; I had hoped that a change of locale, to another ghost's habitat, might buy me a few hours' respite. Curtis's frown increased when he saw that I had been listening to reissues of Hugo's Wagner recordings. "Duncan's here," he said, switching off the CD player. "I'll give him some breakfast."

I rolled stiffly to my feet. "I'll be there in ten minutes."

Duncan was sitting at the table excising raisins from his toast as I came into the kitchen. "Sorry, I had a long night," I said.

"Practicing Beethoven, I'm sure." Duncan sipped from his mug. "Gad, I hate black coffee!"

"There's the milk," Curtis said.

"No milk! Can't you see I've been on a diet?" Duncan snapped. "Sydney wants me to lose twenty pounds before my recital."

I bit into one of Curtis's corn muffins. "I know a good liposuction man in D.C. My father tells me all the senators' wives use him."

Duncan didn't ask for his number. "Let's get going," he muttered, standing up. "I've got a ton of things to do before we leave tonight."

We had a zesty, combative rehearsal. Duncan was playing very strangely indeed, at exaggerated speeds and dynamic ranges. He was throwing his hands into the air and swooning over the keyboard. When I asked why he was suddenly banging out a passage which for years we had played softly, he whined that I was smothering his creativity. Finally I put the violin down. "What's going on, Duncan?"

"I'm trying to balance our act," he said. "Visually speaking. Sydney's inviting lots of people who don't know anything about music. She doesn't want me to just sit there while you strut around with a Stradivarius."

"I see. So what does she want you to wear? I wouldn't think of clashing with your outfit."

We caricatured Beethoven for another hour, until my accompanist suddenly recalled an engagement with his hairdresser and dashed into the fog.

Curtis was at his desk frowning at a few contracts. "Have a nice rehearsal?" he asked.

"You heard it, didn't you? Doesn't he see that Bolt's only using him to make a few points with Godo?"

"Manipulation to you, destiny to Duncan." Curtis returned to his word processor. "We believe what we want to believe."

I was in no mood for sermons so I went to practice. Wars might erupt, earthquakes might split the continent in half, but Frost could never get away for one lousy day without sawing her damn fiddle. Chance called later in the afternoon, wondering if I might feel more comfortable at his New York apartment rather than a hotel. I came within a hair of saying yes before realizing that this was not a good time to wander into that particular quagmire. Would he be at the concert? Perhaps, if he got some work out of the way. I didn't ask if it was Harry's editing crisis. Later, via courier, I received the keys to Chance's penthouse. *Think about it*, the note said.

"More keys for your collection?" Curtis asked. "Let me know if I should cancel your hotel reservation."

"Very funny."

He handed me an itinerary. "This is an easy trip. You only have to show up in Lincoln Center on Thursday night and Chance's studio in Boston on Friday afternoon."

"What?! I told Harry I wasn't doing his editing this time."

"Chance has been doing the editing by himself. Godo's in Boston on Friday and wants to pick up the master tape. Therefore you have to approve it before it goes out the door."

"Can't Chance just send me a DAT for approval?"

"No. He's not done yet. This job's going to go down to the wire."

I didn't have time for any more side trips to Boston. "Why me? Where does Harry figure into all this?"

"He's going to be there, too. Godo told him his presence was required. Look, you'll be out of there on the seven o'clock flight. Appearances are important."

Yeah, yeah. My whole damn life was an appearance.

I flew to New York and caught up with Duncan at Lincoln Center. His hair was now a rich, gluey black: Bolt thought his previous coiffure lacked drama. He was late for our dress rehearsal because Luke the Apostle had been late for a joint interview they had just taped for cable television.

I had never heard him play so badly. "Do you realize we have a concert tonight?" I asked.

"I haven't had a chance to practice," Duncan muttered. "Shopping and interviews took all my time."

"And of course you had jet lag." I put the violin away. "We've got the hall for another two hours. I suggest you use the time to practice." At the stage door I stopped. "By the way, I'm wearing red. Hope she hasn't got you wearing a hot pink caftan or something."

Duncan was preoccupied with his recidivous fingers. I went to my hotel room and tried to sleep but my feet were cold. My head hurt: the thought of walking onstage four hours later and playing the violin in front of two thousand people horrified me. I didn't want to be seen. Didn't want to dress up, force the brain into overdrive, wrestle with the impossible, and again come up imperfect. No, tonight I wanted to be an ordinary mortal. Eat Chinese, get drunk, watch TV, Christ how would I ever survive the next few hours? I lay across the bed, wondering where all the men were when I needed them.

The phone rang. "Did I wake you," said Chance.

"I'm watching the soaps."

"But you're in bed. I can tell from the tone of your voice."

"Where are you, in Boston? Editing your little fingers off?"

"I'm in the lobby, sweetheart. I can't tell you how disappointed I was not to find you at my apartment. May I come up? I brought lunch."

"It's three o'clock."

"All right, I brought tea."

"I was about to take a nap. What are you doing here, anyway? Don't you have a gigantic editing project to finish?"

"Cut the bullshit," said Chance. "What's your room number."

"Twelve twenty."

When I opened the door, several snide comments came to mind. No point in using any of them; he knew why I had let him in.

"Hello, Frosty," said Chance, placing a brown bag on the table. "Thought you might be needing a little company."

I got back under the covers. "Where'd you get that idea?"

"I know all about preperformance dementia." He threw his cashmere coat over a chair and began excavating little white cartons from the bag. "Hungry?"

"No."

"Tired?"

"No."

"Would you like to take a walk, then?"

"It's too cold."

"How about a movie? There's a theater around the corner."

"Forget it."

"Hmm, we're in a great mood today. What's the matter?"

I told him that the concert was going to be a disaster. Duncan hadn't practiced. Bolt was probably going to dress him up like Liberace and paper the house with screaming girls.

"Is Luke going to be joining in?" Chance asked.

"That's all I need!"

"Sounds like the most exciting recital of the season. If I were you, I'd play it for all it's worth."

"What do you think this is, vaudeville?"

"You're on a stage, aren't you? You're getting paid, aren't you? People are buying tickets, right? That's entertainment."

"So I'm an entertainer?" I pouted. "Other people think I'm an artist."

Chance bit into a spring roll. "There's something I don't understand. You're a powerful woman. Why didn't you stop all this nonsense months ago?"

What was I supposed to tell him? The Queen thought my cover needed a little tweaking? "I had no idea it would get out of hand like this," I whimpered. "Particularly with Duncan."

Chance came to the bed and began kneading the knots in my neck. "Look on the bright side. It's going to sell a lot of CD's."

Terrific. More money. "Would you do me a favor," I said after a while.

"That's what I'm here for, honey."

"Take a nap with me." It sounded so infantile. "I haven't been sleeping very well lately."

Chance stripped to his underwear. Maybe he slept better knowing those expensive pants wouldn't get wrinkled. He slid under the covers, snuggled: his body heat alone was relaxing as three martinis. "So what's this crap about everyone going to Boston tomorrow," I said.

"Where's your sense of gratitude, Frosty? I've been working on your project sixteen hours a day for the past week. Godo's going to be in town negotiating a contract with the symphony and I thought it was about time he saw my place. He agreed. I didn't think I'd be finished as soon as I was." Chance kissed my shoulder. "Would you rather I schlepped all the tapes down to some ratty studio in New York so the three of you could listen here?"

I didn't answer.

"Should I have stayed home and pretended I was still finishing up?"

"All right, all right, you win! We'll all go to Boston!"

He lazily untied the knot on my bathrobe. "Why can't you sleep," he whispered.

I smelled limes and warm beaches. "General malaise."

Minutes passed and only his fingers moved. "When was the last time you took a vacation," Chance said.

"I don't remember."

He moved a hand over my abdomen, hardly pressing at all. "How's your bruise?"

"All better."

His fingertips, gentle as morphine, were beginning to nudge me toward a fork in the road I had been avoiding for months. "When was the last time someone made love to you," he said softly.

A thundercloud erupted over a distant ravine. Made love? No man had made love to me in my entire life. They had all fought me and some had won. "I don't remember."

Chance's fingers inched into new territory: despite my acquiescence, he sensed he was cornering a wounded animal. He brought his mouth an inch from mine. I felt his pulse, inhaled his breath, shut my eyes: it wasn't Flick. "You don't remember?" he whispered. "May I refresh your memory?"

I would prefer that he erase my memory. I slowly opened my eyes. The face above mine wasn't that of a lecherous brute. In fact, it was intelligent and rather motherly. Did I really love someone else? Where the hell was he then? When had Flick ever picked up the phone and asked how I was sleeping? Memory flashed to a bridge in Leipzig, a snowy evening when this second slow fuse had quietly ignited. I had been fighting Chance for so long, in favor of what? Nothing at all.

"I'm sorry," I said, rolling away. "This isn't going to work."

His hand crept back to my stomach. "Would you like me to leave?"

God, no. Now I wanted to talk. "Where'd you get all this experience with preperformance dementia? From your first wife—the actress?" I cherished the shock on his face. "Luke told me about her."

The hand on my belly stilled. "She didn't get nervous about anything."

"Your second wife then? Maybe she had the shakes before your dinner parties for two hundred."

"Good old Luke. What else has he been telling you about me?"

"He likes your guitars. So you've been married twice already? *Tsk tsk!* What happened?"

"I was not a very good husband."

He didn't have to explain ambition to me. "How long have you been a bachelor?"

"Five blessed years."

"Don't give me that. You'll get married again."

"I probably will." He turned to look at me. "I want children."

Strange; the statement filled me with lust. "Really?"

"Don't you? You'd make a great mother."

"Dream on."

"What about your obligations to the gene pool?"

"I have other obligations," I said.

"You could hire a nanny. Still play two hundred concerts a year. When they got older, you could take them around the world with you."

The Queen would just love that. "Got it all figured out, eh?"

Chance shut out the light, took the phone off the hook. "Certain things, yes. Other things, not at all. Roll over, I'll give you a massage. Your shoulders are tight." He straddled me. "Don't think about anything."

I shut my eyes, floated away, and was hovering just above sleep, definitely not thinking, when his fingers began to kindle a low-grade flame far back in a deserted cave. If he noticed, he didn't let on; he didn't let up, either. As the afternoon slowly faded, the impossible became improbable became inevitable, all because he had found me isolated in a remote woods, far from home on a winter afternoon . . . was it so terrible to love two men, one for Frost, one for Smith? Each had her necessities. Chance never stopped kissing me and I eventually melted at the bottom of a deep, warm stream.

Chance woke me an hour before the concert. "Show time, Frosty."

I stretched. "Cancel it."

"And disappoint your fans? Never." He aimed me at the shower. When I came out of the bathroom, he was trying to unlock my suitcase.

"What do you think you're doing?" I said.

"Packing your things. We're not coming back here tonight. We're going someplace a little more homey. Less pretentious." He went to the closet. "May I ask which of these you're wearing?"

"The red one."

"Fine choice." He watched me dress and pack. We cabbed across town. It was a clear, frigid night, great for ice skating, bad for sleeping on park benches. Two limousines and one pink hearse were parked outside the artists' entrance at Lincoln Center. "This is not a good sign," I said.

"Remember what I told you," Chance said, pulling me out of the cab. "All in a day's work." He escorted me past an inquisitive crowd hoping to see the Apostle or the accompanist, certainly not the violin player. In my dressing room we found Duncan, Bolt, Luke, and Godo all shouting at each other.

"Leave! All of you! I have a performance to—" Duncan stopped short. "Where have you been? I've been calling all afternoon!"

It was difficult not to stare at the iridescent beads covering his white tuxedo; paint on a moustache and Duncan could have stood in for Wayne Newton. "Practicing," I said, opening the violin case.

"Hey, motherfucker!" cried Luke, embosoming Chance. Bolt had dressed her other artiste in a Mylar cowboy outfit. Mirror sunglasses camouflaged his eyes, which probably weren't focusing too well: ten feet away I could smell the booze on his breath. "Howya doin', buddy? Haven't seen you in an age!"

Bolt's eyes devoured Chance's rear end. "Do I know you from somewhere," she asked, extending her red fingernails. "I'm Sydney Bolt, the publicist."

Duncan charged into the bathroom. "Everyone out of here! Now!"

No one moved. Godo cleared his throat. "So sorry to disturb you, Miss Frost. I insisted Miss Bolt to tell you her plans before we begin concert. Therefore no surprises like last time."

I began tuning the violin. "Now what."

"I want the maximum mileage out of tonight without disturbing our musical integrity," Bolt explained. "Something that will benefit you, Luke, Duncan, and Kakadu Classics."

"You're relocating to Shanghai? That's terrific."

Godo's face fell. "Someone else has hired you?" he asked Bolt. "You break your contract?"

"Of course not! Leslie was just trying to make a joke!" Bolt had to talk a little louder now that I was playing arpeggios. "Luke the Apostle is turning pages for Duncan tonight."

I put the violin down. "Can you read music?" I asked him.

"Sure! Well, sort of."

"Does Duncan know about this?"

"Certainly," Bolt assured me. "They've been rehearsing."

"I turn the page when Duncan nods his head," Luke said proudly.

"What about repeats?" I said. "When you have to turn the music backward instead of forward."

Luke was appalled. "No one told me about this," he muttered. "How many repeats are there?"

"Oh, fifteen or twenty."

Duncan staggered out of the bathroom and fell onto the couch. "Aren't you people gone yet? Get out! I must have quiet!"

"What about these repeat deals," said Luke.

Bolt pulled him into the hall. "This is not a good idea," I told Godo when we were alone.

"But we are number three on the Billboard chart. I have thirty-thousand-piece reorder. Thirty thousand of Beethoven!" He bobbed apologetically toward the door.

Chance hugged me. Under the pants puffed another erection. "I'll try to talk a little sense into Sydney during intermission."

"Make sure that's all you talk into her."

"Must I be subjected to everyone's fucking pillow talk?" Duncan snapped from the couch. He glared at me. "I thought you liked older men."

Chance kissed my cheek. "Have fun." He left.

I changed into the red dress. "Zip this for me, Duncan?"

"Two minutes," called the stagehand.

"I'm so dizzy," Duncan moaned. "This outfit cuts off my circulation."

"Maybe the chemicals from the hair coloring seeped into your brain."

It didn't register. "We haven't rehearsed nearly enough. I can't go through with this. Oh God, why didn't I go to dental school?"

I towed him out of the dressing room. Duncan cheered up when he saw Luke the Apostle nearly puking in the hallway. "What's the matter with you now?" he snapped.

"Can we go over this repeats business," Luke asked. "I don't want to make a fool of myself in front of my fans."

"There are no repeats until the second half," Duncan said. "Can't you take those stupid glasses off? You look like the Terminator."

"They're prescription," Luke answered, following us to the stage door. "I'm legally blind."

Legally drunk, too. I peered into the packed auditorium. The poor subscribers in the first few rows had paid to hear Beethoven. They had no idea they would be blinded by a tinfoil cowboy and a candelabrum with legs. "See that chair next to the piano bench, Luke?" He thought he did. "You're going to sit there quiet as a mouse until Duncan nods his head. Then you're going to turn a page and sit down again. No waving to the audience, no blowing kisses at me. I'm not your girlfriend. Understand?"

"Sure, no problem." Luke blew on his quivering fingers. "I don't believe this, man, I'm scared shitless. All those intellectuals staring at me."

"Don't screw me up," Duncan said helpfully.

Luke fished in his pockets and put a little white pill in his mouth. Meanwhile Duncan began pacing in circles, wringing his hands: beneath the beaded tuxedo he was still, and always would be, a terrified dentist. Finally he took a deep breath. I preceded him onstage.

The aluminum cowboy caused quite a stir, of which he soon became unaware, since he passed out. Just as we were about to begin, I heard a plop and a spongy crack, and knew that a head had hit the floor. I looked toward the piano, saw Duncan. "Get the stagehand," I said, bending over the carcass as the audience murmured animatedly. Luke hadn't broken his neck, only his aviator glasses.

Bolt and her photographer were already in the wings as Luke was dragged offstage. "This is perfect," she kept repeating as I hustled Duncan into the corner, away from the blinding flashbulbs. "Perfect. Get a closeup, Arty. Perfect. Duncan and Leslie, come over here! I need a group shot."

I saw Chance push open the thick doors. He walked quickly

toward Duncan and me. "I suppose you'll be needing a new page turner," he said. "Music onstage? Let's go."

The audience gave us a sympathetic welcome. Duncan played better than he had any right to, all things considered, and I played like a woman who had just acquired a new lover. Beethoven would have been satisfied. At intermission, we found the Apostle prostrate in the Green Room with slices of kiwi over his eyeballs. He looked like a reject from a radioactive lagoon.

"I have good news," Bolt said brightly. "Luke's well enough to do the second half."

"Sorry," Duncan said, "Luke blew it." He went into the bathroom.

"I thought we were in this together," said the mutant on the couch.

"You thought wrong." I looked at Bolt. "Would you mind leaving? You got your mileage out of this concert."

Sighing, she peeled the kiwis off Luke's eyelids. "There are a few too many egos floating around here. Goodbye, Duncan!" she called to the bathroom. "We'll be back after the concert!"

Luke stumbled to his feet. "Sorry, babycakes. I'll try to do better next time." He slapped Chance on the back. "See ya." They left.

I heard someone rap on the door. "Now what."

Harry Paradise swept into the Green Room. He looked as if he had rowed a boat over from London. "Well, I hope you're happy," he said to me, heaving his Vuitton suitcase on top of the kiwi slices. "I nearly lost an arm fighting for a cab. God, this trip is costing me a fortune! Hi Toby, good to see you."

"What are you doing here?" I asked.

Harry brushed a few gobs of banana off his chinchilla coat. "Damage control. Where's Emperor Godo? At the bar again?" He left.

Duncan emerged from the bathroom. "Where'd everyone go?"

Leaving him and Chance in the Green Room, I waited backstage for the auditorium to darken. Nothing like a quiet intermission to prepare the soul for the second half. I was suddenly very tired; too much energy had been squandered on nonmusical distractions. Frost would be playing the rest of this concert on finger memory. It was a luxury amassed only after eons of practice: collateral against that terrifying evening when I looked over the faces of a thousand strangers and realized that my brain was not onstage with me. Tonight I would return to those hours and call in the debt; my fingers would find their way through the maze without me. The audience would have no idea that I was not onstage at all, but somewhere in the auditorium with them, watching Frost the fiddler act a complex pantomime.

Afterward, a debacle of teenage girls crashed the Green Room, clamoring for Duncan the Magnificent's autograph. While waiting, they stared at my dress, my jewelry, tucking the information away in the great female vault. They also stared gaga at Chance. When Arty sidled in with a pair of cameras, I looked at the page turner. "Let's get out of here."

Chance gathered my things. We escaped the Green Room just as screams pealed through the hallway. Bolt and Luke had returned.

"She's history," I said. "I don't care how many records she sells." I didn't care what the Queen said about my new image, either. There was a limit to occupational mendacity.

Chance began to whistle. "Bolt's doing her job, honey," he said, tucking me into the limousine. "All right, where are we going? My place in New York or my place in Boston?"

"Those are the options?"

"We can take a short ride now and take the seven o'clock shuttle in the morning. Or we can take a long ride now and get up at nine."

I instructed the chauffeur to drive two hundred miles northeast. Before leaving Manhattan, we picked up sandwiches and a bottle of wine, which amused us until the Connecticut border. Thereafter we tested the resiliency of the backseat.

Experiments were still in progress when the limousine pulled in front of Chance's button factory on Sleeper Street. He gave the driver a wad of cash and pointed him toward the Expressway.

"Home sweet home," Chance said, defusing the security system. I followed him into his vast living room. It was a little chilly. "Care for a nightcap?"

Not from a bottle, thank you. He led me up the staircase behind his pantry. I had not seen his bedroom before. Furnishings were sparse and exquisitely expensive; beyond a wall of glass, the lights of the Boston harbor twinkled at us.

"I always had a feeling you'd be here one day," Chance said. I didn't congratulate him. "Getting you to stay will probably be the hard part."

Not that night.

14

*H*arry arrived at Chance's studio near noontime, spewing profanities. He had missed the eight o'clock shuttle, of course. He had been seated next to an animal rights activist on the plane who had accused him of electrocuting dozens of adorable chinchillas. Instead of playing deaf, Harry had counterattacked. When he mistook her organic lip balm for a can of spray paint, the crew finally had to separate them. Then he had to wait an hour for his luggage. He had a fiendish hangover and jet lag. He needed this side trip like a hole in the head. He absolutely had to be on the BA flight to London tonight.

"When's Godo showing up?" he snapped, following me down the long spiral staircase to the studios.

"Four o'clock," I said. "He expects to take a master tape away with him, you realize."

"That's ridiculous. It will take until then just to listen to the playbacks."

"That's why you were supposed to get here at ten."

"Please, Leslie, none of your lip today. If you had worked on the editing as I asked, we wouldn't have this last-minute panic."

This time, without even bothering to mark the scores, Harry had sent the session tapes and the track sheets to Boston, telling Chance to "use his best judgment" in culling five

Mozart violin concertos from twenty hours of raw material. Chance had been at it for a week straight, finishing just before he had come to New York yesterday for a little Florence Nightingale duty at my hotel.

"I'll leave you two alone," Chance said after Harry and I had settled into Studio C with coffee and pencils. "If you need me, I'm in my office. Call me when the smoke clears." The heavy door whooshed shut.

"It's stifling in here," Harry complained, throwing his silk foulard on the editing table. "I'll never stay awake."

The air was seventy degrees, electrostatically cleaned, computer-controlled to the proper humidity; unfortunately, the ventilating system was no match for Harry's Eau de Swamp Gas cologne.

"Listen," I said. "Before we start, let's agree to keep corrections to a minimum."

"Fine with me," Harry said. "You're the anal compulsive here."

The phone rang just as we were about to begin. "For you, Harry," Mona the receptionist said over the intercom.

Harry lunged at it. "Yes?" He listened a moment before swiveling his chair toward me. "Would you mind stepping outside? This is private."

I adjourned to Chance's green tiled hallway for ten minutes. Finally the door to Studio C opened. "Mona!" Harry called up to the offices. "How do I get an outside line here?"

Her head popped over the railing. "Top button. If that's busy, try the next one down."

"I'll be quick," Harry told me, enclosing himself behind the soundproof door once again. He didn't come out for another ten minutes.

We listened to the first concerto. As usual, Chance had done a great editing job. I could quibble with his choice in a few spots but I knew that I could go to the trouble of sifting through the session tapes and not find anything better. Different, maybe, but not better. "What do you think?" I asked Harry.

He snapped out of a reverie which I was sure had nothing to do with Mozart. "Excellent. Let's take a break." This time he secreted himself in the kitchenette. When I saw the red button on the phone light up, I went upstairs to Chance's office. He was on the phone, too, but motioned me to his desk, where he managed to kiss my stomach while maintaining a conversation with a recording executive in Los Angeles.

"Nice trick," I said when he hung up. "Bet that took a lot of practice."

"Many years and many women."

I pulled his hair. "I see you got your phone fixed." The new model on Chance's desk was just like the one I had tossed over the railing on my last visit. It, too, displayed the source number of incoming calls.

"Smash this one and you get a whipping," Chance said.

"Where's Harry?" I pointed to the red light on the phone. "Aha. I should have warned you about that. He's very chatty."

"Why don't you tell him to get off the damn phone and stop wasting everyone's time?"

"Time is money, sweetie pie. He's paying two hundred bucks an hour whether he's on the phone or in the studio." Chance licked my stomach. "Need I tell you that the client is always right?"

When the red light blinked out, I went back downstairs. Harry was hunched over the editing desk eating B complex pills. "Where were we?"

"The G Major concerto. It's one o'clock." I punched the Play button.

We got through the first movement before the phone rang. "I've got to take this," Harry said, cutting off the music.

"Who are all these people?" I cried. "Can't they get you in London tomorrow? Godo's coming in three hours, for Christ's sake!"

Harry stared at his watch. "Do me a favor, honey. You listen here while I take this call in the kitchen. Whatever you approve, I approve." Harry didn't return for ages. When he did, he looked pale.

Eventually Chance poked a head into the studio. "How's it going?"

I sighed. "Buzzing right along."

"Anyone interested in a pizza? Come on, Harry, eat. You'll need your strength for Godo."

"Maybe I should lie down," Harry replied. "My head hurts."

"You can lie down tonight," I said. "On British Airways."

"Why don't you sit in the sauna, Harry? Sweat the poison out?" Chance suggested. "It's got a phone. Frosty and I can wrap this up."

Harry accepted before I could protest. As soon as he left the studio, Chance pulled me onto his lap. "Hope you don't mind." He kissed my neck. "I wanted to get rid of Harry for a while."

"Is he always this ditsy when he comes here?"

"Of course. He racks up more studio time than any producer I know. Godo's always impressed with the bills." Chance smiled as the red light on his phone lit up again. "You see how hard he's working."

"Why did he even bother coming?"

"Have a heart. He's terrified that Godo's going to fire him. That's ninety thousand bucks a year down the tubes."

"Whose tubes, yours or Harry's?"

"Irrelevant. Do you want to lose the only producer in the world who puts up with you?" Chance pushed the Play button. "How's Mo?"

"We're never going to finish this in time."

Chance removed his mouth from my neck. "I've got an idea." He went to the machine room, where the noisy end of the Sony panoply was whirring and clicking, gasping cool air. Chance took a blank CD from a box and put it into the Yaba reference system. "Feeling brave? Let's make the master now."

Make a master without Harry or me having listened to his edits? That was like going from manuscript to press without proofreading. I hesitated. "Come on, honey," Chance whispered. "Trust me. I know what I'm doing."

"What the hell," I said finally. "I'm in a gambling mood today."

I watched him type a few instructions on a keyboard, rewind the U-matic tape, press a sequence of buttons: my Mozart was history. Trillions of digital signals leapt from the Sony system into the Yaba, which would translate ones and zeros into a laser beam burning infinitesimal pits into the iridescent plastic. The result would be a perfect copy of the U-matic tape, this time in compact disc format.

Chance and I returned to Studio C, where we sat more or less listening to Mozart until the doorbell rang: Godo, punctual as a time bomb.

"Go get Harry," Chance said, buttoning his shirt. "Mona will take care of Godo."

I went to the rear hallway leading to Chance's gym, where the air was fragrant with eucalyptus. Harry had made good use of the exercise equipment, draping his slacks and turtleneck over the barbell set. Underwear and jewelry graced a small shelf outside the sauna, whence issued his muffled voice. I knocked on the redwood door. "Godo's here, Harry." Zero response. "Harry!"

"I'm busy!" he shouted back.

"Godo's here," I repeated. "I wouldn't keep him waiting."

"Two minutes, for God's sake! Get my towel!"

I got the towel and waited outside the sauna for Harry to stick a hand out. He was in no rush so I put my ear to the door: professional habit. "Tonight," I heard him say in a tone of voice he had never used with me. Then, "That's your problem." He was quiet for a while. "You don't understand. I decide when to see you. You don't decide when to see me."

If this was romantic intrigue, I felt sorry for the lady.

"Wrap it up, Harry," I called, tossing his towel inside. "I'm not leaving without you."

He finally emerged in a welter of hot air. Harry's hairy chest looked like a bastard cousin of his chinchilla coat. The lump beneath his towel gave me some idea of why five women had married him for a few months. "Never seen a man before?" he snapped, stomping around the corner into the shower. "Bring my clothes."

I gathered Harry's pants and shirt from the barbells and hung them in the dressing room. Not to forget his precious jewelry: I scooped it off the shelf by the sauna. The weight of the five gold medallions, Harry's divorce trophies, surprised me. I reckoned he could shed two more wives before his vertebrae started to skid in protest.

Halt: that chain with the triangular links: I had seen it before, in a picture hanging in a music school. The boy on the end, the one whose face was blurred beyond recognition, wore a watch chain just like this. I inspected the smooth yellow gold. The jeweler had nearly succeeded in making a clasp that matched the antique chain. *Paradise Lost—10 XI 82*, I read on one side of the medallion; on the other, *Paradise Found—12 IV 83*. Each medallion was inscribed with the Lost and Found baloney and different dates. Sickened, I went to the shower. Harry, one of them? Impossible. Then I thought about his nervousness at border crossings, his itinerant lifestyle, his dubious vacations . . . they were all sentimental fools, weren't they. Moll had kept his lacrosse pin, Flick had kept his violin, now Harry couldn't part with his watch chain. These mementos were proof that, once upon a time, they had been real people. I tried to picture Harry using a gun, and couldn't. To me, he would always be a scatterbrained record producer. Then again, he had been perfecting his cover for over forty years. "Now what's the matter," Harry said, appearing in the hallway. "Did I part my hair crooked?"

I handed him his jewelry. "Nice gold mine, Harry. Someday you'll have to tell me how you got it all."

His face went momentarily blank. "My goldsmith lives in Florence," he lied. "If you like I can give you his name."

I sighed. "Not my style, dear. You know I prefer diamonds."

We went back to Studio C, where Godo and Chance stood sipping Mona's fresh coffee as the last of the Mozart concertos rippled quietly in the background. "Ah, Mr. Godo!" Harry exclaimed, clutching his benefactor's hand. "Nice to see you! What an honor!"

Smiling faintly, Godo greeted me with his usual mix of deference and dismay. "Did you see your review in the *New York Times* this morning? And a picture of everyone?"

"Wasn't it terrific?" Harry interrupted. "Fabulous exposure."

"But a strange article," Godo said. "So little about Beethoven, so much about a soap opera. Perhaps the critic was making a joke?"

"Perhaps Ms. Bolt was making a joke," I said.

The music ended. Whistling, Chance ducked into the machine room. He looked a little ruddy; then again, he was trying to prevent ninety thousand bucks from evaporating. Through the glass doors, I watched him switch on the tape analyzer, read the error count: clean. Chance hit the Eject button on the Yaba and a shiny new CD slid out. "Here's your door prize," he said, presenting it to Godo.

The president of Kakadu Classics was terribly impressed. "I can play this at home?"

Chance nodded. "What you hear is what your customers will hear."

Tea, tour, handshakes. Godo departed a happy man. Harry, Chance, and I waved to him from the bottom of the spiral staircase before he disappeared over the landing with Mona. Presently we heard the upstairs door slam. "Well," said Harry, "do you think we pulled it off?"

"Cut it a bit close this time, Harry," Chance replied.

"Couldn't be helped!" Harry glanced at his enormous

watch. "I'm going to make the early flight to London after all. What's your schedule, Les? Taking a few days off?"

"Unfortunately not. I'm going with you."

"I'll take you to the airport," Chance said, registering no surprise whatever. He joked another couple minutes with Harry, discussed their upcoming jobs, then followed me to the bedroom. "Okay, what's going on."

I continued packing. "Nothing. I have to get back to Berlin."

"But you just got here."

"I know that." I pulled my suitcase off his wide bed. "Business before pleasure."

"Wait," he said. I almost obeyed. Would the free world collapse if I stayed another day? Chance intercepted me at the door, there to discover that mouth-to-mouth contact would get him nowhere.

I disengaged his arms and became the confused damsel: it was a kinder lie. "I need to think a little. This is so sudden."

Chance lifted my suitcase with a sigh. "I suppose I should be getting used to this." We went back to the office, where Harry was leaning heavily over Mona, helping her type Kakadu's invoice.

"I've run up a bit of a phone bill, darling," he was saying as we entered. "There's no need for Godo to know the specifics. Just bury a couple hundred bucks in studio time for me, would you?"

"Couple hundred bucks?" I squawked. "Who were you yakking with all day?"

"No problem, Harry," Chance said, sending me a remonstrative look. "I appreciate your coming to Boston. Godo won't forget it either." He had Harry initial an invoice for twenty thousand dollars. "We'd better head out."

We took the Jeep, not the Cobra, to Logan. At the international terminal, Chance tried one last time. "I can't talk you out of this?" he said as Harry flitted to the ticket counter.

"No." I kissed him. Chance made me feel warm, safe,

almost home: what was missing? Only the serene despair of age. "I'm sorry to run off like this."

"We'll talk about it later." He handed me my violin. "In bed. It's the only place to have a reasonable discussion with you."

I watched his car pull away. Harry had finished checking in when I joined him at the ticket counter. "Changed my mind, Harry. I'm not going to London with you."

Harry peered outside. "So he finally talked some sense into you."

I walked him to the gate. "So nice of you to fly six thousand miles to take a sauna."

"Win a few, lose a few. See you in Leipzig. Stay well." Harry led a cloud of perfume into the airplane.

I called my old school chum Alfred, said I had a couple hours before my flight to London. Could I drop by? Cabbed to his place on Beacon Hill and spent a few moments with Stella, the kids, and the family television before retreating to his computer room. Alfred deflected my questions about his business, saying only that profits were down and desertion was up. Industry gossip never concerned who had invented what any more. It was about who had gone Chapter Eleven. While Alfred steadily depleted a bottle of Scotch, we amused ourselves poking into this and that, beginning with Harry Paradise's Amex account. Apparently Harry still hadn't straightened out the mess with Kreutzer Music Repair that we had instigated months before. "Should we fix it?" Alfred asked. "Or are you still peeved at him."

"Leave it." I pulled my chair closer. "Are you still playing with phone bills?"

"Please! Are you still playing encores?"

I gave him Chance's phone number. "Look this up for me, would you?"

"What's this?"

"The studio I was in all day," I said. "I've got a crush on the editor but I think he's already got a girlfriend."

"A little background check? Very smart." Alfred tapped a few keys. "He's got three lines."

"Can you get me all the long-distance calls today between noon and six?" I followed Alfred's dexterous fingers: even when drunk, he was a stunning hacker. A long list of numbers appeared on his screen. "Can you identify these?" I asked.

A CD plant, a bank, two calls to Sydney Bolt Inc., then record companies in New York, Los Angeles . . . after two o'clock we began to get twelve- and thirteen-digit numbers. "Sorry," Alfred said. "I can't identify international numbers. Maybe the prefixes might tell you something."

"London," I pointed. France somewhere, Amsterdam, Rome, London again. My finger stopped at an all-too-familiar country/city code. "Leipzig."

"He's got a girlfriend in Leipzig?" Alfred asked.

"I hope not." I continued down the list.

"You've passed that one twice now," Alfred said. He traced the number. "Data Translation Services, Tarrytown, New York."

The name had a bad effect on my insides. So did the location, Tarrytown, New York: Vuota Corda, that little record company: Leon Jurkowsky's CD on Harry's wall, in Flick's apartment. Three bumps into Tarrytown now and that was no longer coincidence. I looked at the time of the call: it was placed exactly when I had gone to fetch Harry from the sauna. "What's Data Translation Services, do you think?"

"Data translation, Les, just what it says. I use one in Concord all the time. You send them your program in one computer language, they translate it into another. Or they translate between media, say if your data's on hard disk but you need it on videotape. Someone's got to make a few bucks off all our incompatible software systems."

"I see." My fingers dropped over the few numbers left: a tape supply house, a record company in New York. "I guess it was a false alarm," I said. "Not many women's numbers here except Sydney Bolt."

"Sydney's a woman?" Alfred asked.

"Sort of." I finished my Scotch. "She runs a PR firm."

"Oh God! Say no more!" Alfred exited his program. "I can keep an eye on this guy if you like. Fax you his most frequently called numbers."

"That won't be necessary. I don't think I'll be going out with him in any case."

"Right." Alfred demonstrated a few new computer routines, all dazzling, all worthy of prison terms. If the Queen ever relaxed her gender restrictions, I had an excellent candidate for the Seven Sisters. "I wouldn't worry about your business, Alfred," I told him when he finally quit. "You could make a fortune selling this sort of information."

He yawned. "That type of business gets people killed. I'd rather be bankrupt than dead."

I got my coat. "How's Clove doing these days? As badly as everyone else?"

"Laying off right and left. They sank everything into the supercomputers and now no one's got the money to buy them." Alfred chuckled. "They had a slight uh-oh with the QV6 series, you know."

"Like what."

"Remember that VP I told you about, who got fired? Know why? One of the software engineers in his department left a bug in the system. A Trojan horse."

"You're kidding."

"Nope. I know the perpetrator. Used to go drinking with him. John Svek. Brilliant but a total nut case."

"How serious was the Trojan horse?"

"Very. Svek wrote a catastrophic crash at thirty-six hundred hours on the computer clock. By sheer luck another employee caught it during routine farting around."

"What happened?"

"They made Svek fix it, of course. Then they plugged it into all the units they had sold, pretending it was an upgrade. Both Svek and his boss were fired and the company's going to sue them dead if they so much as open their mouths."

"That's pretty hilarious." I tried to laugh. "People don't know about this?"

"Are you kidding? Not outside of Clove." Alfred anticipated my next question. "I have my spies, you know. It's the only way to survive in this business."

He passed on a few more industry secrets before dropping me off at the airport. I called Curtis, told him not to expect me. I wouldn't be coming home for a day or two. Then I rented a Mercedes and drove south, fast. It emptied the head. Somewhere near the New York border I pulled into a motel. Forget sleep: too much random input today. I kept seeing Harry Paradise. Who was he, really? I had known him, and socially avoided him, for six years. Strange, now that I thought about it: between wives, during wives, in all this time he had never made a pass at me. Was he the boy in the corner of that picture? Just the right age. He knew that I had been in Boston over the holidays. He could have sent the redhead to Luke the Apostle's concert in Worcester, then. With whom was he speaking today, in such a harsh voice?

I began to worry about Alfred Chung. I really didn't know him very well, either. Why volunteer all that information about John Svek and that crash at thirty-six hundred hours on the Clove? Did a successful executive really spend all that time playing at home with his computers?

Then I began to wonder why Chance had come to the hotel the day before to hold my hand. Now it seemed ludicrous. Any man with a normal-size ego would have stopped pursuing me months ago. He could have made any of those phone calls today, couldn't he. He could have informed the redhead that I'd be at Luke the Apostle's concert in Worcester. Why was it that each time I saw Chance, things spun a little out of control? And why, each time I'd tried to outguess him, I'd guessed wrong?

Then, of course, paranoia would not be complete without Flick, salt of my dreams. He loved me, he loved me not, he knew, he knew nothing . . . I recalled his face as he lifted my sweater, looked at my bruised ribs. No triumph there.

Recognition, rather, as if things were proceeding on schedule. That made me hate him. Perhaps that was what they had planned also.

And finally, the redhead, who had totally eluded me. I intended to change that.

15

$\mathcal{I}$ woke up unsure of where I was, then remembered having driven to a tacky motel forty miles north of New York. Outside I saw a foggy, ashen morning. The earth had broken into a cold sweat, fearful that winter would never end. I dressed and drove to Tarrytown, arriving at Data Translation Services around eight o'clock. The bland brick building occupied one corner of a bland industrial park; inside, I knew it was all polystyrene and fluorescent lights, the kind that made eye shadow look like carcinoma. I parked next to a tubby Chrysler at the far end of the lot and sipped McDonald's coffee. Now what? Walk in and ask for a tour? How about a peep at the employee list? Useless. Coming here had been a rash reaction to a speck of information.

As I munched on an Egg McNitrate sandwich, employees began drifting in to work. A methodical bunch, all sizes and colors, they filled the parking slots in contiguous order, early birds taking places closest to the company entrance. Intent on locking their cars and escaping the cold, they took no notice of my Mercedes off in the mist.

A white Honda nuzzled into its parking space. I saw the red hair, felt my stomach grow cold, but couldn't believe it was she: that would have been too blatant, too easy, almost a letdown. What was that insolent bitch doing here? Employees in places like this had to take polygraph tests. Their résumés were carefully checked and their interviews were attended by a psychologist. They probably walked past an X-ray coming and going: if Data Translation Services couldn't guarantee the confidentiality of the information its clients sent, the company was out of business. I watched her lock the car and wave hello to the fellow who had pulled into the space next to hers. So friendly, so fake. Side by side, their beige raincoats bobbed up the concrete steps and disappeared behind the glass doors.

I slowly finished breakfast, plotting an itinerary of lies and masquerades. This was going to be a long day. I edged the Mercedes out of the parking lot and called Maxine from a palatial Holiday Inn in White Plains. She picked up after one ring: not bad for three o'clock in the morning. "Hi. Did I wake you?"

She knew I wouldn't call her at this hour on open lines unless it was rudely necessary. "What's up." I gave her the Honda's license number. "Anything else?"

"John Svek," I said. "Computer programmer, worked for Clove, recently fired. That's all I know. Also, I want a bio of Harry Paradise, baby teeth to hemorrhoids."

Six time zones away I felt her hesitate. "No problem," Maxine said. "Give me a couple hours."

I drove into downtown White Plains, a mezzo-affluent suburb of New York City. Every chain store in America had acreage on Main Street and the old ladies here were partial to powder blue overcoats and seamed stockings. Maybe the Chamber of Commerce hadn't taken down the Christmas lights yet because people were still returning their gifts. First I bought a ski outfit, complete with face mask. Then I found a computer store. Stashed between two crass boutiques, it was a depressing pit of calculators and video games. The manager's polyester tie had staged many amphibious assaults on many cups of coffee. I rented his fastest computer/peripherals and returned to the hotel.

Maxine called back around noon, six in the morning Berlin time, when her call would be lost in a flood of transatlantic conversations. "The Honda's registered to Hannah Selke," Maxine said. "Does she have red hair?"

"Red hair and evil eyes."

"Bingo." Such congratulations. "Have you got a modem? I'll send what I've got on her and Svek. You'll have to wait for Harry." She zipped her information over.

First I got John Svek on the computer screen. No police record, no tax problem, no credit history. No credit cards? Alfred was right: the man was a misfit. I got his Social Security number, address/phone in Concord, Massachusetts. Age forty-eight, single, decent salary once upon a time. Termination of employment two weeks before, reason health, according to the state unemployment bureau. Good old Maxine had also sent a street map of Concord.

Hannah Selke lived in Briarcliff Manor, New York, a quiet town full of old money and taxidermal moose heads. According to the state motor vehicle agency, she was born fifty-five Novembers ago in Brooklyn. Ah well, at least they got the age right. She had been driving since she was sixteen and of course Hannah had a perfect record. She didn't have an unlisted phone number. Again Maxine had thoughtfully sent me a local road map.

I had no intention of going near Hannah now. Since I had her phone number and a modem, however, it might be useful to do a little preliminary prying, so I ran Alfred Chung's credit card routine on Hannah Selke's MasterCard account. If this billing period was any indication, she had a spotless relationship with plastic. Bought no frills, paid on time. She was a devoted customer of Lufthansa. I was a little disappointed to see that she lived within her means but of course Fräulein Selke would be a much more responsible citizen than the average American.

Maybe she talked . . . I applied Alfred der Hackmeister's methods to Hannah's phone number: *ditditdit* went my printer. After twenty lines it suddenly stopped and I got a message to please reidentify myself. That didn't look too good so I hung up. The feds had zero sense of humor about these things, so I took what hard copy I had from the printer and left the hotel. Took the computer back to the man with the soiled tie, then drove to one of the gigantic electronics supply houses on Forty-second Street in New York.

"I'd like a box of CD blanks," I told the Korean behind the counter. "For the new Yaba system."

Couldn't buy just one, of course. I had to get a box of twelve, which put a major dent in my cash reserves. I headed north on the Merritt Parkway just as the first snowflakes eddied over the frozen concrete. Not good: snow begat footprints. Within a few miles traffic on the narrow, winding road had slowed to a timorous crawl. Night fell at four in the afternoon. I turned up the heat and pressed forward in a dull daze punctuated by the garish blue flashers of police vehicles.

Deep in Connecticut, I pulled over for gas. As the Mercedes was on-loading liquid ballast, I glanced over my printout of Hannah's phone bill, that is, the section of it I had managed to get before someone smelled a rat. She had made one call to Flick's office in Leipzig, three calls to Harry in London. Hannah didn't have many American friends except for one in area code 703: six calls about six minutes each, every couple days. Our thrifty girl had waited until just after eleven at night, when rates were cheapest, before dialing.

I walked to the phone booth. It still smelled of its previous occupant's French fries. "Operator, where's area code 703? Exchange 582?"

"The area code is for Virginia. There is no exchange 582."

I dialed the number, got a computer. No surprise: every intelligence agency in the country lived down there. As the wind whistled around my ankles, I held on to the whining receiver, trying to think. Nothing happened so I called Maxine.

"Having fun?" she said.

I gave her the phone number. "What's this?"

I heard keys tapping, then silence. "Are you flying out tonight?"

"Tomorrow morning." I studied the printout. "She called

that number February five, eight, ten, twelve, fourteen, about six minutes each time, at twenty-three hundred hours.'' The page was already wrinkled with snow and my teeth were beginning to chatter. ''Anything more on Svek?''

''He didn't file a joint return and took no deductions for dependents or alimony.''

Ah, what would we do without the IRS files. ''No roommates? No dogs?''

''That's something you'll have to find out for yourself.''

I skidded along the Massachusetts Turnpike toward Boston. Traffic was minimal and the state troopers were too busy hauling cars out of ditches to bother with the radar guns. I left at Route 128, once upon a time America's Technology Highway, now America's Office Space Available Highway. The last of the rush hour crashes were getting towed away as I crawled to the Route 2 exit.

Concord was still rustic, still rich: by and large the town fathers had succeeded in keeping the colonial homes surrounded by woods. John Svek's place was about a mile from the battlefields of the American Revolution. I knew the area. During my school days, miserable and homesick, I had often visited the modest hills; tangentially, their history was European. Around dinnertime, I parked the Mercedes near a restaurant on the charmingly restored Main Street. Inside I could see couples eating by soft electric candlelight, being served by waiters in billowy white blouses. Two of the luckier diners held hands across the linen tablecloth; they didn't care if they were snowed in for a month. I zipped a tiny DAT player into a top pocket. Weapons? The white knife, a tiny lavender pill, and the eyebrow pencil, one of Maxine's more fanciful creations.

I stepped into the snow. The clean air slapped me awake; I went quickly to the end of Main Street, walking faster as the streetlamps thinned out. At the darkest point I cut into the woods.

As the Queen's map suggested, after a half mile of pine needles I passed three houses on the left. Svek's was the last

of them. Its windows were totally black except for a downstairs room from which issued the macabre, dancing rays of
a television set. I pulled on the ski mask, clamped the eyebrow
pencil in my teeth: no time for third wheels tonight. The old
porch squeaked beneath my boots as I peered inside.

Seated on the sofa, a middle-aged man stared at the boob
tube, absently poking his fork into a tray on his lap, then
lifting it to his mouth. His eyeglasses reflected the glowing
television screen, as did his bald head, although not as crisply.
At his elbow stood a trombone resting on its bell. In the
corner of the room I saw the soft green light of a computer,
on but momentarily forgotten. Magazines, books, boxes cluttered the room: I was looking at yet another variation of
Moll's steeple.

I circled his house, looking for entry. The garage door was
unlocked so I lifted it a foot, rolled underneath. Instead of a
car I saw a dented canoe on two sawhorses. The walls were
lined with transistor radios and receivers, twenty-year-old
technical manuals, and a staggering collection of electrical
components. The congeries smelled of motor oil and rust. I
entered his house, crept along the hall, stopping when I heard
domestic noise: footsteps, mild crash of dishes, refrigerator
opening/shutting, paper crinkling. Svek returned to the television.

He began watching the news, eating an ice cream sandwich. As the commentator spouted off about the latest fairy
tale come true in Germany, I crept behind his chair and slid
an arm tightly around his throat. "John Svek?" I whispered
in his ear, affecting an Israeli accent. "I have a knife in my
hand. It's quite sharp. You will do as I say. Put the food
down." He dropped the ice cream to the floor. "Are you
alone?" He nodded stiffly. "I hope so. Turn the television
off." His trembling fingers pressed the remote control. "Now
close the curtains." I followed him from window to window,
keeping the knife against his ribs in case he suddenly decided
to get noble. "Still playing with your computer? Good." I
ushered him to his terminal and switched the desk light on.

Svek glanced long enough at my knife and ski mask to realize that it was not a promising combination. "Who are you?" he asked. "Mossad?"

Movement on top of the sofa. In a second I had the eyebrow pencil in my mouth. I blew sharply: with a horrid snarl, Svek's cat fell to the floor, twitched, lay still.

His mouth dropped. "My cat," he croaked. "Is she dead?"

"You told me we were alone," I said.

"I was!"

"You are now." I took the DAT player from my jacket and placed it next to the computer. "You're going to write me a small program. Hook that up, please." I watched his quaking hands connect my tiny DAT unit to the computer. "You put a little bug into the Clove QV6 series, I understand. Tell me about that."

"It was just a joke! They're all fixed!"

All except serial number nineteen, currently resting in a steeple, not the Atlantic seabed, as its manufacturers thought. "That's not a very funny joke, Mr. Svek." I put the eyebrow pencil into my mouth and nonchalantly pointed it at him. "Why did you do it?"

"They burned me out for twenty years. Stole all my ideas, all my inventions. They used my brains and treated me like dirt." Ho hum. I didn't bother to ask why, if conditions were so inhuman, he had stayed with the same company for twenty years.

"So you arranged for the computers to have—shall we say—a fatal heart attack." I saw his eyes widen. "I know all about it, you see. Thirty-six hundred hours on their clocks and *poof*, they suddenly die." I let the word hang suggestively in the air. "That was childish of you."

"But I fixed them all! I overrode the virus!"

"You've complicated my life, Mr. Svek. I'm going to give you one chance to save yourself." I put the eyebrow pencil away and stood behind his chair, delicately pricking his neck with the tip of my white knife. "I want you to write a program moving the computer's clock to five minutes before system failure. The operator's clock will remain unchanged.''

"But I fixed them all!'' he repeated.

"Do it,'' I said. "Step by step you're going to show me how to get into the Clove QV6. I'm sure you remember how.'' The knife point sank a quarter inch into his greasy neck. "By the way, you're going to be writing ten-bit words, not sixteen.''

"Ten-bit words? That's for music. I don't know if I can change them.''

"You invented the computer, you write the conversion program. Or you end up like your cat.''

Whoops, overdose: Svek began to cry. "You didn't have to kill her.''

"She's not dead,'' I said. "Just tranquilized. But if she wakes up before you're done, I'm going to shoot her again. So stop sniveling and type.''

As he began to work, brilliantly, I stood over him, challenging every move. Once he saw that I was familiar with his line of work, Svek rose to the occasion; all his life, he had craved an audience. I hoped the knife in his neck would dissuade him from double-crossing me. I would have no way of knowing if his program worked; during my next visit to the steeple, I'd have just enough time to hit the Clove and flee while Moll was downstairs leading the boys through another motet.

My crash course finally ended. "I don't know if this is going to fly,'' Svek whimpered.

I unplugged my DAT player from his computer. "You'll hear from me if it doesn't.''

"I know a lot of information,'' he said. "I could be very useful to you.''

"Get up.'' I led him to his filthy kitchen. The pile of dishes in his sink was almost as high as the pile of garbage in the corner. A nose-curdling odor of sour milk and kitty litter shortened my temper considerably. "Get a glass of water.''

Svek obeyed. I dropped the lavender pill into it. "Drink this."

"You're going to kill me?" he cried. "I did everything you said!"

"No. But you're going to sleep for a while," I said. Didn't need him calling the FBI while I was stumbling through the woods. "Just like your cat. I wouldn't tell anyone about this. You're under twenty-four-hour surveillance and your phone lines are tapped." I couldn't say it with a straight face; thank God I was wearing a ski mask.

"When am I going to wake up," he whined after I had led him to his easy chair.

"In time for Johnny Carson."

"I really could be helpful to you. I know people at the Defense Department."

"So do I. They don't like traitors. Swallow." Terrified, Svek spilled half the glass down his shirt. For an instant I pitied him; then I was angry at the waste of talent, at the indulgence of a man who had spent his entire life serving as his own prison warden. I waited until his head rolled to the side. No doubt in a few months, a year, drunk at some gummy bar, he'd tell someone about me: Alfred, perhaps. By then his story would be so bloated with hyperbole and misremembrance that no one would believe him. And if they did, so what? Check the clocks on all those Cloves? They'd find nothing.

Fresh snow had already obliterated my first footprints. Soon, the storm would erase my new trail in the woods. I tore the ski mask off and ran across Svek's back field, gulping clean air, feeling terrible hunger, terrible energy: postmission fallout. But I wasn't done yet. I drove to Logan, returned the Mercedes, and called Chance's private line, half collapsing at the sound of his voice. It was my only buoy in a heaving sea. In the background I heard soft jazz. "I'm in Boston," I said.

"You are? What happened?"

"I changed my mind about leaving," I lied. "Are you busy tonight?"

Laughter, talking behind him: he was not alone. "I'll be in the studio mixing for a while. Come right over. Please."

"Are you sure it's all right?"

"That's a silly question, Frosty. I'll listen for the bell."

Etiquette degenerated a bit when he answered the door. "Well, well. Life is full of surprises," he said, flinging open my coat, clamping me to his chest. "I won't ask what part of that devious brain brought you back here."

There seemed to be a baseball in his pants. I ran my thumbs over it, checking the seams. "How long will you be working."

"All night." Bad news. Chance took me across the reception area to the door leading to his apartment. "Go upstairs. I'll be there eventually."

"Any food in the house? I forgot to eat dinner."

"In the refrigerator. I still don't believe you're here." He walked quickly toward the spiral staircase.

First, I ate. Then I went upstairs and dropped my suitcase and violin at the foot of his bed. In a few days, somewhere in Europe, I'd have to play the fiddle again: that was unbelievable. I was not an artist, never had been. I was something terribly different. Across the harbor, a few lights peeped intermittently through the snow. I was glad to be here, very glad that Chance was downstairs. For a few hours, he would shelter me from an ugly world. Before going to bed, I rummaged in my cosmetics case. Nice token of appreciation, I thought, tucking one of the Queen's more potent fragrances under my pillow. He deserved better than that, but . . .

When Chance woke me, the gray, diffuse light indicated dawn rather than night. A warm hand grafted onto my side and bad dreams melted, flesh dissolved, ah lovely man, was I really here on business only? How masterfully the libido manipulated available reality. "Why didn't you come back last night," Chance whispered. "Straight from the airport?"

"I needed time to think." That sounded ludicrous so I

made it twice as bad. "I'm afraid I'm falling in love with you."

"Terrible." He rolled me on top of his stomach, dividing my legs. "Horrible." Then he was inside of me. "You know the feeling is mutual."

Tight and tremendous: I knew why I had wanted to come back here. He made love openly, confidently. He knew he'd have many tomorrows and his past had not yet grown heavy enough to sink him. The present? A bustling intersection of ambition and good luck. No demons, no desperation, only the anticipation of an exciting journey. I was included in that journey; that was the most potent aphrodisiac of all.

When his breathing became soft and regular, I slid a hand under my pillow and removed the Queen's atomizer. Held it under Chance's quiet nose waiting for him to inhale. Sorry darling *pfffft*: he slid peacefully into a deep abyss. I gathered my software and crept down the long spiral stairs to Studio C, smelling coffee and a faint bouquet of pot. The area was still warm, still thick with musicians' egos. I turned the Sony editor and the DAT machines back on and went to the machine room. The clock above the Yaba read six-fifteen.

From John Svek I had gotten a tiny DAT cassette containing a program that would alter the time clock of the Clove QV6 in Leipzig. When I returned there in two weeks, I would feed it to the monster in the steeple. Five minutes after Moll next turned the Clove on, Svek's virus would kill everything in it. I intended to transfer my data from tape to compact disc: easier to disguise, safe from X-ray problems at airports. I could slip it right into Moll's CD-ROM, do my damage and disappear.

First I had to make a CD master tape from Svek's DAT cassette. That meant transferring the digits to U-matic tape, adding time code and PQ code tracks, without which the Yaba could do nothing. It needed format and signposts. I put Svek's tiny cassette into the DAT player, timed it: he had crammed all instructions into thirty-three seconds. I connected the DAT to the U-matic machines, laid on the time code, generated the

PQ codes, pressed Forward. Thirty-three seconds later I had a U-matic CD master.

Now to get the digits from U-matic tape to disk. Chance's new machine in the corner would translate my numbers into laser burns on plastic: Yaba read a One, laser On; Yaba read a Zero, laser Off. The system could translate over three megabytes of information per second. I rerouted all the cables into the Yaba and inserted a blank plastic disk I had bought in New York. Tape rolled, laser spat: thirty-three seconds later I had my compact disc. It was almost seven o'clock.

Unplugged the works and rearranged Chance's connector cables in their original positions. I brought everything back to his bedroom and waited for him to wake up; we would have another hour together before I had to catch the flight to JFK.

Curtis picked me up at Tegel and drove straight to Kreuzberg. Maxine wished to see me immediately. We arrived at the nightclub well before her first show. Curtis brought me to the jammed bar, staying close while I inspected the contents of Roland's funhouse: the usual crew plus a dozen East Berliners who didn't realize that eight-inch-wide lapels had gone out of style soon after the bombing of Dresden. Through the smoke a few guests from Roland's New Year's party waved at Curtis and me. He and I were an approved social unit. As always, Roland's table in the corner was open, although its proprietor was nowhere in sight. Curtis and I went there and waited as, onstage, a pianist's fingers somnambulated over the keys. "Any more reviews from New York?" I asked.

"Reviews, no." Curtis reached into his pocket. "Press releases, yes. Sydney Bolt faxed this to me."

Too dark to read anything but the logo of her PR firm across the top of the page. "What now."

"To make a long story short, Duncan and Luke are going to make an album of love songs together. Chance is recording it."

I swallowed alcohol. "Shit."

"Duncan's been calling all day from New York. I wouldn't say he's in a healthy frame of mind. Seems to think the present situation is all your fault."

Across the room I saw my brother teetering toward our table. "Connect him with Roland. They have a lot in common."

"Hi toots," my brother said, flopping onto the banquette. "Curtis. Don't you two make a nice pair. American Gothic without the pitchfork."

Pickled in gin: the fumes rose from his skin and settled sweetly over the table. I had never seen him this bad. "What happened to your face?" I said. "Did you try to shave with a piranha?"

"I fell out of bed." He lit a cigarette. "So where have you been?"

"Duncan and I played a concert in New York."

Roland signaled to a waitress. "Oh. Great. You tag along, Curt? Not that my sister needs protection, of course."

Enough: I stood up. "Is Maxine backstage?"

"Don't hold her up, Les. I've got a full house tonight."

I burst in on the chanteuse, who sat in her dressing room daubing rouge on her fancy cheekbones. "What the hell's happening to Roland?"

"Nothing," the Queen said.

"Come on! Is someone blackmailing him? Did Flick come back here?" She didn't answer. "We should never have gotten him into this, Maxine. He's not strong. He never was."

"He's impotent." She finished her cheekbones. "No more, no less."

"Can't you do something about it?"

She fastened me with a long, chimerical glare. "Not right now." Maxine went to her costume closet and slowly picked through the fluff, waiting for me to compose myself. After a while she pulled a green-and-black number from the rack. "What have you been up to?"

I reluctantly put Roland away. "I saw Svek. Big-time loser

who used to work for Clove. He put a virus into all the QV6's. Programmed them to crash after a couple thousand hours. They caught him and discreetly fixed the problem with all existing units. He's fired. Now he watches TV and waits for a lawsuit."

Maxine stopped fooling with a zipper. "Says who."

"Alfred Chung. My old MIT chum."

"Does Alfred always pass on this kind of information?"

"He's a gossip." In a week she'd have a file on him two inches thick. Maybe it was just as well. "I made Svek write a program for the Clove in the steeple. He moved the clock up. Now the system will crash five minutes after Moll switches it on. If Hannah does any post-mortem checking, she'll find out about Svek and think this was his sabotage."

Maxine smiled at my astounding cleverness. I waited for her sincere congratulations. "You're going back to Leipzig, then?"

"Don't you ever listen? I told you I have recording sessions there two weeks from now." That reminded me of something else. "About Harry Paradise. Did you get the information for me?"

She rummaged in a drawer crammed with hair ornaments, finally locating a tiny cassette. "There's Harry," she said, tossing it to me. "What's this all about?"

"I think he's one of them."

She laughed. "Are you joking? He's much too stupid. He's genuinely stupid. Believe me."

If she hadn't said "stupid" twice, I might have believed her: the Queen rarely repeated herself unless she was lying. "So I'm paranoid."

"May I ask how you came to this conclusion?"

Suddenly it seemed ridiculous that the chain Harry wore around his neck was the same chain I had seen on one of Zwinger's Little Rascals. I sighed. "Maybe it's a little far-fetched."

"Maxine! Five more minutes," Roland shouted, bashing on the door.

We listened to him stomp sloppily away. "About that phone number in Virginia," Maxine said, shepherding me back to easier riddles. "It belongs to the NSA. Top-secret access, of course."

"Hannah got into the NSA?" Even Alfred Chung hadn't been able to do that. "Any particular department?"

"Satellite transmissions. She requested all communications between ground stations and the Russian satellite. They gave her everything she needed. Hannah Selke's quite a hacker, to say the least."

"It must have taken her years to penetrate the network."

"She knew what she wanted and she went after it." Maxine pulled out her lipstick. That was normally my signal to leave. "Now that you've found her, what are you going to do?"

"I don't know yet. First I want to kill the Clove."

I walked through the heat and smoke back to Curtis, who was arguing with Roland. My brother abruptly held his tongue when he noticed me. "Back so soon? You two must have brain-to-brain syringes or something."

"Shut up, Roland," Curtis said. "You're not feeling well."

As Roland's eyes settled blearily on the stage, I realized that his illness could be terminal. "Look at her," he murmured as Maxine came out. "She's so goddamn beautiful."

Maxine began to sing her low refrain as Curtis steered me across the crowded room. He packed me into the M6 and drove quickly away. "You've got to do something about him," he said. "He's going to get you into a lot of trouble one of these days."

"He's my brother. Roland knows when to keep his mouth shut."

"He didn't tonight."

"Maxine's making him crazy. Ignoring him."

"Another Frost ill with unrequited love? *Tsk tsk*."

I wasn't up for another fracas so I slouched into my seat, listening to slush slurp beneath the heavy wheels. After an interminable ride, Curtis pulled into the driveway. He brought my suitcases inside, pausing at the foot of the stairs. ''Why hasn't Maxine sent him away by now? Or does she enjoy sleeping with dynamite?''

I watched his convex rear end mount the stairs and veer into my room. Situations always looked simpler, more distilled, to an outsider. If Maxine had wanted Roland away, she would have gotten rid of him by now. I was a little peeved at Curtis for flinging the ethics of survival in my face at a time like this. When he came back downstairs, I was pouring myself a Scotch.

''Alcohol dehydrates,'' he said, heading into the office.

I followed him there and began leafing through a mound of mail. Someone from Prague wanted to take lessons with me. Someone from Munich wanted to sell me a super violin bow. A composer had sent me his new concerto. Nothing from Flick. In a padded envelope I found the CD of Gregorian chant I had ordered from the record shop on the Ku'damm long ago, with a note reminding me that I had promised to deliver it to that man from Leipzig. I laughed.

Curtis looked up from his pressing correspondence. ''Something funny?''

I drained the glass and wandered around the room, adjusting drapes, pawing magazines, pushing buttons on the fax. ''If you're not tired,'' Curtis said after a few minutes, ''why don't you go practice? You're playing the Berg Concerto in two days.''

''So what? I've played it a thousand times.''

''How many times have you played it perfectly?''

If I swallowed that bait, we'd soon be swinging at each other. Taking the CD, I went to Hugo's study. Before switching on the lights I stood a moment in the dark, inhaling the old leather, the heavy drapes: I was tired of ghosts, even more tired of humans. My faithful manager had propped the score of the Berg Concerto on my music stand. On an adjacent table lay my violin. I tuned and began a flurry of scales, waiting for the sands to shift, the personalities to change.

Eventually Frost the fiddler returned but not without a fight from the other one. Smith was upset: Hannah was too good. From her own house, she had hacked into the most sacrosanct computer network in the country. It made me a little afraid.

After an hour I quit. No sense overdoing it: the Berg Concerto was almost ready for public consumption. It was one o'clock. Perhaps, back from another vigil in the poisoned countryside, Flick would be creaking into bed. As his head touched the cold pillow, would he miss me? I had to smile. Surely I flattered myself. I put the violin away and flopped onto Hugo's green leather couch.

The doorknob turned. "Finished?" Curtis said.

What did that mean? I should go to bed? I should practice more? Christ, he was insufferable! Without answering, I opened the new CD from the music shop. Another hit from Vuota Corda, the people who had made Leon Jurkowsky immortal. I put it into my CD player.

Curtis heard a few moments of Gregorian chant. The uninflected plainsong sounded like a dirge. "Why are you listening to that?"

"Will you get out of here?"

The door slapped shut. Ten funebrial minutes passed. Then the phone rang, my private line. Not many men had that number: perhaps longing was telepathic after all. I tried to keep my voice casual. "Hello."

"Reverse charges from Duncan Zadinsky. Do you accept?"

"Sure."

"You awake?" Duncan rasped. "What's that I hear, chant?"

He had been crying. I turned the volume way down. "When did you get back?"

"I'm still in New York. Things have turned to shit!" On the last word his voice shot hysterically skyward. It sounded like a sneeze. "I'm never going to live this down, never!"

I tried to play innocent. "What's the matter?"

"Don't pull that on me! You know what happened!"

"Curtis did mention something about a new recording contract. That's great, Duncan. You've wanted this for years."

"I wanted a solo contract for years. What happens? Instead of a violinist, now I get a fucking rock star!"

"I thought you wanted to expand your repertoire."

"Oh please! He can't even sing! Did Curtis tell you what we're supposed to record? Love songs!"

"What's so bad about that? People like love songs. They buy them in large quantities. You'll get a lot of name recognition."

"The hell I will!" he screamed. "Do you know what she wants to call us? Luke and Dunk! Dunk with a *k*!"

"Is that one word, Lukendunk? It's a little like Humperdinck, isn't it."

On and on and on we went: Duncan would never live this down, a lifetime of labor was wasted, he was the laughingstock of Cleveland, he would lose his job at that prep school in London. It was all my fault: I had introduced him to Sydney Bolt. Now she wanted twenty thousand bucks for services rendered. "She's going to sue me," Duncan moaned. "I'm going to lose the shirt off my back."

"That's ridiculous. You didn't sign any contracts, did you?"

He began to cry. "I didn't think it was a contract."

I had him read it to me. It was a contract. "Forget it," I said. "She can't do anything."

Duncan was sure Bolt would have him dragged away in chains the moment he stepped onstage for his comeback recital. We went round and round, trading accusations and longwinded apologies. An hour later, I had succeeded only in convincing Duncan that he must make a dash for JFK and fly back to Europe tonight. Everything would be straightened out before he returned to New York for his Chopin recital.

I hung up, needing another drink. Why did men come in only two varieties, collapsible and indestructible? I turned the lights out in the study and was about to leave when I noticed the stereo was still on. During Duncan's jeremiad, the Gregorian chant had come to an end; absorbed in my telephone ministry, I had not noticed the speakers go silent. My finger was an inch from the Off switch when I saw that the CD was still spinning vigorously. Why didn't I hear music, then? I waited a long moment, thinking the CD player was between tracks or perhaps winding down at program end, but the iridescent platter did not decelerate and I was still hearing no music. The counter indicated track eighteen so I grabbed the jewel box, read the program: the monks had sung only seventeen tunes. No eighteenth track here unless it was silent meditation. Mesmerized, I watched the CD spin on and on. When it finally stopped three minutes later I just stood there summing the parts as the chill in my stomach spread. It felt like the time I was running through the woods in Austria, knowing that within a second or two, a bullet would catch up with me.

"Still here?" Curtis said.

I turned my head toward the door. Just as that last time, I came out of a long sleep to see his face; he had seen me through that winter and he'd see me through this one. I put the CD into its box and gently snapped the lid. "That was Duncan," I said.

"What did he want?"

"Absolution. He came to the wrong person, of course." I said good night and went to my room.

It was a brilliant, simple plan, one I would have been proud to have devised myself. Hannah hacked into the NSA data banks and copied all communications between the satellite and its ground stations. She brought her cassette, microcassette, God knows what tape, to work and walked out of Data Translation Services with the information in U-matic format. Handed the U-matic to Harry, who walked it through Naja Ltd., that fly-by-night pressing plant in London. Out came a CD containing music plus, on the last track, sounds only a computer would understand. She would force the system to mute before the last track: Hannah wouldn't want any static rushing through the speakers of unsuspecting consumers when the program shifted from music to computer code. She had been careful to append her data to super-esoteric CD's that would have a run of only five hundred copies, on a tiny record label with no distribution, thus minimizing the chances of detection. Hannah probably owned the record company. If she didn't, she probably bought most, if not all, copies of the infected disc. If Leon Jurkowsky's mother happened to notice her CD player continuing for a few minutes after her brilliant boy's music had ended, so what? Would she suspect she had Russian satellite code on the tail end of her CD? Most people wouldn't even look before pressing the Stop button and on most players the spinning CD was not even visible. No, Hannah was quite safe. Once the CD was made, Harry brought it to Leipzig. If that was inconvenient, the deputy chief of the trade fair had only to place an order, pick up the disc in Berlin, and give it to Moll. That's what Flick had tried to do with the Gregorian chant the night he had visited me. Each CD would furnish the choirmaster with more and more clues until finally Moll would have enough data for the Clove to break the code. Then they owned the satellite.

I introduced Spot to Gregorian chant. My computer recognized the eighteenth track: its configurations matched those on the tape I had made months before in the steeple. I wondered how many CD's Hannah and Harry had had to make before the Clove cracked the code. Three? Twenty? Had Leon Jurkowsky been the straw that broke the camel's back? I should have figured it out the moment I saw the enormous CD collections in the steeple and in Flick's apartment. They were camouflage for Hannah's discs. I had assumed Flick and Moll were ardent music lovers, period. Silly of me.

I put the Gregorian chant aside and gave the computer Maxine's cassette containing the Life of Harry.

HARRY PARADISE
b. 4/22/35 London
mother Elke nee Hildebrandt b. 10/06/08 Stuttgart
    d. 06/08/86 London
father Charles Paradise b. 02/26/11 London d. 05/
    11/50 Shaftesbury
siblings 0

So Mom was a German. Older than Pop, no marriage date: Maxine hadn't thought it critical. Harry's father had died very young. Accident? I read the next few lines describing Harry's education. Before 1945 there was no record at all. Thereafter he had attended English schools and had barely managed to graduate from any of them. No mention of formal music training, no violin teachers on the bio. Harry had graduated from Glasgow University with a degree in French. Very practical. He had then bollixed a half dozen jobs before winding up a record producer for a large English label in the early sixties.

Harry had married five times, for periods ranging from three weeks to eleven months. The list of wives and their approximate tours of duty read like the cast of a B movie: Rosina, Greta, Nina, Eva, Vera. The ladies' last names were all German or Hungarian. Harry had residences in London, Toulouse, and the Grand Cayman Islands. He had almost seven million pounds in his various bank accounts. That was a hell of a lot of recording sessions.

I didn't want to think about Harry Paradise any more so I went to bed.

Next day Maxine and I went to a hair/face/nails salon for a little rehab work. The last few months had been murder on our femininity. In the sauna I told her about the wayward path of Hannah Selke's CD's from Tarrytown to Leipzig. For a long while the Queen just lay on the redwood deck sweating her ass off. Then, rather than express her admiration for my brilliant work, she brought up the same old questions: who were they and what did they intend to do with the satellite? In her opinion, the data pipeline was now irrelevant since the damage had been done. The Queen managed to imply that, had I been a little swifter in my deductions, we could have sabotaged the Clove long before Moll cracked the code. When I mentioned Harry Paradise, she only scowled.

"His mother was German," I said.

"So what? So was yours."

"Where was he during the war? What happened to his father? Where'd Harry get seven million pounds?"

"Why don't you ask him yourself? Get all the gory details he's been withholding all these years." Pebbles of sweat began to roll into her belly button. "By the way, he should really learn to launder money a bit better. He left a paper trail about a mile wide." The Queen refrained from calling him stupid yet again. "I still don't see what makes you think he's involved in all this."

"For starters, his name is on the CD with an extra track on it. Over the past few months his behavior has become bizarre. He disappears for weeks then lies about where he is. Twice I saw him in Leipzig sneaking around at four o'clock in the morning. Last time he was in Boston he spent the whole day on the phone. One of his calls was to Data Translation Services. Hannah's called him three times in the past two weeks."

Maxine took a while to absorb all the evidence. "How well do you know Alfred Chung?" she asked finally.

"We're old friends. Don't start on this, Maxine."

"He feeds you information and you tear off like a dog with a steak. Ever cross your mind that he might be setting you up?" She tossed a cup of cold water over the red-hot stones in the corner. "How about your friend Chance? He knows how to make phone calls too, doesn't he?"

"Chance was entertaining Godo at the time. I overheard Harry in the sauna talking with Hannah."

"How did you meet Chance?" Maxine asked.

"He came in at the last minute when Emory got sick in Berlin."

"Who brought him in?"

"Harry. For Christ's sake! Now Chance is a bad guy?"

"How should I know? He seems a little too good to be true, doesn't he?"

"He's come in very handy over the past few months, you might recall. I've gotten fairly good mileage out of him." The heat was giving me a headache. I stood up. "Forget anyone?"

The Queen yawned. "Why did Emory drop out of sight just as Leipzig was heating up? Where has he been the past few months? Wasn't his name on all those Vuota Corda CD's also? How about that CD pressing plant in London? Who's the contact there? If you're exploring suddenly bizarre behavior, you might take another look at Duncan Zadinsky. He goes to London once a month, doesn't he? Couldn't he be picking up tapes from that CD plant? Where'd he get the money to do this comeback recital?"

I thought I'd faint. "What are you doing to me, Maxine."

"I'm trying to keep your mind open."

Wrong. She was trying to deflect me from Harry Paradise. If, in the process, she turned me into a raving lunatic, distrusting the air I breathed, so much the better. That way the Queen retained control.

"What will you do now?" Maxine asked for the third time.

"Keep my mind open." I saw her smile. She knew I was lying.

Over the next few days I amused myself playing the Berg Concerto in Hamburg, Hannover, and Kassel. The performances were dour, edgy, hell on the audience. The only person who would have understood them was Flick but he was elsewhere playing with matches.

After my last rehearsal in Kassel, I began walking the cold streets in search of the Simler Music Shop. A glitzy neon sign two blocks from the concert hall indicated that the family still sold stringed instruments. Six strings, however, not four: a panoply of electric guitars packed the front window. The most expensive of them bore the Chance logo.

I went inside. A potential customer was testing amplifiers, sending loud, grating twangs through the store. As a young salesman displayed guitar picks to a woman with green hair, I studied the violins in a case behind the cash register. Finally a salesman came over. "May I help you?"

I pointed behind him. "Are those violins for sale?"

"Sure. Are you interested in any one in particular?"

"The oldest one." When he gave it to me, I looked inside its sound holes. The old German script was exactly the same as in Flick's violin. Simler 1901 Kassel. Only the date was different. "Who made this?" I asked.

He peered inside. "My great-grandfather. The Simlers have made violins for hundreds of years."

"Do you still make them?"

"No, no. Grandfather was the last." He paused as the guitarist thrummed a few chords. "No one buys violins any more."

I put the fiddle under my chin and plucked a few strings. "A friend of mine plays a Simler. He's quite fond of it."

"Really? What's his name?"

I almost said Zwinger but lost my nerve. "Flick. Emil Flick."

"Don't recognize the name. He's probably in the book, though."

I lay the violin on the counter. "Which book is that?"

"Our customer book. Everyone who bought a violin signed it. Goes all the way back to 1809."

The book in Hugo's library noted that the Simlers had kept precise accounts of how they made violins, not to whom they were sold. "It must be fascinating," I said.

"Not really. No one who bought a Simler ever became famous. But my grandfather kept in touch with every one of our customers. He sent a card on Beethoven's birthday asking if they were still practicing. Believe it or not, most of them wrote back saying yes."

Musicians were incredible liars. "If I bought a violin," I said slowly, "could I sign your book?"

"Sure, why not? It's right there in the drawer."

I bought a fiddle. With an indulgent smile, the current Herr Simler brought the ancient and precious volume to the counter. "May I?" I asked, turning over the old pages.

Behind me stood a Mick Jagger wannabe with a green guitar. "Take your time," said Simler, attending to his next customer.

I started searching the lists for Zwinger. Serial No. 1 was sold in 1809. Wolfgang Amadeus Simler had carefully noted the date, the lucky customer, and purchase price. One century, hundreds of failed Paganinis later, I had still not come across Zwinger. There weren't many pages left but sales had probably gone flat after World War I. Twenties, thirties, where are you Professor? . . . ah: seven violins for a Herr Stark, Berlin, April 1945, bought at an unbelievably low price. Grandpa Simler was probably off shooting deserters and Grandma was starving. Who would buy seven violins in the last weeks of the war? Beneath Stark's name I saw several addresses listed for him. The only one that wasn't crossed out was an old folks' home in Garmisch-Partenkirchen.

Simler shut the cash register. "Interesting?" he asked me.

I returned the book. "You really should keep up the family tradition."

Screech: another performing artiste was running his fingernails over amplified guitar strings. "I do. But it's with guitars now."

I thanked him and left, relieved but a little sad that he hadn't recognized me. Of course, I played four strings, not six.

16

*C*urtis had made sauerbraten; I could smell it from the garage. I followed the intoxicating aroma to the kitchen, where he stood over the stove sliding potato balls into boiling water. "How'd it go?" he asked. Curtis had already seen the reviews but he always waited for my side of the story.

"Not bad in Hamburg and Hannover. Kassel was a disaster. Try not to book me with Frimmer any more, would you? He's hopeless." I leaned over the stewpot. "When do we get to eat this?"

"Ten minutes." Curtis plopped the last dumpling into the water. "I put your mail on the desk."

I went to the office. Lying on top of my desk was an envelope from Flick. My heart began to pound as I saw my name written in his clear, disciplined hand: days before, miles away, he had thought of me.

> Dearest,
>   Could I see you next time you're in Leipzig? It's been a long winter.
>
> As ever,
Emil Flick

Did the bastard think we were just going to pick up where we had left off? Sorry, there was another man in the picture now. I tossed the note aside, disgusted. How easily his mere signature disrupted my life.

Chance had sent eight faxes, all love sonnets by Shakespeare and Herrick. His five sealed letters were more anatomically specific.

"Dinner," Curtis called. "Bring the calendar, would you?"

I went to the kitchen. We talked over my short-term concert schedule, much of which had been etched in stone for two years. I'd be starting March with a week in Scotland and Wales, going to Berlin for five days, Leipzig for three days of recording, straight to New York for Duncan's comeback recital and Kakadu's Lukendunk party, back to Germany for some chamber music to be filmed for television. In my spare time I was to learn a new concerto, not to mention the crossover album Kakadu wanted me to record with Maestro Blondie later in the spring. "It's kind of jammed," Curtis said. He turned the page to April. "Should I continue?"

"What for? I'll be dead by then." I swallowed another dumpling and a pool of gravy. "When's Scotland again?"

Curtis flipped the calendar back to March. "Thursday. Emory called, by the way. He was pretty upset not to be going to Leipzig with you and Harry. Said he had been promised the job and Harry suddenly gave it to Toby Chance."

"Typical. I'll try to see him in London. Cheer him up."

As we were doing the dishes, I asked Curtis if he knew anyone in Garmisch-Partenkirchen. "Please don't ask me to get you a concert," he said. "The impresarios there are impossible."

"I don't want a concert. I need a sanitarium. One where I could take Roland in the next day or two."

"Roland? What makes you think he's going to go?"

"Nothing."

The next day Curtis found a clinic in Obernach, a tiny village nestled in the Bavarian Alps. Minimum stay one month or results could not be guaranteed. They preferred celebrity addicts but would accept close relatives of famous

people if absolutely necessary. Would Fraulein Frost personally bring her brother to the clinic? Yes? They found a bed
for Roland.

Later that afternoon I drove to my brother's apartment to
announce his impromptu vacation. Caught him in his bathrobe
just as he was finishing breakfast. "Hi Sis," Roland said,
backing unsteadily away from the door. I doubted the bristly
cheeks and pink eyes signified recent literary ecstasies.
"Looking for Maxine?"

"No." I followed him to the kitchen and made a pot
of coffee. "How would you like to take a ride with me
tomorrow?"

Concentrating mightily, Roland diluted a glass of vodka
with a little orange juice. "Where to."

"The mountains." Whoops, too much orange juice. He
adjusted the proportions by sloshing more vodka into his mug.
"I booked you into a clinic for a month," I said. "Kind of
a late Christmas present."

"A month? What for? I feel fine."

"Fine? You look like hell."

"Aha, I get it! I'm embarrassing you."

"Give me a break!" I put my mug in the sink. "Do you
think Maxine likes living with a drunk?"

"You think I like living with a spy?"

Thank God Curtis wasn't there to hear him. I sighed.
"You're ill, Roland. Has anyone been bothering you?"

"Who the hell would bother me? Everyone wants to know
when Luke the Apostle's coming to visit. They want to know
what you're doing, where you've been. Things like that.
Forget me."

"Who asks? What do you tell them?"

"Oh, this and that. I make up stories. Hope you don't
mind. It's my only entertainment."

"Listen," I said. "Let Horst run the club for a while. Will
a few weeks in the mountains kill you? I found a place where
the scenery's nice, food's good. Nurses are nymphomaniacs.

It's costing me an arm and a leg." That perked him up considerably. "You'll come back a new man."

He eyed me distrustfully. "Did Maxine put you up to this?"

"She has no idea I'm here."

Roland somberly swallowed the last of his pale orange juice. "Why are you pushing so hard? Don't tell me this is for my own good. You've got something up your crafty little sleeve, I know it."

"Pick you up at eight in the morning." I got up to leave. "The whole trust fund goes to the survivor, remember. If that doesn't encourage you to outlive me, nothing will."

"Don't tempt me," he called as I shut the door.

Next morning I found Roland on his stoop, seated on a suitcase, smoking. "I don't believe it," I said, swinging open the car door. "You're awake."

"I never went to bed," he answered. "It seemed the sensible thing."

As I was snuggling his suitcase into the trunk, Maxine sauntered to the curb. Seeing me in black leather, she stopped cold. In silence she watched Roland bend himself into the passenger seat. "Going somewhere, you two?"

I slammed the trunk. "He didn't tell you?"

"Oh hi Max," Roland said. "You're up early."

"Where are you going."

That was a command, not a question. Upholding a long-standing Frost tradition, Roland's bravado collapsed. "Leslie's taking me to a funny farm. I'll be back in a month or so."

Her eyes met mine over the roof of the car. Anger, pain: I realized I was kidnapping her only barrier against a cold, choppy ocean that always hit high tide around four in the morning. Hey, she had done the same to me. Now she could take a dose of her own medicine. "A month?" the Queen repeated.

"They had an opening," I explained lamely, gunning the engine. "Seat belt on, Roland?"

He opened his window. "I'll write, Maxine. Take good care of yourself."

I accelerated rapidly away from the curb: the less of her in the rearview mirror, the better. "What are you trying to do, snap my neck?" Roland complained, peering at the speedometer as we cornered onto Mohnstrasse. "I know you're in a rush to get rid of me but this is ridiculous."

I jammed to a stop at a red light. "That was rather cowardly, Roland. You could have told her." He didn't reply as I blew past a Mercedes trying to beat me through the Grunewald.

We hit an outbound traffic jam but it was nothing compared to the inbound lanes: to the East Germans, Berlin was still Disneyland. "Look at that mess," Roland said as we drove past two miles of idling Trabants. "Filthy cars. Rotten roads. Smells like pig shit. God, this place depresses me."

"Cheer up. Your taxes will soon fix everything."

He reclined his seat. "Wake me up when we get there."

An hour later the clouds broke but the pollution didn't. Instead of sunshine, a reddish glow suffused the muddy fields around Leipzig. In two weeks I would be going back there for the last time. The town would be crowded, chaotic, in the throes of its March trade fair; Flick would be up to his neck in mischief. It was absolutely the worst time to have scheduled recording sessions, but Harry Paradise had insisted this was his only opening in months. As I passed a line of flatbed trucks crawling off the E6 at Leipzig, destination fairgrounds, I suddenly wanted Hannah's game to be over. I wanted the page turned so I could get on with my little life. It had not been mine since that night in Auerbachs Keller.

As we wound back into West Germany, I doubled my speed. Roland slept through Bayreuth, Nuremberg, Munich, and most of the Bavarian Alps, finally waking when his bladder signaled that he had ignored it long enough.

That evening, we rolled up the driveway of a white villa. Maybe my mind was already on my next errand. Maybe I couldn't bear the panic in Roland's eyes as I helped him out of the car: suddenly the lid slammed shut on my pity. It was a matter of self-preservation. I smiled as Frau Doktor welcomed us to her retreat. In a few seconds she sized Roland and me up and was probably surprised that he was the one who would be staying. Nevertheless we were both given the grand tour. I shook a lot of hands, signed a few autographs but no, sorry, couldn't stay for dinner. I had a rehearsal in Munich tonight. Hearing that, Roland smirked.

He walked me back to the car to fetch his suitcase. "Rehearsal in Munich? You didn't even bring your violin," he remarked. "Never mind. Thanks for making the side trip. I might enjoy it here. Good clean living. No musicians. No one tossing and turning in my bed all night, muttering in her sleep."

He knew just which screws to turn. "I'll visit you." Kissed his cheek.

"Didn't you hear the doctor? No visitors." He took a few steps along the spotless flagstones. "Look after Maxine, would you? Between the two of us, we've done a pretty good job on her."

No one ever did a job on Maxine. What Roland really meant was Maxine and I had done a pretty good job on him. I waved goodbye and drove through a few fields and villages, checking the rearview mirror. Nothing followed me south but the clear, sharp moonlight. Soon I joined the caravan wending slowly through Garmisch-Partenkirchen. Having invigorated themselves on the slopes all day, thousands of skiers were now looking to exercise other muscle groups. Their well-toned bodies and skintight outfits slowed traffic on Zugspitzstrasse to a voyeuristic crawl. After a few blocks, I pulled the M6 out of the parade and began climbing the steep side streets.

Zwinger, or I suppose he was Stark now, lived in a large and deceptively residential retirement home. It looked like a downscale variation of the clinic in which I had just installed Roland. I waited until finally all of its lights went out. Then

I checked the locks, the windows: security minimum. But who would want to break in here? The residents didn't have any cash or jewelry. Their families had already confiscated it all. I entered through the front door. Inside it was very warm, thick with the sweet-sour smell of old people. A hodgepodge of couches and tables, left behind by the deceased, crowded the foyer. Ramps, rails, and oxygen tanks reminded the guest that this was a holding tank for the local mortuary. I crept upstairs. Two nightlights glowed on either end of a long hall, spreading feeble light over the walkers and wheelchairs parked outside their owners' rooms. Names were taped on the doors.

I found Zwinger sleeping alone in a tiny room. He still looked like the man in the portrait at the Hochstein School. He lay on his back and his skin was cold, but he was breathing, which was all I wanted. I took an atomizer from my pocket. The label at the bottom indicated Chanel No. 5 but the liquid inside had no odor. Perfume nevertheless: instead of persuading men to yield to seduction, it persuaded them to yield to truth. Sleeping men would not wake, would not remember. I preferred injection but that would mean turning on the lights, finding a vein, leaving a puncture, to say nothing of waking the old boy up. No thanks.

I paced Zwinger's breathing, as I had the other night with Chance. Then, just before he inhaled, I misted his nostrils. Dosage? The Queen had only recommended administering as little as possible. I stopped after six sprays. My patient had not moved. I put my lips to his ear. "Zwinger," I whispered. He snorted, didn't respond. Overdose? Maxine's pharmacopoeia was probably not intended for nonagenarians. "Zwinger." I pulled his earlobe.

Damn! Took another demure case from my pocket: smelling salts, more or less. I needed to revive him just to the edge of dreams. I passed the case a few inches from his nose. He jolted. "Zwinger."

"Zwinger," he whispered back.

"You must help me," I said.

"Help."

"Help me find your students."

"Students," he repeated.

The nurse would be breaking in with a breakfast tray before I got any sense out of him. "Do you remember the Hochstein School in Berlin?"

"Berlin."

"You taught the violin there."

This time he remained silent: I had hit a submerged log. Forty-five years later, he still remembered, still fought to protect it. "You taught your pupils more than how to play the violin, didn't you. Who were they?"

He swallowed. "Who . . . are you?"

I'd have to have a word with Maxine about this perfume. Subjects weren't supposed to ask questions, just answer them. I gave him another snoutful of Succubus No. 5. "Who were they? What were their names? What were you doing with them?"

He fought, and lost. "Operation Phoenix."

Not quite what I wanted but at least he was beginning to cooperate. "They were only children. How many were there."

"Seven."

He had bought seven violins from Simler. "How many are left."

Zwinger frowned. "One—two—three—four—some died."

"What was their mission?"

He sighed. "To wait."

"Wait for what?"

"For Germany."

"And then what?" He drifted away from me, or pretended to. I hesitated to give him another bolt of uppers. "Answer me, Zwinger."

He smiled slowly, imperiously, very much like the Queen. "Ask Hannah. She's . . . in charge now."

"Hannah Selke?"

His head dropped to the side. "Women are . . . so crafty."

I slapped his cheek. "Emil Flick. The man in Leipzig. What is his job?"

"Emil. He played the violin. He was a wonderful boy . . . a beautiful boy."

"What is his job?" I repeated. Careful, Smith: keep the voice soft, coaxing. "You must tell me."

Zwinger smiled peacefully. "His job is . . . to obey Hannah."

That got him a noseful of punishment. Zwinger began to rattle and wheeze, loudly enough for the nurse to notice, if she slept with one ear cocked. Then he suddenly went still. Again I bent over him. "What about Harry." No answer. "Harry Paradise."

"Paradise," echoed Zwinger, fading with each syllable. "Para . . . diiise."

"What does Paradise do?"

Zwinger smiled again. "He . . . obeys . . . Hannah . . . Ha . . . H . . ." He left, not to return.

I left him barely breathing and ran from that house of death. I rolled my car down the hill, scuttled through the now-quiet streets of Garmisch-Partenkirchen, and sped to Munich, taking a suite at the Four Seasons. Couldn't sleep I was still so afraid: didn't know at which sentence, which sigh, he had emerged from the netherworld, but I knew that Zwinger had outfoxed me.

The following evening I got back to Berlin. Perhaps to dissuade me from going directly from garage to liquor cabinet, my housekeeper had baked an apple pie. Still warm, it sat on the kitchen counter just begging to be ravaged. In the distance I heard Curtis vacuuming. "I'm home," I called when he shut the machine off. "Can I cut this?"

He came to the kitchen as I was shoving a gigantic wedge into my mouth. "That was quick," he said.

I ignored the implied criticism of my cruising speed on the autobahn. "This is excellent pie, Curtis. Have some."

"No thanks, I'm cleaning. The bookshelves are pretty dusty."

"Why bother with that? No one reads any of the books now."

Curtis washed his hands and wiped them dry over his rump. "Coffee?" He tossed a handful of beans into the grinder.

"Thanks," I chomped. "Any messages?"

"Toby Chance called four times. I'm sure he'd appreciate it if you'd return one call out of twenty."

"I'll try."

"He sounded like a gentleman."

"He's in way over his head."

Curtis frowned. "He didn't strike me as naive."

"What are you, a dating service? What have you two been talking about anyhow? Has he been asking you questions about me?"

Over the years Curtis had developed a fairly reliable method of defusing rampant paranoia. He took my pie away and wrapped me in a bear hug. "Shhh." Until he felt me wilt, he wouldn't let go. Today it took a while; that crafty old Zwinger had pulled a bad switch. Finally he broke away and slapped my rear-end. "Get to work."

Around sundown the phone rang. "Hello stranger," said Chance. "Working hard?"

"I was."

"Did you get my messages?"

"Of course! I've been snowed under here. Sorry."

"I see. Look, I've been thinking. Curtis told me you're going to Scotland tomorrow. Why don't I meet you in London? We can relax for a day or two, then go to Leipzig together."

"Are you out of your mind?" Ouch: guilt hurt. "I don't think so," I said, more contritely. "Not this time."

Chance paused. This was not the same woman who had recently driven through a blizzard to jump into his bed. "What's bothering you, honey?"

Oh, just a couple of *Übermenschen* who had been waiting

forty-five years for Germany to rise again. "Nothing," I said. "I'm just a little tired."

More guilt twinged my conscience the moment I hung up. It was all Maxine's fault for planting a million doubts about Chance in my weakened brain. But she always did this to me. The Queen knew that distrust was my oxygen. Therefore she waited until a case was winding down, when it seemed as if I would once again escape with my life, then *blam!* what about this wrong number, where'd Joe Blow come from, isn't that a strange coincidence . . . afterward she always said it was just mental reinforcement, for my own protection. Bah. She enjoyed watching me spin like a top: revenge for never having thrown her coffee cups away at the doughnut stands. I almost called Chance back, begging to meet him in London. But he didn't fit into the schedule and I had more pressing items on the agenda.

Forty-eight hours later, I was playing a Paganini concerto in Edinburgh. My fingers were agile and Maestro had a fire in his belly; nevertheless, we owed much of our success to a twelve-tone piece that opened the program. In comparison, Paganini's pyrotechnic claptrap sounded exalted. The orchestra and I repeated the menu in Glasgow, then Cardiff. With each performance, the concerto got quicker and lighter while the overture sank deeper into a pit of phony angst. Needless to say, the composer was not speaking to me much by tour's end.

After the final concert, I went to London for a little chat with Emory Morse, Harry's waylaid recording engineer. I had been intending to see him for weeks but wanted the trip to appear innocuous, spur-of-the-moment. Now was my last chance before Leipzig. Since his unfortunate poisoning in Berlin in November, Emory had been too woozy to accompany Harry on his global treks. For months the poor man had been lying in bed worrying that Toby Chance had usurped his place at Harry's side. Harry had not eased Emory's fears by asking Chance to do my next recording in Leipzig. Acting with his usual grace, Harry had hedged until the last minute, then disappeared; Emory got the news about his replacement from Harry's housekeeper.

I wasn't surprised, therefore, to find Emory waiting morosely in a corner of his favorite pub. Many pints of beer had already dissolved his posture into an amoeboid slouch. Deprived of sunshine for months, his skin had acquired the texture of egg soufflé. Lots of Emory's hair had drifted away; those precious tufts still brushing his ears he dared not discourage with scissors. As I walked to his seat, he stared into his beer as if each bubble contained dire prophecy.

"Hi Em," I said. "Feeling well?"

He tried to sit up a bit now that every man in the pub was staring at him in dismay. "Much better."

For the umpteenth time, my mind replayed the scene in the Kempinski Hotel, where the old woman had tapped Emory on the shoulder before scuttling out to the street. Had that been Hannah? Same size, same tight gait, only she never would have hit Emory instead of me. Never. The whole episode still rankled me. "I'm so sorry, Emory. It must have been awful."

"Awful? It was a bleeding nightmare. My faith in doctors is destroyed forever. First they thought it was food poisoning. Then malaria. Then AIDS. Now it's a microbe from another planet." He finished his beer. "Let's drop the subject. It's over."

Not quite. I ordered a magnum of champagne. We talked for a while about Emory's disastrous love life and my manufactured romance with Luke the Apostle. As the bottle emptied, conversation veered inevitably toward the recording business and, finally, Harry.

"Son of a bitch," Emory muttered. "He knew I wanted to go to Leipzig. Why'd he take that pushy Yank?"

"It was a deal," I said. "Chance bailed him out of a last-minute editing crisis. In return he wanted Leipzig."

"What's so special about Leipzig? Why didn't Chance take the New York Phil job or the Paris opera?"

"Because I'm playing in Leipzig. He's become rather fond of me."

Emory frowned, considering the ramifications of an artist-engineer liaison. "Feelings mutual?"

I didn't care who made my recordings but I needed Chance in Leipzig this one last time: he was my perfect alibi. "I don't know. But Harry really does owe him on this one. Chance edited the Mozart project on about twenty minutes' notice." I ordered another bottle of champagne. "It's all Harry's fault. Chance just took advantage of his stupidity."

"Bastard. Without me he doesn't even know which month he's in."

"Do you think so?" I ventured. Emory was not good for too many more polysyllables. "Sometimes I think Harry only pretends to be a moron."

"It's no act," Emory said. "Believe me."

Sorry, I never believed anyone. "But he's so . . . crafty."

"A man's got to cover his ass."

"Was he always so devious?"

"From the moment he realized he had a tin ear, love. That was about thirty years ago, when we did our first session together."

"Why didn't he do something else then?"

Emory took a long time to reply. "He's always trying other things," he said carefully. "I think he feels safest around musicians."

Of course: the neurotic surrounded himself with the paranoid. In comparison, he looked imperial. For a while I watched a game of darts over in the corner. "Poor louse. I wonder if he had a happy childhood."

"I don't think so. His mother was a witch. She never let him forget that she would have preferred a girl."

"What about his father?"

"I never met Harry's father," Emory said. "I'm not sure that Harry did, either. He told me he had no recollection of him at all."

"Harry's mother died only a few years ago, didn't she?"

"Ninety-five years old and sharp as a pin until the bitter end. It was the happiest day of Harry's life when he shipped her to the crematorium." Emory looked oddly at me. "Why are we talking about Harry's mother?"

We ordered lunch and switched to politics, a topic only marginally less ludicrous than Harry's mother. Emory was looking forward to the millennium now that Europe was fusing into one gigantic nirvana. I let him rave on: he'd wake up eventually. As he depleted the pub's champagne reserves, Emory talked about the great new markets opening up in the east and how he hoped to tap into them. Once again, conversation returned to Harry, our mutual millstone.

"Of course, he's got all the connections," Emory said. "Harry's been working in the east for thirty years."

Terrific. "How'd he get started over there?" I asked.

"Don't know. When I met him, he was already thick with Eastern European record labels. And Eastern European women, of course. They've always been his downfall."

"How so?"

Emory's face suddenly reddened. "You don't know about his wives?"

"I never asked and he never brought the subject up."

"Bitches," Emory said hastily. "It's no wonder he never talks about them." He tried to laugh. "First it's his mother, now it's his wives! We must be pretty drunk!"

Intermission: we ate, amused by a darts game. Neither of us was done with Harry yet. "So this Yank is busy?" Emory resumed after a while.

"Afraid so."

"I hope he's got a low-voltage ego. Harry's not into giving credit where credit's due."

"Don't worry," I said. "Chance will get his mileage out of Harry then drop him. He's a pretty slick operator himself."

"Eh? I thought you liked him."

"Chance has many fine qualities. Finessing Harry is one of them."

Emory sedulously finished his pea soup, working up the

courage to ask the question that had been haunting him for months. "Is he a good engineer?" he asked finally.

"Better than you? No." Occasionally a few white lies paved the way to higher truth. "Harry's going to come crawling back to you sooner than you think, Emory." I ordered the knockout round of champagne. "You two have been together for years. Those walls in Harry's apartment are covered with great CD's he's done with you."

"None of them are great. Most of them are mediocre and a few are real disasters. We did it for money, not art."

The window of opportunity had opened a crack: go for it now, Smith. "You didn't do any projects for fun? Look at what you did for Vuota Corda. Krumhorns and Leon Jurkowsky. Don't tell me that wasn't fun."

Emory's face remained vacant: could he really know nothing? "Those were alimony jobs, Les. Harry and I made our money and split. Period. Everything we did for that label was a nightmare. What makes you think of them?"

"The name appeals to a violinist. *Vuota corda* is Italian for 'open string.' No vibrato. Who are they anyway? I never heard of them."

"You never will either, I think. They've gone bankrupt. No surprise considering the drivel they put out. Like that Leon Jurkowsky fiasco. The man thought he was a composer. Got to the sessions and couldn't even read his own music. He just made it up as he went along."

"Why would a label even release that?"

"What can I say? Everything in their catalog was that way. Krumhorns, sackbuts, castrato arias, Gregorian chant. But they paid the going rate."

"You never saw anyone from the company?"

"Harry did all the schmoozing with some woman in New York. I think she got his name from Billboard magazine. In six months we did a dozen projects, bang, out of the blue. All rush jobs. Then she suddenly dried up in December. Harry even flew to New York to stroke her but it was all over."

I sighed. "You did the editing?"

"Inch by agonizing inch, darling."

I played with my sandwich. Better slow up: even a drunk would realize he was being interrogated.

"But he was strange about those projects," Emory suddenly continued. My questions had funneled him into a narrow ravine and the champagne trapped him there. "I had to have everything edited within two days of the sessions. The moment I finished, Harry snatched the tape."

"He actually rushed on something? Hard to believe. Did he at least listen to the master before it went to the pressing plant?"

"I don't know. He just came to my studio and took the master tape."

"Took it where?"

"To the CD plant, love. Naja Ltd. It's around the corner from Harry's new flat. They put it right into production and shipped all the CD's to New York."

I tried to look confused. "Why didn't Vuota Corda just press the CD's in the States?"

"Don't know. I told you this was a lunatic company. The woman who ran it had a lot of money and no business sense at all. That's what Harry said anyway. I think his interest in this was more than pecuniary, if you know what I mean. He never gave anyone this kind of special treatment without a payoff in mind."

"Is she attractive? Petite?"

"I never met her."

"Does she still see Harry?"

"How should I know? He's much too busy to call any more."

I knew how that felt, all right. Until I had to get back to Heathrow, I drowned Emory with sympathy, encouraging him to become more independent of his lifelong partner. What with plane crashes and microbes from alien planets, there was no telling how much longer Harry might be in the record business.

* * *

For two days I imprisoned myself in the music room with the Sibelius Concerto, one of the most difficult in the repertoire. I had recorded it years earlier with Hugo; the moment I was contractually free to record it again, Godo had insisted on an updated version for the Kakadu catalog. He thought it was my calling card, my little show-off number. In fact it was thirty minutes of angina. The concerto was almost impossible to play up to speed, yet fell somehow flat at anything under breakneck pace. After ten years and dozens of performances, I still considered it paper-thin ice from first to last note. Recording it again would be no picnic.

Toby Chance called from the Berlin airport, inquiring after my mental health. I told him in a taut monotone that all was well, yes yes, London was fine. Sorry we hadn't been able to get together. No, no possibility of dinner that evening, I had to practice. By now he knew better than to hang on the phone waiting for me to change my mind. However, he did say that he intended to vent his frustration on certain areas of my anatomy in the near future. "Looking forward to it," I said, and hung up.

Late that night, my doorbell rang. Quite a while later, Maxine let herself into the music room. In her book, turning the doorknob was the equivalent of knocking. I put the violin down. "Well! Make yourself right at home!"

Even in casual clothes, the Queen looked dangerous. It was the way she walked: taut, ready to pounce . . . somewhere beneath that tight sweater, the minimal pants, she carried a razor. Like me, she slept lightly and trusted no one. Unlike me, she looked better all the time. "Curtis tells me you're leaving for Leipzig tomorrow," she said. "Thought I'd wish you luck."

Luck? She should wish me nerve. I wasn't up for crawling a third time into the steeple. "Thank you."

"Nervous?" she said.

I sat opposite her in Hugo's favorite chair. "Extremely."

"You'll be fine." The words circled ominously in the air

like vultures over a carcass. "Roland called today. He seemed in good spirits."

"The nurses are blond and horny. Don't expect him back for months."

She didn't smile. "I understand the trade fair's in full swing."

What did that mean? I was just in time for Flick's laser exhibition? "It's the worst time of year to be recording there. The hotels will be packed, the streets will be noisy. The orchestra's just back from a long tour, so they'll be tired. Harry insisted, though. Said it was his only free slot."

Maxine picked up a crystal paperweight. "Do me a favor," she said, studying the refracting light. "Just do your job and get out of there. We'll take care of the fallout later."

"What are you telling me."

"I'm telling you not to get sidetracked with Harry or your two boyfriends. You've made the soup a little thick this time."

"Since when is my soup your problem?"

The Queen blinked wearily. "Hannah Selke flew to Munich yesterday. She rented a car and drove to Garmisch-Partenkirchen. Right down the road from Roland's hospital, in fact. I followed her." She delicately replaced the paperweight on an old book. "Whom did she see?"

For a moment I was too ill to reply. "Zwinger."

"You found Zwinger?" For once the Queen reacted. "Damn."

"You'd better rethink the formula for that perfume. He wasn't supposed to remember my visit."

"Could he describe you to Hannah?"

"Only my voice." That was enough, of course. "Did she fly back to New York?"

"Are you joking? Hannah's in Leipzig."

I looked at Hugo's old leather books, his old instruments in the corner cupboard. It was really a beautiful, serene room. Once I had felt very safe here. "Flick knows who I am," I said after a while.

I felt her weigh, one by one, the awful implications. "Has he done anything about it?"

"If he has, I guess I won't be seeing you again."

The Queen's face became slightly purple. I hadn't seen it that shade since the day she came backstage in New York to congratulate me for winning a violin competition. "Fool," she muttered. "I hope you don't think Flick's going to be the one pulling the trigger, putting you out of your misery." She started toward the door.

"By the way," I called, "you could get me all the information you can on Naja Ltd. It's a pressing plant in London. I think that's where Hannah and Harry made their CD's. Also, run me a detailed list of Harry's wives. The last one you made for me was a little thin."

She smiled bleakly. "Still hot on Harry?"

"Just do it," I snapped, suddenly aware that this trip to Leipzig was totally out of sequence. I was going too soon and too late, underprepared and overrehearsed, all because of a damn recording session. Hah, Hannah was going to frost the fiddler, all right. The Queen knew it, too. That's why she had come to pay her last respects. I picked up the violin. "Thanks for stopping by. I'll call when I get back."

"Could I ask you to think about something?"

I played a few soft trills. "Sure."

"The purpose of this trip is not to avenge a failed love affair. The purpose is to confound the opposition."

"What about the Sibelius Concerto?"

"Make a great recording, Smith. That's the cornerstone of the confusion." The Queen left.

Harry's limousine waddled into the driveway as Curtis was reviewing my upcoming agenda over breakfast the next morning. "Try not to run the sessions into overtime," he instructed, pouring more orange juice into my glass. "I've got you on the three o'clock flight to New York on Sunday. If you make the plane you'll have just enough time to get to Duncan's concert. Kakadu's throwing a party the next day.

It would be wise to make an appearance. You've got an interview with—''

The doorbell rang. As Curtis went to answer it, I marveled at his compact, curvaceous rear end. Strange that after all these years I had managed to keep my hands off it. Suddenly, I regretted that.

"Smells great in here, Curt baby," Harry called from the front hall. "Save a piece for me?" A few moments later, the chinchilla coat swirled into the kitchen. As usual, Harry's chartreuse ascot accented the yellow in his artificial tan. "Good morning," he said to me, beelining for the coffee pot. "Ready to kill 'em?"

"Ready if you are."

Curtis brought my boots from the hall. The leather gleamed and, I was sure, the white knife in the inseam had been carefully sharpened. "You're wearing these, I take it," he said, lifting my right foot.

Chomping on coffee cake, Harry watched my housekeeper prepare me to leave. "Curt," he said as I slipped into a coat, "if you ever get tired of dressing this pest, give me a call."

Curtis glanced at the clock above the stove. "We'd better get this show on the road." He brought us to the limousine, where Harry and I waited in the backseat as Curtis checked out the chauffeur's credentials. Finally satisfied, he stepped back.

"Coming to the sessions?" Harry called.

Curtis only smiled. "I've seen it all before, Harry." He stared calmly at me as the smoky window rolled shut.

The Mercedes cruised onto the E6. I looked out at the flat, gray fields, cursing myself for not having taken the motorcycle. However, appearances had to be maintained. I pulled out a best-selling biography and passed my eyes over and over the same lines while Harry listened to his Walkman, very occasionally scrawling in an opera score. Today, both of us were sloppy actors. Traffic chugged thickly along the highway. Now that the West Germans had slated Leipzig for early resurrection, so many Mercedes and BMW's occupied the inside lane that passengers in the Trabants didn't even stare at us any more as we blew past them. The limousine ran into a logjam at the Leipzig exit. Everyone was going to Flick's trade fair. Harry and I crawled with the horde to the center of town, arriving at the Gewandhaus as the midafternoon sun flitted wanly above the smog, its light jaundicing the streets. The locals had tried to spruce up the old downtown with a few banners and information booths which were already filmed with mud.

We signed in at the stage door and followed the stacks of shipping cases to the control room, where Chance was just beginning to set up his equipment. The sight of him playing with the buttons on the Sony machines ignited a tiny flame of lust which I knew would amplify as the day slipped away. Pre-mission pyromania? Maybe. He had always had an uncanny ability to override all Stop signs. "Hello," I called, heaving my coat over a table.

The whistling stopped, his eyes caught mine: one of us would not be sleeping in his/her bed this evening. Chance greeted me on the mouth. "Hi, Harry," he said, making no attempt to put a little oxygen between our navels. "Have a good trip?"

"I'm fine. The lady's miserable," Harry said. "Didn't say two words to me the whole way over. She needs round-the-clock attention."

Great move, that. Disengaging myself from the designated chaperone, I went to practice in a tiny room down the hall. Someone knocked a while later and led me onstage to rehearse the Sibelius with Maestro and the orchestra. We'd be performing it that evening in anticipation of tomorrow's recording sessions.

When I returned to the control room afterward, Chance sat alone behind the mixer writing a few notes in his logbook. The equipment was neatly set up, tested, ready to roll. "Where's Harry?" I asked.

"He left hours ago." Chance kissed my hand. "Sounds great."

"He didn't even listen to the rehearsal?"

"I listened to the rehearsal, my dear. Everything's under control." He watched me fidget with my coat. "Going back to the hotel?"

"Going for a walk." There was no reason not to take him along. Outside, the sun had called it quits and the damp, sharp air pressed against the dead earth. I turned right, toward the Thomaskirche.

Probably aware that I preferred to be alone, Chance took my arm but did not talk much. As he had told me often enough, he had had a lot of experience with preperformance musicians. We joined the natives and conventioneers streaming over the wet cobblestones of the inner city. Trade fair or no, the fundamental pulse of Leipzig had quickened since my dip in a barren fountain only five months earlier. It would never again be the medieval village I had known.

We rounded a last corner, my mouth dropped: the scaffolding was gone. The steeple of the Thomaskirche stood naked under an arc of yellow lights. "Pretty, isn't it," Chance said, following my eyes.

We walked past the fountain, past the spot where Flick had ended a policeman's watch. I clutched Chance's arm and began to babble about stupid little things, shrinking from people with cameras. He walked me in a wide circle back to the Merkur and obligingly calmed me down, usual method.

I played a great concert at the Gewandhaus that evening, but Flick did not come backstage afterward. Just as well. He would have seen a proprietary young man at my side and that would have bothered me. Afterward Harry took us all out to the Kaffeebaum, making eyes at a plump woman across the room as he traded vulgar jokes with Maestro. I kept checking over the dark, cavernous café for Flick or Hannah's red hair: nothing, damn them. Chance stayed the night in my room, trying to regain lost ground, but we weren't in Boston anymore, were we, and as Maxine had said, he was a little too good to be true.

17

$\mathcal{T}$ he next morning, I awoke vaguely disturbed, tingling with anxiety, then remembered why: recording sessions at ten and two at the Gewandhaus. At six o'clock, the choirboys sang Bach at the Thomaskirche, ergo one last visit to the steeple. Then I was free. It was all too awful to contemplate so I rolled over and bumped into Chance.

"Good morning," he said.

Damn! Hadn't he had the courtesy to leave yet? The last thing I needed this early was human contact. *"Hmmmfph."*

He thought about that a while before edging to my side of the bed. His mouth was lazily anointing my shoulder when the phone rang. "Leslie," Flick asked, "did I wake you?"

From sleep, no; from the dead, maybe. "I was about to get up." We spoke in German. "How are you, darling?"

"Very well, thanks," Flick said. "You played beautifully last night."

"You were there? Why didn't you come backstage?"

"I could only get away for an hour." In the background I heard Flick's PA system telling everyone to visit pavilion twenty. "You're recording today?"

"Morning and afternoon sessions," I said, pausing as Chance exited diplomatically to the bathroom. "I must see you, Emil. Any time. Anywhere. You name it, I'll be there." Why not beg? We had wasted so much time already.

"There's a reception at eight tonight in pavilion five," Flick said. "We'd only have to stay a few minutes. I'm sorry there's so little time. I'm absolutely stuck here."

"No problem."

"I'll leave you a pass at the west entrance. The pavilion's just a few steps away."

"Eight o'clock, then. Thanks for calling." I hung up.

"Let me guess," said Chance, emerging naked from the bathroom. "Maestro's in the lobby. He needs one more rehearsal."

"That was an old friend. He invited me out tonight."

"I see! And you said yes, of course."

"You understand German?"

"I understand tone of voice, honey buns." Chance began to dress, whistling "La Donna è Mobile." "How friendly is this friend?"

"He's a violinist," I said. "I gave him a few lessons."

"Ah, a fellow artiste!" Chance viciously zipped his fly. "Why is he calling you so early? Does he like to catch you in bed?"

"What? He's got to get to work."

"Where are you two going, the opera? Or are you just staying in and playing duets?"

"No idea. You're jealous? I don't believe it."

"Let's say that, knowing you as I now do, I'm apprehensive."

"You're pretty ridiculous."

"I suppose so." He turned the doorknob. "See you at the sessions."

The day was off to a murky start and Harry didn't inject any sunshine at breakfast. He hadn't slept at all and, once again, had forgotten to bring several vitamins upon which his health depended. When eight people at the neighboring table lit their postprandial cigarettes, I left the dining room. As I walked alongside the squealing trolleys to the Gewandhaus, heavy clouds roiled over Karl-Marx-Platz. From sky to earth, everything in sight was black or gray, filthy, wet, and cold.

I shut myself into a warmup room and twiddled Sibelius. For the next few hours, the brain would acknowledge nothing but these few thousand notes: ten, one hundred years from now, they would be all that remained of me. Just before the sessions began, I found Harry in the dim control room, gobbling antacid tablets as he flipped through the score. Chance sat at his side, eyes closed, hands clamped over a pair of headphones: he was a recording engineer now, not my lover.

"I'm going onstage, Harry," I said.

"Go, go!" he snapped. "I'll tell you when we're ready back here!"

I joined Maestro and the doodling orchestra on the stage we had just left a dozen hours before. This morning we would be playing the same piece but this time the auditorium was empty, we were dressed like slobs, and when we made a few mistakes, Harry would cut us off. For the next three hours we'd be performing not music but tonal surgery. If these goddamn instruments were easier to play, if we didn't have to follow a conductor in orderly columns of sound, we'd probably be doing drugs like every other breed of musician: recording sessions were like making love to a mirror. Pulling them off required massive leaps of the imagination.

"Good morning, everyone," Harry announced through the talk-back speakers. His awful German stunned everyone into immediate silence. "May we take a few sound levels, please?" He directed us to passages which might paralyze the delicate Sony equipment. Chance ran out to rearrange a few microphones as nearby musicians of both genders inspected his body. He didn't seem aware of them, or of me. After a while, we were ready to record.

My fingers obeyed and the orchestra buoyed me like a gorgeous mattress. Sibelius would have been happy. The electronic monsters in the control room quietly munched tape and Harry kept within a page of us most of the time. Exemplary sessions: by late afternoon, we had the first and second movements in the can.

Harry's coat was already on when Maestro and I returned to the control room. "Excellent! Super!" he bellowed.

"I would like to listen to a few places," Maestro said, as Harry was about to put his hat on. "Just to be sure."

"Sure of what? Everything's covered. You have nothing to worry about."

Maestro wasn't worried about anything; like most conductors, he got a hard-on listening to his own performances. "Perhaps a little of the slow movement before I go home? A tiny cadenza?"

Harry consulted his watch. "Dreadfully sorry, Waldemar. I've scheduled another appointment."

With a redhead, no doubt. "Cutting things a little close, aren't you, Harry?" I asked.

He glared at me. "Chance will take care of everything." He quickly left.

Chance leapt to the breach. "Pull up a seat, Maestro," he said, beckoning to Harry's still-warm chair. "I'll change tapes."

I followed the engineer to the machine room: didn't want to leave him, perhaps forever, on a sour note. "Still speaking to me?"

"That depends, darling." He dropped a U-matic tape into the Sony. "Are you sleeping at the Merkur tonight?"

"I expect so," I lied, taking my coat.

I returned to the hotel and took a long, hot bath: purge Frost, coddle Smith. Today my visit to the steeple would be brief and final. I had only to feed the Clove thirty-three seconds of sabotage and run down that dark, winding staircase back to the sanctuary. But today I was more afraid than ever before. Hated going back three times anywhere. First time no problem, total surprise bang, I was gone. Second time, the opposition was a little wary, maybe expecting me. Third time? Goading fate.

I dressed in my Generic Coed outfit, filling my pockets with the Queen's gewgaws, and walked through the dank streets to the Thomaskirche. Motets still at six; Moll still conducting choirboys; Bach still under the bronze slab at the altar. Somber worshipers already crammed the sanctuary, staring at the rafters and the cracked plaster vaults, waiting for Oskar Wildau to begin his organ prelude. When I saw Moll flee from his steeple to the choir loft, his face very much like Harry Paradise's before a recording session, I drifted toward Bach's gravestone. For the last time I tailed a cluster of Poles into the vestry and remained there, communing with the tapestries, until the time came to slide behind the heavy chests in the corner.

At the opposite end of the Thomaskirche, Oskar began a gigantic toccata. Up in the choir loft, two dozen mouths opened and Bach rose from the dead, as he would until the end of history. My silly little life, my games with phantoms, were just passing specks of dust. I unlocked the steeple door with the key I had stolen.

Another world there, without song. I stood a moment acclimating to the soft whoosh of air lost in the cavern. Then I flew up the cluttered steps, following the conduit gleaming against the damp wall, until I stood at Moll's door. I had a gun with me tonight: witnesses *verboten*. Hannah could relate to that even if she were on the receiving end. No light issued from the crack beneath Moll's door. If I had seen light, heard some keys tapping inside, I could bash in and take care of her before she realized I wasn't the choirmaster coming back for some forgotten music. Was she waiting for me in the dark now? If so, I had to know where to aim so I slid a tiny flat microphone the size of a tongue depressor under the door and fanned it 180 degrees, listening through an earplug for movement, breathing: nothing. Flat dead in there. I distrusted that. Unlocked the door.

The room was astonishingly clean, as if Moll were expecting royalty. Stereo equipment still lined the wall, CD's crammed the shelves, but his desk was bare. I stared at the empty space a moment, considering what that void meant, then ran to the trapdoor and yanked the cord, fighting the bile rising in my throat as the stairs eased slowly down to me. The bells still hung placidly from the beams but no more air conditioner, no more dish pointed through the slats toward the fairgrounds. I didn't have to continue because without cables the Clove was defunct, but they had been so damn clever so far that I had to check, so up I crawled to the highest belfry. No hum there and yes the Clove had vanished along with the scaffolding around the steeple. I almost cried.

For the last time I fled down the skewed, dizzying steps to the sanctuary and waited, cowering behind the dusty wardrobe as Bach's polyphony blessed the church. I heard a final cadence, a wondrous silence followed by the commotion of humans. Even when they began wandering again through the chapel, I couldn't move, paralyzed with dismay: it wasn't over yet.

I left with the last of the congregation as the sexton was smothering the altar candles. In the loft, Oskar switched the organ off. As the bellows slowly collapsed, silence limned our forlorn footsteps. We all huddled out of the Thomaskirche, past Bach's statue, into the twentieth century.

Back at the Merkur, I changed from black leather into black silk and took a cab to the fairgrounds, west entrance, where Flick had left me a pass. In the distance the Slaughter Memorial poked into the night like a rogue thumb rising from the center of the earth. "I'm Leslie Frost," I told the guard. "Mr. Flick has left me a pass."

The guard gave me a cheap tin badge along with directions to pavilion five; judging by his generous inspection of my face and legs, I had dressed well for the occasion. Since my last visit to the fairgrounds, construction crews had managed to slap together a few new buildings; however, they had not gotten around to removing their dumpsters and cement mixers from the wayside. Perhaps by next summer they would lay down sidewalks and plant a few trees. In the meantime, broad avenues of mud separated the exhibition halls.

Pavilion five, a primitive cinderblock hulk, contained many booths and a couple thousand glowing cigarettes. As the conventioneers wandered around the grandstands, jabbering in syrupy languages, overhead fans twirled from the un-painted beams, circulating odors of cheap brandy, sausages, and tobacco. I handed my coat to the woman who told me I had to give it to her and stood uncertainly at the head of the steps, looking for Flick. Within a few seconds I picked him out on the right, next to the Technical Information desk. He wore the same black suit that had first arrested my attention in Auerbachs Keller. As he got closer the old, ravishing terror took my stomach. It had never gone away, it had never even been dormant. I waited for him, appalled and overjoyed, as the peace returned.

We picked up where we had left off. "Hello, dear," I said.

His eyes dwelled a moment on the ruby pendant dangling a few inches below my jugular. "I'm so glad you could come."

The safe, classic reply but I believed he meant it. "So this is the trade fair."

"This is the electronics exhibition." Flick took my arm. "Let me take you on the grand tour. We begin with the small items." He strolled me past a few calculators and adding machines, ignoring or perhaps enjoying the stares of many men in blue suits: he was entertaining the only woman in the hall with her knees exposed. Funny, him parading me around like this after all that bitching about my poor reputation. Anyone with an optical nerve could tell I was not a visiting dignitary. I didn't quite know what to make of it all until a shrill voice pierced the baritone thicket.

"Leslie darling!"

It was much worse than just Harry. Next to him stood the redhead. Oh God I was a fool, probably a dead one. "What are you doing here," I growled.

"Took the words right out of my mouth, sugar." Harry blew smoke at the corrugated roof as Hannah's .45 caliber eyes bored into me. "Never mind, you seem to be enjoying yourself. I'd like you to meet Hannah Selke."

I nodded my head, not about to touch her. Ever. Flick was

studying my face. Words were expected so I said, "This is Emil Flick," in English. The two of them shook hands. What a farce!

"Have I seen you before?" Harry asked Flick after introducing himself as my exclusive record producer. "London? Brussels?"

"I don't think so," Flick answered. "I work at the trade fair."

My turn to act natural. "Are you a musician?" I asked Hannah.

"No, no," she lied in that smooth, chilly voice I had hoped never to hear again. "I know nothing about music."

Harry turned his brandied breath my way. "Hannah is the president of Vuota Corda. I'm sure you've heard of it. We've done dozens of projects together. I ran into her at the Kaffeebaum this afternoon."

"That's nice." I smiled faintly at her, she smiled faintly at me. Oh, we were dying to kill each other. "What brings you to Leipzig? Recording contracts?"

"I have an exhibit in the audio building," she said.

"Hannah's always been five steps ahead of the big record companies," Harry crowed. "Can you imagine our Godo having the foresight to come here? She's going to eat up the eastern market before he even finds it on a map." Suddenly noticing Flick's hand circling my arm, he peered at me. "How do you two know each other?"

Flick smiled; this charade was, on one level, amusing. "We're both violinists," he answered. "One of us plays better than the other, of course."

"That's it! I've seen you backstage!" Harry cried.

By now even Flick had had enough: the necessary points, whatever they were, had been made. "Perhaps." He bowed. "A pleasure meeting you both."

Hannah nodded, smirking. "Likewise."

Flick steered me toward the middle row of exhibition booths. "What an unpleasant man," he said, nodding here and there to strangers.

"What a horrid woman. They deserve each other." We ran into heavy traffic. "What's all this?" I asked.

"Personal computers. The hit of the show." As usual the Japanese were out in force, speaking through interpreters to a spellbound crowd. "Care for a better look?"

"I've seen it already."

"Come here, then. You'll like this much better." Flick maneuvered me past the PC's to the last aisle. "Lovely, aren't they?"

I glanced impassively over the row of mainframes. He was going to stroll me past them one by one, clocking my pulse with his fingers so snugly wrapped around my arm: lover's polygraph. As we neared a French computer, the sales rep smiled hopefully at us. "Have any been sold?" I asked Flick.

"None. Not yet, anyway. Maybe in a year. This time the manufacturers are just introducing themselves." Flick shepherded me past two men and a machine from California, finally halting at a modest display in the corner. "I think this is a good-looking system, don't you?"

The mainframe looked much smaller in this setting than it had in the steeple but it was Moll's baby all right, complete with keyboards, video displays, printers, streaming drives, modems. The Clove logo had been replaced with a nondescript monogram that could be English, German, or Japanese. No sales rep and it looked no different from the surrounding wares, so no one paid much attention to it. The Clove was set up in the perfect, forgotten corner of the exhibition hall, smack on top of all the electrical inputs. Moll could easily slip in after the cleaning ladies had gone and party all night. "Very nice," I said indifferently.

"That's all you can say?"

"What do you want me to say?" I snapped. "It's just a machine."

My tour ended alongside a German computer about the size of the Slaughter Memorial. "There you are," said Flick, ushering me back to the pocket calculators. "You've now seen the electronics exhibition."

"Are all the pavilions like this?"

"Yes."

"I can see why you've been busy the last few months." I heard Harry Paradise laugh and knew that, somewhere in this babble, Hannah was plotting my death. "How much longer are we required to stay around here?"

We left, not quite as surreptitiously as I would have hoped but that was the story of my life. "I've had supper sent to my office," Flick said, leading me into the dank night. "It's quiet there."

I told him about the recording sessions as we passed under the heavy cables connecting pavilion five with the communications building. Moll didn't have to worry about broadcasting from the steeple to the fairgrounds any more; he was wired directly to the dishes now. Fine planning. Who would notice an extra cable in that clump? More to the point, noticing one, who would care? We walked past the observation tower, now festively lit like the Thomaskirche for the duration of the trade fair. Visitors choked its upper decks, straining to see the Slaughter Memorial through the smog or, in the opposite direction, the feeble lights of Leipzig.

Flick steered me into a side street. "The back way," he explained, unlocking a door. We went through a long corridor to another dull door, this one the unmarked entrance to Flick's office. He took my coat, kissing the back of my neck. "Wait here." He left me beside his desk and crossed to the other side of the room. No need to turn on the lights; the fairgrounds glowed on the other side of his picture window. As he locked us in, I noticed that his little bed was still in the corner.

Flick drew the drapes and dropped wearily onto a large sofa. "Come sit a moment," he said, patting the cushion beside him.

I sat on his lap and played with his face, his neck, his collar as Flick's mouth languidly, occasionally responded. He was tired. "Hopeless," he said once but I didn't want him wasting his tongue on words. We only had an hour.

His narrow cot, the one he had slept on for so many months

while Moll interfered with satellites, squeaked when he backed me onto it. As Flick took off my shoes, I told him I had missed him, I adored him, always had, always would. Only toward the end did I realize that his fingers were always within reach of my neck and even when his head was between my legs, he gripped my wrists, not letting go until he was in control of my throat again. Each time I opened my eyes, I found him staring at me, answering the questions even as he asked them until finally he gave up and let all questions, all answers, gallop away.

He stopped moving, perhaps slept for a few minutes. Then his arm moved, disturbing the peace. "I have to go," Flick said. He began picking up his clothes. "Could you stay? I'll be back in an hour."

That was impossible: I had a recording session tomorrow. I joined him in a pathetic, despondent hunt for dead underwear. He dressed quickly, monitoring me. No more kisses, no sweet words. As always, his silence confused me; I didn't know why he had brought me here. Before leaving the office, Flick straightened the blankets on his rumpled cot. He handed me my little beaded purse and we scuttled like two thieves through his private corridor to the street where, as if to remind all visitors that today's party was over, the neon lamps suddenly clicked off. "I'm very late," Flick said, stopping suddenly in front of an administration building. "Would you mind if I didn't see you out? The gate is straight ahead. Just follow the crowd." He kissed me. "I'll call you tomorrow." Without looking back, he went inside.

I followed the crowd for a couple hundred steps, then wandered back to pavilion five, waiting behind a corroded dumpster as the merchants went home and the cleaning ladies invaded the fairgrounds. Damn cold out there and I regretted the absence of black leather but that costume clashed with tonight's role. It was nearly midnight when Flick finally returned to the pavilion with Moll, tonight dressed not in choir robes but in a janitor's uniform. They entered quietly through the service entrance. After a few moments, I followed them inside. The lock was a farce but the darkness wasn't so I had to pick my way slowly through the shelves and boxes to the crack of light at the end of the stockroom. Flick's sloppy carpenters had left a fingerspace between the double doors.

I peered into the exhibition hall. Moll, in his dingy gray janitor's uniform, sat at the Clove as Flick paced beside him, referring often to his watch. "Is Hannah there?" Moll asked. It was the first time I had heard him speak. He cheeped like a nervous bird.

Flick looked again at his watch. "Waiting for her demonstration."

"Satellite contact," Moll said at last. He hit a key. "Fire. She's going to like that."

I imagined Hannah in a muddy field, smiling as she watched another barn incinerate. Moll entered many more commands before switching the system off; it was all over in a few minutes. Flick went to the switchbox and killed the low lights in the pavilion. As they headed for the stockroom, I crouched behind a stack of toilet paper. Four footsteps whished past: two of them suddenly faltered. Had someone dropped something? I bristled, listening ferociously. After just a second, four footsteps resumed.

The door slammed behind them and the exhibition hall grew hollowly quiet, like Moll's steeple on a late afternoon. Go! Now! I ran to the Clove, flipped it back on, got Svek's disk from my purse and rammed it into the slot. Type, Smith. Fast! No lights; I had to navigate the keyboard by the green reflection of the video screen. The system was staggeringly fast, eons ahead of my simple brain. As fast as I could type, the Clove obeyed, running circles around my fingers. I understood why Moll never wanted to come down from the steeple, why Alfred Chung never wanted to leave his room: funneling that incredible power to my will made me feel like Zeus bending thunderbolts. This was much more intoxicating than playing a dead violin.

"Stop," Flick said.

He stepped out from the stockroom. At first I couldn't see

a face or a body, only a dim, phosphorescent wedge of shirt, but I had heard the faint click of his gun beyond the tapping keys. In the big picture, I would be no more of an obstruction than that cop in the Thomasplatz, so I did as he said. Flick walked slowly to the Clove, pointing the gun at my heart. His face was grim, alien, absolutely still. But his voice shook. "What are you doing."

Go go go Clove: ten million calculations later I replied. "My job."

He considered that a moment before rapping the side of my head with his gun. Not too hard, of course: Flick wanted me coherent enough to answer a few questions. I tried to slip off the chair, get at him from the floor, but he caught my hand on the way down and yanked me back up, twisting my left elbow at a career-ending angle. That was unacceptable so I bit him hard high on the leg. For my efforts I got my head smacked again and this time I almost passed out. The Clove began to twirl but it needed two-four-six more seconds to finish Svek's program so I held on. He hit me again, harder. I let go. From far away, in slow motion, I watched Flick snap the disk out of the drive and shut the Clove off. He ran his hands roughly over my body, checking for hardware, then pushed me toward the double doors.

The fine, fresh air of Leipzig revived me like a blast of smelling salts. I thought briefly of running away but there was too much open space between pavilions and I didn't want to hear a sharp *pffft* and get a big hole in my expensive new dress so I staggered alongside Flick back to his office. Things had been so cozy there just a few hours before but that scenario had involved a lighter plot and amateur thespians. Flick flipped on a pale lamp and shoved me into a heavy chair facing his across a coffee table. For a moment we stared at each other. His face was no longer a white mask; it was clouded with that pain born only of exquisite treachery. I tried not to be ashamed. He didn't know? Maybe he didn't want to know. I had never really considered that. Respectful and quivering, I waited for his eyes to slowly harden again.

"Why did you come back to the pavilion?" I asked finally.

He didn't have to tell me; on the other hand, I wouldn't be leaving the room with any trade secrets, would I. Flick's mouth turned up at the edges. It was not a smile. "I smelled your perfume in the air as I was leaving. How long have you known about me?"

"I saw you shoot the policeman the evening before you introduced yourself at Auerbachs Keller."

An honest civilian would have reported him, of course. "Who's running you?"

"Run? No one. I'm just a curious person."

"You're a very bad liar. You know all about the Clove in the steeple, don't you."

"What steeple?"

"This won't do, Leslie. If you don't want to talk to me, I'm going to bring you to that woman you met at the exhibition. She's not going to be happy about you meddling with her computer. I'll warn you that she can be quite merciless. So shall we start at the top? Please tell me everything. I'm not going to beat it out of you." He sighed. "She will, however."

"Why? What have I ever done to that bitch?"

Flick let the question slide. "How did you find the Clove in the steeple?"

Ah, hell. He needed the answers and I was incapable of denying him anything. "I saw you dragging in the air conditioner the same night you killed the cop."

"Then what?"

"Moll lent me his keys." I saw Flick's eyebrows shift. "Involuntarily."

"You've been in the steeple, then?" Flick said.

"Three times. I got a sample of the program Moll was running and saw the links to the fairgrounds. You showed me the dishes yourself. All I had to do was find out what was flying over Leipzig."

He paled: I knew much more than he had thought. "You're not alone," Flick said. "Who's behind you?"

"What's your objective anyhow? Blackmail? Terrorism? Don't tell me you're just a bunch of overqualified arsonists."

Fires: barns: those midnight waits: I could see him back-tracking step by step. "So it was you who put the transmitter in my car," Flick said. "Damn you, that caused me a lot of trouble."

"Caused me a couple broken ribs. Did I kill that man who snitched one of my receivers?"

"Almost. When the police fished him out of the Elster, he made a number of contradictory statements about a man in black leather." Flick inspected the barrel of his gun. "He also mentioned a mole above the man's-lip."

Thank you, Maxine. That damn mole would kill me yet. "So you knew it was me?"

"The idea crossed my mind but I dismissed it as fantasy." His face was bitter. "I suppose people like us should recognize each other."

"But you had to suspect! You had me followed."

He shook his head. "Never. Whom do you work for? The East Germans? The Russians?"

"The Americans."

"This is not the time for jokes."

"It's the truth."

"I don't believe it. If you did, I would have heard about you years ago."

"Is that so? How many Germans know about you?"

Touché. This time he slowly pointed the gun at me. "What do you mean."

"I found Zwinger. You were all violinists at the Hochstein School during the last days of the war. Then you scattered."

"How did you find him?"

A slip of the tongue and pure stupid luck! "You shouldn't have kept the violin he gave you. The Simler family kept records." Flick's beautiful face became so pasty that I thought he'd faint. "It wasn't just you. Moll shouldn't have kept a lacrosse stick from Johns Hopkins. Harry Paradise shouldn't have kept a gold watch chain. All those sentimental souvenirs eventually added up.''

Flick glanced at a clock, then went to the window. When he looked at me, his eyes glittered with revulsion. ''America's not going to survive the next twenty years, you know. It's bankrupt.'' He got no argument from me. ''Do you have any idea what it's like to work for the losing side?''

''Not yet.''

''I do. You wouldn't like it.'' Flick returned to his chair. ''Join us. We'll give you everything you want. You're not an American anyway, you're a German. We're going to take back everything we lost.''

''You can have it.''

''You don't want to be on the winning side?''

''What fun is that?''

He was losing patience. ''Give me your purse.'' I tossed it on the table and watched him remove, first, my manicure set: Lockpicker's Special. ''Very clever,'' Flick said. He unsheathed my white comb from its leather pouch. ''That man you nearly drowned,'' he said, ''told the police about a white knife. Ceramic, eh?'' Flick sniffed a lace handkerchief. ''Ah, lovely. You shouldn't have worn that perfume, darling. Or you shouldn't have slept with me tonight. My olfactory memory is quite retentive.''

''There's more of it in the atomizer.''

Flick sniffed the nozzle and buckled, choking, damn mad and damn quick: before I could get anywhere near the disk in his pocket, he caught my foot a split second from his face and lashed it to the side, twisting me through the air like a balsa airplane. On the way down my ribs met the coffee table. Christ, another three weeks in a girdle now. I wormed to the middle of the floor and lay still so he wouldn't have to kick me. ''Why did you do that,'' Flick said from his chair. ''I almost shot you.''

''You will eventually, why not now.''

''Because I have a few more questions.'' He tucked the

atomizer back into my purse. "What's on this disk in my pocket?"

"I don't know. My job was to plug it in."

"That curious mind of yours just plugged it in? Without question? I find that very hard to believe. Impossible, in fact."

"Does Hannah tell you everything?" I retorted. "Or do you just do what she says? Without question?"

That disturbed him. Ah, now we were getting to the heart of matters. Flick's next inquiry had nothing to do with obedience. "Did I mean anything to you, business aside? Or was I just a piece of the puzzle, to be worn down by any means possible."

"I might ask you the same question."

The gun spat *pffft*: the rug hiccuped two inches from my head. "Answer me," Flick said.

"I love you. Business aside."

He didn't say anything for such a long time that I thought Maxine's perfume had, as advertised, knocked him out. I opened my eyes: Flick was still in his chair, studying my legs. The hem of my skirt brushed my chin. "Get up," he said. "I can't stand to see you lying on the floor like that." He watched me slither back to the couch. "Why don't you want to work with us."

"I work for someone else."

"You don't have to tell him. You realize your options are limited."

I turned rustily to the side. "Why did you move the Clove?"

"We had to. Renovations were finished and they were going to remove the scaffolding."

"What are you going to do with it now?" He didn't answer: I suppose that was a compliment. "How long did it take Moll to break the code?"

"Four months." The small clock on Flick's desk chimed once. He stood up. "We're going to meet Hannah. She should be getting back to Leipzig about now."

"Hope she's bringing some roasted marshmallows."

Flick's face hardened. "She's not going to be happy seeing you with me."

"No? I'd think she'd be delighted. She's the one who wanted you to fuck me in the first place." Bull's-eye! When Flick's mouth dropped, I lurched toward the gun. Chopped his wrist straight down, yanked the barrel straight up: the Queen had forced this exercise on us often enough to guarantee results. The gun went spinning across the floor. I lunged for his throat but what Flick lacked in speed, he made up in power and he knew the feints and attacks as well as I did. My only hope was to recover the gun or my knife or Maxine's atomizer but Flick knew that too and wrestled me away from the coffee table. We bashed and rolled from sofa to desk to wall. He fought the way he made love, elegantly, lethally, leaving as few bruises as possible. I was foolish to think I ever had a chance with him in love or war: within a minute I was pinned face down to the old rug, inhaling shoes and dogs. Flick sat on the small of my back, holding my wrists as if they were the reins of a hobbyhorse.

"I've changed my mind," he said, leaning over my ear. "You're a bit too dangerous to move. Hannah will come here when I don't meet her."

"You're hurting my rib," I said.

He reached under my skirt and roughly pulled my panty hose off. With them Flick tied my hands behind my back and propped me on the couch next to him. "Better?" he asked.

"No." I looked away from his face; the grim, black leer reminded me of the statue of Mephistopheles outside Auerbachs Keller. It was disturbing my peace.

"It's such a waste, you know. Why didn't you just stay a violinist? Think of all the recordings you're not going to make now. All the concerts you're never going to play. What's going to happen to your Stradivarius?"

"You can have it," I said. "It's at the Merkur, room two forty-five. Work on your intonation, would you? It stinks."

He resisted an impulse to kick me. "I took those lessons very seriously. You obviously had other motives."

The mole above my lip throbbed; dragging my face across the rug had not been good for it. "Oh, so you practiced your little fingers off for the Muse? Give me a break." My bitterness cut as deep as his and I wasn't about to die without letting him know it. "Hannah went with you to my concert in Amsterdam. I wired your seats. Made a nice tape of your conversation. She told you to screw me, which you did about five hours later. Nice job. Good dog. *Arf arf.*" I laughed. "Bastard."

"I meant everything I told you that night."

"The hell you did."

"Let's not play the violated virgin, darling. Wasn't spreading your legs part of your assignment too?" He sighed. "Why must whores be so self-righteous?"

"Because their jobs sicken them."

Flick slapped me across the face. Above my lip I felt a prick, a tiny trickle, as if my nose were running but too far to the right: the Queen's mole had ruptured. That was a severe problem. I was saving it as a last resort in case Hannah got a little too high-handed with her interrogation. Once the syrup dribbled past my mouth, I'd have no more shot at a medically efficient death, no more chance of dropping dead in front of Hannah's beady eyes, robbing her of the pleasure of killing me, leaving all her questions up in the air . . . damn, damn, I didn't want to swallow now. A guard might knock, the sky might fall. Tomorrow I was supposed to record the third movement of the Sibelius Concerto.

"Forgive me," Flick continued. "You see I still believe your lies."

Open my mouth and I would die contradicting him so I stared at my lap instead as the poison slowly oozed along the top edge of my lip. For a long time Flick studied my profile. "I don't quite know what I'll do without you," he said. "You've been the core of my existence for so long. You know that, don't you?"

I hung my head in silence.

"No need to reply. When I was a little boy, I'd play the violin and dream of heaven. You were there somewhere. Then the war came. Afterwards it was unspeakably bad here. For forty years I existed like a worm in the mud, waiting and waiting . . . then I saw you onstage in Vienna. Funny, isn't it, how just a slip of a girl can resurrect the dreams of a tired old man? I'd play your recordings and feel alive again. I'd go to your concerts and watch you take over a hall with one stroke of your bow. You were I, ten million years advanced on the evolutionary chain. You were above all the decay and the lies. You led the type of life I could barely imagine. I knew we'd meet someday. No one asked me to introduce myself to you in Auerbachs Keller. It was an inevitable event, like waking up after a long sleep. That first night in Amsterdam was something I could never describe to anyone. That would have happened with or without Hannah. I think you know that." He sighed again. "You came into my life at the worst possible time. I don't know why Hannah ordered it. I didn't care—I had to see you. I had waited so long. Yet I was afraid that seeing you would put you in danger. I had no idea that you were quite at home with it. I should have known from the very beginning, I suppose. Under normal circumstances someone like you would never get involved with someone like me. It all happened so quickly, God it felt so good, so perfect. . . ." He turned sharply toward me. "Did you amuse yourself with the lovesick old goat? Get a laugh reading those naive, respectful notes? Have fun sleeping in my miserable little bed?"

I could not answer him. The Queen's poison had dribbled to the corner of my lip and I was beginning to cry. Maxine had explained what would happen if we mixed her potion with saliva but she had not said what would happen if we added a few tears. Perhaps I should open my mouth, swallow now: four seconds, she had said? That was just enough time for I love you, I'm sorry, one last kiss.

"I suppose there's no shame in reaching for the stars and

failing,'' Flick continued. ''Look at me. But you—it's such a waste, Leslie. Just playing the violin would have been enough.'' His voice had become sad and gentle, like my father's after I had disappointed him. ''To think, after all this, I'm still tempted to let you go.'' Flick raised my head, noticed my bloody mouth. ''Did I do that to you, love? I'm sorry.'' He kissed me.

Flick suddenly caught his breath, caught my eyes. Then he began to choke. In ten seconds, his face was very red, his eyes watering. In thirty seconds he was making terrible wheezing sounds, clutching his throat. He staggered toward a pitcher of water on the conference table and tried to drink but the poison had paralyzed him, so he fell to the floor, pounding his chest, slowly turning blue. After sixty seconds the noise was no longer human and he still fought ferociously but now he was getting weaker so he stumbled to the coffee table and picked up his gun, pointing it at me while his eyes could still focus. It would have been dishonorable to kick it away so I sat quietly waiting as the seconds dragged by and still he hesitated to put me out of my misery. Flick finally pointed the gun at his head, tried and tried to pull the trigger but the Queen's poison had disconnected his nervous system so he finally fell to the floor at my feet. I slid off the couch, rolled on top of him and was about to wipe my mouth on his lapel so I could whisper what he ought to hear but then I heard the Queen in my ear saying *Do not leave evidence*.

Flick clutched me with a last surge of strength and I rested my head on his heart as it slowly, very slowly, faded. Finally his hands thumped to the floor and the horror of it all came back to me: once again, the same as with Hugo, I heard no farewells and received no forgiveness. Flick was so warm, still with me really, except his eyes were wide and ice blue. Gone, just like that? Impossible. Perhaps if I just lay there quietly, he'd come back, with the peace. We could rewind tape the way we did in recording studios, go back to the moment before the mistake was made. Then we'd try again and this time do it right.

I waited for ages. No rush; Flick had waited forty years for me. And I was so tired. Maybe I fell asleep, floated away . . . then the Queen's voice was in my ear again, cheerleading. *Get up*, I heard her say, nicely at first, then with increasing disgust. *Get UP*. I lay still. *So Hannah won*, I heard her hiss finally. *Damn you, Smith*.

I opened my eyes and stepped over Flick's body. Bending far backward, I plucked my white knife from the coffee table. I kneeled next to him, poised the knife between my heels, and ran my panty hose over the blade. I heard the Queen whisper *Steady Smith, just cut the nylon, not your wrists*, and wearily obeyed. When my hands were free, I retrieved my data disk from Flick's breast pocket and dragged his heavy body to the cot where we had just made love. I began to strip him, freezing out thought, concentrating on the crisp, classic instructions the Queen's training had imbedded in my brain. I took his gun, neatened the office, and finally washed my mouth off because I was beginning to realize that I might actually get out of here before Hannah caught me. I must flee, resist the temptation to wait in the dark and put a bullet through her: later. My ribs felt like broken glass but I ran and ran past the pavilions, heaving Flick's gun into the first dumpster. Next dumpster I unloaded the floppy disk, next dumpster my white knife and tiny atomizer. In a few hours the crews would slosh to work and bury everything in new garbage. I unbuttoned my dress, lost a shoe, slipped once in the mud: a hysterical wreck screamed to a halt in front of the guard's station. I was going to confound the opposition, all right, even if it cost my life.

"Oh God!" I shrieked. The poor guard nearly dropped his porno magazine. "Help me! Help! Mr. Flick! I think he's dead!"

He dialed for reinforcements before sprinting back to Flick's office with me. This time we entered noisily through the front doors, the secretary's offices: if Hannah was in there, she had plenty of time to scram out the rear exit. When the guard switched the lights on, I ran to the cot. My poor Flick, already cool, had not moved one iota. High on his leg was the set of teeth marks where I had bitten him. His bruise, unlike that on my ribs, would never heal. I didn't have to pretend now and, as the room filled with consternated faces, I stamped and cried, calling him back from wherever I had just sent him. Finally I was taken to the filthy, Stasi-infested police station. I gave a weepy statement that Flick and I had been nuzzling when poof. I donated a semen sample to the lab to corroborate my story; tomorrow the police would find a thousand witnesses who had seen us parading arm in arm through pavilion five, not looking much at the computers. The autopsy would reveal heart attack and Maxine's poison would be untraceable. End of story.

Hours later, hounded by the first set of media vultures, Curtis made a very impressive entrance with a doctor and a lawyer who made all sorts of noise about previous trauma and accidental death with older, overexcited men. The police released me as dawn was leeching the thick night.

Curtis shipped the legal/medical froufrou back to Berlin and took me to my room at the Merkur, where he divested me of clothes reeking again of mud and bile. He took a look at the new blue wounds northwest of my stomach. "Anything else," he asked, taking the phone off the hook.

"I killed him," I said. "It was slow and horrible."

"Shhh." He put me in the shower, then handed me a glass. "Drink this."

"I don't want to sleep." That was first cousin to death. Flick would be there, spitting at me. I tried picking up my violin.

"I'm canceling the sessions," Curtis said. "You can't play."

"No!" I shrieked. If we didn't finish Sibelius today, I'd have to come back to Leipzig again. I had no more business in Leipzig. My business was all with Hannah now. I lay on the bed but began to cry like a sentimental whore as Curtis sat in his chair at the window, listening to the walls.

At nine-thirty, he woke me. My suitcases were nicely packed. Trailed by vermin from the newspapers, we drove to the Gewandhaus. The old lady at the stage door knew. The janitor in the hall knew. The violinists passing us in the hallway knew; or maybe they had just heard vicious rumors. I followed Curtis into the control room. Harry was nowhere; as always, Chance brooded behind the mixing console, checking his equipment. He looked quickly over, saw my sunglasses, then Curtis. The combination confused him.

"Hello," my manager said, extending a hand. "I'm Curtis Porter."

"Happy to meet you," Chance replied. He looked archly at me. "Sleep well?"

He didn't know. I unpacked the violin.

I was just about to leave the control room when Harry swung the door open. If he had bathed, it was in vinegar. He wore no protective ascot against the rank winds; a single nacre button connected the two halves of his shirt. His foul gold medallions swayed over his throat as he stopped cold at the sight of me. I waited: he had many choices. For once in his life, Harry said nothing.

"I'd like to run it twice, Harry," I told him. My voice sounded brittle and defoliated. "Do a few patches and go home."

"Monster," he said.

Chance immediately deduced that a page was missing from his libretto. As I left the control room, he took a step after me: Curtis stopped him. I was glad to leave. Didn't want to see his face when he heard why Harry called me such an unkind name. Backstage I ran into Maestro, who had learned over the years never to involve himself with the sordid personal details of musicians under his baton. Miracle enough that they showed up for rehearsals and produced noise according to his commands.

"So," he said, slipping an arm around my shoulder, "we finish Sibelius this morning?"

I nodded and we went onstage. As always, the musicians

stared at me with curiosity, contempt, sympathy: only special fools dragged them into the Sibelius Concerto. The concertmaster's eyes were particularly solicitous. Having been seated next to me in Auerbachs Keller the night Flick had introduced himself, he would know that the rumors were true. Like Maestro, however, he didn't care. These things happened.

"Are we ready?" Harry cawed over the talk-back speaker.

"Yes, Harry," Maestro replied angelically.

"Tape rolling," Chance said in a thin voice. I couldn't worry about that now. In my path loomed a mountain named Sibelius. I had been slogging through the wilderness for years to get another shot at it. Of the billions of humans alive this very moment, how many could play this concerto? One hundred? One thousand? We had an obligation to remain alive, with or without the peace. Poor Flick.

"Would you like to come to the control room and hear that?" Harry said after the first take.

I looked at Maestro, shook my head. "No, Harry," he called. "We'll continue, if you don't mind."

From another galaxy, Chance slated the next take. We took several runs at the inhuman pages before Maestro turned to me. "Satisfied?" he asked, ignoring the producer completely.

"That's all," I said. The orchestra and I applauded each other.

Maestro escorted me to the control room. Chance sat glumly in front of the Sony 1630 machines labeling U-matic tapes with a black marking pen. Off in the corner, Curtis sat ramrod straight and silent in his black wool suit. A pile of junk food lay untouched on the mixing console: Harry had been too perturbed to eat. He attempted to congratulate Maestro, never me, from the bottom of his heart. "Excellent work," he said, donning his chinchilla coat.

"I'd like to listen a bit," Maestro said.

"Listen to what? You just sent the orchestra home. If you don't like what you hear, it's too late."

The door opened. Polizei: I was dead. At least they had had the courtesy to let me finish the sessions. Across the room, I found Curtis's eyes. The policeman studied me for a long moment, then turned to ask, "Harry Paradise? Come with me."

Harry's jaw dropped. "Me? Why? You've made a serious mistake."

"Just go with him, Harry," Curtis said in English. "It's quicker."

"But I haven't done anything!" Realizing that belligerence was not effective in a police state, Harry tried docility instead. "Could you at least tell me what this is all about, Officer?"

"They know, Harry," Curtis said wearily. "Don't make him angry. He's not used to resistance."

"How long is this going to take? I have an important plane to catch!" Harry continued to object but he looked so guilty now. What could have gone wrong? Had Moll collapsed? Had Hannah been caught in Flick's toilet? The policeman took his arm. Harry's wretched bleating finally faded down the long hallway.

Curtis rose from his seat. "Marvelous sessions, Waldemar. Congratulations." As I put the violin away, he thanked Chance for putting up with "many difficulties," meaning me, and took the liberty of inviting him to Berlin at the next opportunity. Then he put me into my coat.

I went to the lovely man standing behind the mixer. "I'm sorry."

This time Chance didn't whistle. The gray eyes told me I had challenged him once too often. "So am I, Frosty." He turned toward the conductor. "What would you like to hear, Maestro? The last take?" Chance pressed a button on the remote control. "Stand by."

Maestro was already seated at the console, eyes closed, as an ostinato rhythm began pulsing through the control room. For a moment I hesitated, ears riveted to the gorgeous sound coming from the speakers: Chance was a great engineer, an aural Botticelli. No one else had ever made me sound as good. I had never told him how much I respected his work and now it was too late. Not daring to look back at him, I left the control room. I had made a sublime recording of the Sibelius Concerto all right. Along the way I had ruined everything else that mattered to me.

"Hold it," Curtis said, stopping me in the parking lot. Three reporters were dallying beside my car. "I'll pick you up in front of the Thomaskirche. Go." He pushed me away.

I walked dully across the old town square, past the fountain that had been my downfall. Hannah didn't cut me off and Curtis eventually pulled up aside Bach's old, worn church. I got in the M6. "What was all that with Harry?"

Curtis eyed the rearview mirror. "Pornography. During the sessions, the police raided his room at the Merkur. Probably found a couple hundred pictures."

"Who tipped them off?"

"I called Maxine before coming to pick you up." Curtis pulled slowly past the Thomasplatz. "Hope you don't mind."

"She turned Harry in?" I laughed stupidly. "What for?"

"I guess she'd had enough."

I was too tired for any more questions so I watched the smog puff against statues and steeples as we drove quickly away from Leipzig.

ood news traveled fast. When Curtis and I got back to Berlin, a dozen journalists were already waiting on the front stoop, smoking nonchalantly and flipping their butts into the street. Before Curtis shut the gates on them, they got a few shots of a beautiful car, an expressionless driver, and a violinist's dark sunglasses. The raunchier German magazines would probably buy off someone at the Leipzig morgue and run Flick's dead face next to mine, rehashing all the Black Widow stories surrounding Hugo's death. I didn't argue when Curtis put me to bed with a gush of tranquilizers.

Next morning I was sitting in Hugo's study, staring vapidly at the music shelves, when the doorbell rang. Curtis put his newspaper down. "Expecting someone?"

"No." It was probably the Queen, wondering if I got the disk into the Clove all right. Maxine never concerned herself with the corpses, animal or metaphysical, piled on the sidelines. Those were enemy casualties.

Curtis left the study. I heard him open a far-off door and converse briefly. "It's Emory," he said, returning.

"Emory? What's he doing in Berlin?"

"Crying, it seems."

I went to the office, where Emory was fidgeting with an

ashtray. "Oh! Sorry to get you out of bed!" he said, noticing my pajamas .

Bed? I wasn't ever going near a bed again. "I was in the study."

"What's all the excitement outside?" he asked.

"Who cares." I sagged onto the couch. "What brings you here, sugar?"

Emory coughed; his pasty face reddened. I looked away as he recovered. "Harry was supposed to meet me last night. Have you seen him? Did he drive back with you? I'm terribly worried."

"He's in Leipzig," I said. "In jail. They arrested him."

The red drained from Emory's cheeks. "Wha—what for?"

More dismay, more ruptured trust: I was so tired of it all. "He seemed to know."

Emory sank next to me on the sofa. "It was just a matter of time. He never listened to me." He wiped his eyes. "Harry was into porno, you know."

I looked distastefully at him. "So I hear."

"He's been doing it for years," Emory blabbered. "He needed the money. It started out small and just grew bigger and bigger. Harry knew people all over the world. They took pictures and he sold them. It was much more lucrative than making records."

"Who bought pictures of what?"

"Everyone bought everything." Emory blew his nose. "Remember the critic with us at the Kempinski the night I got sick? He's one of Harry's biggest clients. Collects fat women and mutilated bodies. You know the bald usher at the Philharmonie? He has a standing order for little girls. I could go on and on. Harry had a sixth sense about these people. He found them everywhere."

I cut Emory off: lengthy confessions presupposed absolution. "What was Harry doing in Leipzig?"

"Setting up shop. The potential market was enormous."

I thought back to the wee hours of the morning when I had seen Harry's chinchilla coat rush across the parking lot of the

Merkur. I thought about his hasty departures after recording sessions and his absences from his hotel room. Working with Flick? Acting as Hannah's courier? Bah. Harry wasn't an idealist: he was a bankrupt divorcé with an expensive lifestyle. One black dream nudged another and I remembered what had been on the film I had confiscated from Oskar Wildau. "Was the organist at the Thomaskirche taking pictures for him?"

"I don't know." Ho hum, another poor liar. I was tired of that, too.

"I caught him following me with a camera," I said, watching: within a few seconds Emory's flush betrayed him. "So Harry sent Wildau after me? What kind of pictures did he think he'd get? Come on, Emory. Tell me now or tell my lawyer later."

Emory sighed contritely. "Harry has a client who collects pictures of you."

Even after all these years, I was not expecting that. "Doing what?"

"Anything. The man's obsessed. Buys everything Harry gets." Emory daubed his runny forehead with a handkerchief. "Don't be angry, Les. Harry never gave him anything you couldn't show your father."

"What's his name," I said.

"I don't know. Really, I don't. He lives in New York."

"How long have you been sending him pictures."

"Ever since we met." Emory looked hopefully over at me, searching for sympathy. "It was just harmless fun, Les. Until one of your friends beat Harry's photographer to a pulp in Berlin. Then we stopped. It wasn't worth it."

I remembered Flick's face as he gazed out my bedroom window at the Trabant parked down the street. He hadn't known where the car had come from, either. It was just another raven cawing overhead . . . all that agony caused by Harry Paradise? Damn him. I left the couch and stood near the fireplace, away from Emory's throat. "So what was your contribution to all of this?" I asked.

"Harry packed the pictures with the recording equipment. No one ever looks behind the Styrofoam in road cases."

I smiled, prevising another great punchline. "Is Toby Chance in on this now?"

"God no! He doesn't know anything! Harry's been bringing it all in himself!"

That's why he had screwed up, of course. Harry was about as subtle as an attacking army. Now I recalled him almost passing out the last time our limousine was stopped at the border. "No one knows about this but you two?"

"And you. And now the police." Emory chewed his lip. "What's the punishment? Life in prison?"

"Firing squad, I think. They take morality seriously over there."

"Are they going to come after me now?"

"Depends on what Harry's told them, doesn't it? If I were you, I'd take the first plane out of here."

Emory hesitated. "Shouldn't I try to call him first?"

What an amateur! Next he'd be begging me for forgiveness! "I wouldn't. Harry's probably trying to convince them he's been framed. Last thing he needs is his accomplice calling."

Emory stood up. "Could you ever forgive me, Les?"

Because of him, I had been followed with a camera; because of me, he had been tapped on the shoulder with a bubonic cane. Even exchange. "I'll try."

At the door he paused. "We never, ever took any bad pictures of you. Please believe me."

I parted the curtain. At the end of the driveway, five diehards with telephoto lenses waited patiently for the next lie. "I wouldn't chat with anyone outside if I were you, Emory."

As Curtis showed him out, I smiled at my folly. Maxine had tried to warn me about Harry. I had preferred to believe that that one gold chain around his neck solved all my silly little mysteries. Why hadn't she just told me he was a pornographer, for Christ's sake? Cut my theories down cold? Next time I saw her, the Queen would have a lot of explaining to do.

"What time's my flight?" I asked Curtis when he returned.

"Three o'clock. You don't have to go to New York, you know. I'm sure Duncan can play his comeback recital without you."

"What would I do instead? Sit here and count my blessings?"

He drove me to the airport. The flight was jammed with German suits and their New York bankers still toasting the end of the Berlin Wall, as if their courage had directly contributed to its dissolution. I thought about Hannah sitting somewhere by herself, staring hollowly at the walls, trying to separate fact from illusion. Flick dead: was she happy now? Had I done what she wanted me to do? Hah. There was another woman headed for Judgment Day.

Manhattan, more filthy and raucous than ever, choked in slush. As my cab hydroplaned through the lakes at each corner, soaking many mink, I looked at the overcast sky. More snow would fall. I checked into my hotel and called the artiste. About now he should be in his room watching reruns of the Three Stooges. "How's the Comeback Kid?"

An intemperate philippic indicated that Duncan was not on top of the situation. No surprise: my accompanist was not endowed with the two requisites of a performing artist, death wish and a love of the absurd. "Let's get something to eat," I suggested after he had run through a dozen reasons to cancel tonight's concert. "Carbo load."

"Eat?" he choked. "My stomach's in knots!"

"We'll take a walk. Force some oxygen into the system."

"Are you nuts? I have to conserve my energy! You have no idea how difficult this program is, no idea at all."

Now was not the time to remind him that as he spoke, one million Asian pianists were teething on Chopin sonatas. "You've been playing that program every day for almost twenty years, Duncan. It's on automatic pilot now."

"What am I, a fucking robot like you?" He slammed the phone down.

Not particularly gracious, but an invitation nonetheless: I went to his hotel room. "Hello, tiger."

"What are you doing here," he snarled, cracking the door.

I had said the same to Toby Chance the month before when he had come to fill the vacuum between dress rehearsal and stage door. "I brought some food."

Grumbling, Duncan stepped back. I followed his terry robe inside. Judging by the poor light, he had either been trying to sleep or trying to masturbate. Newspapers and magazines cluttered the floor. I cleared the bananas and chocolate bars from the table and opened the bag I had brought.

"If you eat now," I said cheerfully, handing Duncan a white carton, "there's less chance you'll puke backstage at eight o'clock."

While I chomped on a few fried ravioli, Duncan cursed his existence. "This has been the worst week of my life," he whimpered. "I had to give eighteen interviews."

"Fame is a noose, my boy."

"Seventeen of them were with Luke the Apostle. Bolt made us drive everywhere in that pink hearse. People stared at us like we were freaks."

"Isn't that the point?"

"I didn't even get to practice until yesterday. The piano at Lincoln Center is a dog. It belongs in a saloon." He shrugged. "Who cares? No one's going to be at the concert anyhow."

I poured some tea. "Did Bolt sell a lot of tickets?"

"She says this concert is just for exposure. It's an investment in my future. She's got some sort of intermission entertainment planned."

"Aha. Any critics coming?"

"It's kind of hard this time of year, she says."

"You paid her twenty thousand bucks and she can't even get you a critic?"

"She says they're not interested in hearing Chopin any more."

I'd better quit this line of questioning. "I guess your mother's in town, eh? She must be excited."

"She brought three busloads of friends from Cleveland. They're probably all going to clap between movements." He put the carton quietly back on the table and crawled under the covers. "I don't feel very well now."

I turned the lights out, television off, and lay on the other side of the bed. "Go to sleep, Duncan. It's going to be all right."

He didn't sleep and we weren't lovers, so time, fraught with dark, heavy baggage, passed very slowly. Poor Duncan tossed and moaned, enduring agonies experienced only by those who wanted something very, very much. But what did he want, really? Glory? Riches? Acknowledgment of all those solitary hours? Didn't matter: there was no consolation for longing of this intensity. The best I could do was lie close by, warm as a spaniel, and wait with him. Couldn't tell him it would get better because it wouldn't. Before every concert he'd face these same sepulchral twilights and the more famous he became, the worse would be the doubt. Fame would probably kill a person like Duncan; he relied too heavily upon the approbation of others.

Luke the Apostle called as Duncan was taking a shower. "Ehhelloo doll," he said. "What are you doing over there? Holding Dunky's hand?"

"Something like that."

"Say, Sydney just told me about your little uh-oh in Leipzig," he said. "Far out. Something like that happened to me once with a chippie in L.A. I had to pay her parents an unbelievable pile of dough. You really have to watch your ass at all times these days."

"I'll tell Duncan you called."

"Coming to our launch party in Newport tomorrow night? Sydney's arranging a mixed-media bash. I'm not sure what that means but you gotta be there."

As Duncan and I walked to Lincoln Center, snow began to sift between the skyscrapers, flecking a little poetry over Broadway. Duncan's mood lifted considerably when he saw the box office full of teenage girls and pear-shaped women.

In the Green Room we found a tremendous corsage from Mrs. Zadinsky with a note wishing her son luck. Sydney Bolt came backstage wearing a yellow chiffon jumpsuit with large red polka dots. "Leslie!" she cried, seeing me. "You really rang the bell in Leipzig, didn't you!" Then she checked her spiked hairdo in the mirror. "Where's the star?"

I nodded toward the bathroom. "Puking."

She rapped on the door. "Duncan, come out. Let me see you." He emerged. Sydney's face dropped. "What happened to your yellow jumpsuit?"

"Left it at the hotel," I told her. "Red polka dots just don't fit with a Chopin sonata, know what I mean?"

As Duncan fled back to the toilet, Bolt turned toward me. Her odd juxtaposition of smiling mouth and murderous eyes somehow reminded me of Hannah. "I don't think you understand," she said. "This concert is a carefully orchestrated event. I've been planning it for months down to the last detail."

So had Hannah and look what I did to her. "What can I tell you? Musicians are unreliable. Maybe you should stick to beer and deodorant."

"Duncan," she snapped at the bathroom door, "you MUST wear that jumpsuit. Where's your room key? I'm going back to the hotel to get it." She rummaged through his coat pockets and found it. "Don't you dare start without me, Dunky!" she called, running out.

The toilet flushed at precisely one before eight. Duncan wobbled out, declaring that tonight he would definitely die. I pinned the best parts of his mother's corsage to his lapel and walked him to the stage door as he wistfully mentioned again that he should have been a dentist. "Your mother's in the front row," I said, pointing through the peephole. "When you walk out, smile at her." I pushed him into the lights.

Applause, prolonged silence. I looked onstage: Duncan was still twirling the knobs on the piano bench. Then he sat contemplating the keyboard as if it were an infinitely fascinating still life. I knew what was going through his mind, poor bastard. Getting those first notes out was like diving into an ice-cold swimming pool. Staring at the water would not increase its temperature; to think about plunging in would be to remain forever on the diving board. "Play," I whispered. "Play, damn you."

His fingers finally began to move. Perhaps his frozen mind would thaw after a few pages. There was nothing more I could do. For years Duncan had wanted a comeback; now he had one. The sound of music pained me so I left the backstage and wandered along the carpeted corridors as Chopin, applause, Chopin seeped through the padded doors. I was all right until I realized that Flick would not hear music again. That irrevocable disaster made me choke and choking made me cry: my gagging was so puny, so temporary, such a cheap imitation of his. Flick gone? Just because I had jumped into an empty fountain one bleak night in October? NO!

I sank onto a couch. Something amorphous and massive was pressing the soul. It was the same unknown force that overtook me whenever I stood at Bach's grave in the Thomaskirche. It drew me out of the body and placed me on that old, mysterious threshold: if I listened, I could hear movement behind the closed door. Flick was there now, with Bach. I heard them rustling together, untethered to time and mud and me. Happy? I couldn't say. Gone? Oh yes, and Flick had taken the peace with him.

More applause: intermission. At least I thought it was; very few people were leaving the auditorium. I went to the bar, smiling at two obvious alcoholics, desperate men. They were probably the music critics. Then Godo ambled in.

"Ah, Leslie. I knew you would be here." He ordered a double vodka martini. "Duncan plays well?"

"Very well."

Godo would ask a dozen more people the same question before reaching any conclusion. "You have your ticket stub?" he asked, glugging his martini. "We must go to the raffle." He took my arm.

We returned to his loge just as Sydney Bolt, dazzling in

her measled yellow jumpsuit, was blowing sharply into a microphone in front of the piano. She slapped it a few times, then, reassured that the PA system functioned, welcomed everyone to this exciting occasion at Lincoln Center. The woman was quite an entertainer, milking round after round of applause by asking if everyone was having fun, if everyone liked Duncan. Then she artfully veered the topic to Luke the Apostle, working in an apology for all this Chopin which Dunky had insisted on playing. Since Luke couldn't be here tonight with his friend, he was going to compensate by taking someone in this audience for a ride in his pink hearse.

"I won't keep you in suspense any longer," Bolt finally announced, turning to the stage door. "Duncan!"

I turned to Godo, who was eating all of his fingernails. "What's this now?"

"He draws the winning ticket."

Bolt tried once more, but when Duncan didn't show up in a matching yellow jumpsuit with red polka dots, asked for a volunteer. A young girl vaulted onto the stage and drew a ticket stub from a large fishbowl. "Number 816! Who has number 816?" Bolt cried.

The winner collected an oversize certificate good for one ride with Luke the Apostle. Bolt didn't keep the woman in the spotlights too long after learning that she had come in on a bus from Cleveland with Mrs. Zadinsky. The raffle broke up with somewhat crestfallen applause.

Godo and I watched from the loge as most of the audience put on their coats and left the auditorium. "They come back?" Godo asked anxiously.

"It's a school night. Teenage girls have to do their homework."

He stared at the empty stage as a custodian removed the microphone and the fishbowl. Then we returned to the bar for a few more vodka martinis. "The sessions went well in Leipzig, I hear?" he asked delicately.

"Who told you that?"

"Mr. Chance. He is very good about keeping me informed." Godo looked around. "I thought he would be here tonight."

"Did he say he was coming?"

"He said perhaps." Godo swallowed an olive. "I understand there are some complications with Harry Paradise. Most unfortunate."

I wondered what Chance had told him. "I wouldn't worry about it. Harry can talk his way out of anything."

"I hope it will not delay this project. Perhaps we should find another producer for your recording in April."

When I said nothing, Godo changed the subject. "How long will you be in New York?"

"I just came to hear Duncan."

"But Curtis told me you would be at the Lukendunk party tomorrow night! It is a big event!" He looked innocently at me. "Mr. Chance will be there."

I peered at the plump ladies snuggling into their seats as the lights dimmed: Duncan's audience had atrophied about ninety percent. As he returned to the stage, I regretted not having spent intermission holding his hand. Around the eyes his face was deep red; he had been shouting at someone. As his mother's troops applauded, Duncan managed a smile, then began a set of polonaises. I knew from the first note that the vacant seats had unnerved him. As the memory slips accumulated, my heart began to thud unpleasantly. Poor dog! He thought he was going to elevate souls and he got a bad piano, a stupid raffle, and three busloads of uncomprehending matrons.

I smiled reassuringly at Godo after the polonaises, more or less, had ended. "The sonata's his best piece."

Years of mindless repetition did not fail him. Duncan dispatched his final number on autopilot. Since it ended on a loud chord, the audience applauded loudly. Godo stood up after the encore. "Good?"

Ah, how life, comedy, bobbled on. Debate raged around us as we joined the line edging toward Duncan's dressing room. Half the ladies from Cleveland thought Luke the Apostle was a televangelist; the other half thought he made dirty records. No one could figure out how he was connected to Duncan.

Daintily sipping orange juice, Sydney Bolt hovered over her fragile Frankenstein, encouraging him to sign autographs as she scanned the dressing room for meaningful visitors. Godo, of course, was nearly knocked off his feet. "A fabulous performance!" she blurted before Godo could ask. Meanwhile, Duncan morosely swilled champagne, trying to obliterate memory.

I had seen enough burlesques lately so I left Duncan to his admirers and returned to the sidewalks. Heavy plows rumbled by, pounding the snow to mush: in New York, snow was not a miracle of nature, it was war on the Sanitation Department. I walked past my hotel on Central Park South, continuing to the East Side, to Chance's apartment. It wasn't really a conscious destination until the last few steps.

The doorman, remembering me, tipped his hat. "Would Toby Chance be in," I asked.

"No ma'am."

No point using his key, then.

A fax awaited me at the hotel. Unsigned, obviously from Maxine. It was a brief clipping from a Leipzig daily. MUSICIAN FALLS, I read. A review, all right, but not of a concert.

> 16 MARCH—The body of Ulrich Moll, choirmaster at the St. Thomas Church, was found by police, having fallen from the steeple, where he kept his study. Cause of death is accidental although suicide has not been ruled out. According to the rector, Moll had been under great pressure to complete an Easter cantata.

No further explanation necessary: Germans understood the dark side of Prometheus. I wondered how Hannah had managed to toss a man twice her height onto the cobblestones. Maybe she had a cosmetics kit like mine: first knock him out, then heave ho. I suddenly saw Moll's ashen face, heard his robe flapping, as he rushed past the pews to the choir loft. Poor nervous man! A brain like his deserved better than a splotching all over the Thomasplatz. I went to the window overlooking snowy Central Park. Dead, all dead: between us Hannah and I would rid the earth of all distinguished men. It was time to stop her.

I called a few airlines, looking for Hannah Selke. Now that she had two funerals to attend, her return to America had probably been delayed. Yes: TWA found her flying in from London, arriving at Kennedy at two that afternoon. She wouldn't be taking many road trips hereafter so I rented a car and drove north to Briarcliff Manor.

I got to her sleepy little town as harried executives were beginning to dribble into the train station. I called her number, got no answer, no machine. She lived in an unassuming apartment house off the main street. I rang the doorbell, again no answer, so I waited for someone to leave for work. Finally, a bleary-eyed yuppie held the door open for me.

Hannah's apartment locks were no more, no less advanced than those of her neighbors. She didn't have an alarm and I didn't have to annoy any roommates. No surveillance, in fact no security here at all. Hannah's place was modestly furnished, pristine as an operating room. It didn't smell of spices, flowers, or occupancy. She had lived here anonymously and alone, waiting, watching, planning Operation Phoenix. In forty years she had made only one mistake. Me.

Instead of a guest room, she had an office. On the desk sat her computer, same model as poor dead Moll's. Next to that, modem and printer, all totally common. I switched it on and glanced through her files. No passwords, but Hannah didn't have much to hide: household budget, filing program, a few innocuous letters . . . whoa FROST . . . what the hell kind of file was that. I pulled it onscreen.

There I was, in atomic detail, beginning with the moment of my birth. No, before that: Hannah had researched my parents also, noting the early death of my mother and my father's career in the diplomatic corps. Roland was there— including his recent retreat to the clinic—as well as Maxine, who got several paragraphs, but only because she was friendly with both my brother and me. Curtis, Duncan, Emory, Harry, Alfred, Chance, everyone I knew, Hannah knew also. After Hugo's name, nothing but DECEASED and date. After Flick, a note of our meetings in Amsterdam, Leipzig, Potsdam . . . he had not told her about the night he came to Berlin, nor my impromptu visit to his apartment. Now she'd have to type DECEASED after his name also.

But this was only supporting material. The data on Leslie Frost was endless. I waded through psychological profiles, long analyses of my attraction to older men, my school records, my concerts, all my interviews, reviews, my eating habits, my motorcycle—Christ, what an invasion! Rape! It was like reading my own obituary but I plodded through to the end before turning the computer off.

Hannah's desk was unlocked because it contained nothing of value except an antique fountain pen. Beside a paperweight I saw a few envelopes, hastily opened, unfiled. Checked the postmark: they had probably arrived the day Hannah left in a rush to see Zwinger in Garmish-Partenkirchen. She had gotten a new credit card bill and an acknowledgment of her donation to the local Just Say No program. The junk mail she hadn't bothered opening. There was a letter from the personnel department at the Todtech Company, headquarters nearby, thanking her for her job application. Her qualifications were outstanding and would she please call to arrange an interview at her earliest convenience? I folded the letter back in its envelope and tucked it with the others next to the paperweight.

The safe was in her bedroom closet, not very cleverly stashed behind her hat collection. Jewels? Swiss bank account numbers? I whizzed the combination lock a few times around and opened the door.

Pictures, hundreds of them. The photographers had captured me smiling, scowling, nuzzling Chance's neck at a rock concert, shopping with the Queen, eating, oh God, kissing Flick beside a canal in Amsterdam. My stomach rolled and I thought I'd be sick. Swallow it, Smith, he's gone gone gone. I dug through years and years of snapshots, surprised at the number of men I must have slept with. Hardly remembered their first names now. Emory hadn't lied: nothing here I couldn't have shown my father. On the bottom, furthest removed in time, was Hugo. Hannah had about a dozen pictures of us, all unposed, all inhumanly happy. My stomach rolled again, more violently. I stuffed her pornography back into her safe and began looking for the violin.

Small apartment, few hiding places. She kept it in her front hall closet with the umbrellas and winter boots. I opened the tattered case, lifted an old velvet cloth. There lay another of Grandfather Simler's bids for immortality. Three out of four strings were broken now. It smelled of mildew; Hannah had buried it alive. I tucked the red velvet shroud back over it, noticing the elaborate script monogram in the corner. HS. The threads had frayed from their velvet mooring so the intertwined letters looked almost like HL now. Who had embroidered this little coverlet for her? Her mother? Perhaps that was why she had kept it for forty years. Germans were all sentimental fools. I replaced the violin behind her umbrellas and left.

In a coffee shop I sat, dazed, suddenly homeless. Hannah knew everything . . . but did she really know *everything*? I couldn't tell from her files if Maxine and the Seven Sisters were blown. The evidence was all there but I couldn't believe Hannah had put the pieces together. It wasn't what she was looking for. *Was it?* This very moment she was flying one hundred miles a minute toward New York, toward me: frightening. I needed someplace to hide.

I drove to Boston. There was no place else to go, no other men left. I rang the doorbell on Sleeper Street. "It's Leslie Frost," I said to the intercom. The door buzzed, I pushed. Halfway up the long oak staircase, I began to quiver. Odds were high Chance would throw me out.

I followed Mona's blue suede rump to the reception desk, nodding to two men waiting on the couch. One was a tape salesman. The other was either a rock musician or a reject from the Gulag. "Is Toby expecting you?" Mona twittered.

"No. Is he very busy today?"

"He's always busy."

Mona was still exchanging moonbeams with the occupants of the couch when Chance came out of his office, arm around a petite woman's shoulder. For a grisly moment I thought it was Hannah in a black wig. He happened to glance up as the nausea tore my insides. God, I hated this profession! It twisted innocence into guilt, trust into fear, it sought evil where before there had been only shadow. No amount of music would ever redeem me. I stared strickenly at Chance as he approached Mona's desk. Last time I had come crawling to Boston, I had been able to hide behind a Christmas tree. This time, his foyer was empty.

Ignoring us all, Chance helped the woman into a coat and saw her to the door. He remained staring down the oak steps well after the outside door had slammed. Then he returned to the four of us waiting stupidly for him. Which of us would he acknowledge: the salesman, the derelict, the receptionist, the spy?

"I'm pretty busy at the moment," he said to me. "Why don't you wait in the house."

I went to his apartment and sat at his kitchen table. As an hour dragged by, I stared into the cavernous living room, realizing too late that I had been quite content there. I remembered Chance coming to my hotel and getting me through a particularly bad afternoon in February. I remembered a bridge in Leipzig where I had wrapped my legs around his back, where it had all begun . . . no, not there: further back. It had begun the moment I had heard him whistling backstage at the Philharmonie the morning after Emory had been canceled. Then I remembered the disbelief, the hurt, finally the disgust on his face as I left him in Leipzig. It was the disgust that had brought me here. I didn't want it to end that way.

Each time the phone next to me rang, I jumped, then stared at the incoming number displayed on Chance's little box. Recognized none of them and waiting tired me so I put my head on the table. Eventually the door behind me creaked and he walked into the kitchen. Chance stopped short, seeing me there: in times past, I had waited for him on his couch or upstairs in his bed. Without a word, he filled a teakettle, peeled a tangerine. Today he wasn't about to initiate any conversation.

"I've come to apologize," I began. "I wouldn't blame you for never speaking to me again." His silence impelled me to glorious new heights of banality. "Perhaps I could explain the situation. I'm not sure what Harry told you in the control room."

"Harry told me plenty."

"Don't believe him," I wailed. "He's a professional liar."

"He is? I'd say you were." Chance threw a tangerine pit into the sink. "You were screwing the old man the whole time, weren't you."

Ah, bravo, excellent shot. Another hit like that and I'd walk out of there. "I met him before I met you."

"Aha. Head over heels? Love at first sight?"

It was something at first sight. I still wasn't sure what. "I was in Auerbachs Keller after a concert. He came to the table and introduced himself. He was the deputy chief of the trade fair." Why was I telling this to Chance? It was none of his business! But I babbled on, just as Emory had to me two days before. "After that he came to a concert I was playing in Amsterdam. He went to Berlin once and to a concert in Potsdam. I only saw him a few times for a few hours." It sounded ludicrous. "He was a violinist."

"And where do I fit into all this? Spare parts?"

Chance was something else at first sight. I wasn't sure what that was either. "If you recall, I didn't exactly lead you on." I sighed; coming here was a mistake.

Chance poured two cups of tea. "Were you physically attracted to him?"

We were vampire and blood! After Flick my life would just be a watercolor. "A little," I said.

"Did you know he had already had a heart attack?"

Ooof. "Who told you that?"

"Curtis."

He never told me, God damn him! That's why the police had let me go with so little fuss: they knew Flick's track record. "I didn't know."

"Was he the one who called you that morning in the Merkur?" Chance continued.

"Yes. I hadn't seen him in six weeks."

"I guess you made up for lost time, didn't you? Sorry, that was nasty. I have trouble with you rolling out of bed with me into bed with an old man."

"It won't happen again. He's dead." I stood up. "I didn't mean to hurt you." Use, yes. Hurt, not really.

"Wait," Chance said as I was at the door. "Where does this leave us?"

One met many people in a lifetime. Most of them just made momentary contact before floating harmlessly off into the ether. One or two tore the lid off the firmament as they departed. All the rest left a soft hole filled with inaction and stillborn opportunity; enough of those holes and the spirit eventually drowned. "Where would you like it to leave us?" I asked.

He came to the door, looked for a moment at my eyes and the deflated mole above my lip. Then he hugged me. The gesture was paternal, not amorous; Chance was aging fast. "I don't want to lose you, Frosty. You're part of my life." He kissed my head. "Like mumps and hemorrhoids."

"Very funny."

"Cancel a few concerts. Let's disappear for a while. Maybe we can start all over again."

I softened against his chest. Then the phone rang.

Chance looked over and disengaged me. Before picking up the handset, he checked out the source number on the box. "Hi, Aunt Maude." He winked at me. "This is a surprise."

Aunt Maude didn't ask how Chance knew it was she. Typical aunts would have had to be told again and again about that smart little box next to the smart little nephew's telephone. I could have stayed at the door but the old phantoms pulled me softly toward the table. I glanced at the liquid crystal display beneath the telephone. Area code 914: it was Hannah calling.

"You are? That's great!" Chance said. "Of course we can. Haven't been there in ages. Oh, I'm fine. You? Actually, I'm in the middle of some business, dear. Four o'clock, then. The Parrot. Terrific. Bye-bye." He hung up and rolled his eyes. "My aunt's coming to town this afternoon. She wants to meet me for tea." He circled to my side of the table, slid his arms around my waist. "Where were we, Frosty?" he whispered.

Frosty had just died, not as tortuously as Flick, but in agony just the same. Chance was dealing with Smith now. "We were discussing travel plans," I said.

"Right. Ever been to Brazil?"

I went to the sink for water. From this distance he might not hear my voice shaking. "I'm invited to some kind of party in Newport tonight," I said slowly. "Care to go with me?"

"Love to."

For a moment I allowed him to kiss my neck. "What about your aunt?"

"I'm only taking her to tea, thank God." Chance remembered his manners. "I'd ask you to join us, but she doesn't like surprises."

No? She was going to get a bad one. "You take care of your aunt. I have to go shopping for something to wear tonight."

"Remember, less is more." Chance looked at his watch. "I'll get back to the office. Hadn't planned on any family obligations today."

"Why didn't you just tell her to buzz off?"

"Because she's worth millions, sweetheart. I'm her favorite nephew.'' A smooth liar but not yet a professional one: he didn't appreciate the stakes. I wondered how I could have been so far off about both him and Harry. Bah. I was losing it.

"Take this,'' Chance said, handing me a set of keys. "You now have the run of both my residences. Don't stay out too long.'' He returned to work.

I put a few things in my purse and left.

19

I went to The Parrot for lunch, and was surprised to find a long, narrow café bordered by glass all along Newbury Street. It was a terrible place to meet secretly. They couldn't be that careless, that confident, could they? Maybe Chance was innocent after all. Maybe Hannah really was his aunt. Maybe the earth was flat, too.

I hadn't pinned a bug to his lapel and I wouldn't be stashing a microphone in the daffodils on their table. They'd probably recognize me if I dressed up as a waiter, so I decided to put a contact microphone against the glass outside the restaurant. I'd nestle it in the planters lining the windows. They'd speak and their voices would vibrate the glass; my mike would pick up the signals and send them to a nearby receiver. Across the street was a croissant shop where I could loiter with a pair of headphones and not attract too much attention.

"Is everything all right?" asked the headwaiter, noticing my uninterest in the crab cakes.

Fine, fine. On the way out, I handed him two hundred-dollar bills and mentioned that around four o'clock, my fiancé would perhaps be coming to tea with another woman. I described Chance and Hannah. Would it be possible to seat them at that table by the window?

He thought about it a split second before deciding that, although my request might jeopardize my fiancé's life, it would not jeopardize the headwaiter's job. Besides, favors like this went with the turf: his income, to a large extent, derived from a correct reading of lovers' triangles. "Certainly, madame," he said. "I'll arrange it."

I left the restaurant, turning left on Newbury. Skies were thick gray, fecund with snow. As I passed the planter and its evergreen shrubbery, I picked up a handful of wood chips. Then I killed a few hours cruising the boutiques. In a dressing room, I glued the wood chips to a two-inch-square box. Around three o'clock, encumbered with packages, I walked by The Parrot again. The lunch crowd had gone and the tea crowd had not yet arrived; target table was empty and the headwaiter was nowhere in sight. I dropped a package into the planter and, while retrieving it, stuck my camouflaged microphone to the glass. By four o'clock, even Hannah would have difficulty spotting it in the fading daylight.

Eventually I ended up at the croissant palace across the street. Ordered coffee and arranged myself at a window table with a newspaper and headphones.

Ever the gentleman, Chance arrived first. The headwaiter took him right to the table I had requested. My pulse wobbled unpleasantly as I heard him order an expensive brandy. Headwaiter delivered the alcohol with a few polite comments about the weather. I held my breath, waiting for him to warn Chance of an ambush by his fiancée, but the man kept his mouth shut: a woman who could afford two hundred bucks for a seating arrangement could also afford to have his nose broken if he double-crossed her.

Hannah didn't keep Chance waiting long. Shortly after four, she turned the corner on Newbury Street. Mousy anonymous brown coat and she was walking quickly, bobbing like a hen. I had never seen her move in the open and suddenly her gait pricked my memory. That old woman in the Kempinski Hotel, the night Emory had been tapped with a bad cane, had bobbed the way Hannah did now. She had been wearing a dull brown coat and the same brown hat. It was so simple, of course: Hannah had always intended to hit Emory. Remove one engineer, replace him with another. That night I had not been her target at all.

Chance rose, greeting her with a kiss that could be interpreted several ways. Her flat, vitreous voice complained about the traffic before ordering tea and scones. I didn't need to look at the two of them any more so I hunched over the newspaper, pretending to read about Giant Germany while their toxic words seeped through the headphones.

Hannah had been in various airplanes for the last twenty hours. In a foul mood, she brushed aside Chance's preludial flatteries. He finally ordered another brandy and asked what had brought her to Boston.

"You, actually," Hannah said.

"Me? That sounds interesting. Please explain."

She was studying his eyes, trying to make him nervous. "I've paid you a lot of money recently."

"You got your money's worth," Chance replied.

"I'm glad you're convinced. I'm not." She sighed. "I'm afraid you gave me a bad disk. A virus has ruined everything."

"Not possible, dear. The tapes didn't leave my sight from the moment you gave them to me until I made the glass masters." So it was Chance, not Harry, in the CD pressing plant in London. Should have known; he had told me often enough that he spent a lot of time there. I was shocked to hear him so nonchalantly slough Hannah off. He had no idea with whom he was dealing. "Maybe you gave me some bad U-matics," he told her.

"The tapes I gave you were clean," Hannah retorted.

Neither said anything for a moment. "What about your computer operator," Chance said. "Did you check him out?"

"Of course." She didn't mention that Moll was just a big pizza now.

"What about your logistical expert?"

Sorry, Flick was dead, too. "I've checked everyone," Hannah said. "The only one who comes up a little short is you."

He laughed in her face. "Why should I kill the golden goose?"

"For a bigger golden goose. I know how fond you are of money."

"Go home, Hannah. Start from the beginning and use a little more imagination this time. I'm still the same gullible guitar salesman you turned into a recording engineer."

Fifteen years ago, Hannah must still have been a hot tamale. Oy, I was stupid! That night in Leipzig when Chance and I had gone for a walk in the fog, before I had kissed him on a crumbling bridge, hadn't he said that a violinist had turned him from guitars to recording? I hadn't really been listening. My attention was focused on Oskar Wildau following us with his camera.

I watched her casually butter a scone. "I have a new job for you," Hannah said. "Vuota Corda will be making several recordings in Dresden next month. Would you like to be the engineer?"

"I'll check my calendar."

"There are seven extra boxes to bring back with your equipment. The same seven you brought over in September. I don't think the camet will be a problem. Security at the border is nonexistent now."

Change the little nameplate from Clove to Sony and not one border guard, not one customs agent in a thousand could distinguish a computer from a digital tape recorder. "No problem," Chance said. "I'll need a raise, though. One of my primary sources of revenue has recently dried up."

"You're talking about Harry Paradise, I assume."

"That's right. Whatever the poor schmuck did, he sure looked guilty when they dragged him away."

"He was distributing pornography. It carries a severe jail sentence in East Germany."

"God, that's funny!" Chance laughed for a long time. "You really fixed me up with a winner, didn't you."

She didn't join him in laughter. "He was perfect, actually. We won't find another cover like him for a long time."

Hannah poured more tea. "The violinist got into a little hot water herself. Did you hear what she did the other night?"

"The old man? She didn't mean it."

I put the newspaper down and watched them intently. "How would you know?" Hannah asked. "Were you there assisting?"

"She told me."

"A tender confession, I'm sure. Of course you forgave her."

"Of course I did. She came all the way to Boston this afternoon to apologize."

Hannah very slowly looked out the window, up and down Newbury Street. "She came to America simply to see you?" she asked innocently.

"Not quite. She had to go to New York last night for her accompanist's recital. It was some sort of comeback he'd been planning for years."

"Then on a whim she just came to Boston?"

"I know this might be hard for you to swallow, dear heart, but she has genuine feelings for me. She felt badly about the way things were left between us in Leipzig. I was rather unhappy with her when I found out about the old man."

"You shouldn't have been surprised. The little whore's done it before."

"My my, that's vicious. She can't help it if men get overexcited when they're inside of her." Chance swallowed a slug of brandy. "Why did you drag her into it, anyway? She's a temperamental artist. Her mood changes by the minute. Very risky."

Hannah tersely wiped her mouth with a napkin. "She was perfect for the occasion. Like Paradise."

"All right, don't tell me. I don't really want to know. You guessed right, I suppose. She turned into a nice little mule for you. Leave her alone now."

Mule? When had I ever been Hannah's mule?

Hannah buttered another scone. "What do you intend to do with her," she said after a while.

"Well, as soon as I get rid of you I'm going to go home and fuck her brains out. Then we're driving to a party in Newport. I'll probably ask her to marry me tonight. I love her."

"That wasn't part of the plan."

"That wasn't part of *your* plan. It's part of mine. The two of us could be quite happy together. Beneath the crust, she's just a lost little girl. I think she needs father figures. Brings out the protector in me."

"Don't kid yourself. She knows exactly what she's doing."

"Like you? I doubt it. You should meet her someday. Then you'd understand."

"Fool" was all she said.

Chance did not realize that it was a professional, not a personal, comment. "Try not to be jealous, darling. She can't help it if she's everything you're not."

On that fine note, the tea party adjourned. As Hannah stepped onto the sidewalk, a gust of wind suddenly blew her hat away: the hatred etching her face as she watched Chance run after it awed me. He had chosen a bad time to remind Hannah that she was a failed violinist. Perhaps, if she had told him about the loss of Flick, Moll, and the Clove, he would have been kinder to her. Perhaps not. What did I know? I had jumped into a marathon two feet from the finish line. My appreciation of the race was, to say the least, incomplete. Without a word Hannah put her hat back on. Chance proffered his arm and they hurried toward the Boston Common.

I crossed Newbury Street, peeled my contact mike off the glass. No evidence, please: Aunt Maude was no slouch. Then I walked back to the button factory.

Chance was already in the kitchen with a knife and a wide slab of smoked salmon. Beside the cutting board sat a bottle of exquisite Chablis. "Anything left in the stores?" he asked, noticing all my packages.

I tossed him a little box from Tiffany's. "Happy Ides of March."

He inspected the cuff links. "Dice? You consider me a gambler?"

"Name's Chance, isn't it?" I opened a larger box and held up a black dress, a close copy of the one I had ruined that last night in Leipzig. "How do you like this?"

His hands circled my waist. "It'll do."

The smell of lime and beaches confused me so I broke away, toward the wine. "How was your aunt?"

"A pain in the ass, as always. She gets worse all the time."

"Cheer up," I said. "Maybe she'll kick the bucket soon. Is she old?"

"Not old enough." His hands caught up with me again. "God, it's nice to have you here. What time are we supposed to be in Newport?"

"Party starts at eight."

"I'll get you there at ten. We don't have to stay, do we?"

"Long enough to say hello to Duncan and Godo. And goodbye to Luke the Apostle. I'm pulling the plug on that carnival." I broke away from him again. "I'd better lie down a while."

"Would you like some company?"

Didn't he know what happened to men who slept with me? We went up to his bedroom, undressing as downtown Boston glimmered across the harbor. I kissed him a few times and fell asleep.

Dreams only accelerated the riddles, of course, and the commotion soon tossed me awake. Across the pillow, Chance breathed placidly as an innocent child. Mule, he had said. Mule mule mule. I hated mules. They were stupid, slow, sterile. If I was Hannah's mule, I had taken something somewhere for her. But she had never given me anything. Had someone planted something in my violin case, perhaps? In my luggage? Not possible, not with those locks. Had Harry ever given me anything? Headaches. Emory? He had given me a guilt complex. Flick? He had given me flowers and a ruby; the flowers had died and I had kept the necklace. Had Chance given me anything? Several delightful orgasms and a

CD reference disc of Beethoven sonatas . . . which I had given directly to Flick.

Oh dear. I was a mule, after all.

The last track of that CD must have been computer code. Chance had made the reference disc on his new machine downstairs. Once he bought the Yaba, there was no need to go to England and make the CD glass master at Naja Ltd. any more. Emory had said that Harry's recording projects with Vuota Corda had dried up suddenly in December: precisely when Chance had acquired his new machine. He had given me the reference disc in Boston and two days later, I had given it to Flick in Potsdam. How did Hannah know I'd be doing that? Flick hadn't even had to ask. I had just given it to him. That had been on New Year's Eve. Moll had started incinerating barns a few days later. Apparently my sentimental little Christmas present had provided him with the final clue necessary to break the code.

Clever of me to dope Chance and put Svek's sabotage on a Yaba reference disc last month. Too bad I hadn't been swift enough to realize that Hannah and Chance had the same brilliant idea way before I did.

Mule.

Chance slowly opened an eye and smiled. He was glad to see me. "Did you sleep?"

"Yes." I froze as he tried to kiss me. "Please don't."

He retreated and helped me stare at the ceiling. "Are you all right?"

"Not really."

"Can I do anything?"

"No."

Futile hanging around in bed so we dressed. "You're wearing tails?" I asked, noticing his attire. "What's the occasion?"

"Our first date, Frosty. As opposed to business trip. Isn't it?" I didn't reply. "Besides, if I wear tails, I get to wear my new cuff links. And I'd hate to be eclipsed by that little black dress you're wearing." Whistling, he straightened his bow tie.

In the garage, he held open the driver's door of the Cobra. I stared at the steering wheel a moment, then shook my head. "You drive."

"Not in a mood to break the land speed record? Maybe a party is just what you need." He helped me in the passenger side.

As the Cobra neared the end of Sleeper Street, a car pulled quietly into the traffic behind us. "Looks like snow again," I said.

The threat of bad weather encouraged all motorists on the Expressway to rush home: average space between vehicles was about two yards, one yard if a truck was involved. Honda-size potholes gobbled axles. The highway had been patched so many times that the department of transportation no longer tried to paint white lines on it. All told, it was a worse road than the E6 between Berlin and Leipzig.

Chance swerved to avoid a van stalled in the middle lane. Someone was actually trying to change a tire. "Can you believe what happened to Harry?" he said.

"What a fool," I replied. "I don't know whether to laugh or cry."

"Is he going to jail, you think?"

"Depends on what they caught him with."

"I wonder what tipped them off."

I looked at Chance. "It was probably something incredibly stupid, like a cigarette butt in the wrong toilet. Or some drunk crying in a sleazy bar. These things eventually catch up with people. Harry had been lucky for so long that he probably began to think he was cleverer than everyone else. Now he's lost everything. I don't have much sympathy for him."

Chance steered deftly between two trucks. "The poor louse was only trying to make a few bucks, Frosty. Life is expensive."

"So are mistakes in that line of work."

"You seem angry."

"I am. He threw everything away for nothing." I stared out the window, wondering why old Zwinger had recognized Harry's name when I had questioned him that night in the old folks' home. I wondered why Flick had not seemed surprised when I had mentioned how foolish Harry had been for keeping that gold chain around his neck. I wondered why Maxine had never told me about his moonlighting. They all knew there was more to Harry Paradise than recording sessions and a few pictures of naked boys.

"How do you know Harry threw it all away for nothing?" Chance cut past a knot of traffic as big, clumsy snowflakes began to spatter the windshield. "Aren't certain things in life worth risking everything for?"

I watched his eyes watch the road. "What would you risk everything for?"

"It changes. Used to be success."

A button factory, all that equipment, this car: without Hannah's payments, how much of it would he have now? "You have success. What is it now?"

He looked at me. "Love, I'd say. Family."

"That's all? What about country?"

"Are you kidding? Risk everything for country? Definitely not. Not this one, anyway."

Flick, too, had told me I was working for a loser. "What's the matter with it?"

"It's bankrupt, Frosty. Ask your friends in Germany or my friends at Sony. You were quite correct to leave. In fact, that's one thing I admire most about you. You're not really an American."

I wasn't really a German, either. I was one of those geniuses without a homeland. "You do feel some loyalty to America, though, don't you? I mean, you wouldn't betray it, would you?"

He looked slowly at me. "How would I do that?"

"It was a rhetorical question."

Chance switched on the windshield wipers. "I buy Japanese tape recorders and German microphones. That's about the extent of my betrayal."

He hadn't really sold any American secrets, had he? Before accepting payment, perhaps Chance had asked Hannah what exactly was on those tapes. Perhaps she had told him the truth: Russian satellite transmissions. Passing that along wasn't really treason. Theft, perhaps. But how did he know she was telling him the truth? How could he be sure she wasn't stealing vital secrets? Had he ever tried to turn her in to the FBI? Become a double agent? I doubted it.

The highway suddenly split and the Cobra veered toward Newport. The roads were a little messier there so Chance decreased his speed to sixty miles an hour, smiling each time the car tried to slide into the trees. If Flick were still alive, I would have demanded that Chance slow down. Now my survival didn't seem too critical. "What sort of party is this?" he asked as we pulled into Newport. The car behind us snuggled a little closer; it didn't want to lose us now.

"Bolt's launching Lukendunk," I said. "America's newest lieder team."

"Why are you even showing up? This has nothing to do with you."

"Curtis seems to think that humoring Godo is part of my job." We drove through a narrow street. All the colonial homes were now touristy boutiques. "After tonight, I'm not coming back to America for a long time."

"No? Looks like I'll have to move to Europe, then."

We began passing increasingly larger homes. Sydney Bolt had rented a mansion for her kickoff party. She wanted to get all her media buddies out of New York for an evening. Kakadu was probably putting them up tonight in the poshest hotel in Newport; that would generate miles of copy for Godo's newest freak show. Chance didn't have to look for a house number. He had only to follow the traffic to the festivities. The driveway was already blocked with black limousines and one pink hearse so we parked around the corner, aside a tall spruce. The snow had turned to fine sleet.

Inside, wall-to-wall mouths were busily spewing words, englutting extravagant hors d'oeuvres, grinning smarmily. Isolated puffs of smoke rose to the cherubim painted on the ceiling. Through the clamor I heard occasional snatches of adulterated Chopin. No, not Duncan: he was shouting at a bartender. Near a fountain, Luke was autographing rear ends again. I sighed, homesick: this was Flick's trade fair, American style.

"All right?" Chance asked me. I held on to his arm as a few flashbulbs popped.

"Toby! Toby!" Bolt cried melodiously. Tonight she was wearing a red sequined toga and no bra. The effect was relaxed and hostessy although the outfit would have hung better if her nipples weren't the same latitude as her belly button. "I'm thrilled to see you!"

"We're thrilled to be here," Chance replied.

Too thrilled to realize he was mimicking her, Bolt gripped Chance's free elbow. "You look terribly sexy in that tux. Let me get you something to drink." She led us to the bar.

I let go and drifted over to Duncan. Although he had stopped shouting at the bartender, his eyes were still ringed with red. Tonight he was finally wearing the yellow jumpsuit he had neglected to put on for his comeback recital. "Hi there," I said. "Remember me?"

Duncan hiccuped miserably. He had probably not stopped drinking since walking offstage the night before. "There was no review."

He should be on his knees thanking God. "What? Why not?"

"How should I know? It snowed. The critics forgot. I just threw forty thousand bucks down the toilet."

"What are you talking about? You made your comeback recital. Two thousand people heard it."

"But no one wrote about it. Therefore it didn't really happen."

I looked across the bar at Bolt. Her red fingernails were tracing little circles all over Chance's lapels. "What does your publicist have to say for herself? Is she giving you a refund?''

"She says we have to do the whole thing again next season." Duncan held his glass out for another refill. "I think I made a mistake. I should have bought that chalet in the Schwarzwald instead."

He looked as bad as my brother Roland. "Listen, Duncan. I know a great spa in Bavaria. I want to send you there for a month." Why shouldn't I prescribe the same remedy? I was half responsible for Duncan's misery as well.

"Can't. I've got recording sessions with Luke." Duncan suddenly turned his head. "Say, are the stories about you and that old man true? I never know what to believe any more."

"I was there when he died, if that's what you mean."

"I'm sorry to hear that, Les. Poor bastard. He was all right. Why don't you go to that place for a month yourself? Looks like you could use a break."

A stranger interrupted to ask Duncan about Luke the Apostle's potential as an opera singer. Across the way, Bolt was trying to get her sequins caught in Chance's fly and Luke seemed to be edging in my direction, so I followed a rent-a-butler into the kitchen.

"Too stuffy for you up there, sweetheart?" called the chef, glancing up from his shrimp sculpture.

I looked at the coats hanging in the doorway. "Could I borrow one of those? I need a little fresh air."

"Go ahead. Just make sure you come back."

I took a long black coat that hung to my ankles, a hat as well, and followed a cobblestone path into the garden. Despite winter, the shrubbery remained full. I could smell the sea. I walked to the far corner of the garden and sat on an iron bench looking at the sky. The clouds were low and moist, as they were on the night I had crawled into the fountain at the Thomaskirche. If I hadn't done that, Flick would be alive tonight. So would Moll. So would the Clove. Why had I interfered? Was I really saving the world from an unspeakable disaster? Bah. Beneath the curiosity, beneath the talent for dangerous riddles, I was just a bully. I got a kick out of wrecking everyone else's castles in the sand.

Didn't really catch on at first because I thought I was alone out there, but that tiny *rrrk rrrk* on the other side of the trees meant company. The sound was too soft, too repetitive, to be honest. Wasn't the Cobra parked right about there? The local juvenile delinquents were probably trying to pry the insignia off. Such mementos were worth a fortune.

I found a space in the hedges and ducked out to the street. Completely dark, empty, silent except for that small noise coming from the Cobra. I walked very slowly from tree to tree, stopping when I saw the hood up and demure haunches leaning over the engine. *Rrrk rrrrk*—she was loosening something. Impassive as the statue of Bach, or Mephistopheles, I watched Hannah's episode of the eternal comedy. Finished, she gently snapped the hood back in place. Then she stared directly at my face. Felt me there staring at her. From that distance, through this sleet, she couldn't see my face. Or could she? In any event, she walked quickly away.

I waited and waited but she did not return so I ducked back through the hedges, went into the loud house, hung my borrowed coat and hat back on their hook, and rejoined the party.

Chance found me right away, but he had been looking. Sydney Bolt was still hot on his tail. "Where were you?" he asked, taking my arm.

"There's some interesting topiary in the garden," I said. "You might want to take a look at it later."

Luke tottered over. "Hey Les!" He waited for the photographers to catch up before embracing me. "I hear your Beethoven's number two on the charts this week. That's awesome!"

"You're going to be number one in a few weeks yourself," Bolt assured him. "Just wait until this album hits the stands. It's going to make history."

"How can you be so sure, Syd?"

She waved magnificently over the room. "Investments pay

off. They know we're serious when we spend this kind of money." Bolt ran her thumbs over Chance's lapels. "Luke tells me you have a nice car."

"He does," I said. "We're going to drive it away in a few minutes."

"What?" She switched to a baby voice. "Don't you like me any more, Uncle Toby?"

"You're a sweet girl," he said, prying her off.

"Why won't you take me for a ride in your car, then?"

"Because he came with me and he's leaving with me," I said. "Why don't you take a ride in Uncle Luke's hearse instead."

Bolt dropped the baby talk. "Hearses are for your boy-friends, dear. Not mine." She walked away.

"Disregard that statement," Chance said to me. "I'll get our coats."

"Eh, sweetheart," Luke said awkwardly when they had both left, "don't get me wrong, I really think you're smart and terrific, but are you aware of current events?"

"Like what."

"Like Sydney and Chance? I mean, they're not exactly strangers."

"They're not?" It was too hilarious. "Since when?"

"I guess they met backstage when I was turning pages for Duncan."

I laughed curtly. "He's been seeing her?"

"Every square inch, scout's honor. Sydney tells me all about it. I thought you knew. Hey, here comes Chance. Please don't tell him I told you. He'll skin me alive."

Chance slid my coat over my shoulders. "Nice seeing you, Luke. Tell Sydney she really knows how to throw a party."

I stepped away from him. Double-crossing me with Hannah I could forgive: that was business. Two-timing me with Sydney Bolt was another matter. I could never trust him again. "Luke just offered me a ride in his hearse," I said. "I've been meaning to talk with him about a few things."

Chance thought I was referring to my farewell speech.

He winked at me, grinned at Luke. "Beware. She drives fast."

"Come on, Luke." I took his arm. "One last buzz for the press corps."

"Last buzz?" he echoed. "I don't like the sound of that."

Bolt caught up with us at the pink hearse. "Where do you two think you're going? I have a party to run and you're supposed to be there."

"Fresh air," I said. "Go inside and start some more rumors."

A cute little smile crossed her face as she considered more attractive opportunities posed by my absence. "Uncle Toby," Bolt said, reverting to baby talk, "do I get a ride in your fancy car, too?"

"Stay away from his car," I snapped. "I mean it."

Chance looked indulgently at me as he slid a hand over Bolt's shoulder. Traitor, liar: I never wanted to see him again. "Back to your party, Sydney," he said. "Have a nice ride, you two."

"You really handled that excellently," Luke said as we rolled down the gentle hill. "I would have strangled him."

"Then you would have gone to jail and never sung again," I said. "Just drive around a little, would you? I'll be all right."

We got back to the party half an hour later. Around midnight, when Chance and Bolt still hadn't returned from their little joy ride, I exited to New York with Duncan. Sure that Bolt and Chance had run away together, Luke was almost crying when he said goodbye to me. Somehow he felt that I had been shafted. Nonsense, I told him. Chance and I had been only casual friends.

20

*N*o use hanging around America anymore so I took the first flight out of JFK. Curtis met me at the Berlin airport. "No luggage?" he asked.

It had been in the trunk of the Cobra. "I lost it."

We led a boisterous parade of photographers to the parking lot, where a video team was waiting in ambush next to my car. The reporter holding the microphone had interviewed me for some women's magazine a few months before. Her boss probably thought I'd bare my soul to her now. Noticing the competition yammering at me, she limited herself to yes-and-no questions. "Was Emil Flick trying to rape you?" she shouted. "Did you bite him in self-defense?"

Curtis shoved me in and slammed the door, almost crushing her oversize microphone. As he rounded to the driver's side, she knocked on my window. "Do you think there's a curse on you? Nod yes or no. I'll understand."

The car pulled away. "I'm afraid this is going to take a while to simmer down," Curtis said. "It's the *Götterdämmerung* of the month." Once we got onto the ring road, he took my hand. That was a bad sign. "Did Duncan play well?"

"Not really. It was more circus than concert. I told him to demand his money back from that shyster Bolt."

Curtis did not rise to the defense of Kakadu's brilliant publicist, nor did he ask if I had attended her party in Newport like a good girl. He didn't inquire how I had managed to lose my suitcase. Instead he cleared his throat and concentrated on the rainy road. When he wasn't shifting gears, he held my hand.

"Hear anything from Harry?" I asked.

"He's busy buying himself out of jail. Don't worry, he'll probably succeed in time to make your next recording."

Ah, but Chance would not be at my next recording. I would have no more calm, whistling stranger ruling the control room, teasing me between takes, turning my dead Stradivarius into a perfect, velvet fire. So what if he had amused himself with a bit of wayside flesh? Who else had ever dared call me Frosty? Without him, I would never make a great recording again.

Ignoring the Nikon squad outside the house, Curtis pulled into the garage. He quietly followed me into the kitchen. On the table was a new batch of spice cookies, my favorite. That was a very bad sign: Curtis only baked them when the bottom had fallen out. "Hungry?" he asked, taking my coat. "Thirsty?"

"You can tell me, Curtis," I sighed, slouching into a chair. "I'm a big girl." He pulled his chair next to mine, took my hand again. Such a long silence passed that I imagined the worst. "Maxine?" I croaked.

He shook his head. "Godo called this morning. I'm so sorry to tell you this. Toby Chance was killed in a car crash last night."

I knew that and yet . . . yet . . . now it was true. Done, forever. I had tried to warn them. I thought of the Cobra spinning out of control on a straightaway just as Chance got it up to one-twenty for Sydney. He had probably been whistling Schubert when the lock nut rattled off the steering arm. Distance from earth to the other side of that mysterious door what, five seconds? Ten? Flick had had four minutes to curse me forever. I would never know how Chance had ceased thinking about me. His ability to deceive had been absolute. "Was it quick?" I asked.

"Instantaneous."

"What about Sydney."

Curtis sat very still a moment. "She's in critical condition. Broke about every bone in her body." His eyes leveled slowly with mine. "You already knew, didn't you."

"Chance was sleeping with her the whole time he was seeing me." I chuckled, remembering his indignation when he had found out about Flick. Hypocrite. "Is Maxine in town?"

"Of course. Would you like me to take you to the club?"

"No. I'm expecting a visitor." Hannah was going to be incensed when she learned which two birds she had killed with one stone. I figured she'd be in Berlin in a day or two. "Cancel the concerts for a week, would you? Tell them I'm in shock."

I went to Hugo's study and fell deeply asleep, dreaming about the various expressions on people's faces the last time I had seen them. Flick's beautiful face was distended in agony, a horrible kaleidoscope of primary colors and all hell welling in his blue eyes as he slipped away from me. Chance, on the other hand, had grinned and told Luke to obey the speed limits. I had even smiled back at him, kissed his pink mouth goodbye, smelled the lime and warm beaches. . . . Sydney Bolt? I hadn't really paid attention to her face. Its expression had meant nothing to me because it was all paint, applied in the morning, washed off at night. And then there was the face of Harry Paradise, smeared with guilt but never remorse, yellow with surprise and shallow denial. Even as he protested his innocence, Harry had been sizing up the policeman, calculating a price. I could never quite get a grip on Hugo's face but I began to dream again about the sounds he had last made. That pulled me right back to Flick.

Occasionally, from an upstairs window, I checked the pack of media hounds in the street. Once or twice, I practiced the violin. It couldn't be helped. The phone rang steadily; if Maxine called, she spoke only with Curtis. Duncan dropped by but didn't say much. He had come to the wrong place for sympathy. Luke the Apostle called, in hysterics: without Bolt, he was ebb tide. I spoke briefly with the Newport police and confirmed that Chance had left the party with Miss Bolt. Yes, he loved to drive fast. Recklessly fast? Definitely.

I listlessly pulled Spot out of hibernation. Nothing could be undone but I still had a few loose ends, a few last rites. First I hit the American file and asked for the Todtech Company.

Headquarters: Nyack, NY
Annual Revenues: $32,073,000
Net Income: $4,924,000
Employees: 400
Product/Services: weapons guidance systems/components
Year Founded: 1972

Todtech is a multinational company that develops, manufactures, and assembles weapons guidance systems for the military. It is considered one of the leading smart bomb suppliers and is a major recipient of SDI research grants. For further information see Bomb (Smart), Laser, SDI.

I went back once more to Harry's file because he still bothered me. Old Zwinger had not flinched when I had mentioned his name, nor had Flick when I mentioned Harry's divorce medallions. I went back to the bio that Maxine had given me and looked again at the list of Harry's wives. His third, commemorated by that medallion with the triangular links, was named Nina Schmidt. The name, common as Mary Jones, meant nothing to me. I called London.

"Hi, Emory. Hear anything from Harry yet?"

"Not a word. Have you?" He had been drinking and crying.

"No."

"This does not look good. I'm worried sick."

What was Emory whining about? Harry was alive, wasn't he? "Give it a few more days. You know how persuasive

Harry can be when his ass is on the line." I wasn't up for any more boozy jeremiads so I came right to the point. "Speaking of Harry, I have a question. Did you know his wives at all?"

"Wives? Harry's wives?"

No, Harry's husbands, jackass. "His third one, to be exact. Nina."

"Eh—Nina? Let me think—"

A pathetic liar. "He was married to her for four months and you never met her? Didn't you go to the wedding?"

"I don't think I liked her," Emory said slowly. "She had shifty eyes."

"Where'd Harry meet her?"

"I have no idea, darling. She just appeared."

"Just appeared? Like a mushroom? Come on, you can do better than that."

"Wait—it was right after some sessions in Budapest. We were doing a Kodály oratorio. The soloists kept going flat." He coughed and squirmed. "Maybe . . . she was a singer."

Maybe? Give me a break. Singers announced themselves a mile off, like hippopotamuses. "Where did she live?"

"Why are you asking me all this?" Emory blurted. "Shouldn't you be asking Curtis?"

"Why should Curtis know anything?"

"He's a manager," Emory said weakly. "Everyone knows everyone else in this business."

I hung up. Curtis?

I went to the window, aiming a pair of binoculars at the crowd on my curb. A pale, petite redhead had finally joined them. Beneath the lackluster raincoat she was wearing the same crisp suit she had put on for Toby Chance. Her tiny, taut face did not reflect her recent losses; in fact its expression had not changed much in almost fifty years. Attach a pair of pigtails, put on a pinafore, and she'd fit right back into Zwinger's class picture, next to Flick. I felt my pulse return to life: Smith was aching for one last ride.

I dressed quickly in black leather and went downstairs. The

office door was shut; my manager was inside talking. I went to the kitchen, the mud room. My boots stood in the corner and a new white knife was in the boots. I carefully slid it behind my belt and returned to the office.

Curtis was on the phone explaining that yes, yes, of course I would be well enough to make that crossover album next month. Seeing me, he suddenly went quiet. Maybe it was my dead face and the black leather; maybe he noticed my hands stiffening near my belt. Curtis had been living with me long enough to appreciate the meaning of my absolute stillness. "I'll speak with you later, Irwin," he said. "Don't worry about a thing." He hung up.

I closed the door and walked slowly toward the desk. "I was just talking to Emory. He said you might be able to tell me something about Harry's third wife Nina."

Curtis got up and approached to within a few paces of me. God, he was big. I would have a hard time overpowering him if he tried to jump me. "What's that behind your back?" he said. "Take it off." I dropped the knife onto the table beside us. "You weren't intending to use that on me, were you?"

When I didn't answer, he tugged me in with those colossal biceps. "Listen," he said. "It's all over. You're going to be all right."

I looked him in the big brown eyes. "Who's Nina Schmidt?"

His breathing halted for a tiny moment. Then he finally answered me. "Hugo's wife. The one he divorced to marry you."

"That sow married Harry? I don't believe it."

"She married someone named Schmidt first. Then she got Harry. They lasted about four months. Nina was Harry's best-kept secret. She was a nightmare, I understand. Shortly after he divorced her, Harry became your producer."

"Why didn't he ever tell me?"

"How could he? Hugo's divorce was sensational. There were all kinds of cross-accusations. Harry was terrified that you'd drop him if you ever found out he'd married the woman who had said all those vile things about you. In fact, he swore me to secrecy before taking his first job with you."

"Why didn't Maxine tell me, then? She knew, didn't she?"

"You'll have to ask her yourself."

I broke away from him and walked to the door. "I'm going for a ride. Give me ten minutes, then tell the people outside I've gone to visit my brother. Don't tell them anything else."

Curtis opened his mouth, about to protest, then shut it. I gunned the Harley past the photographers on my stoop and rode south, wondering how long Hannah would need to catch up with me. Three hours? Five? Depended on how fast she drove. Hannah was the only one in that crowd who knew that Roland was not in his nightclub but in a clinic near Garmisch-Partenkirchen.

I raced south all night, intercepting occasional pockets of warm, damp air: spring dissolving winter. It was almost April, after all. By dawn the fog was slithering steadily down the mountains, inhibiting forward motion on the autobahn. I passed two chain-reaction accidents before coming to the exit near Roland's sanitarium. The ramp ended at a crossroad: I puttered the Harley to a bench across the street and waited.

She drove almost as fast as I did. At eight o'clock, a white VW squealed down the ramp. Hannah was so agitated she didn't even notice my chrome monster across the street until she was almost past me. Jammed on the brakes, reversed the engine . . . I didn't move as she came to a halt right in front of me. "Need some help?" Hannah inquired, getting out of the car.

"No." I stared haughtily at her. "Haven't I seen you somewhere before?"

"We met at the Leipzig trade fair. The electronics exhibition." She extended her hand. "Hannah Selke." I didn't move. "President of Vuota Corda."

"Oh, right," I said finally, itching to pull the leather loop in my boot. If she made one move toward me, ever tried to touch me, Hannah would find a ceramic knife in her windpipe. "You're Harry's girlfriend. What are you doing here at this hour of the morning?"

"Looking for a gas station. I have a breakfast conference in Garmisch," she lied. "I must say, you were the last person I expected to see sitting on a bench."

"I'm visiting my brother in a clinic nearby. I've been driving all night and thought I'd catch my breath before seeing him."

"You've been driving all night?" Hannah tried to sound incredulous.

"Sure. It clears the brain. I've had a spell of bad luck lately. If you read the newspapers, you'll know what I'm talking about. First my lover drops dead on top of me. Then my recording engineer drives his car into a tree. He's killed and my publicist's in traction for a year. It's really aggravating."

Now Hannah tried to look confused. "She was with him?"

"Of course! We were at a party and she kept bugging him for a ride in his fancy car. Finally he gave in. You know what really spooks me, though? That could have been me instead!"

"How awful."

"The pits. Oh yeah, I forgot to mention that my record producer was just arrested for distributing pornography. Everyone I work with either ends up dead, in jail, or in the hospital. Someone must be sticking pins into a voodoo doll. Anyway, why am I telling you my problems? You have no idea what it's like when everything turns to shit on you."

As Hannah tried to laugh it off, her tiny mouth wobbled and I realized that she was swimming a bit. I tried to put myself in her position: Clove wrecked, Moll dead, Flick dead, Chance dead, Operation Phoenix not a success and she still didn't know what had started the chain reaction. All she knew was that I had been in a lot of places at the critical moments. My behavior here today corroborated all the stories she had been reading about me for years: Leslie Frost was a spoiled brat. On the other hand, Flick had apparently died making love to me and Chance, an accomplished connoisseur of women, had told her in Boston that he intended to marry me. It made no sense. Intuition told Hannah that one of us had deceived her. I was her only remaining clue.

"Anyway," I said, flinging it in her face, "now I've got to cheer up my brother. He's an alcoholic. I dropped him off here a few weeks ago."

Hannah blinked quickly a few times, not believing what I had told her: too blatant. She knew that Roland had entered his clinic the same day a woman had broken in on Zwinger. Could that be me? Or was I innocent as a cow? The evidence was overwhelming but she could not accept it because of one pivotal detail: Hannah had sucked me into all this in the first place. She had told Flick to seduce me, she had planted Chance in my path, and now those two clever ploys had run their natural course. The possibility that I was something more than a designated mule was something she had never planned, thus could not accept now. It presupposed too much blindness on her part. Stupidity of that magnitude in a precise, analytical brain like Hannah's could have only two causes: intense hatred or intense love.

I got up from the bench. Until four months ago, I hadn't even been aware of her existence. She had been hating me for years. What had I done to deserve that but slide out of my mother? Ah, such waste, such mismanagement. Life was a wicked game of unanswered questions and broken midnights. I would never know why she wanted to ruin me and Hannah would never know that the moment I lost Flick, she had achieved her goal.

"Guess I'll be on my way," I said, rising. "Enjoy yourself in Garmisch." Kill Hannah? What a waste. Allowing her to wander in the ruins, suspecting all and nothing, was a much worse punishment.

Her malevolent eyes glinted one last time at me. "Poor girl. Your first husband died too, didn't he? Wasn't that Hugo Lange? The violinist?"

I felt a harsh, cold pain behind my ribs. "No, he was a conductor."

Hannah smiled with her thin lips closed. "But he began as a violinist," she said, her voice sharp. "I know because I went to school with him."

The cold began creeping up my throat. "Is that so?"

"Yes. So did Emil Flick. Didn't he ever tell you?"

The only time I had mentioned Hugo to Flick, he had left my bed. "No."

"How strange! We were all in the same class! It's quite a coincidence, isn't it really?" When I didn't answer, Hannah smiled again. "We were all so surprised when he married you. So hasty! But of course, your father was such an important diplomat."

I breathed slowly in out in out, waiting for the cold to leave my chest. It only expanded upward into my brain, cutting off mercy. "I was in Newport the other night," I began, staring not at her eyes but her red hair. "Sitting in a garden, smelling the sea. All by myself. Then I heard a noise beyond the hedges. Can you believe it? Some fucking little urchin was messing with the Cobra."

Out of practice, Hannah: the moment she tried to pull the gun from her coat I kicked it across the street. Then I put an elbow in her stomach, hard but not hard enough to knock her to the wet grass. I wanted her to come after me, foaming at the mouth, stopping at nothing. I gunned the Harley the wrong way on the exit ramp back onto the autobahn and sure enough, several seconds later, Hannah followed. The VW was practically on two wheels.

The mountains were sweating fog all over the highway but I kept my speed at the maximum, shooting past cars with a horrible roar. Oddly enough, she seemed to be gaining on me and then *zzzzzink!* the Harley shivered. At this speed, this distance, driving a damn VW, she had hit it with a bullet? I didn't like that at all so I blew onto the grass dividing the highway and made a sloppy U-turn, heading back toward

Munich. Hannah plowed wildly right after me. The fog was worsening because spring was more insistent here: I had to slow to ninety or I'd be driving into the backseats of the cars ahead of me.

The Harley hadn't liked getting nicked and began burping delicately whenever I tried to accelerate. I'd be out of gas in twenty miles. Each time I looked in the rearview mirror, the white VW was a little closer. How was that possible? Just as I overtook a Mercedes, its left taillight shattered. Good shot! Christ! While my body gasped for breath, preparing for another bullet in the back, my brain amused itself with the interesting ballistic problem posed by my speeding away from a speeding bullet. If I stayed at one hundred miles an hour, how deep would it go, one inch? Four? Would it come out the other side? Didn't matter, really; if I crashed on the Harley at that speed, Hannah's little bullet would end up in a piece of hamburger five hundred feet up the autobahn.

Just before the highway curved around a mountain, I glanced in my mirror. She was so close now I could see her hand out the window aiming the gun at me, then *whoppp* I hit a pillow of fog and couldn't see an inch beyond my nose. Downshifted *crunch* from fifth to fourth, then I saw the pileup ahead of me all over the highway so many cars at a standstill, each with its snout in someone else's rear end. I was going to hit them.

I stomped on the brakes, plummeting to forty-five. The Harley squealed and skidded like a banshee, about to die: then I found a narrow gap between two wrecked vehicles. If I concentrated with all my might, approached this test of nerves like a very tough leap in the Sibelius Concerto, I could just squeeze through that opening and come out on the other side. Kill the brakes before she rounds the bend, Smith! Don't warn her with the bright red lights! I squeezed my brain, my existence, into a pellet and aimed that pellet at the gap in the pileup ahead of me. I heard screams, smelled smoke and rubber and then it all went into slow motion. With just a few inches on either side of my handlebars, I seemed to float between two crushed cars, emerging onto the vacant, peaceful highway beyond them.

I heard the next squeal of brakes then a crash that shook the mountain. Another farewell, acerbic and final. There could be no more of them.

When I got back to Berlin, I went to the cupboard in the corner of Hugo's library, where his old violin had been lying untouched for years and years. The battered case looked familiar so I pulled it off the shelf and opened the rusty clasps. Inside it smelled musty and fragile, exactly the same as Flick's and Hannah's violins. I lifted the red velvet and recognized the angular frets, the carving in the bridge: it was a Simler, all right. All four strings were broken. No need to take it out so I let the old shroud fall back in place. Then I noticed the embroidered initials in the corner of the velvet: HS, definitely HS. Not HL. I sighed like an old, weary fool. The HL was in Briarcliff Manor, around Hannah's violin. She had probably done the needlework herself and given it to Hugo before the group had dispersed. So he wouldn't forget her.

I returned the violin to the cupboard. Far back on the shelf lay Hugo's old, worn book about German instrument makers that I had been looking for. I slowly opened the green leather cover; it felt alive, thick with ghosts. Deep in the brittle pages I found a small photograph of Hugo and Hannah. The children were sitting on a bench by a lake, apparently on a picnic. The gold watch chain dangled from Hugo's belt loop and he was smiling proudly. Hannah was not really smiling but her young eyes brimmed with that soft peace I knew too well. After Hugo left, it had never come back to her.

I guess Hugo's gold chain had gone from Hugo to his wife Nina to Harry: small world, connected by lust and miscalculation. I went out to my backyard and rolled under a big fir tree, listening for a long time to the needles rustling over my head. As the wind came and went, the ancient, rickety tree shimmered and whispered, then was silent again. How strange that, all these years, I had believed that Hugo married me for love. Eventually Curtis came and took me back inside.

As winter slowly dissipated, so did the cadre of photographers on my doorstep. After a few weeks, to pass the time, I began to practice more. When tiny green leaves returned to the trees outside my window and blossoms shyly engaged the air, I told Curtis to stop canceling my engagements. The mud was going away.

On a fragrant, limpid night in April, he drove me to the Philharmonie, wedged me into my dress, and took his seat in the auditorium. Onstage, the orchestra began the overture to *A Midsummer Night's Dream*. I was fiddling softly to myself when someone knocked on the backstage door.

Roland came in. "Hey! Long time no see!"

He wore a charcoal gray suit that complemented his salt-and-pepper hair. Roland had gained some weight and looked relaxed, alert, extremely potent. Reminded me of Chance. I hugged him. "Guess I got my money's worth, eh? When did you get back?"

"Maxine picked me up this morning. It was a great loony bin, Les. Thanks for sending me." He studied my face. It was unchanged. Even the mole above my lip looked the same although its insides were gone. "Sorry to hear you've had a rough winter."

"I'm over it."

"Can you come to the club tonight? We'll celebrate. Maxine would love to see you."

"I'll try."

The door moved again and Maxine stepped in. She hadn't really changed, either. Her skin still spanned the fine cheekbones like a taut brown tarpaulin. The eyes still bored holes in her subjects and the lips moved slowly as snails as she deigned to speak. "Hello," she said.

"Guess that's my signal to scram," Roland said. "See you later, Les. Play well." He left.

The Queen eyed the purple-and-black dress I had bought on our last shopping trip. "Looks good," she said.

I drank some water. Throat dry. "You lied to me."

She didn't move. "In what regard."

I pointed to the mole above my lip. "Four seconds, you said. Quick and painless. It was four minutes and it was agony."

"What can I tell you, Smith? It's not the type of thing we can run too many lab tests on."

At least she didn't try to tell me that mine had been the first complaint. I cradled the violin back under my chin.

"I was in London last week," Maxine said. I didn't care where she was so I continued to practice a tricky double-stop scale. "Visited the CD plant."

Damn, it was impossible to make music with her hanging around. I put the violin down. "Sweeping up after me?"

Her face moved but she didn't really frown, didn't really smile. "Toby Chance owned Naja. I'm surprised you didn't figure it out yourself."

"How's that?"

"*Naja naja* is genus and species for cobra."

What a cheeky boy. I would miss him. "Biology was never my strong suit. Why didn't you tell me about Harry Paradise?"

The Queen had had a month to make up a good reply. Still, she hesitated. "I wanted to preserve your peace of mind."

Not to mention my cherished memories. "And thanks for telling me about Flick's heart attack. Most kind of you."

"Would you have behaved any differently?"

I didn't answer.

The Queen sighed. "I'm very sorry, Smith. You were more stable than I thought."

She had actually apologized to me. Maxine must be desperate. Maybe Barnard had gotten herself eliminated in the last couple weeks and I was the only one left to torment. What the hell, I might as well forgive her. "I went to Hannah's house," I said. "She was applying for a job at Todtech."

"What's that?"

"An electronics company. They make the other half of smart missiles. The half that follows the laser beam to the target. Screw those Todtech seekers to a stupid missile and away you go." I adjusted the horsehair on my bow. "Launching a missile is easy, you know. You can do it from anywhere. Designating a target is the dangerous part. You have to send a team into enemy territory and get them out again afterward. Anyone who could figure out how to illuminate a target from a satellite would have a great advantage. Hannah was more than halfway there."

"On behalf of whom?" Maxine asked.

"Germany. Big Germany." I began softly playing Sibelius. "Unification's going to be expensive. They've got to start upgrading their arsenal somehow."

"Do these smart missiles actually work?"

"They've been around since Vietnam. No one's really tried them yet on a grand scale."

Onstage, far away, the orchestra hit the final stretch of the overture. I pressed my fingers into the strings, finding my first high, solitary notes in the Sibelius Concerto. "It's interesting," I said dreamily. "Hugo married me because I was a diplomat's daughter. Not because I was a great violinist."

When I opened my eyes, the Queen was still watching my fingers. "Does it matter?" she asked. "You were happy for a while, weren't you?"

The stage manager knocked. "Miss Frost?"

I checked my face in the mirror, toying with the ruby around my neck. I had found the peace a second time, with a nobler man. There were worse fates.

Overture ended, applause began. I went to the padded door, taking deep breaths as Maestro bobbled back and forth for a few bows. All those people, all those notes . . . I couldn't do it. I wanted to run away, back to my father, back to Flick, away from the terror waiting in the auditorium. I looked over my shoulder. The Queen was standing in the hallway, arms crossed, reminding me who I was, or who I was supposed to be.

Maestro readjusted his cummerbund. ''Are we ready, my dear?''

Never. I nodded and we walked into the warm yellow lights.